THE Shadow
and the GOLDEN MASTER

WALTER B. GIBSON

The Mysterious Press
New York

For information address The Mysterious Press, 129 West 56th Street, New York, N.Y. 10019.

Library of Congress Catalogue Number: 83-63032
ISBN: 0-89296-073-6 Trade Edition
0-89296-074-4 Limited Edition

FIRST EDITION

It took nearly eight and a half years, with a total of more than one hundred and seventy novels, for The Shadow to meet up with Shiwan Khan, the Golden Master, yet that confrontation was inevitable almost from the start. To appreciate this, it is necessary to review the saga of the Shadow, which began and ended as an unfinished story, running up a total of more than fifteen million words which carried it into its twentieth year before it suddenly ceased publication although further adventures were still in the offing. That marks the conflict between The Shadow and Shiwan Khan as a definite peak in the series.

The factor that rendered The Shadow series decidedly unique was that it opened with only the semblance of a plot; not just as a single story, but as one of four. Henry W. Ralston, general manager of Street & Smith Publications, had decided to produce a new magazine featuring a character to be called The Shadow, which required at least four issues to establish it as a regular periodical on a quarterly basis. To get it under way as soon as possible, Ralston instructed Frank Blackwell, the editorial director, to have someone update a leftover dime novel on a rewrite basis.

This confronted Blackwell with two dilemmas. None of his regular writers was anxious to take on a rewrite assignment; and since The Shadow was to be more of a mystery figure than a stylized private detective, the job itself raised too many complications. But I had already been thinking in terms of a mysterious character who would become a controlling force in the affairs of lesser humans, so I was naturally intrigued when he asked me if I would like to take on The Shadow. That offered the prospect of developing the character in the course of the story itself, and when Blackwell agreed that if the first story proved acceptable, I would get the order for the other three, that meant that the process could be continued right on through.

I delivered the first story within a month, following a pattern discussed with Blackwell, and went right ahead with the rest on the same basis, building The Shadow from a nebulous concept into a more solid figure who swayed the ever-wavering balance from the side of crime to that of justice. I delivered those at the rate of one a month, so when the first story, *The Living Shadow,* made its appearance in mid-March of 1931, I was just finishing the third novel. I turned in the fourth around the middle of April and began catching up on other work, now that I had fulfilled The Shadow quota.

One reason for pushing ahead was that I had taken on the editing of a new magic monthly, *The Seven Circles,* which made its appearance only a few weeks after the first issue of *The Shadow.* Much of my work had been the gathering and writing of new tricks and articles, as well as contacting potential advertisers. I had started that late in January, soon after delivering the first Shadow novel. So later, when it was decided to use a pen name for The Shadow stories, I was asked for suggestions and it occurred to me that it would be a good idea to combine the first and last name of two magic dealers to form a link between the two publications.

Two names were standouts on the list. One was Maxwell Holden, who had just retired from the stage to open a magic shop in New York and was doing a column for the new magazine. His specialty in vaudeville was a "hand shadow" act in which he formed life-sized silhouettes that moved across a screen. The other was U.F. Grant, of Pittsfield, Massachusetts, who invented an illusion used by the Great Blackstone in which a magician walked away from his own shadow, leaving it in full view. Since these were both devices that I intended to attribute to The Shadow as a means of baffling or intimidating crooks, I felt that the pen name of Maxwell Grant would be appropriate; so I appropriated it, with due respects to Maxwell Holden and U.F. Grant.

By May 1, however, my brief respite from The Shadow came to an abrupt end. Word came from Street & Smith that newsstands were selling out *The Living Shadow,* so the magazine would definitely be continued beyond the first four issues. I was to go ahead with another story at a full word rate, but with no immediate deadline; and since The Shadow was now a recognized crime fighter, the most appropriate location would be Chicago. Having plenty of data to work from I was getting under way when I received word from Blackstone that he was taking on a two-week engagement in Bermuda and wanted me to go along to do publicity and help with his show.

So I took The Shadow along as well and wrote about Chicago between times while viewing the Bermuda locale as a potential setting for future novels. This policy of writing on the rove proved so satisfactory that I continued it, taking about seven months to complete my new quarterly quota of four stories. During that period, I attended a magicians' conclave in Michigan, did magic at a Lions' convention in Toronto, and traveled to Atlanta and New Orleans with the Great Raymond, doing publicity for his show.

In the meantime, the second issue of *The Shadow* had sold out like the first, but with a much larger print order, so with the third, the publishers decided to go monthly. I was called on to deliver accordingly and came up with six stories in four months. It was well that I did for by then Street & Smith were planning to go twice a month and offered me a contract on that basis. Wisely or otherwise I took it, and the race against time was under way.

From the first issue of *The Shadow* on, the editing had been assigned to John Nanovic, who, like myself, was a newcomer at Street & Smith. Since the stories had been following a general pattern, there had been very little discussion of coming plots or future development, nor radical changes in finished stories. Now, however, time was of the essence; and since The Shadow was still in a formative stage, it was possible to shape the future along more productive lines. The farsighted Mr. Ralston had foreseen all that and more. He had placed Nanovic in charge of a group of character magazines spearheaded by The Shadow, so that stories could be discussed, outlined, and fully plotted in advance, thus consolidating writing, editing, and sales toward an ultimate purpose.

With The Shadow, ideas came fast as a result of this coalition. Crimes became more varied, The Shadow acquired new devices, stories with an Oriental background gained occasional precedence, and output zoomed so rapidly that I was six months ahead of schedule. Not only was the pressure off, this gave John Nanovic a backlog of a dozen stories to choose from, which in turn sped my output, since I could turn out stories of a similar type or background in rapid succession before going on to something else.

Most important during this formative period was the question of villains. Avid readers of *The Shadow Magazine* began listing villains from the very start, but very few of them were worthy—or unworthy—of more than passing notice. Mostly, they simply crossed paths with The Shadow to their own deserved misfortune, although there were some whose schemes were so fiendish that they demanded rapid counteraction on The Shadow's part. But by the time the magazine was entering its third year, it was evident that crimedom would be on the way out unless a new breed of supercrooks arose to match The Shadow's might with machinations of their own.

An early example of this was found in *The Red Blot,* symbolizing a master crook who appeared in the issue of June 1, 1933; while several months later, three superfoes, *The Wealth Seeker, The Black Falcon,* and *Gray Fist,* succumbed to The Shadow in three successive issues. They were followed by *The Cobra,* who lived up to his title with the aid of highly vicious subordinates called "Fangs" who tried unsuccessfully to combat The Shadow's agents. By then, readers were writing in to say how greatly they appreciated this wave of supervillainy, but the best compliment of all was one I received in person without the donor's knowledge.

In New York, I went to see a movie involving scenes of the Parisian underworld. One set showed a stone-walled chamber, with heavy doors and stone steps winding into view from a darkened corner. While I was admiring this sinister architecture, I heard someone in the row behind me confide to a companion in a hushed, awed tone: "It looks like The Cobra's lair!" It did, too, and the fact that a reader had realized it before I did simply pleased me all the more.

Other superfoes followed at intervals in the persons of *The Crime Master, The Condor,* and *The Python.* That was more than forty years ago, yet only recently I saw a Gothic novel entitled *The Shadow of the Condor,* which proves how far the long arm of coincidence can carry. But the real breakthrough came with *The Voodoo Master,* dated March 1, 1936, which marked the end of The Shadow's fifth year and was the ninety-seventh novel in the series. The Voodoo Master, whose real name was Doctor Mocquino, was so wily that even when defeated he twice escaped The Shadow's toils to return for two more matches before finding oblivion.

This represented the second stage in the development of The Shadow, an expansive period during which he encountered a variety of supervillains and a series of fantastic situations involving battles to the bitter end. With *The*

Shadow Unmasks, in which the cloaked avenger resumed a true identity which he had up to then—August 1, 1937—kept strictly secret, the constant readers gained an inside knowledge of their favorite hero that added new zest to his incredible quests. To those "in the know," it seemed a certainty that this presaged the advent of a supervillain whose aims, capabilities, and resources would be comparable to those developed by The Shadow, but geared for evil instead of good.

It took more than two years with a total of more than fifty novels before that happened; but The Shadow was not idle meanwhile. After disposing of a formidable candidate known as *The Murder Master,* he met up with a five-man cartel known as *The Hand* and eliminated them one by one in intermittent stories, despite the fact that each seemed to profit by the mistakes of his predecessors and therefore became more formidable than those who went before. To test his expanding powers further, he disposed of three more supermen of evil, *The Lone Tiger, The Vindicator,* and the *Wizard of Crime,* who put him in fettle for the test to come.

That was provided by Shiwan Khan in *The Golden Master* of September 15, 1939. Since The Shadow in his early years had visited Tibet, there to acquire hypnotic powers that helped him to triumph over fiends of crime, it stood to reason that his nemesis—if he should ever have one—would have to come from that mystic land in order to challenge The Shadow on his home ground. Shiwan Khan not only came from Tibet, he claimed that he owned it, along with outlying territories, which made him formidable, indeed.

Even The Shadow wondered how far he had defeated this superfoe and marked the case as "Unfinished" in his archives, to which, as Maxwell Grant, I had sole access and therefore can vouch for his uncertainty. So it seemed likely that the two would meet again, which they did, in *Shiwan Khan Returns,* dated December 1, 1939; and now, after forty years, readers who missed one story or the other—or both—will find them in their original form in this combined volume.

Walter B. Gibson
Maxwell Grant

HIGHLIGHTS ON THE SHADOW

You've had one fine Shadow novel after another in the past, all of them well above the average story, and many of them really exceptional. But in this issue you'll find one that is more than exceptional—one that is really a yarn that will make you tingle. And right off the bat we'll tell you one thing—the Shadow *doesn't* get the Golden Master, for Shiwan Khan, master of the power of the mystic East, is more powerful than any adversary The Shadow has met thus far. You see, we are not afraid that we will give the story away by telling you this; even with this thought in your mind, you will still find the novel by far the best mystery story you have ever read!

We can expect some argument on this point, of course, and we'd like to have your comments on it. Do you really think Shiwan Khan is a man worthy of the great talents of The Shadow? Can the power of the East, the control of mind over matter, conquer the power of skill, science, and daring? It's a question that can cause plenty of discussion, so let's talk it over!

Incidentally, we think that Gladney has done an excellent job on the cover on this issue, picturing Shiwan Khan in his robes of glory, and getting all the cunning and shrewdness of the master villain into his features. Many of you will want to put a frame around this painting and hang it on the wall of your room or your den.

Robert C. Blackmon, Jack Storm, and Arthur J. Burks, the trio furnishing the short stories in this issue, are all familiar to you. You know that they turn out stories which give you something to think about, and to get excited over. "When the Blind Die," by Jack Storm, is especially interesting, since it deals with a racket that is particularly vicious in appealing to the finer senses of us humans. "Banana Oil," by Blackmon, and "Something Queer About Murder" are also good yarns. Mr. Blackmon is a Southerner—lives in Florence, South Carolina. He comes to New York occasionally to talk over ideas and plans for future stories with us. He was here the other day, to take in some of the World's Fair, and do his usual business. He just happened to hit a particularly warm week, so felt quite at home in the climate.

If some of you missed the Blackmon story in the last issue, "The Funniest Thing," dig up your copy of The Shadow now and read it. It's one of the most unusual stories we've printed in a long time.

Our next issue will bring back to you another Whisperer story, and Danny Garrett, the shoeshine-kid detective. The Whisperer story is "The Mouse Became a Rat," and Danny Garrett's yarn is "The Kid With a Song." They're both sweet stories—and of course there will be others.

"Castle of Crime" is the title of the book-length Shadow novel in the next issue. It is something different from ordinary crime; a scheme bigger than the average crook could possibly conceive, and one that embraces everything from a common murder to international complications.

Still a few Shadow pictures left—or we hope there will be by the time this reaches the stands. If you'd like to have one, send three cents in stamps to Picture Editor, The Shadow Magazine, 79 Seventh Ave., New York, N. Y., and get yours. It's the same picture we gave for three successive coupons appearing previously in this magazine, but many readers asked that we give them a chance to get it more quickly than waiting for three issues. So, the ones we have left, we offer this way. Hurry up, if you want yours!

You've probably noticed that we have printed a few pictures of The Shadow's agents on covers recently. Harry Vincent has appeared on one. We've had Hawkeye in a full figure on another. We've had the entire group of agents on a cover some time ago. We're interested in the reactions of you readers; whether you want us to give you more of such pictures, or whether you want to have us stick close to The Shadow in the illustrations.

We're justly proud of our Shadow covers, because they are admitted the best on any magazine. From the very beginning they have set a new standard in covers for mystery magazines, and we have kept stepping in front of the parade all the time. Usually, innovations we try are copied by others—and we are always glad to find out what our readers like so we can follow their suggestions and not only meet public demand, but keep ahead of it!

It's been some time since we've been able to find space to print some of the letters from our readers. We'll try to make up for this in the future, and give you some each issue, so you can see how others agree or disagree with your opinions on this magazine, crime conditions in general, and any other related subjects which may come up.

"You have a wonderful magazine, the best ever written. I enjoy all magazines, and have read them extensively, but The Shadow tops them all. I especially liked 'Smugglers of Death,' 'The Three Brothers,' and 'Nose of Death.'

"Ed Cartier's drawings are very, very good. Without his fine drawings, you couldn't *feel* the story so well. Keep producing such a good magazine, and you will have my support and the support of many others for a long time.

"Franklyn Larson, 1005 North Main, Mobridge, S. D."

"I don't think there is a more interesting and thrilling book than The Shadow. The stories always hold me spellbound all the way through the book. Every story is just a little better than the one before.

"Mrs. W. E. Jones, 1218 E. Henry St., Savannah, Georgia."

"I have been a constant reader of The Shadow magazine for the past three years. I think that it is the best magazine of its kind on the market today. Will you please send me a complete list of back numbers available, as well as titles of Shadow stories that have been published in book form?

"The best kind of short stories in your magazine are the Danny Garrett stories and the Sheridan Doome stories.

"Are pictures of The Shadow available?

"James E. Farina, 91 Fort Ave., Roxbury, Mass."

Back-number lists are mailed to readers on request, showing all back issues available, as well as Shadow stories published in book form. Up ahead in this department we tell you how you can get your Shadow picture.

Francis English, 647 South Main St., Butte, Montana, is collecting back issues of The Shadow, and is also making

Continued on page 93

Spotlighted in the terrible power of

THE CRIME RAY

The Shadow fights for justice!

It's going to be a **SHADOW CHRISTMAS**

For Christmas all the stores will be featuring The Shadow merchandise pictured here. If you can't buy it at your local store, send direct to us the amount which each item costs and we will have it mailed to you without additional charge.

This year you can wear The Shadow Hat and Cape and melt into the shadows. You can hide your face in The Shadow Mask. You can disguise yourself as a Chinaman, porter, or ranger. Write letters in invisible ink or in code on your own Shadow Stationery. Strap on The Shadow Official Holster Set, use the keen Shadow Tectolite, which you can hide in the palm of your hand. Write in the dark with the Pencil Lite just as The Shadow makes his notes. And play The Shadow Game—the finest fun.

THE SHADOW PENCIL LITE, a 5¼" automatic pencil that lights up so you can write in the dark....................50c

SHADOW DISGUISE KIT, six different face make-ups, Chinese and Frenchman's mustache, goatee, sideburns, mask, invisible ink, fingerprinting records, Shadow code book...........$1

THE GOLDEN MASTER

A Complete Book-length Novel from the Private Annals of The Shadow, as told to

MAXWELL GRANT

The mysterious power of the Orient against The Shadow's automatics, as Shiwan Khan attempts to rule the world!

THE GOLDEN MASTER

BY MAXWELL GRANT

CHAPTER I.

DEATH'S WHIRL.

THE lights on the electric sign had begun their strange whirl again. Paul Brent stood watching them from the window of his hotel room. Over him came the same fascinating spell that he remembered from previous evenings.

Tonight, the lights did not cease their spin. Gripped by their curious magic, Paul felt a surge of recollections as rapid as the lights themselves.

Odd, about that sign.

It stood atop a low building on the other side of Broadway. It had a flapping, birdlike figure in the center, with three circles around it. Red, green, finally an outer circle of yellow lights, which matched the color of the central bird.

Viewed from Broadway, the sign caught the eye, but did not captivate it. The only times that it produced a mental daze were when Paul stared at the sign from his window. Probably that was because he was looking straight at it.

If the matter of angles explained it, Paul was the one person in New York who could feel the bewildering effect of those lights. His window was directly opposite the sign, and on an exact level with its center.

Why did he happen to be in this hotel room?

Even that simple question could not be precisely answered. Paul Brent had never heard of the Hotel Grayland, until receiving the circular with the offer of special rates. The letter had been waiting for him in Miami, when he stopped there on his way back from South America.

Deciding to try the Grayland, he had found a room already reserved for him. This room. So Paul had taken it. Simple enough, but the rates, he had learned today, were higher than the circular said.

Who had sent that fake advertisement? Who had reserved the room in Paul's name? Who—the final question jarred Paul, despite his increasing daze—was responsible for those devilish lights, with their crazy flip-flops and maddening whirls?

The questions seemed to jumble, like the circles. Of a sudden, the lights went blank. So did Paul's thoughts. He saw the blackened square of the extinguished sign, but the roar of Broadway traffic was gone. Paul was in the midst of a vast calm, from which he actually expected the token that came.

He seemed to hear a voice, like a distant call, yet cold and level in its pitch:

"Paul Brent . . . Paul Brent—"

Paul's squarish face was frozen. Its tan gave it the effect of a cast molded from bronze. His eyes were fixed in an unseeing stare. His lips did not move, yet he felt himself speak a word in answer:

"Yes?"

"You have heard me," said that far-off voice. "You know my name."

This time, Paul's lips opened. Without knowing where the thought came from, he replied spontaneously:

"You are Shiwan Khan."

"I am Shiwan Khan"—the icy tone seemed closer, yet its pitch had not changed—"and you are ready to obey.

Follow every thought that comes to you!"

Slowly, Paul turned from the window. He sat at a writing desk that was strewn with papers. From them, he brought a cardboard folder, opened it and mechanically thumbed the papers that he found inside.

They were orders for commercial airplanes, to be delivered to South America. They were made out to Globe Aircraft, the firm which Paul represented as a technical expert. Paul had gone to South America to arrange the final specifications.

He had the needed details on another sheet of paper. He could have copied them directly to the orders. But the paper that Paul picked up from the desk was blank. His eyes, though, saw writing on it, in a hand other than his own.

The hand of Shiwan Khan!

First, Paul added amendments to the orders. He increased the number of certain planes, eliminating others of a definitely commercial type. To the specifications for those that he increased, Paul called for a special wing design, used in military aircraft. With that, he wrote the comment: "Required for flights across the Andes Mountains."

Next, he changed the motor type from KJ4 to WI7, code numbers used by Globe Aircraft. The orders for WI7 would please them at the factory, for they already had a few hundred of those new-type motors in stock. It would also puzzle them, for Globe had built those new motors for delivery to the United States government.

On the South American orders, Paul wrote: "For immediate delivery." Finally, he produced a government order that he had picked up while in Washington. It called for delivery of three hundred WI7 motors within two months, specifying that following such delivery, future motors of that type must be built for the government only.

A conniving chuckle came from Paul's lips. It was a forced tone, a gloat that seemed rather to belong to the unknown Shiwan Khan.

The government contract showed a figure "2" to specify the number of months. Paul inserted a figure "1" in front of it, producing "12" as the total of months. With a year to go, the Globe factory could easily ship the South American orders, and then begin producing motors for the government.

No longer puzzled, they would be doubly pleased at this chance to make a big commercial sale ahead of the government's deadline. This would win Paul real approval from the factory. Until Washington heard about it.

Thought of an unpleasant future did not deter Paul from his next action. Still following the controlling thoughts of Shiwan Khan, Paul folded the order sheets into a large envelope that was already stamped and addressed to Globe Aircraft. Putting on his hat and coat, he walked stolidly from the hotel room.

The elevator operator noted Paul's trancelike expression, while he was riding down to the lobby. So did the bell captain, when Paul dropped the envelope in the mailbox. But neither observer made comment, for the tan-faced man seemed to know what he was about. They saw Paul Brent walk out through the side door.

On the sidewalk, Paul waited for a taxicab. That was the first real evidence that his brain probably wasn't right. No cabs ever stopped on the obscure side street; they always pulled up to the front door.

Tonight was the exception.

Paul had not waited a dozen seconds, before a cab wheeled from a parking place and stopped for him. The young man stepped into the cab as if it belonged to him; which, in a sense, it did.

That cab, like Paul Brent, was under the control of Shiwan Khan, the unseen master of many destinies.

HARRY VINCENT, young and personable, is the main aid of The Shadow. His life once saved by the man he now serves, Harry gives completely his time and services to The Shadow, particularly passing on information about pending crime he might pick up in social circles.

The proof was the muffled driver. Despite his upturned coat collar, the man's features were momentarily visible. They were yellow, with sharp black eyes that kept watching Paul in the rear-view mirror. Gleaming teeth showed the driver's grin; straight black hair matched the fellow's scrutinizing eyes.

The man at the wheel was a Mongol. He belonged among the guerrilla bands of western China. Any passenger other than Paul Brent would have wondered what strange quirk had made the man a cab driver. But Paul was scarcely conscious of time, space, or surroundings. The will of Shiwan Khan controlled his thoughts as it did his deeds.

WHEN the cab stopped in back of a small apartment house, Paul stepped to the curb mechanically. Across the sidewalk he saw a door, and he entered it. Following a hallway, he turned when he came to a stairway and ascended to the third floor. Passing one door, he stopped, laid his hand upon the knob of the next. It was the last door in the hall.

Entering the room by a little passage, Paul was immediately attracted by the glow of a single lamp that stood, unshaded, on a table. It had a greenish tinge, that light, and though it possessed brightness, it didn't hurt Paul's eyes. Instead, it held them.

There was a radio cabinet in the corner and Paul heard the music that was coming from it, for the tune seemed to catch the same vibration as his thoughts. Standing motionless, Paul observed something that glittered on the table. His eyes were blurred by the greenish light, so he groped for the object and gripped it.

The music ended. There was the voice of an announcer, but it wasn't what Paul expected to hear. There was something else—what it was to be, he had no idea; but another voice—the singular tone of Shiwan Khan—told him to wait and listen. It came suddenly, from the radio: the stroke of a Chinese gong.

The very air seemed to catch that vibration. It quivered about Paul's ears, made him shudder with a hard shake of his head. The spell of Shiwan Khan seemed to crash apart, like the breaking of a wave. The circling lights, the ethereal voice, Paul's own recent deeds, were the slipping recollections of a hideous, tangled dream.

His hand clenching tight, Paul felt weight, and coldness. He looked at the object that he held. It was a .32 revolver. His eyes, no longer blurred, gazed beyond the gun, to a thing that lay on the floor beside the table with the greenish lamp.

It was the body of a man, clad in pajamas, lying face down. Blotched in the very center of the man's back was a mass of crimson that dyed the striped pajama jacket. He was dead, that victim, a bullet in his spine.

A bullet from the very gun that was gripped in the tight-clenched hand of Paul Brent!

CHAPTER II.

FIGURES FROM GLOOM.

"I KILLED him."

Paul Brent spoke the words calmly, with a trace of satisfaction. Then, the memory of his own voice alarmed him.

"I . . . killed . . . him—"

It was almost a query, that higher pitch. Paul uttered it desperately, as if to fight off a conviction that must have been inspired from someone else. Panic caught him; he wanted to dash from the place, raving the news of murder.

Then came a flood of reason.

Paul couldn't remember coming here; he'd never seen the place before. The gun wasn't his; he had no idea who the dead man might be. It didn't make sense, this murder.

Or did it?

Doubt was back again; not the sort, however, that made Paul Brent want to scream a guilt that might not be his. This was a doubt induced by cold consideration, grim enough to prove disconcerting.

Actually, Paul could not account for the past half hour, except as a period of mental haze. He remembered starting to his hotel room, but wasn't sure that he had really been there. The spinning lights visible from his window were an occurrence that he associated with previous nights.

It could be that he had come directly here; that he had murdered the man who lay on the floor!

Such a deed, committed in a frenzy, could numb the senses and produce a haze. Confessed killers often stated, honestly enough, that they had no recollection of anything that happened. Paul's own words: "I killed him," spoken aloud to himself, loomed anew as damning evidence.

If only he could snatch some tangible detail from that recent whirl of thoughts!

There was a name somewhere in the medley. A name about which everything revolved. A name that Paul would know instantly, if he heard it; but every effort to recall it made it more elusive. The name that Paul sought and could not find was Shiwan Khan.

With an effort, Paul jolted himself back to the present. He faced the fact that he had a revolver in his hand; that a dead man lay on the floor. The gun could tell him nothing, but the victim could, despite death's intervention. One way for Paul to test his own sanity was to learn if he knew the dead man by sight.

Probably he didn't. That settled, he

would feel better. People didn't go about killing strangers merely for the fun of it. Stepping boldly forward, Paul knelt beside the body. Still gripping the gun, he used his free hand to turn the dead face up into the light.

The sight jarred him. Even in death, he recognized those drawn, dissipated features, tight-lipped and bulge-eyed. The dead man was Bob Ryndon, stunt flier and adventurer, whose path had crossed Paul's a few times too often.

They had argued it out heavily, nearly a year ago, when Ryndon had wanted Paul to O. K. some old crates that were being shipped to China. It wasn't a Globe job; the planes were some that Ryndon had bought on his own. But the purchaser would not accept them unless the specifications were approved by a person of recognized ability.

Paul had refused to lend his name to it, on the ground that Globe wouldn't like it. Ryndon hadn't believed him. He had called Paul a fool who put integrity ahead of easy money. Nobody would ever know the difference, Ryndon had said, since a lot of incompetent Chinese aviators were going to crack up whatever ships they received. Paul had coolly told Ryndon to ask someone else to do his dirty work.

Who else knew about that argument?

No one, unless Ryndon had talked about it, which he would not have found good policy. Unless he had found some way to twist the facts against Paul. Nevertheless, it wasn't pleasant for Paul to find that this dead man was an acquaintance, even though he hadn't seen Ryndon for nearly a year.

SUDDENLY sure that he had not killed Bob Ryndon, Paul decided upon immediate departure. He was somewhere in New York; that was certain. If he could find his way to the street, he could go back to his hotel and forget Bob Ryndon. The stunt flier knew plenty of other people; the police would probably find the real murderer long before they reached Paul.

Almost to the door, Paul realized that he still held the gun. He was wondering what he ought to do about it. An incriminating thing to have, yet something he would need if he met the real killer just outside of here. Paul was speculating upon that unpleasant prospect, when he stiffened.

A *click* of the doorknob told that someone was entering the room!

To late to get out of sight from the passage, Paul dropped back, aiming the revolver. He was ready to give challenge, when he found that words were unneeded. The person who entered wasn't formidable. Quite the contrary.

The arrival was a girl. Stepping in from the passage, she faced Paul, a faraway stare in her eyes. That distant expression suited her costume. The girl was clad in Chinese dress that made her a symphony in silk.

Her colorful costume had the appearnace of pajamas, topped by a loose, wide-sleeved robe of an exquisite pattern, combining poppy leaves and peacocks. She was one of those rare creatures who might have delighted an opium smoker's dreams.

Her oval face was beautiful: dark eyes with languorous lashes, ruddy lips that were not too bright. Her nose was short, but without the wideness that sometimes marred the symmetry of Chinese features.

Despite her costume, Paul would have classed the girl as an American, rather than Chinese, if it had not been for the olive tinge of her complexion. Since she showed neither fear nor antagonism, Paul lowered the gun and waited.

The girl spoke in English, not with singsong pitch but in a slow monotone:

"My name is Lana Luan."

There was a rippling sound to the name, even with that slow pronunciation. Paul bowed, but did not introduce himself. He watched the girl gaze about the room.

She looked toward a large box-seat couch at the front wall, then toward the radio across the room. Her eyes passed the rear window and settled on the corner where Ryndon's body lay beneath the greenish light.

Sight of the dead man produced no surprise. Lana Luan acted as though she expected to see Ryndon lying there.

It was the body of a man, clad in pajamas, lying face down.

Turning to Paul, she eyed the gun and stated, very simply:

"You killed him."

Almost on the point of nodding, Paul restrained himself. Lifting one hand slightly, Lana Luan carried a broad fold of silk cloth with it.

"Let me have the gun," she suggested. "I shall dispose of it. I think it would be wise for you to leave."

There was no malice in the eyes that met Paul's. Their depths revealed a simple sincerity. Perhaps Lana Luan had wanted Ryndon's death, though Paul was convinced that she had not murdered the man. It might be that she was protecting someone else. Whatever the case, it offered an end to Paul's own predicament.

He placed the revolver in the folds of silk, gingerly keeping his hand in readiness, should Lana Luan make a grab for it. His trust was complete when he saw the girl stand motionless, merely waiting for him to leave.

With a quick stride, Paul stepped toward the passage. He was through it, closing the door, before the girl could possibly have disentangled the gun, to aim it. His parting glimpse restored Paul's momentary loss of confidence. A statue in silk, Lana Luan had made no move whatever.

Not until Paul had time to reach the street did the girl stir from her position. Then turning her head mechanically toward the door, she watched it, while her hand folded in the corners of a silken square. The gun was not lying in a portion of her sleeve. It was in the center of a handkerchief that matched her costume in all its gorgeous pattern.

In the same tone that she had used before, Lana Luan announced:

"He has gone."

THE lid of the box-couch lifted. From the interior came an ugly Mongol face, quite like that of the taxi driver who had brought Paul to this apartment house. The leering Mongol was the actual murderer of Bob Ryndon, and Lana Luan accepted him as another portion of the scene.

Lifting the handkerchief by its corners, she grave it to the Mongol, who carefully wrapped the folds more tightly. He paid no further attention to the girl, as she stepped toward the doorway to make her own departure. Even before the door had closed, the Mongol was engaged in other business.

The silk-wrapped gun pocketed in his American garb, the killer stepped to the radio and lifted the lid of the cabinet.

It was a combination phonograph and radio. From the turntable, which had stopped automatically, the Mongol lifted a ten-inch phonograph record and slid it beneath his dark vest. Moving past the corpse, he was careful not to crack the phonograph record, as he made a rapid search of Ryndon's clothes.

With a dozen pockets to turn inside out, the job took several minutes, despite the Mongol's expert touch. Finished with the clothes, he tapped the pocket of Ryndon's pajama jacket, then had a look through a suitcase that stood in the corner. Satisfied with his task, the Mongol fixed his gaze upon the greenish lamp.

Though his leer did not alter, the Mongol's eyes took on the same distant stare that Paul Brent had noted in the case of Lana Luan. At that time, it had not occurred to Paul that he, too, had held a similar fixed expression, back in his hotel room. He might have realized it, had he remained to witness the actions of this Mongol.

"Yes!" hissed the leering man, suddenly. "It is I, Hoang Khu. I hear you, master. All is done, Kha Khan!"

There was a pause, as if the evil brain behind the yellow face had received an important reminder. A clawlike hand moved toward the greenish light. About to touch the glowing blub, Hoang Khu quivered, as under a vibrating impulse.

Slanted eyes lost their stare as the Mongol's fingers gripped the light bulb, prepared to loose it from the socket. An instant later, Hoang Khu gave up that purpose. Leaving the light aglow, he whisked from the table and bounded, with a rubbery silence, to the open box-couch at the front of the room.

Clutching one hand to protect the precious record, Hoang Khu vaulted the couch edge with the other. Landing noiselessly, he sped a claw upward, drew the hinged top into place with an action as silent as it was speedy.

A streak of blackness stretched inward from the passage. It formed a hawkish silhouette upon the floor, then dwindled, as the figure that cast it moved into the green light's glow. Of all intruders upon the scene of death, this arrival was the most remarkable.

He was a being cloaked in black, whose slouch hat obscured the profile that had momentarily registered itself upon the floor. Unlike Shiwan Khan, who ruled evil from afar, this being, foe to crime, preferred to visit danger zones in person.

The green glow had welcomed a final figure from the gloom: The Shadow!

CHAPTER III.
CRIME'S EVIDENCE.

FROM the moment of his entry, The Shadow began an intensified survey of the murder scene, accomplishing his work with most efficient tactics. Starting with Ryndon's body, he noted its position, the condition of the wound, as well as the dead man's face.

With one black-gloved hand, The Shadow tilted Ryndon's chin into the light. All the while, another gloved hand was waiting, half-concealed within The Shadow's cloak folds. The slightest move on the part of any foe, hidden or otherwise, would have brought that ready hand into sight, armed with a .45 automatic.

In inspecting the body, The Shadow used a process that had occurred to neither Paul Brent nor Hoang Khu. He stooped in the corner beyond the flattened form, so that he retained a view of the entire room. It was impossible to tell whether he was actually looking at the body, or keeping camouflaged watch on other portions of the room.

True, there were moments when The Shadow's eyes displayed a reflected glow when they caught the rays of the lamplight; but those moments were seldom, and afforded no opportunity to Hoang Khu, who was watching from the crack of the couch top.

The Mongol considered his own concealment safe. The interior of the couch was dark; no one, not even The Shadow, could have discerned the peering eyes of Hoang Khu.

At intervals, the Mongol eased the couch top a trifle upward, while his other hand sought the handle of a long-bladed knife beneath his coat. But always, Hoang Khu was forced to let the top inch down again, when The Shadow made a timely turn in his direction.

Ryndon's clothes showed plainly that they had been searched. Therefore, The Shadow gave them a very brief examination, which did not allow Hoang Khu time to get busy with the knife. Gliding about the room, The Shadow passed close to the couch, but he was gone before Hoang Khu could take advantage of his nearness.

Reaching the radio, The Shadow used his system of standing against the wall beyond it, thus watching the door, as well as the rest of the room—the couch included—while he made an inspection of the cabinet. He learned, by lifting the lid, that the radio was also equipped as a phonograph.

He also discovered something more.

Though the combination cabinet contained no records, there was dust on the phonograph needle. Peeling away a glove by pressing his left hand beneath his right elbow, The Shadow stroked the needle point with his finger tip and assured himself of the telltale clue.

One of Shiwan Khan's devices, that of influencing persons by sound, was definitely indicated to The Shadow.

During his roam about the room, the cloaked investigator had given passing glances to the green light. His interest in the olive-tinted bulb had been quite as frequent as Hoang Khu's efforts to bring a knife into play.

Back at the table, The Shadow was comparing the position of the light with that of Ryndon's body. A whispered laugh stirred the room.

Like the stroke of Shiwan Khan's gong, the tone was shuddery. But the air seemed to absorb it, repeating an echoed sibilance, rather than be jarred. The Shadow's laugh remained a recollection, whereas the gong clang had broken off the chain of previous memories.

The green light, as The Shadow saw it, had the sort of glow that would produce a hypnotic effect, the longer that one watched it.

Just how the bulb had been placed here, did not demand immediate consideration. Certain it was that Bob Ryndon had stared at the curious glow, until too puzzled to do anything about it. His mind focused upon the eye-gripping brillance, the victim had gone into a tracelike condition that had made his murder a simple matter.

Ryndon had never sensed an intruder's entry. He hadn't felt the gun muzzle that had been planted squarely against his spine. It was doubtful that the death shot had jarred him from his coma. Crime had been merciful, in this case, but that did not indicate charity on the part of the insidious master who had ordained Ryndon's death.

Contrarily, a supercriminal who dealt in such calculating methods could resort to wanton cruelty, if it would better serve a purpose. The Shadow had learned that often, in his campaign against living fiends.

GLOATING within the box-couch, Hoang Khu was hopeful that the light would rivet The Shadow's attention, as it had done with others. The Mongol was promptly disappointed.

The Shadow, it seemed, had timed the brief limit in which it was safe to watch the light. Stepping from the table, he began to inspect other portions of the room.

The slight crack on the edge of the box-couch was gone. Settled inside, Hoang Khu was making rapid changes in his plans. The knife was beneath his coat, with the phonograph record. Frantically, he was tugging at the silk cloth in his pocket, to get at the death gun.

Shiwan Khan wanted that revolver as it was, with Paul Brent's fingerprints implanted upon it. Hoang Khu, the tool, was spoiling one design of the hidden master, in an effort to save his own yellow-hued hide. He had no other choice.

If The Shadow lifted the couch top, a knife would not suffice the Mongol. It would be a question of gun against gun, and Hoang Khu's leer, though lost in darkness, was proof that the Mongol considered that he, rather than The Shadow, would be the survivor, should such a duel arrive.

With passing minutes, Hoang Khu realized that The Shadow had apparently ignored the big couch as the possible hiding place of an assassin. That was not entirely unreasonable; outwardly, the couch had an appearance of solidness. Working the top upward with his free claw, the Mongol shoved the gun muzzle to the crevice, along with his eye.

What Hoang Khu saw, pleased him. The Shadow, apparently satisfied that the room was empty, had returned to the light. This time, to test the glow fully, he had seated himself before the table. The green glow had done the rest. The Shadow was slouched forward toward the light, exactly as Ryndon had been when Hoang Khu murdered him.

Lifting the couch top higher, Hoang Khu aimed straight for The Shadow's back. Then, as a chance breeze from the partly opened window stirred the cloak sleeve, the Mongol changed aim with a snakish action of his claw. Tugging the trigger, Hoang Khu dispatched a bullet to the green light, instead of the black cloak.

Amid blackness wherein glass tinkled to the echoes of the gun blast, Hoang Khu sprang from the couch and dived for the window. A figure shot from the doorway passage, caught the Mongol in a low, fast drive.

Hoang Khu's gun blasted again—above The Shadow's shoulder. The shot told where the weapon was. A gloved hand clamped the Mongol's gun waist.

Wrenching wildly, Hoang Khu managed to dodge the stroke of The Shadow's gun. Letting his own revolver scale from his hand, he clawed at the long-limbed adversary who had sped in, cloakless, to intercept him. Hoang Khu was fighting with the fierce writhe of a giant python, which told that his present desire was escape.

Hoang Khu's hearing was no keener than The Shadow's. The Mongol had caught the creak of a door hinge before The Shadow entered. Similarly, The Shadow had heard vague indications of the Mongol's rapid sneak to the box-couch. After lulling the hidden killer, The Shadow had tricked him into showing his hand.

Noting the betraying crack along the couch edge, The Shadow had seen it disappear. Whisking off cloak and hat, he had draped them on the chair near the table. Choosing the passage, The Shadow had watched for Hoang Khu's thrust. Only the chance breeze from the window had prevented Hoang Khu from completely gobbling the bait. By shooting out the light, the Mongol had somewhat equalized matters.

His gun gone, Hoang Khu was after his knife. If gripped by the twisty yellow hand, the blade could prove a powerful weapon in this grapple. The Shadow was not deceived by a crackle that came from beneath Hoang Khu's coat. It was the phonograph record, not the Mongol's ribs, that had cracked.

To get the range he wanted, The Shadow whirled Hoang Khu toward the window, then loosed him with a half fling. Dropping back, The Shadow aimed his gun. But the quick-witted Mongol didn't wait.

Head foremost, he crashed through the window, ruining the half-lifted sash with his huge shoulder. Landing on a low roof, a story below, Hoang Khu made a lope for the roof edge.

By then, The Shadow was at the window, aiming his automatic. Had his finger tightened in its squeeze, there would have been one less Mongol in the service of Shiwan Khan. But The Shadow was forced to hurry the shot, with a jerky motion. A man lunged in from the doorway; behind him came the glare of a flashlight.

Jabbing his shot at Hoang Khu, The Shadow let the recoil carry him about. A tall figure in evening clothes, one arm raised to hide his face, he drove squarely upon the pair who had arrived to start a combat of their own.

THEY were headquarters police. The Shadow learned that as he tussled with them. The flashlight had clattered to the floor, and in the darkness the two men handled their guns earnestly, but with bluntness rather than speed. The Shadow treated them to jujitsu tactics, which they recognized but could not duplicate. The police guns, when they talked, merely shot into darkness.

One detective was flung in a backward somersault that brought him, gunless, against the box-couch. The other was launched into a spinning dive that ended when he crashed into the radio cabinet. Whipping his cloak and hat from the chair, The Shadow sped out through the doorway.

The half-groggy dicks were groping for their guns. Finding them, they performed individual crawls toward the glowing flashlight on the floor. Their paths crossing before they reached it, they locked in a well-matched grapple. By the time they had taken a few wild slugs at each other, they discovered their mistake.

By then, it was too late for them to even trace the combatant who had so suddenly left them. The Shadow had reached the rear street, where he, in his turn, was learning the futility of gaining an immediate trail.

Again wearing hat and cloak, The Shadow used a tiny torch to discover small blobs of blood, that ended after a few yards.

His shot had clipped Hoang Khu, but probably not seriously. The Mongol had reached friends and was safely away Those blood splotches, however, were not the only clues that he had dropped. Along the sidewalk, The Shadow found a few fragments of a broken phonograph record, which he promptly gathered.

Then, with a swift glide across the street, the cloaked being merged with the opposite darkness. Like others whose paths had crossed the trail of Shiwan Khan, The Shadow was gone into the night.

CHAPTER IV.

THE CEYLON RUBY.

It was dusk again and Paul Brent, staring from the hotel window, was hoping that the lights of the Broadway sign would begin their vivid whirl. The circles were moving, as they always did when the sign was illuminated, but they had not swung into that peculiar effect of opposite revolutions, timed to the rhythm of the lifting bird wings.

There was reason enough for Paul to seek the hypnotic opiate of those lights. He felt that they, alone, could cure him of a different sort of bewilderment, which the day's events had induced.

On the writing desk lay a newspaper, with an account of Bob Ryndon's death. It told that the murdered aviator's body had been found, following a phone call to the police. Who had given the tip-off, the newspaper didn't say, but it had been a timely one. Headquarters men had almost managed to capture a well-dressed intruder on the premises. Unfortunately, the man had slipped them.

Paul agreed that it *was* unfortunate. He was convinced that *he* wasn't the man in question. Whatever else he might have done, Paul hadn't wrestled with a brace of detectives. He at least remembered leaving Ryndon's apartment and coming back to the hotel.

In his opinion, the murderer had returned to the scene of crime, and the police had nearly trapped him. A near-capture, however, did not lessen Paul's own dilemma. The newspapers said that the police had recovered the death gun and were checking it for fingerprints.

Only too well did Paul realize that he had left his own imprints upon the revolver handle. Between him and arrest stood a barrier: his fingerprints were not on file.

But that would not help, if the police learned that he was a friend of Ryndon's and decided to question him. Once his fingerprints were taken, and compared with those on the gun, Paul Brent would be charged with murder.

He remembered how Lana Luan had let the gun nestle in the folds of silk. Was the lovely Chinese girl a party to

The Shadow whirled Hoang Khu toward the window, then loosed him with a half fling.

the plot that might brand Paul as the killer? He did not know, but he hated to believe that she was. The arrival of the returning murderer could have forced Lana Luan to drop the revolver and flee. In fairness to her, Paul was ready to accept that explanation.

What bothered him most, was a telegram from Globe Aircraft. It acknowledged receipt of the orders, and stated that they were being put through with the recommended changes.

Paul had received that wire this afternoon, and the fact that the order sheets were missing proved that he must have mailed them. Unquestionably, he had done so during the same dazed period in which he had gone to Ryndon's place.

Paul could remember the lights. He was sure that they were responsible for all that had happened. That was why he wanted to see them spin again, in hope that while under their influence, he could recapture some important details of yesterday.

WHILE Paul watched, the circles began their concentric revolutions. By the time they had returned to normal, he was receiving the projected thoughts of Shiwan Khan.

Under the control of the being whose name he again could have spoken, Paul went to the writing desk. Picking up a pencil, he wrote mechanically upon a sheet of paper, following the mental dictation that came through his own brain.

SHIWAN KHAN—Oriental master mind, who would conquer the world.

The quiver of a gong rang through Paul's head. With a shudder, he found himself at the writing desk. The name of Shiwan Khan was erased from his memory, but upon the paper, in handwriting that was Paul's own, the young man saw:

> It would be unwise to deny that the orders are as stated. Mistrust by Globe would result, demanding full explanation. Such details would produce a link to Ryndon's death and bring suspicion from the police.

Though the statements were not Paul's own, they might just as well have been by the time that he had read them. Until then, he had not connected the altered orders with the scene at Ryndon's. Knowing at last that they were joined, Paul saw the entire logic.

Some master brain had forced him to an illegal action, then had framed him as a murderer. Should he repudiate the deed that he had actually performed, Paul would be convicted for a crime that he had not committed!

Self-preservation demanded that Paul Brent take no step to free himself from that dilemma. He could only trust that in some way, the schemes of a master plotter might be frustrated, thus releasing Paul—and perhaps others—from the insidious, invisible control.

Circumstances enmeshing Paul Brent were not as bad as he imagined. There was bluff behind the message that Shiwan Khan had forced the dupe to write. The Shadow had scored definite points against his invisible superfoe, and at present was reaping the fruits of his partial victory.

During the periods when he discarded cloak and hat, The Shadow frequently posed as Lamont Cranston, a wealthy globe-trotter who spent many of his idle hours at the exclusive Cobalt Club. The membership list included Cranston's friend, Police Commissioner Ralph

Weston, who liked the quiet of the club for after-office conferences.

As was usual, when crime was on the rampage, Weston was at the Cobalt Club chatting with his ace inspector, Joe Cardona, while Cranston sat by, almost a disinterested listener. Actually, The Shadow was learning just how far the law had advanced with the Ryndon case.

"THERE's not enough prints on that gun to convict a flea!" Cardona was growling to the commissioner. "Whoever handled it last, smudged it so badly that we might as well forget it."

The Shadow's lips framed a slight smile. Though he had not learned of Paul's visit, he knew that the death gun, if kept by Hoang Khu, could have proven a valuable tool in the incrimination of an innocent party. Lack of Hoang Khu's fingerprints did not matter. The Shadow intended to find that murderous Mongol himself.

"I let the reporters think we had the prints, though," added Cardona. "I told them, too, what we'd found out about Ryndon. How he had gone to a place called Sinkiang, to sell a lot of old crates to the government there, after he couldn't unload them in China."

"Sinkiang is part of China," corrected the commissioner. "They call it the New Dominion. Am I correct, Cranston?"

The smile was traceable upon the hawkish, masklike features of Cranston. His tone was leisurely when he spoke.

"Sinkiang is not precisely what they call it," said The Shadow. "A new dominion, yes, but in a sense its own dominion. It lies between Tibet on the south, and Mongolia on the north. It is a restive land in some ways—the strangest that I have ever visited."

"Why so?"

"It is close enough to feel the influence of Tibet, the one country where mind rules supreme, yet it feels the force of Mongolia, where brute strength has long been a standard. Sinkiang may some day become the very heart of Asia."

Weston decided to test Cranston's knowledge of geography further. The commissioner nodded to Cardona, who produced a small, ruddy object that glimmered in the light. Holding it upon the palm of his hand, Weston displayed it to Cranston. The object was an exquisite ruby, of ancient cut.

"Could this have come from western China?"

"Not originally," was Cranston's reply. "Stones of pomegranate-red, like that one, are mined only in Ceylon."

"I told you!" Weston gave a nod to Cardona. "This must be one of the rubies from the Twindell collection. Ryndon probably bought it from one of those dealers in Maiden Lane."

The Shadow was instantly intrigued. He knew of the famous gem collection owned by Benjamin Twindell, a wealthy and eccentric New Yorker. Twindell had been disposing of his gems in batches, during the past six months. He wanted cash, so he said, to buy up more famous precious stones.

A connection between Ryndon and the Twindell gems offered new angles. In Cranston's casual tone, The Shadow asked:

"You say this ruby belonged to Ryndon?"

"We found it in his vest pocket," informed Cardona, "tucked down in the corner. Whoever turned those pockets inside out missed finding it. All right, the ruby didn't come from China."

"It could have," remarked The Shadow. "Ryndon was in Sinkiang. He might have obtained the ruby there."

Cardona didn't agree.

"Maybe they kick people's heads around for footballs in Sinkiang," he said, "but they don't shoot marbles with rubies. I talked with a lot of gem dealers. They say the only valuable stuff that comes from the territory is jade. Besides, Thorner says it looks like one of old Twindell's rubies."

"Who is Thorner?"

"Twindell's representative. He buys up whatever Twindell tells him. Right now, Thorner says the old man's gone nuts over the Chinese curios. Thinks they're bargains, because a lot of them have been shipped over here for sale. But Thorner argues the opposite. He says the market is glutted. But when Twindell says buy, Thorner buys."

"How often does that happen?"

"Whenever there's an auction down in Chinatown, to hear Thorner talk. But to get back to the ruby, Thorner is sure it was one of Twindell's lot, so there's no use wasting time by going to see a few small-fry dealers."

WHEN Cranston strolled from the club, he left Weston and Cardona checking lists of Ryndon's friends. From the names and addresses already compiled, it appeared that they would have to get out an international search warrant, if such a thing existed, to even find the people that the dead stunt flier knew.

They had picked a tougher task than rounding up all the gem dealers in New York; but The Shadow, meanwhile, had set himself a simple and direct task. He intended to visit the next important auction that was held in Chinatown.

From a blue-lit room that served him as a sanctum, The Shadow called his contact man, Burbank. Soon, he was connected through to Dr. Roy Tam, an influential Chinese business man, who had co-operated often with The Shadow.

From Dr. Tam, The Shadow learned that the next auction was scheduled for tonight, in the curio shop managed by Loo Look, a Chinese merchant.

Dr. Tam knew little about Loo Look, but he had much to say regarding other matters that The Shadow mentioned. The call finished, The Shadow glanced at the clock upon his table, noted that he had ample time to reach the auction before its scheduled hour of nine.

From beneath the table, The Shadow brought a portable phonograph. Upon its turntable, he placed a patched record.

There were cracky sounds as the disk revolved beneath the needle. Snatches of music, then intervals of silence. The record was composed of the fragments that Hoang Khu had dropped. They had been fitted into a blank disk, cut specially to receive them!

Listening to the reconstructed record, The Shadow heard a few words from the voice of a pretended radio announcer; then came the finish that he wanted. With clearness, the phonograph gave forth the sounds of a gong, that had a sharp, vibratory effect.

Shrouding curtains quivered upon the sanctum walls, as the black drapes took the vibrance of Shiwan Khan's weird token. When their waver ended, another shudder seemed to stir them. Through the sanctum throbbed the whisper of The Shadow's laugh.

The bluish light clicked off. A deep hush gathered in the solid gloom. The sanctum was empty. The Shadow had departed, bent upon another opportunity that might prove a setback to the schemes of Shiwan Khan!

CHAPTER V.

THE CHINESE AUCTION.

Loo LOOK's store resembled many others in Chinatown. It was on the ground floor of a building near the corner of Mott and Pell Streets, and it was the sort of place that usually attracted out-of-town visitors when they came to Chinatown.

A bland, rather squatty Chinaman, Loo Look had rolled in from somewhere and had bought out the merchant who occupied the premises. He had promptly closed the shop for alterations, then had begun a series of auctions to clear out the old merchandise.

This was the third sale of the sort, and the placards in the windows advertised it as the last. There were not very many patrons, because the junk on display in the window would hardly attract a connoisseur, and the Chinatown bus drivers were herding their patrons past Loo Look's toward other shops, where the managers appreciated tourist trade.

Certain it was that Loo Look had an independent way about him, even to the point of discouraging customers, which caused The Shadow to hope for real developments the moment that he entered the almost-deserted auction room.

Coming to the auction as Lamont Cranston, The Shadow naturally arrived in a limousine. The chauffeur had to drive away to find a parking space, but his departure did not deprive The shadow of American acquaintances.

There were three on the street: Cliff Marsland, who looked like a tough guy visiting Chinatown for a laugh; Hawkeye, a stoop-shouldered fellow who had the shifty shamble of a panhandler; and Clyde Burke, a newspaper reporter on the *Classic,* who frequently visited Chinatown for human interest stories.

All were agents of The Shadow. Of the three, Clyde was the one most likely to happen into the auction shop. He wasn't needed for the present; two other agents were already there.

One was Harry Vincent, a clean-cut young chap who seemed to have a genuine interest in Chinese curios. The other was Rutledge Mann, a portly, round-faced individual who ran an investment and insurance broker's office, which also served as The Shadow's clipping bureau.

Tonight, Mann was needed for a duty other than cutting out news reports and filing them. His mission was fulfilled when a sallow, quick-eyed man entered the auction room and immediately began an expert survey of art objects on display. Mann gave a thoughtful nod that was meant for Lamont Cranston.

It signified that the arrival was Herbert Thorner, the purchasing representative of Benjamin Twindell.

Perched on a small platform flanked by two wide Chinese screens, Loo Look began the sale. His audience was enlarging, but most of it was Chinese. Loo Look grinned broadly as he hammered the table with a gavel.

If the Chinese buyers thought that they were going to get merchandise at prices less than wholesale, to sell to other shops, they were mistaken. Loo Look's glance toward the side room told that much. He was gazing at Herbert Thorner.

Each time the auctioneer offered an item, Thorner announced a bid higher than anyone would normally give. Meeting with no competition, he won the chance to purchase. Thorner's whole attitude justified the statements that he had made to Cardona; namely, that old Twindell wanted to buy curios, hence it was Thorner's business to get them.

There was one feature of the auction, however, that held The Shadow's interest. The wares that Loo Look offered were objects of worth, better than the odds and ends displayed in the window. Thorner was getting his money's worth, even though he was the lone bidder.

Evidently, Loo Look had discouraged other buyers, in order to give Thorner full call. The Shadow saw some hidden motive behind that practice.

LIFTING a little curtain at the back of the platform, Loo Look brought out new items. A pair of exquisite vases produced a babble from the Chinese present. They entered the bidding, but stopped when Thorner offered five hundred dollars. Loo Look was ready to knock down the sale, when The Shadow spoke in Cranston's tone:

"Six hundred."

In quick, sharp tone, Thorner raised the price to seven hundred. The

Shadow offered seven hundred and fifty. Thorner shrugged, and let him have the vases at that price.

Later, an ivory pagoda was auctioned off. Again the bidding waxed between The Shadow and Thorner. When Cranston's calm tone announced twelve hundred dollars as the bid, a wince appeared upon Thorner's sallow features. With another shrug, Twindell's representative let the sale go through.

A change was noticeable on Loo Look's fattish face. The auctioneer was troubled because Thorner had a rival. He glanced over toward the sallow man, who coolly ignored him. Whatever else was due, Thorner was shifting the burden to Loo Look. The auctioneer became more crafty.

Instead of bearing down on Thorner, Loo Look tried to impress Cranston, and found it did not work. Actually, Loo Look was pleased. He thought that he had found the system by which he could eliminate the unwanted buyer.

Turning to the curtain, Loo Look fumbled a few moments, then brought out of a porcelain dragon, excellent from the artistic standpoint, despite its hideous appearance.

Setting the dragon upon the table, where it stood a foot high, Loo Look tapped it affectionately and let his roaming gaze center finally upon Cranston.

"Velly fine item," said Loo Look, as though he did not mean it. "Who buy?"

Like Cranston, Thorner was indifferent. A Chinaman offered five hundred dollars. Loo Look lifted the gavel, was about to swing it, when Thorner stepped in with a six-hundred-dollar bid. Before Loo Look could pound the bid through, The Shadow had casually raised the offer by a hundred dollars.

From then on, it was a duel of price, and with good reason. Anyone could have risked a large offer for that dragon. Like Thorner, The Shadow knew it to be a work of the Ch'ien Lung period, which any collector of Chinese porcelain would prize beyond mere money.

Hundred by hundred, the bids were jumping into the thousands. With every increase, Loo Look became more nervous —very odd behavior for an auctioneer. Thorner, backed by the Twindell wealth, seemed quite unconcerned. At last, there was another shrug, this time from Cranston. It came when Thorner offered ten thousand dollars.

Loo Look's gavel hit the block from its own sheer weight. Glad that the ordeal was over, he wiped his forehead with the curtain when he turned in that direction. He offered a few more items, but none was important. After disposing of a small bronze incense burner that Thorner bought for a mere ten dollars, Loo Look closed the sale.

Some of the Chinese onlookers were leaving the auction room. Vincent and Mann went out with them. The Shadow, of course, remained, because he had made purchases. Thorner was getting first service.

Helpers were carrying his trophies out to a car, the porcelain dragon along with them, but Thorner was not paying for his purchases. He simply signed a receipt, which Loo Look accepted, then turned and followed the men who lugged his weighty packages.

From the platform, Loo Look met Cranston's gaze. Shifting his eyes, the auctioneer saw the bank notes that long-fingered hands were peeling from a large roll. Looking farther, Loo Look observed that only Chinese were still in the auction room. Leaning forward, he inquired in confidential tone:

"You like Ch'ien Lung dlagon?"

The Shadow acknowledged that he did. Lo Look gripped him by the arm, drew him to the platform.

"I show you velly good one."

STEPPING to the curtained shelf at the rear of the platform, Loo Look probed beyond it. From the motion of his hands, he was trying to indicate that he was drawing another dragon from the shelf, but there was something wrong with the action.

Loo Look's hands were too far apart. Before he could finish whatever he was about, The Shadow was making a long leap in the auctioneer's direction. He caught Loo Look's left wrist, clamping it tight. The Chinaman's right hand gave a jerk.

Instantly, the platform slid apart beneath The Shadow's springing feet. The quick slither of those separating halves was not swift enough to trap him. Like a skater leaving a layer of crackling ice, The Shadow reached the safety of the ledge where Loo Look stood.

With the failure of that thrust, another came. The ornate screens beside the platform were overturned. From each side sprang a pair of murderous Mongols, four assassins of the Hoang Khu type, whipping long knives into play. They did not have to cross the opened floor. They could throw those blades.

Their hands went back for the hurls that The Shadow, in his present position, could not hope to stop. The knives flashed wildly. A splitting surge of human forms had bowled in on the Mongols.

Those alert allies, springing to The Shadow's aid, were not his own agents. They were men from whom neither Loo Look nor the Mongols had expected an attack: the crowd of Chinese who had remained clustered in the auction room!

His head bobbing frantically from side to side, Loo Look saw the Mongols fighting off a human flood. With a high-pitched cry, the treacherous auctioneer managed to complete the pull of his left fingers, despite The Shadow's grip. He tugged the switch that he had tried to yank before he slid the floor apart.

Every light was extinguished. Amid the blackness, the excited babble of many voices, Loo Look gave a frenzied writhe. It did not take him from The Shadow's clutch, but it produced another result. Twisting, Loo Look was overbalanced from the ledge. He had launched himself into the blackened pit that he had opened.

Perhaps Loo Look preferred the fate that lay below, if it would only free him from The Shadow. But even his suicidal effort did not bring release. The Shadow retained his tenacious grip, though it cost him his foothold on the ledge.

Into those yawning depths went two locked figures. They were bound for the same destination, Loo Look and The Shadow!

CHAPTER VI.

LOO LOOK SPEAKS.

THE plunge was short, but with a solid finish—for Loo Look. Even in the swift dive from the ledge, which he had accepted at a moment's notice, The Shadow had calculated the result and found time to gain a suitable advantage.

Bland Chinamen like Loo Look didn't throw themselves away while they still had hope of life. The auctioneer's dive was one of hope, not suicide.

It jarred Loo Look, however, much more than he had expected. Dropping from the ground floor to a stony basement was not healthy, with another man's weight plunging with him, to land on top of him. That was exactly what happened to Loo Look. In his twist, he had gone first, with The Shadow following.

Rising from the floor, The Shadow flicked a tiny flashlight upon the prostrate auctioneer. Loo Look was stunned, and would remain so for a while. From the open trap above him, The Shadow could hear excited yells, too babbled to interpret. It might be that his loyal Chinese needed help.

Looking for a way out, The Shadow saw a single door to the stone-walled cellar room. It had a knob, but before The Shadow could grip it, the door did the unexpected. It opened, not on a hinge, but in a sliding fashion. Guided by a gleaming light behind them, a pair of Mongols hurled themselves upon The Shadow.

He met them in between their knife-lunging hands. A fist to a jaw floored the first. The Shadow took a throat grip on the second killer, twisted him about and flung him toward the man who held the light.

There was a sweep of a bobbing flashlight, that glared upon the face of Hoang Khu. Then The Shadow was locked with the chief assassin of the lot.

Shiwan Khan had taken no chances in disposing of The Shadow. He had ordered Hoang Khu and two others to be ready to deliver the *coup de grâce* after Loo Look dropped The Shadow in the pit. But none of the trio was able to supply the finishing touch. Even certainties were apt to fail, against The Shadow's strategy.

Upstairs, four of the Mongol fighters were having a tough time with a horde of Chinese. Meanwhile The Shadow, lone-handed, was giving three others an unexpected battle. He had flung Hoang Khu aside and was somewhere in the passage when the three performed another fling in his direction.

Knives, whirling through the air in the blanketing darkness, were met by stabbing tongues of flame that brought howls from the Mongols. One sprawled on the passage floor; another staggered, locking with The Shadow. Twisting that wounded fighter aside, The Shadow let the third go by.

Their knives had missed in the darkness, for they thought The Shadow had dived toward the end of the long passage. The one man who had heard the others stumble was making for a stairway that offered a chance of escape. The fleeing Mongol was Hoang Khu.

In the struggle, there had been no chance for any Mongol, Hoang Khu least of all, to identify The Shadow as anything more than a whirlwind fighter. By producing immediate darkness, The Shadow had been quite as formidable in Cranston's guise, as if attired in his habitual garb of black.

Hoang Khu had recognized The Shadow by deed. With his mates fallen, Hoang Khu had known enough not to stay around.

SHAKING off the wobbly grappler, The Shadow started after Hoang Khu. As he reached the stone steps, a light gleamed above. Someone had pressed the switch that Loo Look had cut off. With The Shadow at the bottom of the stairs, Hoang Khu's flight seemed due for a sharp finish.

Again, The Shadow's finger was on a gun trigger, ready to drop Ryndon's murderer, when intervention saved Hoang Khu. This time, it was not The Shadow who received the attack. Instead, flinging men hurled themselves upon Hoang Khu. They were the victorious Chinese coming from the auction room, to learn what lay below.

Hoang Khu became the center of a human tangle, with The Shadow unable to risk a shot. At no moment was the Mongol entirely visible; sometimes his head bobbed into sight; at others, The Shadow glimpsed one of his swinging arms.

A white bandage showed on Hoang Khu's left wrist, a souvenir of the flesh wound that The Shadow had given him the night before. Knifeless, and partly crippled, Hoang Khu's chances looked slim against the half dozen Chinese who grappled with him.

Numbers, however, seemed to matter little to the wiry, heavy-muscled Mongol, provided The Shadow was not among his antagonists. He was shedding his Chinese opponents with heaves

From each side sprang a pair of murderous Mongols . . . whipping long knives into play.

of his broad shoulders. Landing on hands and knees, they were crawling back toward Hoang Khu, when he finally disposed of the last pair who clutched him.

Turning his twist into a drive, Hoang Khu sent the pair down the stairway, straight into the path of The Shadow's gun. Springing upward, The Shadow met the light forms of the pitching Chinese and halted their fall, but the delay cost him his chance to settle matters with Hoang Khu. The Mongol was gone, pursued by the scrambling Chinese who had been crawling back to battle him.

Knowing that trouble still lurked below, The Shadow swung about and reached the bottom of the stairs. He dropped back on the lowest step, as a Mongol made a lunge toward him. The Shadow's adversary was the wounded man whose tussle had led to Hoang Khu's escape. With a knife plucked from the floor, the fellow was seeking another chance of murder.

His lunge was staggery, too high. As the knife descended past The Shadow's shoulder, the Mongol received a gun muzzle against his chest. He heard The Shadow's sharp words in a tongue he understood, ordering him to surrender. Before the Mongol could halt his stagger and snarl a reply, a revolver spoke instead, from the top of the stone steps.

Thrusting aside the crumpling body of the Mongol, The Shadow arose to receive a bespectacled Chinaman, who was hurrying down the stairway. The arrival was Dr. Tam, and he became ardent in his apologies.

He had seen the Mongol's lunge, but had not realized that The Shadow had the assassin under complete control. It would have been well, Tam recognized, to have kept this Mongol alive.

"The others have all escaped," said Tam, his tone quite sorrowful. "They broke through panels that we did not know about. It is unfortunate, very, that the men I sent here to help you were unable to do better."

The Shadow insisted that they had done well enough. He conducted Tam along the passage, beyond the prone Mongol who had been the first to fall. By the light that came through the open trap to Loo Look's auction platform, they found the auctioneer himself, blinking as he rubbed his head.

Yanking Loo Look to his feet, The Shadow spoke to him in Chinese. He was demanding the name of Loo Look's master, but the fellow did not want to give it. Finding his voice, he uttered a high-pitched jargon that both Tam and The Shadow understood.

Loo Look was saying that he had been paid to run the auction house, but he did not specify why, nor did he state the name of the man who had hired him. Loo Look's evasive speech ended abruptly when The Shadow pressed a gun muzzle against his forehead.

"Speak the name!"

Loo Look spoke it, with a gulp. Fearful of the foe who now gripped him, he discarded his allegiance to his former master. His expression, though, was one of terror as he uttered:

"Shiwan Khan!"

As if the loosing of that name had wrenched his lips, Loo Look's mouth stiffened into a frozen writhe. The scream that he gargled came deep from his throat, issuing wildly through his half-opened mouth. With a sudden convulsion, he twisted his body free from the hands that gripped him.

Before The Shadow could halt Loo Look's torturous forward lurch; before Dr. Tam could thrust himself in front, to break the fall, Loo Look, his hands clasped tight to his stomach, struck the floor, shoulder first, jolted with a twisty shudder and flipped face upward, dead.

Seemingly, he had been struck down by the invisible hand of Shiwan Khan, in new evidence of the controlling master's unfathomable powers Nor was that all. Like a token of delivered death, there came a muffled *clang* from somewhere beyond the confines of that stone-walled pit.

Alarm flashed from the eyes of Dr. Tam as the bespectacled Chinaman stared toward his friend, The Shadow. But there was no expression of awe upon the masklike countenance of Cranston.

Imperturably, The Shadow pointed to the face of Loo Look. Dropping his gaze, Tam saw the stream of blood that was oozing from the dead auctioneer's lips.

Internally injured by his fall from the floor above, Loo Look had succumbed from the straining effort when he forced himself to utter the name of Shiwan Khan.

As for the *clang* that followed, it was likewise a coincidence. It came again, louder, ending with a smash. There was an echo of tinkling glass.

The police were breaking through the front of Loo Look's auction house. Shaking Dr. Tam into motion, The Shadow started him out through the passage and up the stone stairs. They were crossing the landing, when the invading police saw them and raised a shout. But there was no chance for the Chinatown Squad to overtake those departers.

Just as Hoang Khu had woven a path through broken panels and short zigzag passages, to escape Tam's loyal crew, so did The Shadow and the estimable Chinese doctor elude the blundering police. Through outside alleys, The Shadow let Tam lead the way.

They were bound for Tam's own headquarters, where The Shadow could contact his agents. After that, The Shadow and Dr. Tam would mark out the next step in their common cause; the trailing of Shiwan Khan!

CHAPTER VII.

QUEST OF THE DRAGON.

WHILE rapid battle raged in Loo Look's place, some of The Shadow's agents had scattered a flock of tough-looking Chinese out front. Dr. Tam had expected such trouble, when he concentrated some of his men at the auction house. Though tong wars were a thing of the past, lesser feuds still existed in Chinatown.

The dispersed Chinese rioters knew nothing about Shiwan Khan, nor did they unwittingly serve him by making trouble. Others of The Shadow's agents had sped away on another appointed quest. They were trailing Herbert Thorner and his load of curios, which included the rare Ch'ien Lung dragon.

Paced by Moe Shrevnitz, a speedy cab driver in The Shadow's service, the agents had caught up with Thorner's car when it reached its final destination, an old brownstone mansion on an isolated stretch of avenue. They recognized the house the moment that they saw it; the home of Benjamin Twindell.

The car was expected. Two stocky servants came from the Twindell mansion and helped the chauffeur unload. Thorner was no longer in the car; he had dropped off somewhere along the route. From the wheel of the cab, Moe made terse comment to Harry Vincent, who sat in back:

"Pennsy Station."

Harry remembered that the pursuit had led near Pennsylvania Station; that Thorner could have dropped off there. The purchasing agent had left for parts unknown; perhaps he had taken the porcelain dragon with him. Among the wrapped packages being carried into the mansion, it was impossible to tell if the Ch'ien Lung masterpiece was included.

Twindell's mansion was built like a citadel. The only policy was to watch it and check on anyone who entered or left. When Moe wanted to follow

Twindell's chauffeur, Harry said no. The fellow could supply no information. Moe might be needed later.

Soon, Harry's foresight was proven. A cab stopped near Twindell's house. When it drew away, Harry was sure he saw a yellow face behind the wheel. He ordered Moe to trail the other cab, and signaled the deployed agents to be alert.

The order was too late. Instinctively, every agent had glanced toward the moving cab, then back toward Twindell's house. During the interim, a figure in darkish gray had crossed the sidewalk and taken a short passage that led to a side door.

There was no haste to the newcomer's motion. When he reached the side door he stood there, apparently confident that the drab hue of his attire would render him unnoticed.

He was by no means invisible, but his outline was vague, much like a camouflaged pattern. Even his saffron face was no more than a blur that could have been a portion of the dingy yellow brick that formed the house wall.

The human chameleon lifted one hand slowly, let it glide to a bell button beside the door. Oddly, his finger did not actually press the button; it merely remained against it, then folded into the hand as it descended. Nevertheless, the summons was answered by one of Twindell's husky servants.

He was close enough to see the face outside the doorway, that servant, but, curiously, he didn't. The gleam of eyes faded as the man in gray let his eyelids droop. The servant's puzzled gaze went past him, almost through him. Then, as though impelled by an idea, the servant nodded.

Stepping from the doorway, he looked along the house wall. Seeing nothing, he went back inside and closed the door.

The thing in gray was no longer outside the doorway. With its same slow motion, the figure had moved into the house. Watching the servant, The Shadow's agents did not see it go. Again, a conspicuous sight had drawn their attention the wrong way.

GLOOMY as a morgue, Twindell's mansion had a grand stairway leading to the second floor. Like an ancestral ghost come back to haunt the place, the gray shape moved up the steps, undiscerned by servants who were in the lower hall.

At the top, the unheralded visitant turned to the right. At the end of a short passage, he stepped into a lighted room and waited.

The room was Twindell's study. It had desks, filing cabinets, and other office furniture; but it also served as a curio room. Except for a few old weapons, which included Turkish scimitars and African spears, the place was filled with the Chinese items that Twindell had begun to collect.

Large screens and garish tapestries dominated the scene; but on a mantelpiece above a fireplace opposite Twindell's big desk sat a row of porcelain dragons, four in all. They were placed where Twindell could stare directly at them, whenever he sat at his desk.

Old Benjamin Twindell was at his desk at present, but he was not looking at the mantel. Instead, he was cackling gleefully over a new prize, a fifth dragon that stood on the desk.

Against the black background of a large safe set in the wall behind his desk, Twindell's face looked very white and withery. But his eyes were sharp, and his hands, despite their tight-skinned thickness, were very quick.

Those hands were fondling the new dragon as they would stroke a pet. At moments, Twindell's fingers went tight and clutched the smooth porcelain. Those moments marked his greatest glee, and Twindell had a habit of tilting his head back when he cackled. In the midst of one tilt, his chortle ended in a sharp croak.

Twindell's eyes had sighted the figure in the doorway. His lips gave a fishlike gasp; then from his thin throat came the name:

"Shiwan Khan!"

Small wonder that Shiwan Khan excited such complete awe from the man who viewed him. His very arrival was uncanny, in a house so thoroughly guarded. His appearance went with that weird ability. When Shiwan Khan wanted eyes to look elsewhere, they did not see him. When he wished them to fix upon his face, they remained riveted.

Shiwan Khan's loose-fitting clothes were American. Considerably oversize, they had a baggy appearance. His features made that drab garb fade from mind. After meeting Shiwan Khan face to face, one retained a mental picture of him as a being clothed in a robe of dull gold. Benjamin Twindell could recall that phenomenon from other times when he had met Shiwan Khan.

The saffron color of Shiwan Khan's face was the exact hue of the room lights, which produced the curious impression that the features were actually

MOE SHREVNITZ is a New York cab driver, smart as a whip and can drive with the best of them. He, too, is one of The Shadow's agents, and transports him on many of his battles against the underworld.

colorless, but gifted with the ability of absorbing the light about them.

Wide at the forehead, the face tapered to a pointed chin. Set in the center of that triangle was a thin, straight nose that stood as sharply as a ruled line. Beneath thin eyebrows that curved almost to the temples were green eyes that had a catlike glow.

Thin mustaches hung down from his upper lip, and on his chin was a slight dab of whiskers.

Shiwan Khan's mouth seemed lipless, until he opened it. Then, from lips that were thin streaks of brown, his voice dropped slow, well-accented words that broke the hush like tinkles of a bell.

"I HAVE come," said Shiwan Khan, "to speak with you about our future plans."

Twindell's scrawny hands clutched the dragon tighter.

"Have no fear concerning your dragon," added Shiwan Khan. "Five are already yours. The remaining two shall be delivered."

A pleased grin spread across Twindell's withered face.

"It will not be wise for Thorner to buy them as he did before," spoke Shiwan Khan, in his singular tone. "I shall have a messenger meet him with the next one. As for the final dragon, I shall choose a special method of delivery."

"Then our plans are unchanged?"

"My plans are *never* changed!" Shiwan Khan's slitted mouth widened into a contemptuous smile, that could have been meant for The Shadow. "You know my plans, Twindell."

"To rule the world—"

"From my hidden domain in Xanadu, beneath the barren reaches on the borders of Mongolia. You remember, Twindell, who I am."

Twindell nodded.

"I am the descendant of Genghis Khan!" For the first time, the visitor's voice showed change in tone. "Of the conqueror who could have ruled all the world, had he so chosen. I hold the treasures of his descendant, Kubla Khan!

"Treasure is not power. Like my ancestors, I am destined to become the Great Ruler. All the world shall call me Kha Khan! I shall have power, Twindell, supreme power! And you, because you have served me, shall have—"

Shiwan Khan paused. His strange green eyes roved from the desk to the mantel, then back again, to the object that Twindell so eagerly clutched. His voice restored to its accustomed level, Shiwan Khan concluded:

"You shall have your dragons."

Happy, Twindell was nodding. Then Shiwan Khan was close beside the desk. Close to Twindell's ear, he was reminding:

"In Tibet, I learned the power of the distant mind; with that mastery, I control the ways of men. To gain the instruments that I need for conquest is simple, where ordinary persons are concerned. But there are others—especially one other—who may interfere.

"There was trouble tonight, in Chinatown. I know its maker, a creature who calls himself The Shadow. All that he can have learned from Loo Look is my name. But he, or someone sent by him, may seek more from you.

"Should you be questioned by The Shadow, give him this casket"—Shiwan Khan produced a small, square silver box from beneath his baggy coat—"and say that it contains the answer that will satisfy him. From its contents, he will learn more than you could tell him.

"Yet what he learns will not destroy my plans, nor yours. But remember, Twindell—with all others, you know nothing. You are competent enough to deceive them. With The Shadow, I can trust no strength but my own."

Nodding, Twindell received the silver casket and placed it carefully in a desk drawer. There was a bell button on the desk; Twindell saw Shiwan Khan place his finger upon it. The greenish eyes were fixed in a glowing stare, but Shiwan Khan did not press the button. Then, turning to Twindell:

"I have projected the impression," said Shiwan Khan, "that will bring your servant. When he arrives, ask him who rang at the side door. When he says no one, tell him to make sure that he bolted the door."

"But he will see you—"

"He will *not* see me. The human form that remains motionless is seldom seen. When the brain behind that form can suspend its action of thought, it gives off no impressions. That accomplished, the bodily form is never seen."

STEPPING halfway toward the door, Shiwan Khan became rigid. His eyes stared into space, then closed. Twindell watched him, half expecting him to fade away. Then Twindell's attention was attracted by the entering servant, who came into the room wearing a puzzled expression.

Walking straight past Shiwan Khan, the man stopped before the desk and queried:

"Did you ring, sir?"

Twindell ignored the question, to put one of his own.

"Tell me, Harper, who was at the side door?"

"I'm glad you asked that, sir." The servant was relieved. "I am sure that someone rang. But there was no one there, sir."

"Very well. When you go downstairs, see that the door is bolted. You may have forgotten it."

As Harper went out, Twindell looked for Shiwan Khan. The green-eyed visitor was no longer in the room. Like Harper, Twindell had become unconscious of his presence. Shiwan Khan had left, unnoticed!

The side door was unbolted when Harper found it. Shiwan Khan had drawn the bolt, to move outdoors. He was a gray shape, timing his slow-motion advance to the approach of a cab. It was the one that The Shadow's agents had seen before. It had simply kept circling, with Moe on the trail, until the appointed time for its return.

After a halt, the cab pulled away. None of the watchers had seen a passenger enter it. Moe still followed, but Shiwan Khan took care of that by giving an order to the Mongol driver.

Swinging a corner, the cab halted at the curb. Its occupants remained motionless, as Moe wheeled past on an imaginary trail. Again, Shiwan Khan had demonstrated the power of mind. His cab turned about, sped away in the opposite direction.

A black-cloaked figure was arriving, meanwhile, among the agents stationed outside of Twindell's. Receiving reports in person, The Shadow was told that no one had entered or left the mansion.

Only The Shadow could have detected the weird coming and going of Shiwan Khan. And The Shadow had reached the scene too late!

CHAPTER VIII.

MESSAGES AT MIDNIGHT.

LIKE The Shadow, Shiwan Khan had devious routes in darkness; ways that led him to a hidden headquarters. The base that Shiwan Khan used was quite as remarkable as The Shadow's sanctum, and it possessed some features decidedly its own.

The walls of the lair were hung with dull gold cloth, the same color of the robe that Shiwan Khan was now wearing. It was odd that Twindell, who had never seen that robe, should picture it as part of the master Mongol's make-up. Perhaps it was the powerful force of Shiwan Khan's thoughts that had given

Twindell the correct impression.

Alone in his lair, Shiwan Khan could wear the habits of a mighty ruler. It was not mere whim that made him don that robe. From here, Shiwan Khan showed the power of his rule—over the minds of men!

Opposite the door of the gold-walled room was a small alcove. There, Shiwan Khan seated himself in a chair that had the ornate appearance of a small throne. Coupled with that ancient touch, the chair had a modern feature. It swiveled when Shiwan Khan turned about.

Facing a glass board that covered the rear wall of the alcove, Shiwan Khan gave further evidence of his ability at thought projection. He was using telepathy, the art that he had learned in Tibet, in combination with a scientific apparatus that he had designed.

In the East, the reception of projected thoughts was common. To apply it in America, something was needed to obtain the attention of untrained receivers, and Shiwan Khan had the required method.

He placed his long forefinger upon a button and actually pressed it. Immediately, lights showed upon the glass in front of him. Shiwan Khan gazed at a bird with moving wings; at circles, of different colors, that ran riot around the central figure.

In miniature, those lights formed an exact replica of the Broadway sign visible from Paul Brent's hotel window. Connected by a distant control, the sign was speeding up just like the lights on the glass board. To that extent, the whole device was mechanical; but it induced the mental result.

His eyes fixed, Shiwan Khan went into a self-induced trance. Finally, in bell-like tone, he spoke:

"Paul Brent . . . Paul Brent—"

He must have sensed an answer, for his next words were:

"I am Shiwan Khan. The thought that next comes to your mind is one that you shall remember."

From the small table beneath the board, Shiwan Khan drew a photograph of Lana Luan. He brought the picture between his own eyes and the revolving light. Slowly, he announced:

"Lana Luan. You have met her in reality. You meet her in your dream. Lana Luan."

Lowering the picture, Shiwan Khan lifted a small hammer, struck it lightly against a large gong that hung beside the flashing board. Golden curtains gave a quiver, that persisted even when the tone had ended. Shiwan Khan turned off the whirling lights.

He had given Paul Brent an added impression, another link that would keep him committed on the matter of the airplane contracts. Lana Luan was the link. Paul would remember that name from his brief haze. But again, as before, he would not recall the name of Shiwan Khan.

Pressing a second switch, Shiwan Khan produced a new array of lights upon the board. They showed a many-colored sign advertising a brand of cigarettes. The lights came on with a long glow, then unexpectedly went off.

The blank seemed timed, for when the glare appeared again, it came at an instant that produced a pulsating throb from Shiwan Khan's gold-clad form.

THE same effect jarred a gray-haired man who was pacing the veranda of a penthouse near Times Square. He saw the lights of the real sign, a huge affair, a dozen blocks away and stopped his incessant walk.

Many persons would have recognized that gray-haired man. He was Guy Chadbury, who held controlling interests in several companies that manufactured explosives. Chadbury had recently been in the news because of his testimony to congressional committees in Washington.

Chadbury had been authorized to manufacture munitions, chiefly bombs for airplanes, to determine the potential output of his factories in the event of war. At present, quantities of such munitions were ready for delivery to the government, along with Chadbury's reports.

In New York for conference with the managers of his factories, Chadbury had obtained this penthouse at a bargain rate, to complete an unfinished lease.

Every night, he had been attracted by the lights of the cigarette sign. They had a timing that caught the eye and held it; but only at certain hours. Chadbury had watched them often, wondering if the effect would occur again. Again, the lights had found the rhythm which fascinated him.

His arms propped on the railing, Chadbury became motionless. The world was a void, except for those repeating lights. Even they seemed to blur as Chadbury heard a slow, faraway voice, which struck him as familiar.

"Guy Chadbury—"

"Yes."

"I am Shiwan Khan. When I speak, all obey."

From then on, the voice was closer, wording thoughts that seemed to grow in Chadbury's own mind. It was calling him a fool to sell the full supply of munitions at cost, when he could rate his factories on one month's output, instead of two.

Those voiced thoughts were reminding him of recent orders for blasting materials, to be shipped to South American copper mines. If the munitions were sent instead, they would be welcome when received. Chadbury would profit through his own mistake, and no one would be the wiser.

Striving to fight off the urge for double-dealing, Chadbury was swept with a thought that had troubled him the night before. It concerned his niece, Beatrice. She was his brother's daughter, but close enough to Chadbury to be his own.

Through his mind throbbed the uncontrollable conviction that Beatrice was linked with the plan in question, that her safety depended upon his going through with it.

Turning in trancelike fashion, Chadbury walked into the penthouse. Seating himself at a table in the corner of the living room, he began to pencil notes upon a sheet of paper. He was thus engaged when his secretary entered and stood waiting with a handful of papers.

After a few minutes, the secretary ventured to interrupt Chadbury's thoughts. With a slight cough, he remarked:

"Mr. Chadbury?"

Chadbury did not hear the interruption. At that moment, his brain was ringing from the jarring note of a discordant gong. Jolting up in his chair, he gripped the table, as if waking from a nightmare. Blinking, he saw the secretary.

"Oh, hello, Briggs!" Chadbury's long face showed a tired smile. "I must have been asleep. What is it?"

"About those reports. You said that you would have the figures ready, sir."

"Of course!" Chadbury glanced at the desk. "Yes. Here they are. Take them down, Briggs, as I give them."

In the midst of his dictation, Chadbury paused.

"That's odd," he said. "I've put these on a basis of one month's output. If we double them—"

He stopped himself. Written below the hurried figures was the one word, a name: "Beatrice." Chadbury looked at the papers in his secretary's hand.

"Anything from the *Queen Anne?*" he demanded abruptly. "Did Beatrice answer that radiogram I told you to send last night?"

"Why . . . why, no, sir—"

"There is an answering radiogram in

those papers, Briggs. Let me have it at once!"

"Yes, sir. I intended to give it to you."

TAKING the radiogram from the troubled secretary, Chadbury read it. The message fitted his worriment. It stated that his niece was not on board the steamship *Queen Anne,* the ship on which she had booked passage for a Mediterranean cruise. The liner was four days out. Beatrice had been missing all that while.

Chadbury was drumming his desk.

"She's still in New York, Briggs!" he exclaimed. "At least, let us hope she is. I should have gone with her to the pier. I would have, if it had not been for that appointment with a man who did not arrive here!"

"Shall I call the police, Mr. Chadbury?"

"No." Chadbury's eyes were back upon the desk. "After all, there is no need to worry." Chadbury was speaking grimly, his gaze upon his own notations. "We shall hear from Beatrice. She probably missed the boat, and did not want me to be alarmed. By taking a regular liner, she could meet the cruise ship at Marseilles, or some other port. Let us finish these reports, Briggs."

"Very well, sir."

"Write the figures that I give you. The government only wants delivery on one month's output."

"Are you sure, Mr. Chadbury?"

"Yes. I talked with Washington today, while you were out. The rest of the supply"—Chadbury was tracing his own scrawled notations—"is to go to our New Jersey storage plant, along with the blasting materials."

With that, Chadbury crumpled the paper that lay on the desk and flung it into the wastebasket. He had lied to Briggs about that talk with Washington. But Chadbury knew that he was no longer his own master, not if he wished to see his niece alive.

He was fighting to recall a name—the name of Shiwan Khan—but it escaped his recollections. Like Paul Brent, he was fighting for some chance to shake off a baleful influence. At heart, however, Guy Chadbury felt that he was helpless.

IN Shiwan Khan's golden lair, three lights were glowing on the glass-fronted board. In the living room of a Long Island residence, a heavy-jawed man was leaning back in a chair staring at the room lights, which made the same triangular arrangement.

The man with the bulldog countenance was Mitchell Dorron, manager of the Tropical Export Line, which owned a fleet of freighters. His eyes were fixed on the room lights; his lips were moving slowly, as Dorron talked to the shining lights.

"On the *Aritoba,* bound for Chili," muttered Dorron, in a rumbling tone. "Shipments from Globe Aircraft and Chadbury Enterprises. Arrangements to be made tomorrow."

There was a pause, then Dorron repeated back his next impressions:

"Through the Canal, the *Aritoba* will change course for the Orient, with her cargo, duplicating the trip of the *Southern Star.* Yes, I shall remember."

The lights in Dorron's living room lost their glow at the distant touch provided by Shiwan Khan. Dorron heard the stroke of a gong; it seemed to echo from the dome of a reading lamp beside his shoulder. His eyes lost their stare, and Dorron smiled in the slight glow from the lamp.

He could remember the name of Shiwan Khan, though he knew that it soon would fade. But he would not forget instructions. Dorron was writing them down.

This was not the first time that he had served his invisible master. The

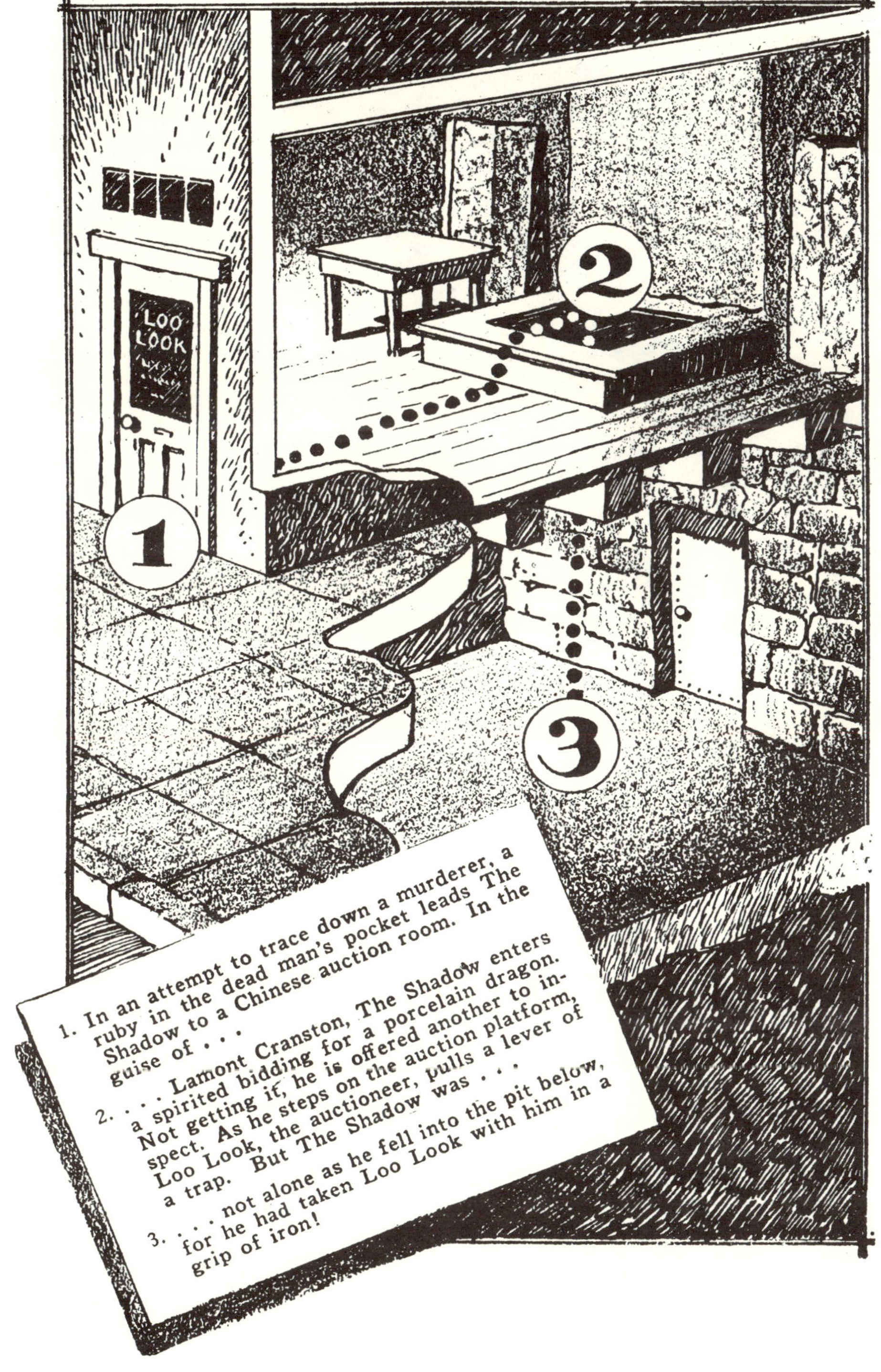
LOO
LOOK
1
2
3
1. In an attempt to trace down a murderer, a
ruby in the dead man's pocket leads The
Shadow to a Chinese auction room. In the
guise of . . .
2. . . . Lamont Cranston, The Shadow enters
a spirited bidding for a porcelain dragon.
Not getting it, he is offered another to inspect. As he steps on the auction platform,
Loo Look, the auctioneer, pulls a lever of
a trap. But The Shadow was . . .
3. . . . not alone as he fell into the pit below,
for he had taken Loo Look with him in a
grip of iron!

CLYDE BURKE, gay, debonair newspaper reporter, gets around New York, and because of his press connections comes on much inside information. Thus his connection with the New York *Classic* makes him invaluable as an agent of The Shadow.

trip that he was arranging for the *Aritoba* was identical with a voyage that the freighter's sister ship, the *Southern Star,* had made one month ago.

Reading the names of Paul Brent and Guy Chadbury, men with whom he would soon have dealings, Dorron gave a chuckle. They were new to the ways of Shiwan Khan. Dorron fancied that they were not enjoying themselves tonight. In fact, they were not.

Paul Brent was seated in his hotel room, staring at the ceiling, trying to recapture portions of odd experiences that had ensnared him. All that he could see was the ever-appearing face of Lana Luan, the Chinese girl that he had met in actuality, as well as in the strange dream-world ruled by Shiwan Khan.

In his penthouse, Guy Chadbury was gazing solemnly at an actual photograph of a very beautiful girl with dark eyes and raven hair. She was his niece Beatrice, and in the photograph she was wearing an evening gown.

Chadbury could picture Beatrice in various other costumes. But it never occurred to him that a high-collared jacket adorned with peacocks and poppy leaves would cause anyone to imagine Beatrice to be a Chinese girl.

Paul Brent could have informed him on that subject. He would have identified that lovely face immediately, could he have viewed the photograph. But he did not know the girl as Beatrice Chadbury. Paul Brent had met her as Lana Luan!

CHAPTER IX.
THE HIDDEN HAND.

AFTERNOON sunlight, glinting through the windows of Twindell's study, brought a sparkle from many gems upon the broad-topped desk. Benjamin Twindell, a smile upon his dryish face, was alternately nodding and shaking his head at prices offered for his wares. He was selling another portion of his jewel collection to an eager group of dealers.

Prices settled, the purchasers gathered in the gems that they had bought. There were sapphires, emeralds, and many other precious stones among the lot. Three witnesses, however, were interested in gems of a different species: rubies.

For the benefit of Commissioner Weston and Inspector Cardona, Lamont Cranston was pointing out the different types of ruddy gems. He indicated the pigeon's-blood stones from Burma, the garnet-hued type of Siam, finally the pomegranate-red of Ceylon.

By the time the sale was over and Twindell had gathered in the checks, both Weston and Cardona were convinced of the fact that they had come here to prove: that Ryndon's ruby had once belonged to the Twindell collection.

When the dealers had gone, Twindell had time to talk to his distinguished visitors. Weston showed him Ryndon's ruby, and Twindell gave a slow nod.

"It was probably mine once," he affirmed, "but I have sold so many, how should I remember them? To me, each new gem was something to admire, then store away."

He gestured toward the closed safe behind his desk. Then, thoughtfully:

"Gems still intrigue me. But I shall purchase only those of historical importance, after I have disposed of those which remain in my present collection. Meanwhile, I have found another interest."

He pointed to the mantel, where five Chinese dragons sat in a stately row. Though similar in size and shape, each had distinctive features. Noting them, The Shadow picked out the one that Thorner had bought the night before.

"Those procelain dragons," said Twindell, "belong to the period of Ch'ien Lung. They were designed by the celebrated T'ang Ying, who had charge of the imperial porcelain factory at that time. T'ang Ying left several treatises on the manufacture of porcelain, and in one of them he mentioned the seven dragons.

"Gentlemen"—Twindell's eyes fairly gleamed with enthusiasm—"I believe that I have acquired five of those seven dragons! Should I find the other two, I shall be the only man in the world owning a complete series of Ch'ien Lung masterpieces!"

TWINDELL'S manner impressed two listeners, Weston and Cardona. To The Shadow, though he carried the calm pose of Cranston, the collector's talk was froth. The Shadow was familiar with the treatises that Twindell mentioned and knew of no reference to a series of seven dragons. Unquestionably, the objects on the mantel came from the Ch'ien Lung period, but The Shadow doubted the rest.

With one proviso. Twindell's mention of the number, seven, indicated that he was cagily expressing a half truth. Evidently, Twindell expected to have two more dragons later, and therefore had emphasized the coming total.

The Shadow hefted the dragons, at Twindell's suggestion. They were hollow, open at the bottom, and therefore quite light. Remembering how Loo Look had thumped one dragon on the auction table, The Shadow planted his in the same manner on Twindell's mantel.

The old man gave a sharp cackle, fearing that the dragon had been injured. Seeing that it wasn't, he beamed again.

Casually, Weston asked Twindell if the fifth dragon had come from last night's auction. Twindell acknowledged that it had. He said that his purchasing representative, Thorner, had bought it for him, and had fortunately left the place before the trouble started. To-day, Thorner was out of town seeking more curios, but Twindell hardly dared hope that he would be lucky enough to uncover the sixth dragon.

"I believe that all are in this country," asserted Twindell, "but there will be no way of telling, until we have found them."

That ended the questioning, though The Shadow would have liked to ask Twindell more. It was evident, though the law did not suspect it, that Twindell was in some way connected with the mysterious master mind, Shiwan Khan. Neither Weston nor Cardona had heard of Shiwan Khan, nor of Hoang Khu, for that matter, though the police had found a few dead Mongols along with the deceased Loo Look.

Somewhere, somehow, Kiwan Shan, the unfathomable, might even now be plotting new crime. But The Shadow, recognizing the mighty power of a foe who could keep his very existence veiled, considered the task of finding Shiwan Khan as something that could be best accomplished alone.

The Shadow's guess that Shiwan Khan's new machinations were under way was definitely correct. At the very time when Commissioner Weston and his party were leaving Twindell's, Mitchell Dorron, a prominent shipping man, was talking with two visitors in his office: Paul Brent and Guy Chadbury.

Mitchell was arranging for the freighter *Aritoba* to take on a cargo of Globe airplanes and motors, also a shipment of blasting materials from Chadbury Enterprises. Both Brent and Chadbury were promising an answer by the next day.

The reason was that each intended to await a message from the brain controlling the mysterious lights. Without such approval, they could not finally commit themselves. Neither, of course, gave any inkling of the reason for postponing a decision.

THE conference in Dorron's office was the very type of event that The Shadow would have expected Shiwan Khan to produce. The case of Twindell proved that Shiwan Khan dealt with persons of wealth and influence. There was every indication that he either held a complete mistrust of crooks of the American variety, or had no cause to use them.

In that surmise, The Shadow was placing too sharp a limit upon the activities of Shiwan Khan. Like The Shadow, Shiwan Khan preferred to supply the unexpected. He was branching out along the line that The Shadow had eliminated, and Shiwan Khan was making his preparations this very afternoon.

Among the so-called big shots in Manhattan, a crook named Flash Gidley could well have regarded himself unique. Flash, dapper, suave of manner, was one crook who was willing to wait for certainties, rather than risk chances.

Weeks at a time, Flash would sit about his sumptuous apartment, attended only by his lieutenant, Herk Duvan, indifferent to many opportunities for crime that were phoned in by members of the mob. This afternoon, Herk, a big and bulky rowdy who preferred strong-arm work to strategy, was complaining about Flash's methods.

"That theater job would be a pipe!" insisted Herb. "They bank a pile of dough every week. All we got to do is barge in before the armored car shows up, and grab off the cash."

"With a couple of cops outside the place?" purred Flash. "And about a thousand people inside, to get a look at us? Forget it, Herk!"

"The boys think it's good—"

"And the dough I'm paying them is good! As long as I keep them on the pay roll, they've got no squawk. Sit down, Herk, and help me listen to the radio."

Thumbing the dials of a brand-new radio set, Flash listened intently to the news reports. He was interested in the fact that a gentleman named Benjamin Twindell was disposing of rare jewels, in order to collect Chinese dragons. Twindell, it happened, had willingly talked about his new hobby to reporters, who had called up after Commissioner Weston left.

Herk Duvan had a comment.

"Say, Flash!" he gruffed. "Maybe there's something in them dragons. If a guy collects them, they're worth dough, ain't they?"

"Who ever heard of trying to fence a dragon?" snapped Flash. "Listen, Herk, if you want to put that clockwork brain of yours to work, I'll give it something to tick about."

"What's that?"

"Tell me who shipped us this nifty radio set. Some guy that's trying to suck in with us, I'll bet. Give it a gander, Herk. It's class!"

The radio set was an unusual one. It was large, and among its ornate features was one that Flash had never seen before. Three lights were set above the dial. When a station was tuned in just right, a yellow light glowed. A variation in one direction brought a green light; in the other, a red.

The set was faulty, though. If the yellow light glowed alone for more than half a minute, both the green and the red would light up. After that, all three lights would flicker continually, in a manner that Flash said made him woozy when he watched them.

As the news bulletin ended, the three lights were busy with their flickering. Looking at Flash, Herk noted that he was bowed close to the radio set. Flash was intent, though he could not possibly be hearing anything. Then Herk heard him mumble.

Mechanically reaching for a pencil, Flash began to scrawl something on a piece of paper. Herk stared in awe.

Suddenly, Flash jolted upward. He looked at the radio, then at Herk. As he shoved the switch, he saw the paper in his hand. He read it, whirled to Herk.

"Did I write this?"

Herk nodded.

"Am I nuts?" queried Flash, softly. "Or did I hear it? A voice—a gong—and this!" He tapped the paper. "If this stuff is the real McCoy, it's worth fifty grand to us!"

Amazed, Herk reached for the paper. Flash shoved him aside, nudged toward the telephone.

"Get hold of the boys. Tell them to be ready."

"I must have heard a voice," murmured Flash to himself. "Anyway, this job is worth going after. The guy means it"—Flash crumpled the paper and dropped it in an ash tray, to burn it—"because he even had me write down his moniker—Shiwan Khan!"

It was an hour later when Benjamin Twindell received a telephone call from Herbert Thorner. The purchasing agent was back in town in response to a telegram that he thought Twindell had sent him. He gave an address over the wire, and Twindell repeated it aloud.

"You're to go there at nine o'clock?' asked Twindell. "Very well, Thorner." The old man gave one of his cackles. "Perhaps you will find a dragon waiting for you. I expect another, very shortly."

There was not a shade of doubt in Twindell's mind. Thorner had received the telegram from Shiwan Khan. But when Twindell stared at the study floor, his nerve almost left him. He thought he saw a long, streaky shadow there.

The stretch of blackness faded while Twindell was reaching in the desk drawer for the silver casket that Shiwan Khan had said would satisfy The Shadow. Twindell chuckled his relief. He thought his imagination had bothered him.

The blackness was real enough. It became a solid shape, descending Twindell's grand stairway. On the ground floor The Shadow, a living figure, glided past Twindell's servants and made his exit by the side door. For a moment, he was visible in the dusk outside the house; then he was gone.

Eyes from across the street had glimpsed The Shadow's fleeting shape. A gray-clad form no longer remained immobile. Entering a Mongol-driven cab, Shiwan Khan delivered a monotoned laugh as he rode away.

Tonight, the master who knew the mysteries of the East was confident that he would dispose of the only enemy who could ever hope to balk his plans of world-wide conquest.

Shiwan Khan was sure that he had prepared The Shadow's finish!

CHAPTER X.
WEST MEETS EAST.

It was eight o'clock, and Beatrice Chadbury was looking at the lights. Only she wasn't Beatrice Chadbury; she was Alice Haywood. The very thought made her laugh, because she knew that her name was not Alice Haywood, after all.

She was Lana Luan.

She was registered at this little hotel under the name of Alice Haywood, but that was because she was wearing American clothes. Actually, she believed herself to be Lana Luan, and in her case, the lights that she watched did not produce a merely temporary daze.

Beatrice Chadbury was completely under the control of Shiwan Khan. When the lights began their vivid changes, they took her into a world that

CLIFF MARSLAND, big, tough, and known in the underworld as a killer, is The Shadow's main contact with the realm of crime. Because of Cliff's hard appearance, criminal characters invite him to partake in pending deals of crime—which information he passed on to The Shadow.

she had come to consider as her own. The lights belonged to a sign above an uptown Chinese restaurant called the Green Pagoda.

When they changed, the lights made Chinese characters, and Beatrice could read them, which was one reason why she felt sure she was Lana Luan. A message spelled itself as she watched. Calmly, Beatrice left the hotel room and went down to the street.

At the door of the Green Pagoda, the girl was greeted by the bowing Chinese proprietor, who conducted her to a corner booth, set in an alcove near a large Buddha, that rested on a high pedestal.

Beatrice did not remain in the corner boot very long. Reaching to a partition on the side toward the Buddha, she slid back a panel. A dim stairway showed below, leading beneath the Buddha. Beatrice took that route, closing the panel after her.

After following a few twisty passages, the girl reached a stairway that had evidently belonged to an old house. Walled in on both sides, it made a route to the second floor, above the Chinese restaurant. On that floor, Beatrice unlocked the door to a small room.

This was her room, where she became Lana Luan. The place had a table, two chairs, a wall mirror, and a curtained closet. Drawing back the curtain, Beatrice gave a happy sigh as she saw her costume of thick silk pajamas, short kimono of peacock and poppy pattern, along with a pair of soft, dark Chinese slippers.

Rapidly disrobing, she flung her American clothes disdainfully upon the nearer chair. Sliding into the Chinese costume, she smiled at herself in the mirror. These clothes were comfortable; they seemed a part of her. She was Lana Luan.

The change was really remarkable. When she entered the room, Beatrice had looked decidedly American. When undressed, her figure had shown entirely white. But the moment that her new attire covered her sleek body, she seemed definitely Chinese.

It was the effect of the costume's pattern. Even in dress design, Shiwan Khan could work deception upon observers. One glance at Beatrice's exotic costume marked her as Chinese; from then on, anyone who saw her looked for Oriental traces in her features. With dark hair and eyes, long lashes, and pursed, ruddy lips, Beatrice was the proper type to produce the illusion.

The pajamas had long sleeves and legs. Her hands were only half visible, her ankles not at all. Thus, chance traces of whiteness were eliminated, and in Paul's case, an added element had strengthened the Chinese appearance of Lana Luan. He had met the girl in a room illuminated only by a greenish light, which had given an olive tint to her complexion.

LEAVING her Chinese boudoir, Beatrice stole along a short passage, passed a spiral stairway and came to a golden door. It opened as she stretched her hand. Shiwan Khan was waiting on the threshold of the golden throne room.

Smileless, Shiwan Khan presented the girl with a porcelain dragon. As she clutched the object weightily in her arms, the master plotter repeated slowly in English:

"Enter the house where the driver takes you. Give the dragon to a man named Herbert Thorner. When he has gone, leave by the same way you entered."

Beatrice nodded. Shiwan Khan pointed her back along the passage. She descended the usual stairway to the level of the restaurant; but, instead of returning to the booth, she opened a panel that led to a service exit. She always took that path, leading to the rear street, when she was Lana Luan.

Stepping into a cab driven by one

of Shiwan Khan's Mongols, Beatrice paid no further attention to her journey. The cab eventually reached a dark street and rolled slowly along it.

The Mongol strained his eyes toward the rear alleyway leading to a darkened house; then, catching a signal, he wheeled around the block to reach the front of the building.

In the gloom at the rear crouched Mongols who were listening to the whispers of Hoang Khu and another, called Shan Juchi. Between them, they were dividing their forces. Hoang Khu was posting men outside the house; Shan Juchi had charge of a group that entered the rear of the basement.

Motionless as they guarded the empty building, the Mongols showed training ordered by Shiwan Khan. Like human statues, they had rendered themselves unnoticeable in the darkness. The path that they left open was the sort that could be turned instantly into a trap.

From his post in the rear passage, Hoang Khu saw another cab stop, watched a man alight and come slowly through. The arrival was Thorner. As the man passed, Hoang Khu looked toward the house, then let his gaze go higher, to the roof.

As Shiwan Khan had planned it, Thorner was going to enter that house and leave it, unmolested. But for anyone who followed, there would be disaster.

Anyone, in this case, was The Shadow.

On the front street, Beatrice Chadbury was stealing up the gloomy front steps, visible to another band of watchers. As the girl opened the front door, Flash Gidley spoke to mobbies about him.

"Two of you lugs come along with me and Herk. The rest of you spread out and be ready with the wheelers, when we lam. No gats, unless the going gets tough. You'll know when to pull the rods, if you need them."

Posting the two men just inside the front door, Flash led Herk through a moldy parlor filled with old furniture. They came to a curtain, a dim light glowing beyond it. Herk wanted to hold back, but Flash pulled him along, nudging Herk's pocket with the comment:

"Just in case."

They looked into a barren room, illuminated by a single light. The only article of furnishing was a battered brass gong that hung inside another doorway, leading to a downward stairs. On the other side of the room was a passage to steps that went up.

Beatrice was standing in the center of the little room, the dragon nestling deep in her arms. Her eyes had a faraway stare, in the general direction of the brass gong.

"Say!" gulped Herk. "The dame's a Chinee! I didn't know that when she ankled in here."

"She's no Chinee," undertoned Flash. "She only thinks she is. Her uncle is worth plenty! He's worried about where she is, but he's scared to squawk to the Feds. He figures something may really happen to her if he does."

"You doped all that today, Flash, while you was sitting at the radio?"

"Yeah, and more. See that dragon the dame's got? It's one of the bunch you were talking about. We don't want it. The dame is going to give it to a guy, and he can have it. We're going to grab the doll, after she's knocked out of that trance she's in. Then we let her uncle know."

"For how much?"

"Fifty grand! On the line! He'll pay—and why not? He don't even know what's become of her. The trouble with the snatch racket is staging the snatch itself. This case is different. It's been done for us."

Twindell stared at the study floor, thought he saw a long, streaky shadow there.

JUST as Herk was about to voice agreement, the two heard creeping footsteps from the lower stairs. Shouldering into the light came Herbert Thorner, his shoulder grazing the brass gong. Herk inquired who he was; Flash said he didn't know.

"He's here for the dragon," whispered the big shot, "and he thinks the doll's a Chinee. Which suits me. Nobody knows different, except us."

In the slow tone of Lana Luan, they heard Beatrice inquire the arrival's name. Thorner answered, not loud enough for them to hear, and the girl gave him the dragon. Another figure had appeared from the lower stairway; Herk eyed the newcomer askance. He whispered to Flash:

"Look at the big guy!"

The "big guy" was Shan Juchi. Watching the interview between Beatrice and Thorner, the Mongol was weighing a hammer, ready to strike the gong.

"He's a stooge," Flash told Herk. "He's here to wake up Sleeping Beauty. Give him time."

Thorner had stowed the dragon half beneath his coat. He was not returning by the lower stairs; instead, he crossed the room and took the steps to the upper floor. Beatrice was watching his departure; half turned, she was ready to step toward the curtain where Flash and Herk waited.

The stage was set exactly as Shiwan Khan had planned it. Shan Juchi had actually raised the hammer for the gong stroke, when a wild shout came from the upper stairs. Following his own shriek, Thorner dived into sight, tripped, and rolled toward the lower stairway, clinging tenaciously to the dragon.

Flipping the gong hammer to his other hand, Shan Juchi whipped out a knife. Slashing aside the curtain, Flash Gidley yanked a revolver from his pocket, a move that Herk Duvan instantly copied.

Yet, with all their speed, none of the trio was fast enough to stave off the threat that sprang from the same stairway that Thorner had so frantically rejected as an outlet. It was a living threat, in black.

Instead of the gong stroke, a mocking laugh quivered through the room. Uttered by hidden lips beneath a downturned hat brim, that mirth was accompanied by the forward shove of a gun muzzle, thrust by a gloved fist.

Wheeling to the very center of the room, the living blackness became a cloaked shape, ready to combat a horde of foemen. Small wonder, for this conqueror of crime had outguessed the measures planned by Shiwan Khan.

Suspecting the Mongol trap in back, noting the crew of thugs in front, The Shadow had chosen the house roof for his entry. By that stratagem, he had blocked Thorner's escape with the dragon, and had arrived in time to rescue Beatrice Chadbury from whatever fate awaited her.

Finally, he had reached a focal spot from which he could fight off two dangerous bands of foemen. In the very heart of the enemy's present domain, The Shadow had raised his challenge to battle!

CHAPTER XI.

THE SHADOW'S CHOICE.

THOUGH Thorner, in his inarticulate way, had shouted an alarm, The Shadow was so close behind the frantic man that no one expected the cloaked fighter until they saw him. Which amounted to the fact that The Shadow's enemies were not ready for all that came their way, whereas the black-clad invader was prepared for anything.

Whirling into view, The Shadow sized matters in a glance. Thorner was out of it, for the fellow's only thought was to save the precious dragon and leave the battle to others. Beatrice's half-dazed stare told that she was no menace, yet she figured as a factor.

The girl who called herself Lana Luan was standing in harm's way. Getting her out of it was one of The Shadow's instantaneous problems, as important as that of battle.

The Shadow saw Shan Juchi starting a swing with the knife. He saw the whipping curtain; beyond it, the glitter of guns. But he picked Shan Juchi as his first antagonist, rather than the gunners in the other room. The Shadow's gun spoke flame.

A stabbing bullet caught Shan Juchi as the Mongol hurled the knife. The blade skimmed the ceiling above The Shadow's head. Shan Juchi was lunging for that whirl in the center of the room. The Shadow spun in reverse so suddenly, that he was away from the path of fire when Flash and Herk let their guns blast.

Shan Juchi was staggering through the space where the bullets had whined. Bewildered, Flash and Herk could not understand how The Shadow had reversed his course so suddenly, considering the speed of his drive. They had the answer, when they saw that Beatrice was spinning with him.

The Shadow's free arm had encircled the girl, as he stabbed that shot at Shan Juchi. Her weight had halted his charge sufficiently for him to wheel instantly in the opposite direction and carry her along.

Though they wanted to capture Beatrice, the crooks preferred to get The Shadow, no matter what the cost. Again, they fired together, but before they tugged their triggers, the whirling blackness split. Herk saw a figure pitch headlong into a front corner of the room. Swinging through the doorway, he took aim—at Beatrice Chadbury!

FLASH gave a yell. He had recognized the flying form. He was looking for The Shadow, instead of the girl, and for a half second Flash was utterly baffled. Literally, The Shadow had vanished from the center of the room, as completely as if the floor had swallowed him.

Then Flash's quick eye had seen Shan Juchi reeling backward. In the dimness of the room, Flash could not see The Shadow just beyond. But he realized that the cloaked fighter had grabbed the giant Mongol as a shield, for the muzzle of a .45 was poking out from under Shan Juchi's arm!

That gun had swung straight for Herk. It wasn't Flash's yell that saved the lieutenant. The curtain performed the rescue, as Herk tripped over it while taking aim at Beatrice. A gun boomed: The Shadow's. A bullet pinged the wall mere inches above Herk's stumbling form.

The timely shot was proof that The Shadow would have dropped Herk before the latter could have fired at Beatrice. The Shadow intended to dispatch another bullet in Herk's direction, to prevent the fellow from using his gun at all. But there was time in between to halt Flash at the doorway. The Shadow jabbed a quick shot there.

Flash was gone. With his yell, he had dived for safety. He was at an angle where The Shadow could not reach him; in turn, Flash had no chance to shoot at anyone. But his gun was ready, and he used it, on the only target that he could see—the single ceiling light at the center of the barren room.

The bulb shattered. From the instant darkness came a weird laugh smothering the echoes of Flash's well-aimed shot. The crook had simply saved The Shadow trouble. The cloaked fighter had intended to douse that light, after settling Herk.

Flash saw the reflection of a gunburst from deep in the other room. He thought that Herk was through. A moment later, the lucky lieutenant flopped beside him, uninjured. Half wrapped in the curtain, Herk had made a rolling scramble through the doorway, just as the light vanished.

The thugs from the front door were on hand with revolvers and flashlights. Their arrival told that more were coming. Flash pointed toward the other room and hoarsed the order:

"The Shadow! Get him!"

Not having witnessed The Shadow's deadly fire, the two thugs took the chance that Flash was anxious to avoid. At the doorway, they halted, staring at the scene their flashlights showed. Wild yells from the other room brought Flash to the scene.

A squad of Mongols had bobbed up from the lower stairway. The crooks had seen The Shadow launch himself into that throng with one tremendous dive. There wasn't a chance for thugs to aim. The Shadow was gone, down the stairway, in the midst of a tangled, milling mass.

There were sounds of a clash between sledging automatics and swinging knives, but The Shadow was carrying the fight below.

Viewing the whole room, Flash saw Thorner crawling for the passage to the upper stairway. Trampled by the arriving Mongols, Thorner had managed to protect the Ch'ien Lung dragon, and was taking the trophy with him.

Beatrice was lying motionless in her corner. She had struck the wall heavily, and the blow had stunned her. The fault was not The Shadow's. He had expected the girl to thrust her hands before her as she hit the wall. She should have done so, even though she had been standing dazed.

But dazed conditions, when induced by Shiwan Khan's hypnotic lights, were by no means ordinary. The self-styled Lana Luan had been living in a dream world. Her whirling trip toward the wall had seemed pleasant, with no need for worry. She had scarcely felt the blow that crumpled her.

Another figure was in the room that The Shadow had deserted: Shan Juchi.

Mortally wounded, the big Mongol was concerned only with a final effort that would complete a duty ordered by Shiwan Khan. Close to the doorway, where The Shadow had dropped his human shield, Shan Juchi had found the gong hammer. He was raising it slowly, painfully, as he tried to rise against the wall.

His hand, wavering backward, reached the gong level. Shan Juchi gave a slash that carried his tottering body forward. The hammer met the gong, clanged it with a force that startled all who heard it. The room seemed to shudder with the brazen reverberations that carried through the house.

Huddling to the floor, Shan Juchi raised his head. With the last echo from the clashing gong, he babbled:

"It has been done, Kha Khan!"

Oddly, the hammer stroke seemed to have banished tumult below. Perhaps the other Mongols, hearing the brassy sound, had felt their work accomplished and were choosing flight, instead of further battle with The Shadow.

They had certainly heard the cry of Shan Juchi, and would carry word to Shiwan Khan that he had fulfilled his mission with the gong. In dying, Shan Juchi failed to realize that the stroke of the gong had been unheard by the one person for whom it was intended: Lana Luan.

He lay silent, stiff, Shan Juchi; and it suddenly occurred to Flash Gidley that other Mongols might have fared the same way.

From below, Flash caught new sounds: the faint, muffled shots of a revolver; vague howls, with the clatter of running feet; finally, the weird shiver of an echoing laugh, too much like the mockery of The Shadow!

Two more thugs had arrived. Flash pointed all four toward the lower stairway. Springing to the corner of the room, he lifted Beatrice, shoved her limp form into Herk's arms. The big lieutenant was looking at Thorner, who had come to his feet near the passage to the upper stairway.

"Forget that guy!" snapped Flash. "I told you we didn't want the dragon. We've got the dame—"

A roar came from the lower stairs. Guns blasted with the force of a cannonade. The Shadow's automatics were recognizable when they began the fire; they kept up their staccato punches amid the wild, disjointed bark of revolvers.

Flash's trouble shooters had found trouble that had shot them up instead. Trouble in the person of The Shadow. Thuds and howls told that crippled mobbies were tumbling down the stairs, while a strident laugh, pealing from a corner of the room, announced the safe return of The Shadow.

"Come on!" Flash tugged at Herk. "Get going—and hang onto the dame!"

Flash headed out to the front. He was away from the sweep of the flashlight that The Shadow flicked from the lower stairs. The Shadow spied two men starting a mad race for safety. Each was carrying a valued prize.

One was Thorner. Stirred with wild desire for flight, he was taking to the upper stairway, clinging to the Ch'ien Lung dragon. The other was Herk; he was following Flash. Across Herk's shoulder, The Shadow caught a glimpse of a girl's face, far paler than the usual countenance that represented Lana Luan.

Choice of pursuit lay with The Shadow. Overtaking Thorner would be a certainty, the capture of the dragon included. From such a chase, The Shadow would obtain the very reward that he had come to claim.

Following Herk meant new battle against risky odds, with only a slight chance of rescuing an unknown girl who, from The Shadow's last view of her face, might be already dead.

The flashlight blackened. Through the solid gloom of that barren room where Shan Juchi lay dead beneath the brazen gong, there came the tone of a sibilant, whispered laugh. A few moments later the sound, like its author, was gone.

His trail chosen, The Shadow was on his way. Whether he was seeking the sixth dragon or the captive girl, his laugh did not proclaim. Even Shiwan Khan could not have guessed The Shadow's choice, had the master plotter been present in that very darkness!

The path that the cloaked fighter had taken in the gloom was known to one person alone:

The Shadow!

CHAPTER XII.
THE CHOSEN TRAIL.

OUTSIDE the deserted house, Flash Gidley made quick plans for a getaway. He shoved Herk Duvan toward the nearest car, an old sedan, that had another mobbie occupying it. The man hopped out to help Herk put the limp girl into the back seat.

Reaching a car across the street, Flash quickly pointed a pair of thugs to the steps of the old house. Crouching on each side of the front doorway, they waited for The Shadow to appear, provided he was coming this direction.

By the time that motors were throbbing, there had been no sign of The Shadow. Flash, swinging his own car about, provided the glare of headlights on the house steps; for an instant, he sighted what looked like a flinging streak of blackness, passing from the steps to the curb.

Then, Flash was seeing other shifting shadows, produced by the swing of the car. Those distorted patches were proof enough that Flash hadn't seen The Shadow, particularly when the men from the doorway, clambering into the car, reported that they had heard no one pass them on the steps.

Herk's sedan was already started—further evidence that The Shadow was taking the trail of the dragon instead of trying to trace the girl. Passing the sedan, Flash saw Herk at the wheel and signaled him to fall behind. A third car was joining the procession, manned by a reserve squad. The safe bet was to keep Herk in between.

Glancing over his shoulder, Flash noted the roof of the old house. No gunshots were sounding there, but Flash hardly expected any. Though he didn't know who Thorner was, Flash had seen enough of the fellow to know that he wasn't the sort who would put up battle.

Thorner was the type who might lie in wait and bag his man; but once in flight, he certainly would not stop. When The Shadow overtook him, Thorner would simply hand over the dragon and beg for life.

Meanwhile, Flash and his caravan were having what they considered an easy getaway, until they reached the corner. There, a coupé suddenly cut in front of Flash's car and forced it to the curb. Flash snapped an order to the men in back; grabbing up sawed-off shotguns, they blasted at the coupé.

But there was no one in it when the barrage hit. The occupants, springing from the far door, had joined companions who were under cover along the street.

Flash and his mob were meeting The Shadow's agents, and finding them a tough squad to battle. In the midst of gunfire, Flash yelled at Herk, who sped away in his sedan. The third car wheeled up, its gunners raking the street with their fire.

The Shadow's agents were gone. They had done what their chief had ordered. He had told them to slow the escape of the mob, and leave the rest to the police. Sounds of shooting in the old house had been reported; sirens were already shrieking in the neighborhood.

Managing to get their cars started, Flash and his mobbies were driving right into trouble, enough to keep them busy. The Shadow's agents, abandoning the old coupé that they had sacrificed, were heading toward another duty.

Reaching the rear street, they saw a frantic man come tearing from the back of another house. It was Thorner; he had fled across the rooftops and taken a route to the street. He had the porcelain dragon with him, but had been making speed despite his burden.

His goal was a taxicab parked under a street lamp, where he could see it. At the wheel sat a Mongol driver.

Before The Shadow's agents could intercept the cab, shots greeted them from the passage behind the deserted house. Hoang Khu and his Mongols were still on the loose, amplified by a few of Shan Juchi's crew, who had survived their fray with The Shadow by taking flight.

Fortunately, the Mongols did not handle guns as well as knives. Dropping away from the poorly aimed barrage, The Shadow's agents suffered no casualties. In their turn, they began to pepper Hoang Khu and his party, with very good effect.

The cab got away, while The Shadow's men were taking shelter. But they routed the Mongols so rapidly that another cab was able to wheel in pursuit. Moe Shrevnitz was driving the second cab, and he was tailing the other taxi closely.

Though he heard no words from the rear seat, Moe had an idea that he was carrying a black-cloaked passenger. Generally, when Moe took up an important chase, The Shadow entered the cab when it started. Thanks to the

Continued on page 94

Whose Law

HERE is a story as given to us by a friend who spends quite a bit of time traveling from court to court in line of business. He is a detective whose work is mostly of a commercial nature; he checks into attempts on the part of various types of people who seek to take advantage of business concerns one way or another, and his work takes him all over the country. He would not give us the scene of his story, but we feel that the scene may be anywhere; that no doubt it is repeated in all parts of the country from time to time. And we also feel that something should be done about it.

Picture the courtroom. On the witness bench is a man who is well known in his community. He is there as a witness to a robbery. The robbery was committed by crooks well known in the locality; in fact, the "big shot" of crookdom in that place is behind the crime, and there is no doubt about it. The "big shot's" own crack lawyer is defending the criminals, and it is he that is cross-examining the witness.

It would take too long to repeat here the series of questions which led up to the point of this story. Nevertheless, one after the other, these questions became more personal, more sarcastic, more insinuating. Finally, the witness got fed up with all this legal tomfoolery. He stood up from the witness chair, turned to the judge, and in about so many words said:

"I am a decent law-abiding citizen of this community. I have no record of any crime against me. All my life I've lived here, and all my neighbors know just what I do. I have no secrets from my friends or this community.

"I have come here as a citizen to do my part in convincing people who have committed a crime, because I saw them do it. I am losing good time from my business; I am undergoing inconvenience in that I am away from my family and my ordinary mode of living. I am actually losing money in performing this task—and now, this lawyer is doing his damnedest to try to make me out a monkey by his questioning! I don't attempt to parry wits with him; that is his business, not mine. But I don't think that anyone in my position should have to submit to such questions. I can tell my story in a few words, and I can prove all of those words. Other than that, I don't see what he's driving after, and I think I certainly ought to have as much rights here as does a criminal!"

That is something which many people have noticed about the part witnesses play in crime proceedings today. Witnesses, it seems, have practically no more rights than the accused. In many cases, they are held in jail, either for their own "protection," or because the prosecutor may think they might otherwise go away. In many cases, too, they have no more conveniences in their jail quarters than have prisoners. When they do get into court, they are at the mercy of the defense attorney who, in some cases, goes pretty far afield to bring out either some long-forgotten phase of the life of the witness, or otherwise twist his questions so as to make it embarrassing for him.

Of course, a witness must be open for questioning, to make sure his testimony is right. And, according to law, that questioning must stick pretty close to the case in hand. But clever lawyers find many ways to twist questions in a manner aimed to belittle the witness, and in doing this they certainly overreach themselves.

What can be done about this we do not know. It is a job for lawyers; or else it is a job for judges who have it within their power to control the questioning. However, any man or woman who is willing to give his or her time and effort to the support of the law should be given better treatment on the part of the law. Perhaps, if there were more provision made for the comfort and convenience of witnesses; if they were considered more than mere pawns in the game of justice, they might become more willing, and more people would make it a point to do their part.

This is a subject which will benefit by discussion. If you have the chance at any gathering, why not talk about it? Ask others of their experiences, and see if they, too, do not feel that something might be done about it. If enough people really get excited over this question, you can be quite sure that steps will be taken!

Navy Fingerprints

FINGERPRINTS is being used more and more everywhere. Now all civil employees of the United States navy, both in the departmental and field services, are to be fingerprinted and the prints registered in the navy department.

All civil employees who have been appointed or reinstated by the Civil Service Commission since 1938 have already been fingerprinted, and the new order affects employees appointed before 1928, and those who are not selected under Civil Service, including those of the island possessions which are governed by the navy.

The use of fingerprints as a system of identification is really of very ancient origin, though it is only during comparatively recent years that most of us have heard so much about the practice. Fingerprinting really had its roots away back in the earliest days of the East, when the impression of his thumb was the monarch's sign-manual. A relic of this practice is still preserved in the formal confirmation of a legal document by "delivering" it as one's "act or deed." The permanent character of the fingerprint was first put forward scientifically in 1823 by J. E. Purkinje, an eminent professor of physiology, who read a paper before the University of Breslau, adducing nine standard types of impressions and advocating a system of classification which attracted no great attention.

Then Bewick, the English draftsman, struck with the delicate qualities of the delineation, made engraving of an impression of two of his fingertips and used them as signatures for his work. It was some time after this that, gradually, fingerprints were started in use by the police of many countries for the detection of crime.

The taking of fingerprints of civilian employees of the United States navy is, of course, merely a precautionary measure. At present, the greatest number of civilian employees ever on the navy pay rolls is at work in the navy yards and other shore stations and in departmental service. The number in the field service, which includes the navy yards, is now said to be well upwards of 75,000. The largest number of civilians are in the navy yards at Philadelphia, New York, Norfolk, Portsmouth, Boston, Charleston, South Carolina, Puget Sound and Mare Island.

An order similar to the one issued by the navy department became effective in the war department several months ago.

Fingerprints depend upon a peculiarity seen in the human hand and to some extent in the human foot. The skin is traversed in all directions by creases and ridges which are absolutely ineradicable and show no change from childhood to extreme old age. The persistence of the markings of the fingertips has been proved beyond all question, and this universally accepted quality has been the basis of the present system of identification.

As the result of much experiment, a four-fold scheme of classification was evolved, the various types employed being styled "arches," "loops," "whorls" and "composites." There are subclasses, and all are perfectly distinguishable by an expert, who can describe each by its particular symbol in the code arranged, so that the whole "print" can be read as a distinct and separate expression.

75 Years of Secret Service

THE United States Secret Service is celebrating its seventy-fifth birthday this year.

This may be real news to most folks—for the United States Secret Service lives up to its name and keeps news concerning its own bureau very secret. It has never gone in for publicity. Its works quietly, efficiently.

It has done work, though, that was done at the risk of the lives of many of its operatives, and at times these operatives even sacrificed their lives in the line of duty. It has instilled fear in the hearts of counterfeiters. You'd see a great deal more counterfeit money if it were not for the United States Secret Service. It keeps after the makers of phony money, spies on them, trails them, brings them to justice. Since the Secret Service is a division of the treasury department, this business of keeping after counterfeiters is one of its main activities.

News of counterfeiting activities come to the Secret Service in various ways. When a new counterfeit bill or coin is discovered in circulation, Uncle Sam's sleuths start to trail it to its lair. They use persistent and scientific methods. Yet sometimes their clues are picked up so haphazardly that the stories about them are almost humorous.

For instance, a Chicago postman was delivering his letters one day when he was hit on the head with a hard dollar. He picked up the coin. It was hot—actually hot. The postman's main job was to deliver letters, but he was also a loyal employee of the United States, and he got in touch with the Secret Service, told of his experience, gave the address of the house he was passing when he was struck by the hot dollar. It didn't take the bureau long to solve that case, getting the band of counterfeiters.

Secret Service operatives often stake out at places of business which criminals who try to "shove the queer" victimize most. Gasoline stations are among these. The "passers" drive in, get gased up in a hurry, pass over a bill and get their change and make a quick getaway. They don't make any getaway at all if a Secret Service man is under cover there.

The United States Secret Service men have many other duties, of course. Their counter-espionage service during the World War is a record of which they're rightfully proud. They also guard the president, and did very good work in supervising the protection of England's king and queen during the recent visit of those rulers to our country.

Getting to Be a Policeman

POLICE work today is not just a job—it's a career. The tests are difficult, particularly in the very large cities. The police heads expect—and get—a lot. And the applicants who average highest on physical and mental requirements get the first vacancies.

At this writing there are thousands of eager young applicants being put through the paces in New York City. The Municipal Civil Service Commission has been using New York University's intramural field, which is situated in the Bronx, away uptown. These men had passed their mental examinations previously. When they pass the severe physical tests set up for them, they'll be as good as members of New York's famous "Finest."

They'll be picked men. Police types in this country have always been rather outstanding since police organization here had its origin away back in colonial days. Of course, the policeman's duties were not so varied, in those days. The office of constable, invested with the powers and duties prescribed by the English common law, was established by the inhabitants of townships in different colonies, and to this day the office of constable remains in rural localities and in many cities, but the duties were not so exacting—and consequently requirements were not so high.

The first step in evolution from constable to modern police system came in colonial times with the establishment of night watches in the larger cities as a supplementary force, and under supervision of constables, and even in those days the night watch had to be able to handle pretty tough customers.

The future of the present young applicants for the New York City force—these young men who have been running miles, climbing walls, dashing up ladders and juggling weights to prove their physical prowess—is interesting to contemplate. Some of them may "pound the pavement" for a considerable time, as a part of the uniformed patrol distributed through the city on beats. These men, of course, are the first line of defense and protection against crime and disorder. The better they're equipped physically, the better they'll be able to handle tough gunmen, burglars, pickpockets and other criminals. Man for man, they'll be much stronger than the criminals they stack up against, as instance this test: Each police applicant had to run a full mile on the board track outside the college gymnasium. The mile had to be completed in seven minutes for the passing mark of 70 percent. This was the first such running test required by the commission, and all who covered the distance in five minutes and 30 seconds—and a number did even better than this—received a mark of 100 percent. They deserved it. If you don't believe it, try to equal this mark.

It's tougher these days—but it's fairer. With the passing of political interference, definite progress is being made in the direction of professionalizing police service, and a higher type of man is being attracted to the police service. Political influence won't help the applicant do that test mile in seven minutes or better. It won't help him scale or hurdle walls, or compete in the obstacle race—one of the most difficult tests, by the way. This involves a ten-foot broad jump, a three-and-a-half-foot hurdle, a four-and-a-half-foot vault, climbing an eight-foot fence and traversing a horizontal ladder hand-over-hand. The entire distance was fifty yards—and all had to be completed within 35 seconds for a passing mark. Some of the applicants did almost twice as well as this. Twenty seconds or better was considered a perfect score.

Also, candidates had to lift dumbbells weighing up to seventy pounds and dummies up to 170 pounds, and had to rise from a prone position to a sitting position while carrying a bar ranging in weight from twenty to forty pounds behind their necks.

Remember, too, that the 3700 applicants trying these rather servere tests had previously passed the mental examinations. The ones who get through will be qualified, in time, to become not only ordinary "cops"—a rigorous-enough job in itself—but with their bodies in a healthy, normal condition, should be alert enough to strive for other branches of metropolitan police work—work in the detective bureau, organized as a separate unit having to do with detection of the more serious crimes. They will also progress, some of them, to the special unit of plain-clothes operatives devoting their attention chiefly to suppression of gambling, illegal sale of narcotics, and liquor-law violations. Many of these men, too, may in time aspire to traffic squads, or the division of police work having to do with the keeping of most important records, installation of systems of communication by signal and patrol and emergency service.

It's a question of just which is more important for a police applicant in New York City today—mental alertness or physical strength. Probably both are equally important. Neither one will get an applicant by, he must have both.

The importance of the mental tests, though, is pretty well proved by the fact that those who come out of the mental tests with a mark of 80 percent or over are to be placed on a special list to be available for temporary detective work at the discretion of the police commissioner.

There were college athletes, of course, among the men taking the tests. They were regarded as having good chances, with their higher education and previous physical training.

So when you see a man in a police uniform today—more particularly in the great cities—though the smaller centers are also getting more particular about the quality of applicants—you may be sure he worked for that job of his. He worked hard. He has reason to be proud of his place in society and his job of protecting the health, safety and moral of his community.

Sometimes when you're in a hurry to get some place and run against a traffic officer, you may think he's pretty hard-boiled. Maybe he is. But he's more than that. He's qualified. He's one of your best friends. He's there to protect you against the wolves of society. He seldom if ever fails in his job, and many, many policemen have stuck to that job right down to and through the door of death.

Policewomen

POLICEWOMEN are being employed in increasing numbers in the larger cities. Of course, many of their duties have to do with the protection of women and children. They are qualified to do this better than the average policeman. But any offender who thinks they're a soft touch—well, he's in for a surprise and a shock! Policewomen today have been known to pick up tough guys wanted by the law and get them to the hoosegow just as fast as any policeman could do it. A bullet from a policewoman's gun can be just as hard as one from the gun of the biggest and toughest male cop. Jane Law is to be respected by the law-abiding and feared by the lawless today, just as much as John Law.

The city of Sacramento, California, paid a big tribute to women "cops" recently. During the annual safety week there, a corps of two hundred women took over police-traffic duties.

Sacramento is a good-sized city. It's the capital of the Golden State. It has several airports and is a station on the Chicago to San Francisco air-mail route, and is served by the Southern Pacific, the Santa Fe, the Western Pacific, electric interurban railways, many auto-stage companies and passenger steamship lines. So what women accomplished in Sacramento they could accomplish in almost any other city. And they accomplished plenty.

In this attractive city, which over ten years ago had an assessed valuation of property of well over a hundred million dollars, the ladies went to town on all traffic violations. They weren't any bossier than the male policemen had been. And they weren't any less efficient, either. They gave out tickets without fear or favor. If some male drivers took them a little humorously at first, they didn't feel very humorous when they were taken to the hoosegow and then to a court—presided over by a woman judge, by the way—and forced to pay fines.

The women's uniform consisted of pith helmet, white sports blouse and dark skirt or riding breeches. They looked efficient, and their appearance was not deceiving. Chief of Police Alec McAllister had only the highest praise for their work. Chief McAllister was still in command, though all police traffic jobs, from captain down, were taken care of by women.

And there are some proud women in Sacramento, California, today—and proud husbands, fathers and sons. During the annual safety week there was another solid chapter added to the glory of American womanhood.

CODES

By Henry Lysing

Author of "Secret Writing: How to Code and Decode," "The Cryptogram Book," "Men Against Crime," etc.

**Codes
Ciphers
Cryptograms
and
Secret Inks
for the expert
or the novice**

PROBLEM XVI

If you've been having trouble solving some of the harder problems that have appeared here—and some of them were really tough babies, we must admit—we'll give you a break on this one, which is comparatively easy. Of course, we have to give some of our more experienced readers problems which take work and experience, thus slighting those who are only beginning this fascinating game. So, whenever you see a problem that looks real hard, don't be discouraged; try it, and if you can't make it, the next issue or so will bring you one that is meant more for fans of your experience.

Now try this:

OVG 20 8 9 19 YV 1 14 VZHB 5 24 1 13 16 12 5 LV 3 15 4 5 ULI 25 15 21 GL 12 5 1 18 14.

Let's see you go to it, now. Remember, you have time until the next issue appears in which to solve this one. If, by some chance, you cannot get to this code within that time, we will accept answers later, provided you state you have not seen the solution in the following issue.

When you have solved this code, send your solution to Codes Department, The Shadow Magazine, 79 Seventh Avenue, New York, New York. Be sure to include your name and address, or, if you wish, use whatever name you prefer for our published list, but please give us your correct name for our own records. We print names of all solvers as soon as we can find space. Some are printed in practically every issue, so you can be sure yours will appear in about a month or six weeks after your solution is mailed in.

ANSWER TO PROBLEM XV

Problem XV was really very simple, although it might not have been entirely fair to you. It was simply the omission of a regular letter of the text, marked by the repetition of the letter B. If you simply looked at that message long enough, you were bound to hit upon the idea that that constant repetition meant something.

Here is how the message was printed:

**Y B U B A
N B O B V
E B H B S
C B D B W
I B H B U
T B U B H
T B O B B
L B I B Y
O B T B K
E B C B A
N B E B N
G B E B S
I B G B H
E B Y B E**

And it was to be read:

"You can solve this code without much trouble if you take a chance in guessing the type."

That's all there was to it! Now, if you have a pet code which you think might stick our readers, why not send it in and see if it proves hard or easy for them? Send in your solution together with the problem. We may use exactly the problem you send in, or, if it seems too hard, make another one from your code.

A NICE CODE

Bill Meyer and Tom Garrett, 1200 N. W. Forty-second Street, Oklahoma City, Oklahoma, are very much interested in codes, and have followed this department for a long time. They now submit one of their own codes which is very easy to handle, yet will furnish many a headache to one who tries to break it without knowing the manner of its construction.

First, we take the alphabet and break it into three sections, calling the first section A or X, the second section B or Y, and the third section C or Z. Then we write the alphabet with five letters for the first section, thirteen for the middle section, and eight for the last section.

Now let's find a word which we can use as a key word. The word "insupportable" has thirteen letters. Twice that gives us the entire alphabet, so we repeat that word twice beneath the present arrangement of the alphabet. We now have:

A or X	B or Y	C or Z
abcde	fghijklmnopqr	stuvwxyz
insup	portableinsup	portable

Now, in order to write your message, simply pick out the group in which your letter is, and the letter in "insupportable" above which it stands. You've broken your word apart so that with one exception, your group break makes all the letters different. First, write the letter for your section, and then write the key-letter for your text letter, and so on. This way you will have one capital letter and one small letter for each letter of your text message.

In order to make the code look better, you take each word after you have encoded it, and separate the capital letters and the small letters, and write them each separately as all small, or all capital letters. This will lessen the chance of someone catching on to your system.

Here is a sample message to illustrate how the code works:

Example: The Shadow Knows.

CoYrAp CpBrXiAuYnCa YbBiYnCaZp

Now by taking every other letter you get this:

cya orp cbxayc priuna ybycz binap

DISCOVERING SECRET WRITING

Continued from previous issue

You might also look upon the back of the paper to see if there are any indentations or other marks. Sometimes the secret message is written on the back of the regular message, and therefore the back needs just as close scrutiny as the front. If the paper looks in the least crinkly, as if it had been wetted and then dried, be extremely suspicious, for something is afoot there! Also watch for the spacing of the lines and words. In many cases, secret messages are written in invisible ink between the lines of the regular message, or between words or even between letters, so be careful in looking over these points. The way letters go above or below lines might also be a means of secreting a message, and if there is any form or pattern to these deviations, check on them. If there is any blurring at certain points, it may be caused by the regular ink flowing into traces of secret ink.

If you happen to be a photography fan, or know a friend who is, take your message and hold it over his ground-glass light frame—nothing more than a piece of somewhat frosted glass with a strong light underneath. He uses it to put his negatives on in order to identify them quickly. You can put your message on that glass, and by means of the strong light see if there is any message inside the paper, put there by acids which leave their impression something like the watermark you see on bond paper. The light may also show you some breaks in texture in the paper, and give you more leads. If you can't take advantage of a device like this, an ordinary strong frosted bulb will serve the purpose. Just hold the paper up against this light. Be sure you don't burn the paper.

That, incidentally, is an important point. Whatever you do in looking and checking over the message, be sure you do not damage the paper in any way so as to interfere with other tests. If you must do something which might harm the surface of the paper, confine that activity to a small portion of your message, leaving the rest untouched for future tests.

Of course, remember that the message need not necessarily be on the regular piece of correspondence paper. Messages have been hidden under stamps, inside the envelope, even on the outside of the envelope itself. If you have no luck with checking the letter, try the other points, and see if there is anything on any of them.

Of course, if you are in a position to use some of the scientific instruments to detect secret writing, take advantage of them. They include infrared light, ultraviolet light, or some other of the standard bulbs used for this purpose.

Trying the paper in various gases also is important. Iodine vapor gases very often reveal some sort of writing not seen in any other way. If you wish to make an iodine vapor bath, construct a box with a glass top, and provision for hangers so that several sheets can be inserted at one time. At the bottom of the box is a container of iodine crystals, with provision so that they can be gently headed, thus causing the vapor to rise. After some time in such a box, secret writing, if it exists, will most likely appear. The glass front of the box allows you to see what progress you are making.

Of course, immersion in water is another way to check on secret writing possibilities. Some secret inks react to water. Others react to heat, and one of the best ways to give heat treatments to suspect messages is with an ordinary electric iron. Be careful not to burn the paper, of course—and, too, remember to keep these immersion and heat and vapor tests until the last.

HIGHLIGHTS ON THE SHADOW

Continued from page 6

a collection of covers in good condition. Further, he wants to know whether The Shadow is printed in foreign languages.

Yes, it is. The Shadow is being published in foreign countries right along, as well as in our South American countries. We rarely bring this to the attention of our readers because it would mean hundreds of requests for these copies, and none of them are available in this country. Duties and customs regulations make it extremely difficult to get any more than the required file copies, so we cannot possibly hope to have any for interested readers, much as we would like to. We hope our friends will understand our position in this respect, and not send in requests for them.

Continued from page 52

delaying gunfire, The Shadow could easily have reached the street before Moe started.

The trail led exactly where Moe expected: to Twindell's mansion. There, Thorner hopped from the other cab, which promptly shot away. Moe saw Thorner run for the side door, which evidently opened to receive him. Parked close to the mansion, Moe looked into the rear of his own cab. It was empty.

Grinning, Moe decided that The Shadow had dropped off and followed Thorner to the gloomy side of the large house. Thorner had carried the dragon during that final dash; perhaps, by this time, gloved hands had plucked it from him.

However, Moe was not supposed to wait here. His job was to get back to where the chase had started and help The Shadow's agents to clear the neighborhood. After that, he could report to Burbank.

Meanwhile, Herk Duvan had completed a roundabout trip to a disreputable neighborhood far from the scene of battle. Parking the old sedan in the depths of a blind alley, Herk turned to the mobbie who rode with him.

"We made it, Brodie," said Herk. "Like I told you we was going to."

"Yeah," returned Brodie, "because Flash covered for us."

"So what?" demanded Herk. "That was the way Flash wanted it. He gave me the high sign, so we could get away with the moll."

"Yeah, but suppose the bulls got Flash—"

"He'll shake 'em," interposed Herk, in confident tone. "Leave that to Flash. C'mon! Let's lug the dame up to the hide-away. She won't give no trouble. She ain't let a peep out yet."

They could see Beatrice's pale face in the darkened rear of the sedan. Opening the door on the right of the car, they drew the girl out and carried her between them, through a ground-level door, down a short flight of steps.

"She slid out easy," commented Herk, "but she seems heavier, now that we're lugging her. Cripes! I hope she ain't croaked! She's worth fifty grand."

"Yeah?" demanded Brodie. "Her old man must be King of China!"

"She ain't no Chinee," returned Herk. "She's an American, and it's her uncle has got the dough. Flash didn't say who he was, but he's got fifty grand that he can cough over."

They were in a squarish stone-walled room, where Herk turned on a hanging light. They placed Beatrice on a rickety cot; and Brodie, noting the whiteness of her face, gave a nod that disposed of the Chinese theory. Herk was holding the girl's limp wrist, trying to detect a pulse beat.

"Get out and bolt the door," he told Brodie, "while I find out if there's any life in her. Maybe we'll need a sawbones—"

A SHARP snarl from Brodie ended Herk's remarks. Swinging about, Herk saw his companion thrusting a quick-drawn gun straight toward the door. He was fast with a rod, Brodie was, as fast as any member of the mob. That was why Flash had given him to Herk tonight.

Brodie's hand was snakelike. It seemed to uncoil and whip in with the gun all in one action, that usually ended with a trigger tug. There was a muffled report close to Brodie's body, but the revolver did not blast the shot. As Herk sprang from beside the couch, pulling his own revolver, Brodie's figure sagged.

Through a drift of grayish smoke, that floated from an automatic muzzle, Herk saw a cloaked figure in the doorway. Burning eyes were fixed upon the gang lieutenant. So was the muzzle of the automatic; the same .45 that had just disposed of Brodie!

Herk heard a whispered laugh: The Shadow's. A revolver clanked the floor, as Herk's hands lifted.

The last thing that Herk Duvan expected was mercy from The Shadow. But Herk received it, for a price. A passenger during the trip, The Shadow had overheard all that Herk said to Brodie.

"You will return to Flash," The Shadow told Herk, "and tell him that the girl is here, being watched by Brodie."

Herk gulped agreement.

"Once you have told that story"—The Shadow's tone was sibilant—"you will be safe! It is your only story! Flash would not be pleased if he learned that you turned yellow"—a whispered laugh taunted Herk's ears—"when you met The Shadow!"

With a quick sweep, The Shadow gathered Herk's revolver from the floor. Cracking it open, he shook out the cartridges. He handed it to Herk, made him turn around. Finding the crook's reserve ammunition, The Shadow took it from Herk's pocket.

Marching Herk out to the car, The Shadow forced him to get behind the wheel. Waiting at the mouth of the alley, he beckoned for Herk to start. The sedan rolled past and kept going. Herk Duvan did not intend to stop until he was far from The Shadow's range of gunfire.

Rapidly returning to the hide-away, The Shadow gathered up the feebly stirring form of Beatrice Chadbury. Stepping across the dead form of Brodie, the cloaked avenger again reached the darkness of the alley and disappeared with his living burden.

The Shadow had gained the prize he wanted. He had followed the path of the girl; not the trail of the dragon!

CHAPTER XIII.

THE POWER OF MIND.

BEATRICE CHADBURY awakened. It was daylight and she was in a little bedroom, quite different from the hotel room where she had recently stopped. This room looked as if it belonged in a hospital. In fact, it could have been termed a hospital room, for it was connected with the offices of Dr. Rupert Sayre, a young Park Avenue physician.

The surroundings did not trouble Beatrice. She was still indifferent to such matters. Her life was still the half-trance that Shiwan Khan had produced. Failure to hear Shan Juchi's gong stroke had kept Beatrice in that condition, even after her unconscious spell.

She was tired, though, and her head ached. So she decided to remain in bed, as she had frequently done, during recent days, until lights began to blink outside the window. Beatrice did not stop to reason that the window might not offer the accustomed view of the Chinese restaurant called the Green Pagoda.

As she leaned her head back against the pillows, Beatrice saw her clothes fixed neatly upon a chair. Sight of the colorful Chinese costume brought eagerness to her eyes. Getting out of bed, the girl slid from the nightie she was wearing and put on the Chinese clothes.

Dressed in the silken garments, Beatrice gave the rippling laugh of Lana Luan. Opening the door, she walked into a passage, followed it until she came to an office. A white-jacketed man looked up from his desk; his face showed a serious expression. Dr. Sayre pressed a desk button, to bring the nurse.

Beatrice watched him with a vague smile.

"My name is Lana Luan," she announced slowly. "I have come here because—"

She couldn't finish the sentence. Nothing prompted her. Without the inspiring action of another brain, Beatrice had no thoughts of her own, except the memory of lights that shone at dusk. The nurse arrived, and Sayre told her to take the patient back to the hospital room.

Nothing impelled Beatrice to object. When she reached the hospital room, she let the nurse undress her. But when she realized that she was in bed again, wearing the night dress, she reached for the Chinese clothes that were over the nurse's arm. The nurse left immediately, taking the garments with her.

"These were the trouble," she told Sayre, as she hung the clothes in the office closet. "She saw them, and wanted them. As soon as I took them along, she started to go to sleep."

"Lana Luan?" repeated Sayre, thoughtfully. "I must make a note of that name, to tell Cranston when he arrives."

WHEN Lamont Cranston reached Sayre's office, a half-hour later, he was quite interested in the physician's report. Sayre repeated the girl's unfinished sentence. When Sayre expressed the opinion that Beatrice's condition was hypnotic, and not due to a brain concussion, Cranston nodded.

"Quite right," he said. "She is controlled by a powerful brain, upon which she depends for all complex thoughts."

"You mean the influence is telepathic?"

"Exactly!" Cranston smiled. "Does that surprise you?"

It didn't surprise Sayre. He had delved into the subject of telepathy himself. But he doubted that the influence could be as effective as Cranston seemed to think it was.

"I have studied the tests conducted at various colleges," said Sayre, "and while they prove telepathy to be a fact, they show that it works only at irregular intervals, even when the subjects are hypnotized."

"Let us review the facts of hypnotism," suggested The Shadow. "The first man to demonstrate it properly was Mesmer. His basic method was to gaze into the subject's eyes and thus command a fixed attention. But Mesmer, despite his results, was denounced as a quack and his findings rejected."

"For many years," agreed Sayre, "until Braid again discovered hypnotism. When Braid proved that trance could be induced by gazing at a fixed object, such as a bright light, no one could doubt that hypnotism was a fact."

"And Mesmer's findings were accepted, at last?"

"Why, yes. It stood to reason that he had been able to make people obey his spoken commands, as any hypnotist can do."

"But Mesmer claimed more than that. At times, he controlled his subjects *mentally,* without speaking to them. We cannot fairly reject that claim, if we accept the rest. Instead, we must look for the reason behind Mesmer's peculiar power.

"The answer may be termed mutual hypnotism. Mesmer's eyes were the bright objects that hypnotized the subject. In his turn, Mesmer was staring into the subject's eyes. Fully concentrated, he became partly hypnotized himself. When that occurred, his mental commands were obeyed."

The facts startled Sayre. He had always considered mesmerism and hypnotism as identical in result, differing merely in method of procedure. The logic of The Shadow's statements gave the case a new status.

"A man who calls himself Shiwan Khan is putting that system into practice," declared The Shadow. "He is using lights to fix their attention, a gong stroke to break the trance. The mental commands of Shiwan Khan are being obeyed.

"It seems obvious, therefore, that Shiwan Khan must gaze into an identical light, whenever he hypnotizes a subject. In that way, he could induce a mutual state of hypnotism, perhaps to a degree exceeding ordinary mesmerism."

Sayre asked about the lights. The Shadow described the green bulb that he had seen at Ryndon's. He mentioned the gong note on the phonograph record. He then produced a small metal gong and hammer, and pointed to the closet.

"Have the nurse take those Chinese clothes into the other room," he suggested. "We shall let the girl resume the part of Lana Luan, the false personality that Shiwan Khan has built for her."

SEVERAL minutes later, Beatrice Chadbury entered wearing the colorful clothes and blank expression of Lana Luan. She repeated her statement of identity; when she halted, The Shadow announced in a slow, impressive tone:

"I am Shiwan Khan!"

A change flickered over the girl's features, but she seemed to note an oddity in the voice. Then The Shadow was approaching her; she was gazing into burning eyes that held her full attention. Beatrice was gripped by the same fascination that the glittering lights commanded.

"I am Shiwan Khan," repeated The Shadow. "When I speak, you hear, wherever you may be!"

"Yes!" Beatrice was breathless. "Yes—"

"And the place where you listen—"

"—is the hotel room, where I can see the lights."

"And the lights are—"

"—above the restaurant. The Green Pagoda. That is where I go. And then—"

Beatrice halted. Long in that automatic trance, she could carry her memory no further. The matter of the lights was implanted upon her brain; the rest had been erased. Both results were the design of Shiwan Khan.

He had forced the girl's mind to retain the first details of her journey. The rest came back when she had actually passed the portals of the Green Pagoda.

Even the effort that she had displayed was a strain for the girl's dazed mind. She wavered; The Shadow caught her instantly and let her settle in the waiting arms of Sayre. Seizing the hammer and gong, he gave the needed stroke. Sayre could feel the sudden convulsion that quivered Beatrice from head to foot.

Then, the blank expression fading from her face, the girl stared about in genuine bewilderment. She looked at Cranston's face as though she had never before seen it. The Shadow's eyes had lost their burn. They had a mild, friendly expression that won Beatrice's confidence.

"Where in the world am I?" she gasped. "What can have happened to me?"

With Cranston's calmness, The Shadow explained that she was in New York; that she had met with an accident while attending a masquerade. All that amazed Beatrice as she listened, weakly, from a chair where Sayre had placed her. She began to explain that she was supposed to be on a cruise ship. The effort taxed her. Sighing, the girl said:

"Anyway, my name is Beatrice Chadbury. My uncle is here in New York. His name is Guy Chadbury. I suppose he thinks that I am on the ship."

Her eyes went shut. Those days of living in a trance had produced a complete nervous exhaustion. Sayre summoned the nurse.

No longer walking with the slow stride of Lana Luan, Beatrice shuffled her slippered feet wearily toward the bedroom. She sighed gratefully when the nurse undressed her. Beatrice was glad to be free of those thick silk garments.

During the last few minutes that she wore them, the clothes of Lana Luan seemed to be dragging Beatrice back into some horrible, nameless past, that could never have been part of her real existence. Unclothed, she felt the terror leave her. In bed, she sighed again, and fell asleep while the nurse was lowering the window shade to cut off the bright sunlight.

In the office, Dr. Sayre was congratulating his friend Cranston upon the remarkable results that he had produced. In response, The Shadow said:

"You may depend upon me to notify Guy Chadbury that his niece is here. I shall, of course, use my own discretion in the matter. It may be preferable to wait until we can give a satisfactory report upon her condition."

Dr. Sayre agreed. He knew the meaning of what Cranston termed discretion. Sayre had long recognized a connection between Lamont Cranston and The Shadow. If news of Beatrice's rescue should be withheld from her uncle, it would be for their mutual benefit.

Nothing should be done to obstruct a coming event that Dr. Sayre could foresee: a duel wherein a plotter named Shiwan Khan would meet The Shadow!

CHAPTER XIV.

DOUBLED TRAILS.

Two days had passed—strange days for The Shadow! In all his dealings with master criminals, he had never encountered one whose ways were as baffling as those of Shiwan Khan.

The Shadow knew of Shiwan Khan's existence; that was all. The rest depended upon sheer reason, but not of a deductive sort. It was necessary for The Shadow to build a theory, test it with every fact, yet even then accept it without positive proof.

A slender link began the chain. It started with the fact that a murdered stunt flier named Bob Ryndon had come from a vast province of western China—Sinkiang.

The Shadow knew that territory, its present state of unrest. He could see deep causes behind the trouble in Sinkiang, at a time when all China was supposed to be united. Between Tibet, the land of brain, and Mongolia, place of brawn, Sinkiang was a terrain where both could unite.

There was proof that they had been united through the effort of Shiwan Khan. His power was that of mind, as he had demonstrated; his followers, fierce Mongols, were men of muscle. Behind that combination lay Shiwan Khan's ambition: to rule all the world!

Even The Shadow, a few weeks ago, would have considered such a scheme fantastic. But in this strange campaign, the seemingly unreal was plausible Things that others would regard as unimportant were solid links, welded in The Shadow's chain of evidence. One was the cry of the dying Mongol, Shan Juchi, which The Shadow had heard follow the clash of a gong:

"Kha Khan!"

The name "Shiwan Khan" alone meant little. Coupled with the term "Kha Khan," it meant much. The title by which Shiwan Khan's Mongols knew their master was the same used by Genghis Khan, greater conqueror of history. It meant "Great Ruler," in the parlance of the Orient.

In days of old, Genghis Khan had conquered empires by superior military measures. In this modern age, such a result could be accomplished only by present-day preparations. To bring an invisible kingdom into reality, Shiwan Khan would need munitions. Another link that fitted into The Shadow's chain!

Shiwan Khan's control of Beatrice Chadbury, the temporary Lana Luan, was proof that his machinations concerned her uncle, Guy Chadbury, the one man—The Shadow had been studying Chadbury's case—who could secretly supply a shipload of bombs for delivery to Sinkiang.

Through Harry Vincent, The Shadow had been carefully seeking facts regarding Chadbury; so far, without result. The trouble was that Chadbury was king man with his own enterprises; it was difficult to check his actions.

Obviously, there would be other implements required by Shiwan Khan: airplanes, for one. Unfortunately, Beatrice had not met Paul Brent during her waking life, hence she had not supplied a clue to Globe Aircraft. So far, The Shadow had obtained no lead along that line.

As for the matter of shipments, The Shadow had considered that phase of the question. Through the investment office managed by Rutledge Mann, he had acquired reams of data pertaining to international shipping companies. None had shown a flaw in the affairs of the Tropical Export Lines, managed by Mitchell Dorron.

WHILE keeping tabs on Chadbury, The Shadow had not forgotten other persons who were definitely hand in glove with Shiwan Khan. There were three: Flash Gidley, Benjamin Twindell and Herbert Thorner. It was possible to check on all of them.

Flash was serving Shiwan Khan on the promise of collecting fifty thousand dollars from Guy Chadbury for the safe return of the latter's niece, Beatrice. That indicated Chadbury to be as honest as Flash was crooked. In this case, The Shadow had scored one on Shiwan Khan.

Beatrice was already safe, in The Shadow's custody. Flash Gidley hadn't guessed it, because his lieutenant, Herk Duvan, was afraid to tell him. With Hawkeye watching the hide-away where Beatrice was supposed to be a prisoner, The Shadow would learn immediately, if Herk spilled facts. But Herk probably wouldn't.

Having double-crossed Flash, Herk's only game was to play ball with The Shadow. It was an axiom in the underworld that when a crook went straight, The Shadow became his friend.

Herk had gone straight—under pressure, of course, but that did not change his new status. He would remember and know that The Shadow would not let him down, provided he adhered to his present policy.

Benjamin Twindell was a different proposition. It was easy to understand how Shiwan Khan was using him. Twindell was serving as a "front" for the purchase of munitions and airplanes, probably supplying cash through various well-covered channels. In return, Twindell was receiving porcelain dragons, which, for some curious reason, he valued more than his famed jewel collection.

Of all persons, Twindell was the one that Shiwan Khan would watch most closely. Close to Twindell, however, was another person, who might be overlooked. That man was Herbert Thorner. Whatever profit he might gain would come from Twindell, not from Shiwan Khan. Like Herk, Thorner offered real possibilities.

That fact explained why The Shadow's complete review of the Shiwan Khan intrigue took place in a limousine bound for Twindell's mansion. Trusting to his guise of Cranston, The Shadow was visiting another of Twindell's jewel sales, on the chance that he would find Thorner present.

The Shadow was not disappointed. Thorner was on hand. The police had not connected him with a crazy fight in an empty house, where they had discovered dead and crippled mobbies and Mongols, along with a battered Chinese gong.

While he watched the jewel sale, Thorner occasionally glanced toward Twindell's mantel, where six squatty porcelain dragons formed a grinning row. Just after one of those off-guard glances, Thorner happened to meet the steady gaze of Lamont Cranston. From then on, Thorner looked worried.

When the sale had ended and the visitors were gone, Benjamin Twindell cackled pleasantly as he thumbed a pile of checks. His total sale from the jewels amounted to many thousands of dollars. Since Thorner was available, Twindell gave him the checks and told him to take them to various banks.

Twindell added other instructions that Thorner accepted as quite ordinary, until he was on his way to make the rounds. Riding in a cab, he happened to notice that Cranston's limousine was following him. It kept on the trail from bank to bank.

At one bank, where Thorner paid a visit to the cashier's office, the sallow man was sure that he saw Cranston watching from near a teller's window. From then on, Thorner plotted a cute move of his own. He tried it when he left the last bank.

Thrusting a bill into the cab driver's hand, Thorner told him to speed away. Ducking into another cab, Thorner trailed the limousine. The big car lost the trail of the speedy cab, and finally took a different course. It stopped on Twenty-third Street, where Cranston alighted near an ancient office building.

The limousine did not wait. Leaving his cab, Thorner stole into the building. He trailed Cranston up a stairway; at the top, Thorner saw no further sign of his quarry.

He noted a short passage, with an office at the end of it, the only place where Cranston could have gone. That was all Thorner wanted to know. Smiling shrewdy, the sallow man stole down the stairway and out to the street.

IN a more modern office building, two visitors were seated in a private office connected with the Tropical Export Lines. Both looked glum, although Mitchell Dorron was smiling from the other side of his big desk. Handing a sheaf of papers to Paul Brent, the shipping man said:

"The Globe shipment has gone aboard the *Aritoba*. Mr. Chadbury's shipment is waiting to be loaded, so that the ship may leave the Hoboken pier tonight."

Looking toward Guy Chadbury, Paul Brent saw a hopeful expression come over the munitions magnate's face.

"I am still waiting a payment for my materials," said Chadbury. "I am afraid, Dorron, that you will have to delay the departure of the *Aritoba* for a few days, at least—"

There was an interruption, as Dorron's secretary entered bringing an envelope that had been forwarded from Chadbury's office. Opening it, Chadbury drew out a check. It was from a company that he had never heard of, but that did not matter. The check was certified by the cashier of a large New York bank.

Chadbury grimaced, as he thrust the check into his pocket. He told Dorron that the loading of the *Aritoba* could be resumed. With bowed head, Chadbury left the office. At the elevators, Paul Brent overtook him.

"I've got to talk to you, Mr. Chadbury!" exclaimed Paul, eagerly. "We're in the same mess! I just realized it, when I saw you put away that check. We've got to talk this over!"

Chadbury caught the earnestness in Paul's tone. Tightening his lips, the gray-haired man nodded, then said:

"Come to my penthouse, Brent."

Back in his private office, Mitchell Dorron was pacing the floor, worried. He had noticed Paul's look at Chadbury. Staring toward the ceiling, Dorron watched three lights, fixed exactly like the ones in the living room of his Long Island home.

Suddenly, those three lights gleamed, pressed by a distant switch. To Dorron's blanking brain came the far-away tone of Shiwan Khan. Dorron began to speak in answer, steadily but anxiously.

In the outside dusk, Harry Vincent had seen Paul Brent enter a large limousine with Guy Chadbury. Trailing in Moe's cab, Harry followed the big car to an apartment house, saw the two get out together. Paul was evidently going up to Chadbury's penthouse.

Who Chadbury's friend was, Harry did not know, but he had come from a shipping office that Chadbury had visited. Over a telephone in the corner drugstore, Harry contacted Burbank.

Word was going to The Shadow. Word that might mean the turning point in the long struggle to frustrate Shiwan Khan!

CHAPTER XV.

PAYMENT DEFERRED.

THE radio program had ended, but Flash Gidley was still staring at the dial. He liked those little lights—green, yellow, red—that blinked with a pulsating throb. Herk Duvan, watching nervously, could hear Flash's low-purred answers to questions that seemed unspoken.

Herk always kept far enough away so the lights would not get him. While he watched, he worried about questions that Flash might ask later. One came soon after Flash finally swung about, no longer fascinated by the lights.

"What did Brodie say when he called up last?"

"Nothin' much," returned Herk. "Everythin's jake, Flash, just like it always was."

"You're sure he's sticking close to the joint?"

"He ought to be, Flash. He looked all set to stay there, when I seen him last."

Flash leaned back in his chair, quite satisfied. He nudged his thumb toward the telephone.

"Call the boys."

"What for, Flash?" Herk tried to curb the anxiety in his tone. Then, hopefully: "Another job?"

"No. The same one. Tonight we collect. Have a couple go over and case the apartment house where Guy Chadbury lives. Tell them we'll be along later, with the rest."

"Who's Guy Chadbury?"

"The dame's uncle," replied Flash, with a grin. "Her name is Beatrice Chadbury. The reason why I told you not to worry about asking her to spill her name, was because I knew it all along."

Two facts were proven by Flash's statement. One: that he had not understood Shan Juchi's real purpose in striking the big gong in the deserted house. The other: that Herk had successfully managed to keep Flash thinking that Beatrice was still a prisoner in the hideaway.

QUITE unaware that he might soon be receiving visitors, Guy Chadbury was finishing a long discussion with Paul Brent. They had dined together at the penthouse; following dinner, they had finally come out with their full stories:

Each found it impossible to recall the

name of Shiwan Khan, but when Paul described the lights outside his hotel room window, Chadbury promptly pointed out the large cigarette sign that had started him on the road to ruin.

"It looks like we'll sink together," declared Paul glumly. "I can't trust my story to anyone else, Chadbury. You're the only man who has been through the same sort of experience. The moment I open my mouth, I'll be arrested for murder."

Chadbury gave a sympathetic nod.

"I'm ready to talk, though," declared Paul, grimly. "At least, it would stop those shipments. It seems more sensible, however, to wait a few days more. Something might turn up to help us. In that case, we could have the *Aritoba* flagged before she gets through the Panama Canal."

"Wait, by all means!" insisted Chadbury. "A move on your part would be as serious as one on mine! We can't take any risk, until we know that Beatrice is safe!"

Stepping to the corner, Chadbury brought out Beatrice's photograph, showed it to Paul with the simple comment:

"My niece."

To Paul, the gown that the pictured girl was wearing seemed to transform itself into a Chinese jacket.

"It's Lana Luan!" he exclaimed. "The girl I met at Ryndon's! She must have looked at lights the way we did! If—"

Paul did not finish. Chadbury was staring off through the window. His eyes were fixed on the changed glimmers of the cigarette sign. Quickly, Paul flung his arm across his own face.

He did not intend to feel that same influence that had again gripped Chadbury. He was listening, though, hoping to hear Chadbury utter words. They came:

"Yes. I hear you, Shiwan Khan!"

The forced voice of Chadbury gave Paul a missing recollection as vivid as a lightning flash.

Shiwan Khan!

That was the name of the hidden master who made all obey his dictates. Hearing it while in a waking condition, Paul intended to remember the name. While he repeated it in undertone, he heard more words from Chadbury. The entranced man was speaking of his niece, and Paul caught his final response:

"Yes. Fifty thousand dollars."

Chadbury's shoulders jarred. He had heard the stroke of the distant gong. He blinked at Paul, then asked:

"What . . . what did I hear?"

Paul repeated it. Chadbury had the same electric effect at mention of the name Shiwan Khan. Then, when Paul had barely finished with the remaining details, they heard the telephone bell.

Chadbury's secretary was out, so the munitions man answered the call himself. When finished, he let the telephone clatter heavily on its stand.

"They're here!" Chadbury bit the words. "To get the fifty thousand! Some racketeer, and probably a crowd with him. I could hear them talking, when he called from downstairs."

"You're sure?"

"He mentioned Shiwan Khan. They're coming up, and if I don't have the door open when they get here, they'll take it that I called the police. In that case—"

"You'd better get to the door, Chadbury. Keep a stiff lip. I'll stand by you!"

Hurrying through a darkened outer room, Chadbury had the door open when his visitors arrived. Leaving two thugs near the elevator, Flash Gidley stalked through to the living room, with Herk Duvan at his heels. Chadbury introduced Paul Brent, whereupon Flash grinned.

"My name is Flash Gidley," he announced. "This is my side-kick, Herk

Duvan. It don't hurt if you know it. The lid's off on the whole works. Shiwan Khan says so. You aren't the only guys that have been looking at funny lights. I've been seeing the glims, too.

"Only I'm on one side of the fence, you're on the other. Shiwan Khan says you've got fifty grand here, so fork it over, Chadbury! That's to pay your niece's room and board."

Chadbury opened a little safe to get the money. He was remembering, rather vaguely, that he had brought the cash here a few days ago. He had made a notation that he might need it. Probably he had been watching Shiwan Khan's lights and thereby had been influenced to draw the money from the bank.

As the front of the safe swung open, Chadbury turned suddenly about.

"What guarantee do I have?" he questioned. "How do I know that my niece will be safely returned?"

"Herk here will take care of that," replied Flash. "He's going to stick with you until tomorrow. This guy Brent" —he gestured toward Paul—"is getting a good break, too. Shiwan Khan says he won't have to worry about a murder rap, after the dame gets back."

There was no question as to the prime purpose governing Flash Gidley. He wanted to get the fifty thousand dollars with as little delay as possible. He was purring other arguments—that he hadn't abducted Beatrice, but had actually saved her from danger. He hadn't known who she was, he added, until afterward.

That smooth talk was glossing over the matter of the money, making it look more like a reward than a demand for ransom. Flash wanted everybody to be happy, himself included. He talked about concluding the deal, and calling it quits. To that, Chadbury agreed; he had caught a glance from Paul.

Both had the same idea. With Beatrice returned, bringing the gun with which Hoang Khu had murdered Ryndon, Shiwan Khan would have no hold over either Paul or Chadbury. They would then be able to have the *Aritoba* brought back to port, through an arrangement with Dorron.

They had correctly figured the shipping man to be a dupe like themselves, though they did not know the extent to which he had come under Shiwan Kan's baleful influence. What they did not realize was the fact that Shiwan Khan did not intend to deliver either the girl or the death gun.

As matters actually stood, Shiwan Khan was unable to keep either term of the agreement that Flash proposed. But Flash had no idea of the real situation. He was bluffing because Shiwan Khan had ordered him to do so, but he thought his bluff was backed.

Chadbury reached for the box that held the money. There was a loaded revolver beside it; he felt an urge to produce the weapon instead, but he resisted that desire, until he heard a voice he recognized speaking firmly from the doorway.

Beatrice's voice!

FLASH and Herk wheeled, reaching for guns. They were too late. Side by side, they were under a muzzle that moved slowly, left and right, keeping them both covered. It was Beatrice Chadbury who stood in the dorway, and she had both crooks covered.

The girl was dressed in dark-blue American clothes. No longer Lana Luan in mind or attire, she had come here somehow ahead of the crooks. Flash, his hands raised and clenched, realized that he had given his game away by sending men ahead to look the place over.

While they were reporting back to Flash, Beatrice had slipped into the apartment house. Coming up to the penthouse, she had waited in the darkened outer room.

But who had released her from the hide-away, and told her to come here? Both questions had a single answer:

The Shadow!

Flash glared at Herk. Thinking that Flash's guesses were going deep, Herk gulped the whole story.

"The Shadow took her, Flash! The night we went to the hide-away, Brodie and me. Brodie tried to croak The Shadow, but got his instead. After that he—"

"He made you pull a double cross, huh?"

"What difference did it make, Flash? You tried to pull a double cross yourself, on these guys"—Herk nudged a raised thumb toward Chadbury and Paul—"telling 'em the dame was coming back, and to forget the murder rap. You was going to lam with the fifty grand, and leave me and the boys here to croak these lugs so they couldn't squawk."

While he talked, Herk didn't heed Flash's interrupting snarls. Meanwhile, Chadbury had the revolver from the safe and was prodding Flash in the ribs. To Paul, Chadbury said:

"There's another gun in the table drawer. Get it and cover this chap Herk. Beatrice can probably tell us what we are supposed to do next."

"I can," announced Beatrice, very calmly. "We are to hold these crooks as prisoners, until—"

Chadbury interrupted with a warning cry. Swinging away from Flash, he aimed his revolver wildly toward the window. Paul made a grab for the gun in the table drawer, hoping he would be in time to aid. Beatrice, startled, let her gaze go toward the window.

Over the still had come a leering Mongol face. The yellow hand above it was starting the hurl of a long-bladed knife, with Beatrice as the target. Crime's counterthrust was on its way.

Out from the blackness of the night, Shiwan Khan had provided another of his lawless killers, to furnish new murder that would defeat The Shadow's plans!

CHAPTER XVI.

WITHOUT THE SHADOW.

A GUN spoke from the darkened doorway of the penthouse living room. It was scarcely noticed, the blast of that automatic, for immediately afterward came the rattle of revolvers. But the spurt of that big .45 was the one thrust that found its mark.

Again, The Shadow's skill was demonstrated; the superiority of a bullet was proven, when compared to a knife fling. The impact of the leaden slug jolted the Mongol at the window, just before his slinging hand completed its arc.

The knife scaled forward as the killer flew back. The blade whirred as it flashed a foot above Beatrice's head, to bury itself, hilt-deep, in the living room's oak-paneled wall. A wailing, long-pitched cry came like an answer to the knife's useless *zip,* as the Mongol began a whirling journey of his own.

He was bound for the ground, twenty-four stories below, striking projecting cornices on the way. Somewhat amazed, Paul and Chadbury were jabbing revolver shots through the window's empty space.

Beatrice knew where the rescuing shot had come from, for The Shadow had brought her here. She turned about to greet her black-cloaked friend; a moment later, she was spinning toward the side wall of the room, sent there by The Shadow.

No longer in the daze of Lana Luan, the girl was able to halt herself as she reached the paneling. She saw why The Shadow had again supplied a rapid rescue. Flash and Herk had spotted the black figure at the doorway. No longer covered, they were yanking their revolvers, to fire at The Shadow.

As he flung Beatrice in one direction,

The Shadow faded in the other. Their first shots traveling through space, the two crooks shifted aim immediately. This time, they guessed the direction correctly, but their tactics differed.

Flash was stepping back to fire, Herk was lunging forward. Beating both to the shot, The Shadow took the closer man. Herk received a fitting reward for his latest double cross—a bullet that turned his lunge into a dive. His gun spurted, but its aim was high. Flash supplied a direct shot at the same moment, but it did not reach The Shadow.

Herk's twisty pitch had thrown his shoulder in the bullet's path. The Shadow's cloaked head ducked away before Flash could fire again. Catching Herk's sprawling body as he had grabbed Shan Juchi, The Shadow blasted a quick reply at Flash.

Though luck had partly served The Shadow, it did the same for Flash. A chance writhe of Herk's body destroyed the black-cloaked fighter's aim. Flash sped for the door with two men after him, before The Shadow could chuck Herk aside.

Paul and Chadbury were out to capture Flash alive. They didn't realize that they blocked The Shadow's fire.

As Flash flung himself into the lighted corridor by the elevators, his pursuers at last decided that shots were necessary. They were aiming, about to tug their triggers, when two men sprang in to block them. They were the thugs that Flash had stationed outside, and they realized their folly too late.

Before the pair could even pick out targets, Paul and Chadbury cut loose. The bullets meant for Flash took the mobbies instead. From the living room doorway, The Shadow saw the pursuers clear the sagging bodies of the thugs. Then came the clash of an elevator door; it was echoed by *clang* of bullets against metal.

Flash had made a getaway under gunfire. The only way to halt him would be to get quick word downstairs, by telephone. Any excitement in the lobby would be spotted by Hawkeye, who would relay word to Cliff Marsland, outside. With Moe's cab available, Flash might be overtaken.

Before The Shadow could reach the telephone, he heard Beatrice's scream. It came from the corner of the living room, a heartfelt shriek, its horror proclaiming some new menace.

THE SHADOW knew the only place from which danger could come; he did not stop to take a look. With a low dive, he made straight for the window, bringing his eyes upward with his gun.

He heard the *whim* of knives that almost skimmed his back. He saw the extended hands that had flung them. Two Mongols were half across the broad sill. They were reserve assassins who had climbed up together, undeterred by the fate of the slant-eye killer who had tried the previous thrust.

They had been swinging their knives when Beatrice saw them. Behind a chair in the far corner, the girl was safe. Both killers were loosing their knife throws at The Shadow, when he had made that instinctive dive. Fast and long, his low, headfirst surge had carried him just below the launched blades. But The Shadow had not ended his plunge until he reached the window.

Grabbing the cloaked arms, the Mongols tried to haul The Shadow across the window ledge. Beatrice had a gun but could not fire, for The Shadow was tangled with his foeman by the time she aimed. The girl dashed to the living-room door, shouting for Paul and Chadbury. They came on the double-quick.

There was a muffled shot from the window. One Mongol sagged from the ledge, losing an elbow hold. As that killer went outward, The Shadow's free hand gripped for the ledge, almost had it, when the remaining Mongol clawed the gloved hand away.

There was a babbled shout of triumph as The Shadow slid outward; but as he went, the cloaked fighter delivered an upward shot. Beatrice saw the Mongol jolt, claw his chest with his hands. Shrieking, the assassin took a forward pitch out into the dark.

Blackness ruled the window space. Wildly, Beatrice hoped that it would materialize into a cloaked shape. She was telling her uncle what had happened; he and Paul hurried to the window. They were dejected when they turned about. There was no sign of The Shadow, as Beatrice realized when she also looked below.

The girl saw the ornamented edge of a cornice, a floor below the penthouse. It was the ledge upon which the Mongols had perched themselves, prior to the arrival of Flash Gidley. Farther down, Beatrice could see other ledges, like vast steps, all showing blank against the glare of the city's lights.

Somewhere below the lowest ledge that she could see, was a sheer stretch to the ground. At the bottom of it lay the bodies of those victims who had taken the long fall. Mournfully, Beatrice pictured a cloaked form lying among a trio of crushed Mongols.

The Shadow had settled three desperate assassins, but there was no possible chance that he could have survived a plunge as long as theirs. Sobs racked Beatrice, as she thought of her rescuer's fate. Gently, her uncle drew her from the window.

"Tell us," he said, solemnly, "what do you know about Shiwan Khan? It is up to us to avenge the death of our lost friend, by tracking down the enemy that caused his death."

Beatrice nodded. Grimly brave, she was ready to do her part. The Shadow was gone, and the one way to serve his memory was to settle scores with Shiwan Khan. Beatrice knew that she could provide the beginning of a trail to the headquarters of the heinous master villain.

Dr. Sayre had told her what she had said while she was Lana Luan. The girl told of the lights that had blinked nightly above the Green Pagoda; how she had been lured by them into the restaurant, there to visit a hidden domain that she knew existed but which she could no longer remember in detail.

NEITHER Paul nor Chadbury could doubt what Beatrice told them, for they knew the hypnotic power of Shiwan Khan's lights. They were pleased, too, when Beatrice remembered a message that The Shadow had ordered her to give them. She questioned her uncle:

"Do you know anything about a gun that was used to murder Bob Ryndon?"

"I do!" exclaimed Paul. "I gave it to you, when you were Lana Luan. What did you do with it?"

"I don't know," replied Beatrice. "The Shadow simply said that the gun no longer mattered. The police found it, but could distinguish no fingerprints upon it."

Chadbury thwacked Paul on the shoulder.

"That clears you, Brent!" he exclaimed. "With Beatrice safe, we can both tell all we know. We can call in the police, to help us find Shiwan Khan."

"We ought to see Dorron first," insisted Paul, "so he can hold the *Aritoba*. Maybe he was duped like we were. If so, he will support our story."

Chadbury nodded while closing the safe, to lock up the fifty thousand dollars. He remarked that Dorron might still be at his office; the shipping man usually remained there evenings when freighters were being loaded.

Taking Beatrice with them, Chadbury and Paul left the penthouse. They were solemn as they rode down in the elevator. Despite their elation over the chance of balking Shiwan Khan, they had not forgotten The Shadow. Their tones were hushed when they spoke of him.

Silent, too, was the cloaked form that soon rose from the blackness outside the penthouse window. Wavering inward from the darkness, The Shadow settled upon the living-room floor.

Crawling farther, he was blocked by Herk's body; managing to circle it, he reached the telephone. His gloved hand failed, however, when it tried to lift the instrument.

Unlike the Mongols, The Shadow had not taken a long pitch from the window. Their plunges had been inspired by bullets. The Shadow had dropped straight; his plummet fall had stopped on the cornice from which the diving Mongols had bounced.

Managing to cling there, The Shadow had rolled inward from the edge. Strength returning, he had climbed up to the deserted penthouse.

Exhausted, The Shadow lay motionless. It would be minutes, perhaps many of them, before his senses came back. Precious minutes for Shiwan Khan, whose evil cause had received a bad setback tonight. For Shiwan Khan, perhaps, would have a chance to rally his depleted forces while The Shadow's recovery was under way.

True, measures were being taken to defeat Shiwan Khan. But such measurs could bring only failure, when employed without The Shadow.

CHAPTER XVII.
THE PERFECT THRUST.

Shiwan Khan was seated in his golden throne room, a silent, immobile figure. He was engaged in a period of contemplation, in accordance with the teachings he had learned while in Tibet. The golden room seemed to flow with the supreme villain's vital thoughts.

Last of the long line of descendants who had come from Genghis Khan, this new seeker of conquest had not always dreamed of power. As a youth, he had been meditative, while he dwelt in the wilds of Sinkiang. He had considered which way his future lay: whether in Tibet to the south, or Mongolia to the north.

He had chosen Tibet. Reaching the forbidden city of Lhasa, he had studied under the lamas, learned their mystic ways. He had gained a mental power which his teachers had informed him he should use to accomplish good. Thus gifted, Shiwan Khan had set out for Mongolia.

In that land where brawn and cruelty reigned, Shiwan Khan had experienced his ancestral urge for power. His mental mastery over the Mongolians had caused him to foresee the rise of another Kha Khan, or Great Ruler—himself. He had gone back to his birthplace, Sinkiang, the dividing land that suited his complex nature.

And there—

A sharp interruption ended the contemplation of Shiwan Khan. An intruder had dashed into the golden room, to fall kneeling at the throne. Shiwan Khan, fixing his eyes upon the arrival, saw the upturned face of Hoang Khu, the lieutenant who governed his Mongol horde.

"We have failed, Kha Khan!" babbled the Mongol. "I saw, with these eyes, from the ground below. There was trouble in the little house on the great building where the man Chadbury lives. Unless there had been trouble, my faithful men would not have entered there.

"They came from the window, all three"—Hoang Khu lifted his hand, keeping his forefinger bent with his thumb, so that only his last three fingers were raised—"like tiny dolls! They were thrown to the ground!

"Only one enemy could have accomplished that, Kha Khan. He alone could have saved the girl, her uncle, and the man Brent, for they came, all three—

the Mongol lifted his other hand—"from the house above. The one who did those deeds was Ying Ko!"

By Ying Ko, the Mongol meant The Shadow. He was using the name that the Chinese employed when they spoke of the intrepid, black-clad fighter. Yet Hoang Khu's excitement did not perturb the placid Shiwan Khan. Lifting a gold-sleeved arm, he pointed to the door.

"Go!" The word was like the tone of a bell. "Await my orders, Hoang Khu. I shall learn more facts than you can tell me. We shall yet destroy The Shadow."

As Hoang Khu left, Shiwan Khan turned to his glass board. Again coupling the mechanical methods of the West with this wisdom of the East, he began to flicker various lights. He pressed one switch, then another, staring at each glow that appeared upon the board.

"I am Shiwan Khan—"

The words brought no mental answers. They proved what Hoang Khu had said. Neither Paul Brent nor Guy Chadbury were where they could feel the hidden master's influence. There was a response, however, when Shiwan Khan pressed Dorron's light.

"I am Shiwan Khan. Speak!"

A mental answer came back. Probing Dorron's brain, Shiwan Khan received the impression that Paul and Chadbury had called his office and were on their way there. Calmly, Shiwan Khan gave instructions. His mental advice was exact.

Dorron was to pose as a complete dupe, like the others; although, actually, he had accepted the rule of Shiwan Khan. Through cunning argument, which Shiwan Khan detailed, Dorron was to dissuade Paul, and Chadbury from mentioning the *Aritoba* shipments to the police.

He could attend to the *Aritoba* quietly, while they took up a more important cause: the trapping of Shiwan Khan. After turning off Dorron's lights, Shiwan Khan monotoned a chuckle. He liked trappers. He had a way of enmeshing them in their own snares.

Three little lights glittered as Shiwan Khan pressed a switch. They corresponded with the bulbs on Flash Gidley's new radio set: green, yellow, and red.

Flash answered. Probing the crook's thoughts required patience on the part of Shiwan Khan, for Flash was a less adaptable person than Dorron. Soon, though, Shiwan Khan had learned enough.

He sped new thoughts to Flash—orders for him to leave his headquarters before the police called on him. He instructed Flash to gather a mob and have them ready.

As soon as that was done, Flash was to be at a specified place, to meet a person sent by Shiwan Khan. Flash would then be started on another mission. At the end of it—this was Shiwan Khan's final mental statement—Flash would be paid fifty thousand dollars, in lieu of the money that he had failed to get from Chadbury.

Extinguishing the three little lights, Shiwan Khan gazed at the blank glass board. His lips phrased a melodious laugh, a change from his usual monotone, as he pressed a different switch. Chinese letters began to flicker from the board. Shiwan Khan had started the flashing sign that hung above the Green Pagoda Café.

Though he knew that Beatrice Chadbury was no longer living the life of Lana Luan, Shiwan Khan still believed that the sign would bring results; and it did. Across the street from the Green Pagoda, a man was watching that sign. Harry Vincent was on new duty, for The Shadow.

Harry had definite instructions from his chief. He was to watch the sign, in case it showed odd flickers. Thereupon, it would be Harry's duty to report to Burbank. Harry had been warned, too, that he was not to watch the sign more than a few seconds.

Without realizing it, Harry stared at the glow too long. He was counting the changes of the Chinese letters, thinking that they were shifting at the rate of one a second. Instead, the letters had a slower progression.

To his amazement, Harry was reading those curious characters. With one of them, he seemed to hear the spoken words: "Come!"

MECHANICALLY, Harry crossed the street. A man in a trance, he entered the Chinese restaurant and was shown to the little booth beside the idol. Thoughts were coming to his mind without the aid of the lights. Sliding back the panel, Harry took the route that Beatrice had so often followed.

Passing the closed door of the room where the girl had discarded her own clothes for the garb of Lana Luan, Harry followed the passage that went by the spiral stairway and came into the throne room of Shiwan Khan. He halted like a stalled mechanical figure, to meet the green-eyed gaze of the gold-garbed master mind.

"Your name"—Shiwan Khan seemed to probe Harry's brain to find it—"is Harry Vincent. Once, you served The Shadow."

Unwittingly, Harry gave a nod.

"From now on," said Shiwan Khan, "you shall serve me! I promise you a vast reward. You shall come with me to the heart of Asia, to the underground city of Xanadu, where the sacred River Alph runs through measureless caverns, into a sea where the sun never shines!"

Harry's eyes seemed to light, as if they caught a vision of the splendid capital which dominated Shiwan Khan's underground kingdom.

"Genghis Khan, my ancestor, conquered half the world," announced Shiwan Khan, proudly. "He used gunpowder, other implements of warfare that were modern in his day. His descendant, Kubla Khan, feared no one, and was able to use the wealth that Genghis Khan had left him. With it, Kubla Khan built Xanadu.

"Thoughts are things. Sometimes they are sent 'on the wind,' as we say in Tibet. Once, a fragmentary vision of the famed city, Xanadu, reached an English poet, Coleridge, who wrote his impressions. The words of a dream? No! The description of a vision!

"I, Shiwan Khan, have again discovered the lost city of Xanadu. Far beneath the earth, on the banks of the sacred River Alph, it forms a vast bombproof shelter. No puny bombs could blast the mountains that cover the forgotten sea of Manja."

Inspired by his own description, Shiwan Khan was sweeping Harry into a state of ecstasy. Leaning forward, the golden-robed master drove home the utterance:

"I shall be Kha Khan, the ruler of Xanadu! Through the wealth of the ancients, I am acquiring aircraft and munitions. My air fleets shall travel everywhere, conquering unprotected lands. Should enemies attack my country, seeking reprisal, all they will find will be dry deserts and barren mountains.

"I have stirred the people of Sinkiang, so that they are dissatisfied. When I return to Xanadu, I shall assemble them. They will populate my hidden kingdom, and later, as conquest proceeds, the craftsmen of all nations will be drawn to Xanadu. There, our factories will supply the planes and bombs for still greater conquest!"

Harry was approaching the throne, drawn by the powerful green eyes of Shiwan Khan. They were face to face, and Shiwan Khan's lips were moving, but the words that he merely whispered seemed to thunder through Harry's brain:

"To you, I promise high honor in Xanadu, if you obey my present mandate. You will accept—"

Harry punctuated the comment with a nod.

"—the duty," continued Shiwan Khan, "of destroying the one enemy who alone can hope to block my ambitions—The Shadow!"

Entranced by the glare of the green eyes, Harry continued to his slow nod. The lips of Shiwan Khan formed a livid smile. The master plotter was ready to give the perfect thrust.

Harry Vincent had become the tool of Shiwan Khan. Doom was scheduled for The Shadow, to be dealt by the agent that he trusted most.

Doom that The Shadow could not possible foresee!

CHAPTER XVIII.

BLACK DEATH.

WHILE Harry Vincent stood rigid before the throne, Shiwan Khan probed his pockets and found an automatic, fully loaded. He placed the gun in Harry's own fist, with the ominous comment:

"For The Shadow!"

Harry nodded. His brain, fully controlled by Shiwan Khan, gave him no inkling of his present opportunity to deal finally with The Shadow's greatest foe. A gun in hand, Harry was facing Shiwan Khan; like the other agents, he was sworn to end that monstrous murderer's evil career, should he find the chance to do it.

The chance was here, and so was Harry. But the urge for the promised stroke was totally absent.

Contemptuously, Shiwan Khan brought a telephone from behind a golden curtain. Lifting the instrument from the stand, he placed it in Harry's free hand. He wanted Harry to communicate with his chief, The Shadow, and a mechanical means was necessary.

The Shadow, however great his prowess, had not yet acquired the skill to project thoughts, with his agents as receivers.

Mental jolts were reaching Harry's brain. They were the commands of Shiwan Khan, standing close beside him. They told Harry what to do, then gave him leeway. His mind, so to speak, was on leash. Freely, it started along its accustomed channels, then pulled up short at the beck of Shiwan Khan.

Harry called a number that came from his own memory. He heard a quiet voice across the wire:

"Burbank speaking."

"Vincent reporting," announced Harry. "Important information regarding Shiwan Khan."

"Report in detail."

Eyes were close to Harry's. Across the telephone, he met the green glare of Shiwan Khan, looming like the vast sea of Manja, ready to swallow him in its forgotten depths. An uncanny shrewdness governed Harry's next words.

"I can't report from here," undertoned The Shadow's agent. "There is danger. I must see the chief alone."

Burbank inquired if Harry could safely hold the wire open. Inspired by Shiwan Khan, Harry gave an affirmative whisper. Burbank then informed that The Shadow had not been heard from since he went to the penthouse.

Cliff Mardsland had gone up there to look for him. Burbank was expecting Cliff's report over another wire.

Soon it came. Burbank made a connection, so that Harry could listen in. Shiwan Khan did not have to hold the receiver. He was getting everything that Harry heard, through the agent's own brain.

Cliff's voice first, then The Shadow's.

Shiwan Khan was ready to pluck the telephone from Harry's hand, in case the power of The Shadow's voice should influence him. There was nothing force-

ful, however, in The Shadow's tone. On the contrary, it sounded weary.

Besides, The Shadow was not talking directly to Harry He was hearing the agent's request through Burbank. The Shadow gave instructions, which Burbank relayed:

"At the Jonas office," said the contact man. "As soon as you can get there within the next half hour."

"Instructions received."

With that, Harry let the telephone drop into the waiting hand of Shiwan Khan. Lifting the curtain, the master criminal placed the instrument behind it.

Then, reaching to a shelf beneath a large brass gong, Shiwan Khan brought out a porcelain dragon. He let the curtain fall again, covering the gong.

Fixing the dragon under Harry's arm, where it settled heavily, Shiwan Khan ordained:

"You will follow my directions, until you meet a man named Flash Gidley. Give him the dragon. Then continue to the place where you are to meet The Shadow."

Harry nodded.

"Have the gun in your pocket"—Shiwan Khan pushed Harry's hand into his coat—"and shoot through the cloth. Remember"—the words had the clarity of a tinkling bell—"that to you, sight of The Shadow means to pull the trigger!"

TURNING Harry about, Shiwan Khan started him through the broad door leading from the throne room. He did not strike the small gong standing beside the glass board, as he had done when cutting off his projected throughts to Dorron and Flash.

Shiwan Khan had supplied an influence under which he intended to remain until an event, quite as jolting as a gong stroke, would suffice to waken him.

In leaving Shiwan Khan's, Harry went down the spiral stairway just outside the throne room. It took him to a basement level, where he followed a long, interminable passage. The low-roofed corridor dipped at one point, then rose again. Reaching what seemed a solid wall, Harry pressed it with his fingers.

To the left, straight up, then to the right—the moves came naturally. They were inspired by the urging thoughts of Shiwan Khan, who at that moment was standing, eyes half closed in concentration, near the center of the throne room.

Though the motions of the wall were imperceptible, Harry's pressure produced the proper combination. The wall slid aside like a door. As Harry stepped through, it glided back into place. In a small cellar, Harry saw a flight of steps. At the top, he opened an ordinary door, that took him to an outside passage.

The underground corridor had carried him beneath two streets and the short intervening block. Going along the outside passage, Harry reached a street that was three blocks from the one which fronted the Golden Pagoda. No one would have connected this outlet with Shiwan Khan's headquarters above the Chinese restaurant.

Harry had not gone five steps along the sidewalk, when a man stepped from a parked car and halted him. Flash Gidley had seen the dragon that Harry carried. He gave his name when Harry asked it. It served as well as code words. Harry handed over the seventh Ch'ien Lung dragon.

As Flash's car pulled away, a taxicab shoved into the space. Though he still stared straight ahead, Harry was forming thoughts that were in a way his own, though they had come originally from Shiwan Khan. He wanted to get to an address on Twenty-third Street. The cab would take him there. Stepping into the cab, Harry muttered his destination.

It was heard by a Mongol driver.

Shiwan Khan was taking no chances on anyone trailing persons who came from his hidden lair. After a circuitous route, the cab finally stopped in front of the building that Harry wanted. Without thinking to pay the driver, Harry stepped from the cab and walked into the building, his hand deep in his coat pocket.

The Mongol at the wheel was not at all disturbed because he did not receive the fare. He was leering, in a very unlovely fashion, when he drove away. He had delivered another of the walking figures who could hardly call themselves human, while under the sway of Shiwan Khan.

This one was just like the others. He would do whatever Shiwan Khan had ordained.

UP a rickety stairway, Harry turned into a passage where wavering gaslight threw its uncertain rays upon a glass-paneled door that had a letter chute on a level with the knob. On the panel, in faded letters, was the name:

B. JONAS

Who B. Jonas was, Harry had never inquired. This office was simply one where special reports were delivered to The Shadow. Usually, Rutledge Mann dropped them in the mail chute, but Harry had also performed that duty.

The glass panel of the door was very grimy. The lock was the sort that could be opened with almost any skeleton key, but usually, thick cobwebs, showing through the glass, gave indication that no one—neither B. Jonas nor any one else—had been in the place for months.

Tonight, the cobwebs were missing. The fact didn't interest Harry. He had a mission to accomplish. Through his dazed mind ran visions of a dream city with glorious palaces, glowing under some strange light that came from neither sun nor moon.

It was real, that city, and Harry wanted no one to destroy it. Only one person intended to destroy it: The Shadow. Therefore, it was only right that Harry should prevent the terrible deed, by disposing of The Shadow first. The place where The Shadow could be found was beyond the grimy old door, so Harry reached for the knob.

Before Harry's hand could twist, the door whipped inward. The gaslight threw a block of light into the Jonas office. Beyond that glow was darkness, that suddenly disgorged a cloaked figure.

Harry saw the brim of a slouch hat, cloaked shoulders beneath. A gloved hand swung a gun straight toward Harry, as its owner suddenly realized that Harry's pocketed hand meant business.

Had Harry's reactions been normal, he would have dropped back at sight of that quick-moving muzzle. Instead, his brain seemed to click a signal that controlled his trigger finger. A burst of muffled flame flashed through the cloth of Harry's coat, spurting a bullet with it.

With the gunburst, Harry's trance snapped. He was in the midst of new amazement. He saw The Shadow jolting upward, backward, to coil upon the bare floor of an unfamiliar room. His hand coming numbed from his pocket, Harry found himself holding a smoking gun.

Harry's vision went black at the sight of death before him. Struck with the terrible thought that he had slain The Shadow, through some hideous mistake, Harry slumped to the floor beside the dead body of his black-clad victim!

CHAPTER XIX.
GONG OF DOOM.

THROUGH Harry's gritted teeth came groans that drowned a muffled *click* from a closet in the corner of the squarish office. Recovered from the staggering sensation that his own gunshot had brought, Harry was unable to lift the slouch hat from the face of the cloaked figure beside him.

He felt that another hand would have to perform that sorrowful rite. Another hand did—a gloved one, that came suddenly past Harry's shoulder, to tug the hat away.

Swinging about on hands and knees, Harry stared upward at The Shadow! If ever a daze had swept him, it was then. The torpor produced by Shiwan Khan was nothing, compared to the stupefied bewilderment that Harry felt at seeing The Shadow alive and dead at the same moment!

From The Shadow that stood beside him, Harry heard a solemn whispered laugh. He saw the burn of amazing eyes that could only be those of his chief. Letting his gaze turn to the floor, Harry viewed the face of the dead man, the masquerader whose hat The Shadow had removed.

It was the face of Herbert Thorner.

"He was a party to murder," expressed The Shadow, "as deep in crime as the rest. His death was deserved!"

The Shadow's statement was self-evident to Harry. He realized that he had fired his own shot in self-defense, even though the action had been involuntary. Thorner, lurking in the Jonas office, had swooped out, intending to drop Harry with a gunshot. He had been waiting for a chance to kill The Shadow, or any of the latter's agents.

Calmly, The Shadow explained how he had led Thorner to the Jonas office during the afternoon. Taking the old cloak and hat from Thorner's body, he hung them in the closet where he had kept them, so that anyone penetrating here would think that they had found The Shadow's actual headquarters, instead of a mere way station.

There was an opening at the rear of the closet, where a specially constructed panel formed The Shadow's usual route to and from the dingy office, instead of the cobwebbed door.

Crossed snares had produced a curious result. The Shadow, talking to Burbank, had correctly supposed that Harry was in the power of Shiwan Khan, because of the unusual request for a special meeting. Thinking that Thorner had contacted Shiwan Khan, The Shadow naturally supposed that he was being duped to enter a trap that he already knew about.

He had said for Harry to meet him at the Jonas office, merely to satisfy Shiwan Khan.

But the master plotter, who usually knew so much, had not been acquainted with Thorner's little game. It happened that Thorner had cooked up the cute idea all on his own, as the results had definitely proven.

In sending Harry to kill The Shadow, Shiwan Khan had doubly injured his own cause. He had lost the services of Thorner and had also released a valuable prisoner, in the person of Harry Vincent.

The Shadow, too, had made a mistake. He had taken his time, coming in to surprise Thorner, not suspecting that the fellow would be due for a clash with Harry. His purpose had been to capture Thorner and make the fellow talk, in hope of learning just where Harry was. Thus Thorner and Harry had fought it out together. Since Harry had won, the episode was closed.

It was Harry—not Thorner—who might now provide a worth-while trail. Questioning his agent, The Shadow learned the same facts that Beatrice had disclosed; namely, that the Green Pagoda was the route to Shiwan Khan's lair. But Harry's experience had been short and recent. It was possible that he could remember more.

Behind the closed door of the Jonas office, The Shadow faced Harry toward a brilliant gas jet, then turned him so that he could gain the proper glitter from The Shadow's own eyes. Under that burning gaze, Harry felt the creeping return of his recent daze. The Shadow talked of lights outside the Green Pagoda; gradually, Harry carried the story further.

He remembered the panel beneath the idol, the trip to Shiwan Khan's golden throne room. He described all that had occurred there, even mentioning two gongs that he had seen: a little one beside the glass board, and a large one when Shiwan Khan had lifted the golden curtain.

Memory of the porcelain dragon returned; with it, Harry described the long corridor that he had used for exit. He told how he had given the dragon to Flash Gidley, then started for the Jonas office.

There the story ended; Harry was suddenly brought from his trance by a jolt that The Shadow pounded to his chin.

LEAVING by the secret route, The Shadow told Harry to contact Burbank and arrange for the removal of Thorner's body.

Outside the building, The Shadow entered Moe's cab and made a rapid trip to the neighborhood of the Green Pagoda. Skirting the block, The Shadow saw a forming police cordon. He knew that Paul Brent and Guy Chadbury must have summoned the police, to begin a hunt for Shiwan Khan.

The Shadow's surmise was correct. More than that, the hunt was making progress. Inspector Joe Cardona was in charge, and he had taken over the Chinese restaurant. Under rapid persuasion, the proprietor had begun to talk.

He was pointing out the panel that led beneath the idol. He didn't know what lay beyond it. He had been paid to put it there, for the use of persons who seemed to know where it was. He had always been able to identify them, by the way they stared.

One reason the restaurant man talked was because Beatrice Chadbury had come along with her uncle and Paul Brent. Recognizing her, the owner of the Green Pagoda thought that she had already imparted the information and that it might be to his benefit to corroborate the story.

The bluff was Cardona's idea. The ace inspector was quite pleased with himself when they began the trip to Shiwan Khan's lair.

Posting men along the line, he stopped at the top of the stairs to watch Beatrice Chadbury open a door that she had suddenly recognized. Close behind Cardona, Guy Chadbury and Paul Brent heard the girl give exclamation.

"Those are my clothes!" declared Beatrice, pointing to a chair. "I remember taking them off in this room, so I could put on the Chinese costume. This is where I became Lana Luan."

Joe Cardona was suddenly impressed that he was on the trail of something important. So far, the story had made him rather dubious, because Guy Chadbury had confined it to a kidnap charge. Cardona had believed the part about Flash Gidley demanding fifty thousand dollars ransom. But Beatrice's talk about a master mind named Shiwan Khan had sounded like a pipe dream.

Finding the clothes made it different. If Beatrice had worn them in here, and left them, she must have put on other garments in order to go out. Either she had left as Lana Luan or Lady Godiva, and Cardona decided that a Chinese costume was more plausible than none at all.

He posted his last detective to guard the clothes as evidence. Turning to Beatrice, Cardona said:

"All right, Miss Chadbury. Your story stands to date. What about this Shiwan Khan? Do you think he's around here somewhere?"

Beatrice nodded emphatically. They followed her along the passage to the throne room.

Seeing the light from the golden room, Cardona pressed ahead, drawing his gun. As he stopped at the wide doorway, the other men stepped up beside him, with Beatrice in the background.

Shiwan Khan was seated placidly in his throne, facing the door. He had drawn aside the cloth at the side of the little alcove, revealing the large gong hanging above the vacant shelf where the seventh porcelain dragon had lately rested.

UNPERTURBED by the bristle of three revolvers, Shiwan Khan gave a slitted smile and bowed. His eyes seemed to focus on the four pairs of eyes at the door. Each person felt the power of that stare, and tried to fight it off.

"I have expected you," announced Shiwan Khan, in his singular tone. "Three of you have already been tuned to my mental vibrations. Your thoughts, to some extent, are still mine!"

Shiwan Khan's words were sheer bluff. Without the hypnotic influence of his lights, he could not place other minds under immediate control. Only a person willing to be hypnotized could succumb to his powerful eyes, though their influence did have a marked effect when accompanied by his persuasive speech.

"You have told little," remarked Shiwan Khan, his gaze shifting between Paul and Chadbury, "but not all. Therefore, the law is still uninformed on my most important secrets, and shall remain so."

The verbal bait was too much for Cardona. He started into the room, the other two men with him and Beatrice close behind.

Shiwan Khan's only weapon was a small wooden hammer that he weighed between his long-fingered hands. He looked helpless against the guns; in fact, he raised his arms wide apart as the group approached.

As they crossed the threshold, Shiwan Khan gave a hard backstroke with his upraised hammer, a move designed to bring his enemies forward in a surge. But before they could spring to action, a black-clad avalanche came whirling from the spiral stairs outside the throne room.

Slicing through the edge of the doorway, The Shadow wheeled upon Cardona and the others, flinging himself into a dive that carried all his weight with it. Bodily he carried them back across the threshold, sprawling them in the hall. Their guns were barking wildly in his ears at the moment when Shiwan Khan's hammer clanged the great gong.

Shiwan Khan had spoken of vibrations. The golden room received one, of a devastating sort. Instead of merely quivering, the golden drapes collapsed. With them came thundering walls, a crashing roof. Beams, rafters, bricks and mortar roared destruction that Shiwan Khan had meant to swallow four unsuspecting victims!

Except for the alcove in the far wall, the entire room was gone. Three rescued men and a girl were blinking upward at the open sky, when they heard The Shadow's laugh, dispelling the final echoes of Shiwan Khan's great gong!

CHAPTER XX.
THE SEVENTH DRAGON.

So thick was the cloud of piling débris that The Shadow's shots were useless when he opened fire with a brace of automatics. He was trying to get bullets through to Shiwan Khan's alcove, where complete darkness had enveloped the gold-clad master foe.

Everywhere, the bullets met obstruction, a fact announced by the harsh laugh of Shiwan Khan filtering through the wreckage. The laugh continued when The Shadow's shots were spent, and with it came a purring rumble.

Situated in the solid wall of the next building, Shiwan Khan's alcove was an elevator. From the direction of the sound, The Shadow could tell that it was going up, instead of down. Evidently, Shiwan Khan preferred escape across the roofs, the sort that he had once prepared for Thorner.

Perhaps he had guessed that The Shadow had entered by the route that led underground, three blocks away, and was therefore neglecting that advantage. Probably Shiwan Khan did not know that the police had formed a cordon around the single block to which his flight was automatically restricted by his choice.

Gripping Cardona in the darkness, The Shadow informed him of Shiwan Khan's direction and announced that he was leaving the fiend's capture to the law. The Shadow mentioned the underground passage, however, in case Shiwan Khan reversed his course. Then, with a final trailing laugh, The Shadow was on his way.

Leading his rescued companions, Cardona started down through the Green Pagoda, to start the hunt for Shiwan Khan.

The Shadow had gone by the underground passage, so as not to be delayed by the cordon. He had another objective, where he intended to operate alone. He had not forgotten the dragon that Harry Vincent had handed to Flash Gidley. The Shadow was headed for the home of Benjamin Twindell.

MATTERS were brewing at Twindell's before The Shadow reached there. Flash and a few of his mobbies were grouped in the passage near the side door; the rest were stationed in front and in back of the house. It was Flash alone who approached the door, to ring the bell.

Harper, the butler, answered. Flash lifted his coat, to let the servant see the dragon. As Harper nodded and stepped back, Flash jabbed him with a gun. The men at the side door entered, and soon had Twindell's servants covered. Opening the other doors, they admitted the rest of the mob.

Benjamin Twindell first learned of the invasion when Flash entered the study and found the old collector at his desk. Twindell showed immediate alarm at sight of the gun Flash pointed at him. He gave a peculiar gulp when the smooth-toned crook placed the dragon heavily on the table.

"We're friends," informed Flash. "Good friends! Why? Because we both know a guy named Shiwan Khan. He's the fellow who sent me here."

Twindell blinked. He didn't fully understand.

"The idea is this," said Flash. "You want this dragon, to match up with six others sitting there on your shelf. I want fifty grand—fifty thousand bucks to you—which Shiwan Khan owes me. He says I can collect from you."

"But I have already paid for the last dragon!"

"You'd better take a gander at your books," returned Flash. "The way I got it, you still owe dough to Shiwan Khan."

Twindell brought a ledger from the desk.

"Ah, yes!" He nodded. "I had forgotten this extra credit. It comes to forty thousand dollars. I suppose I can spare the extra ten."

Flash grinned.

"You can, all right!" he said. "I'll tell you why! Because you're buying a special service; get it? With us barging in here, the cops will think that

Continued on page 120

The Shadow tops them all!

● What is the leading dramatic show in America?

What is the leading daytime show in America?

What is the proven favorite of young America?

THE SHADOW!

This famous program is now heard on the following stations:

WCAE	Pittsburgh, Pennsylvania
KGFL	Roswell, New Mexico
KHJ	Los Angeles, California
KFRC	San Francisco, California
WTAR	Phoenix, Arizona
KTSM	El Paso, Texas
WGRC	Louisville, Kentucky
WKRC	Cincinnati, Ohio
WQAM	Miami, Florida
WSIX	Nashville, Tennessee
KOH	Reno, Nevada
KGU	Honolulu, Hawaii
WDNC	Durham, North Carolina
WGH	Newport News, Virginia

You can hear THE SHADOW in your own city if you'll get in touch with your local station now! It's the most thrilling dramatic show of all time . . . as proven by ten years' leadership in the Crossley and other polls!

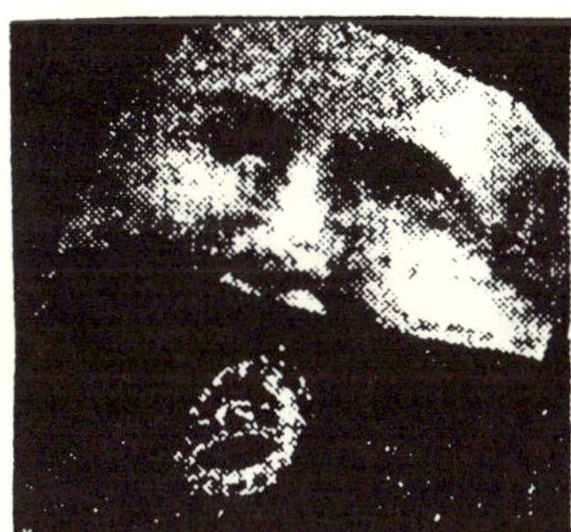

THE SHADOW MASK, a perfect disguise that will fool even your closest friends 10c

THE SHADOW TEC-TO-LITE, a powerful 2¼" x 1¾" flashlight. Hide it in the palm of your hand 50c

SHADOW BIG LITTLE BOOKS, grand stories and pictures. Buy them at your 5 & 10c store 10c

THE SHADOW HOLSTER SET, gun, holster, belt, Shadow mask, handcuffs, Shadow's whistle and The Shadow flashlight $1

OFFICIAL SHADOW STATIONERY & ENVELOPES, with Shadow Club insignia embossed in black and red 20c

THE SHADOW GAME, size 20" x 20", printed in beautiful colors. A pair of dice, 4 colored tokens, play money, 4 Shadow "black hats," dice cups and colored disks $1

SHADOW OFFICIAL HAT & CAPE, black hat (indicate size: large or small), and 36" red-lined, black cape $1

Continued from page 117

somebody was trying to rob the joint. They'll never figure we brought the dragon, instead of cleaning out the place.

"That's worth ten grand, ain't it? Ten grand, for a real alibi? It's cheap for a guy like you, who's got plenty of dough and a rep he's got to watch out for. Forty grand from his nibs, ten from you—that makes up the kitty."

The arguments produced a pleased cackle from Twindell. Hearing it, Flash was sorry that he hadn't asked for more money. He decided, though, that it was best to follow Shiwan Khan's instructions.

While Twindell was opening his huge safe, Flash went out to the stairs and called down to his men, telling them to march the servants up to the study.

"Tell these guys of yours that we're all right," Flash said to Twindell. "Then we can give them back their gats. When we lam, we'll do a lot of shooting, see? They're to do the same—only, it's all in fun. When the bulls get here, you can tell them that you beat us off."

Twindell explained matters to the servants. Harper and the others grinned, when they understood the game. Rogues in their own right, they knew that Twindell was crooked. Any measure that covered their master's methods was a help to them.

PARTIES to a crooked game designed by Shiwan Khan, both Twindell and Flash sent their followers from the study, to get posted for what was to follow. A few of Flash's mobbies remained, looking around at the curios. Flash wanted them with him, so the fake battle could begin as they started downstairs.

He was expecting Twindell to bring money from the safe. Instead, the withered man produced several check books, which Flash eyed askance. Flash began an objection:

"Say! Checks won't go!"

"Why not?" cackled Twindell. "My name will not be on them. These are accounts belonging to imaginary companies, with false names of officers. I have used them in all the transactions that I have performed for Shiwan Khan."

"But if you stop their payment—"

"Why should I? Forty thousand dollars of the fifty belongs to Shiwan Khan. As I have already told you, I consider the remaining ten thousand a mere trifle for the service rendered."

Flash made no further objection. Twindell was making out many checks, all for small amounts, payable to cash. They would be easy to cash. Gathering the checks as Twindell wrote them, Flash was too interested to note what occurred outside the room.

A black-cloaked figure had arrived in the little passage at the top of the stairs. The Shadow, entering while all hands were getting instructions in the study, had found later opportunity to move upstairs. From the doorway, he could see the porcelain dragon squatting on the desk. He watched Flash reach for the last of Twindell's checks.

It was almost the time for action. Drawing back, The Shadow was ready to let Flash and the mobbies pass. Then he could cower Twindell in the study and cover the departing crooks from the doorway. Flash and his whole tribe could not dislodge The Shadow, if they came from one direction only.

At the moment, however, The Shadow's position was unenviable. If discovered, he would be between two fires. A minute more, the odds would be his. All seemed perfect for The Shadow, when he caught the clatter of footsteps on the stairs.

Something had happened below, bringing a pair of Twindell's servants and one of Flash's thugs up to the study!

Trapped in the very spot he didn't want, The Shadow was faced by a serious emergency. His time limit of a minute was cut down to a few seconds, with disaster, not victory, waiting at the finish.

There was a way, however, to make those brief seconds serve. It depended upon an important fact that The Shadow had long ago learned.

Coolly, The Shadow leveled a .45 at the porcelain dragon that stood on Twindell's desk. He pressed the trigger. With the impact of the bullet, the foot-high dragon shattered.

From its interior gushed a cascade of shimmering gems: rubies, sapphires, emeralds—a galaxy of jewels worth half a million dollars!

FLASH heard the gunshot, so did his slouching thugs. But they saw the flood of gems that the dragon had released. The sight made Flash forget everything else. He thought that one of his own men had blasted the revealing shot. Flinging the checks aside, he snarled:

"Fifty grand—for all those!"

Flash made for Twindell. The old man screeched. Driving into the room, The Shadow blasted shots at the astonished thugs. They were sprawling, The Shadow was wheeling to a corner, as Twindell's servants entered. Flash was full about, bellowing as he fired, and Twindell's howls were louder.

It was gang against gang, with The Shadow handy to even up the odds. The cloaked fighter let Flash drive past, then followed. Flash wanted his crew to clean up the servants, to make sure the path was clear. He didn't understand why shots from above the stairs were clipping the mobbies, until he wheeled to see The Shadow.

Two guns spoke. The Shadow's was

perfect in its aim, but Flash's was not.

While the mob leader was still tumbling down the stairs, to join his crippled pals and the battered servants, The Shadow wheeled back into Twindell's study. The scrawny man was waiting fo. him, but not with a gun. Between his palsied hands, Twindell was proffering a small silver casket.

"I'm innocent!" he whined. "I swear it! Shiwan Khan is to blame for all! The facts are in this casket. Look!"

Before The Shadow could reach Twindell, the old man in his eagerness had flipped the casket open. It was Twindell, not The Shadow, who received the answer which Shiwan Khan had said would satisfy the man who asked for it.

A coil of silver writhed within the casket. A darting head slid out, jabbed its tiny fangs into Twindell's wrist. The old man staggered as he let the casket fall. The Shadow fired a shot at the silver snake that wriggled across the floor.

The bullet blew away the snake's head, but the creature's body still wriggled as The Shadow watched it. Twindell, though, was motionless when The Shadow turned to look at him.

Slumped across the desk, Twindell's hands were buried in the jewels that lay about the shattered Ch'ien Lung dragon. The man who had aided Shiwan Khan's schemes was dead, served with a poisonous dose that had been intended for The Shadow.

Every dragon on Twindell's shelf had carried its quota of jewels, which had been turned to cash at Twindell's sales, for Shiwan Khan's purchases of supplies, airplanes, and munitions. The contents of the seventh dragon were the reward that Twindell was to keep for his services.

He had his reward: the jewels on the desk. But Benjamin Twindell had not lived long enough to really enjoy the prizes that crime had brought him.

A solemn laugh crept through that room of death. With the fading of that tone, The Shadow was gone.

CHAPTER XXI.

THE JEWEL ROOM.

POLICE were arriving when The Shadow reached the street. It must have been their approach that had caused members of both bands to hurry to the study. During the quick battle in which one gang had turned against the other, The Shadow had noted some men sprawl as they flung themselves from the front door.

Officers were entering that same door when The Shadow departed from the side, but they didn't account for the fact that a cordon was forming all around the block. As he finally left the neighborhood, The Shadow saw the commissioner's big car arrive. On that account, he soon returned to Twindell's.

The Shadow came as Lamont Cranston, in a big car of his own. Recognized as the commissioner's friend, he was admitted. On the ground floor, he met Beatrice Chadbury, who introduced him to her uncle and Paul Brent. The girl told Cranston that the commissioner was upstairs in the study, with Inspector Cardona.

At the study door, The Shadow met Weston, who looked very sick. Jabbing his forefinger back into the room, the commissioner told Cranston not to look. So The Shadow looked, and saw what he expected, though it wasn't at all pleasant.

The thing was Twindell's body, no longer scrawny. It was swelled from the poison that had brought such rapid death. The face was covered with splotches, mostly green and purple, and the wide-open bulge of Twindell's eyes was something very hideous.

A police surgeon had just decided that

Twindell was dead, a statement that pleased Joe Cardona, because he was reaching Weston's state. The body was lying on a stretcher that had come in from an ambulance, so Cardona covered it with a silk Chinese banner that he plucked from the wall.

Coming out with the police surgeon, Cardona detailed two detectives to guard the body. Entering the study, they stared curiously at the gaudy drape of red and gold, as though they wondered what was underneath it. After Cardona gave a terse but graphic description of what the body looked like, the detectives lost their curiosity.

On the way downstairs, The Shadow learned what had brought the turnout. Shiwan Khan had been sighted near the Green Pagoda. Still wearing his golden robe, he had made an excellent target for police bullets; but the trouble was that none had hit him.

"Either he ducked that lead," growled Cardona, "or that smock he was wearing fooled the eye. Anyway, he got into a cab, with a big Mogul driving it—"

"A Mongol," corrected Weston. "Be precise, inspector!"

"With a big mongrel driving it," resumed Cardona, "and we took after him. When he headed up here, I had a hunch where he was going, so we spread out and closed in on him."

"Thereby losing trace of Shiwan Khan," added Weston. "From what I have heard, we practically had the world's greatest criminal in our hands, and let him slip out!"

"He's in this house," insisted Cardona. "We nabbed the mongrel out back, and while he won't talk, we know that his boss isn't very far away."

Guy Chadbury joined the group.

"I have just talked to the Federal agents," he said. "We called them up a while ago, and they went to the Hoboken pier. Evidently Dorron was really working with Shiwan Khan. He let the *Aritoba* get under way.

"She won't get far, though. They intend to intercept her in the lower harbor, remove most of the crew and tow her back to dock. I told them about the cargo, and said that Brent and I could explain the reasons for our mistakes."

Oddly, Chadbury felt a confidence as he spoke. Perhaps it was because he found himself addressing Lamont Cranston. He realized that Cranston was the man who had found Beatrice, and he was sure that this friend could supply real evidence to prove that all crime was due to Shiwan Khan.

In fact, Cranston could already do so.

"The proof is quite plain," said The Shadow. "Shiwan Khan must have purchased many supplies and shipped them to Sinkiang, with Dorron's aid. I can produce a man"—The Shadow had reference to Harry Vincent—"who talked with him and learned his plans.

"Shiwan Khan intended to start a kingdom in the wilderness, with himself as ruler. Buying supplies was simple, but airplanes and munitions promised him more difficulty. So he established fake companies, in Twindell's name, very early in the game. With Dorron already controlled, he merely needed to force two others to do his bidding."

The "two others" were Paul Brent and Guy Chadbury. Having already admitted the fact, they were relieved, rather than worried.

"Shiwan Khan's chief Mongol is named Hoang Khu," continued The Shadow calmly, as though he had learned the fact from some informant. "Hoang Khu murdered Bob Ryndon, because Ryndon had learned too much in Sinkiang. The ruby that Ryndon had was probably one of many that Shiwan Khan used to bribe the local trouble makers."

There was another link that The Shadow did not mention—the fact that Bob Ryndon knew Paul Brent, and that the death was intended to incriminate Paul. That detail was a thing forgotten, for which Paul was quite grateful.

Sudden enlightenment had struck Commissioner Weston, in regard to the matter of the jewels. He spread a large cloth upon the table, to display the gems that had been brought from Twindell's study.

"Then these gems," exclaimed Weston, "came from Sinkiang!"

"Certainly," returned The Shadow. "Shiwan Khan has masses of them, the spoils that his illustrious ancestors took from conquered nations. Look at the stones, commissioner. Any expert will tell you that they are ancient."

"But how can we prove they came from Shiwan Khan?"

"Very easily," replied The Shadow. "Find Twindell's own collection, which he did not sell. It is probably somewhere in this house. When you find it, you may also find Shiwan Khan. Though he considers jewels to be baubles, he would certainly appreciate a hiding place."

The search of the house had been completed, but Weston decided to go at it again. He and Cranston were at the top of the stairs, when Weston heard his friend suggest that they look at the room next to Twindell's study and note the thickness of the wall between.

Cardona was shouting up the stairs that the dead wagon had arrived. While Weston and Cranston were busy in the other room, the two detectives came from the study, bearing the stretcher with the silk-draped body. Evidently their vigil had not agreed with them, for Cardona noted their fixed expressions when they were going past.

Hearing the call from above, Cardona hurried to the study. He found the commissioner standing by the desk, pointing to a section that had lifted like a hinge. Lights were shining from the open space.

"Cranston found these," expressed the commissioner. "An odd thing: the panel, like the lights, seems to be controlled by a switch—"

WESTON interrupted himself. Cranston was finding more. He was half inside of Twindell's big safe, working at the back of it. He found a spring along the edge. The rear of the safe slid smoothly into the wall. The Shadow emerged to say something, but Cardona did not wait to hear it.

Sighting a light beyond, the police inspector lunged through the big safe and the opening at the back of it. He came into a tiny room that sparkled with the brilliance of many jewels, arrayed upon a table. The Shadow had found Twindell's missing collection, but that was unimportant at the moment.

The sight that really gripped Cardona was that of a gold-robed figure crouched at the end of the table, bent forward as if gloating over the massed gems. Recognizing Shiwan Khan's attire, Cardona decided not to give the master mind a chance.

Pumping away with his Police Positive, Cardona literally punched the gold-clad figure from its chair; then bounded past the table to add a few more bullets, in case Shiwan Khan still offered fight. He hoped, too, to recognize the face of Shiwan Khan, which he had seen once before.

In that hope, Cardona was disappointed.

He recognized the face he saw, but it did not belong to Shiwan Khan. Joe Cardona was staring squarely into the bloated, bulge-eyed features of dead Benjamin Twindell!

His own eyes shut, Cardona groped back through the safe. He was remembering the lights and the dead wagon.

He was realizing something that The Shadow had understood before Cardona had made that unneeded surge into the secret jewel room.

From that new lair, which he had gained as a hiding place, Shiwan Khan had pressed a switch controlling lights in Twindell's study. The glowing bulbs had attracted the two detectives who were guarding Twindell's body.

Obeying the bidding of Shiwan Khan, they had carried the corpse into the jewel room, where Shiwan Khan had adorned it with the golden robe.

No wonder the two detectives had passed so stiffly in the lower hall! Still obedient to Shiwan Khan, they were carrying crime's master out to the dead wagon, under the brilliant cloth that had previously covered Twindell's body!

Weston was shouting when Cardona dashed past him. Something about Cranston having disappeared. Cardona didn't wait to talk about it. Tearing downstairs, he passed Chadbury, Beatrice and Paul as they came from a side room.

Reaching the avenue, Cardona saw tiny lights, no larger than distant pin points: the taillights of the hearse that was carrying Shiwan Khan away to safety. Before the ace inspector could yell for men to follow, he heard a roar from the curb, a half-block ahead.

A taxicab shot away, in pursuit of Shiwan Khan. From the speeding cab, Cardona heard a taunt that promised sure results before the chase was ended.

It was the laugh of The Shadow!

CHAPTER XXII.

CRIME'S FINAL RIDDLE.

THE hearse that carried Shiwan Khan was far speedier than the dead wagons that took murdered victims to the morgue. The detectives who had placed the stretcher aboard it had not noticed that it was a high-powered car, with a hearse body.

Controlled by Shiwan Khan's vibrating thoughts, they had simply delivered

their burden and waited outside the house. The Shadow had seen them when he passed, and knew they would remain in their stupor until someone clanged a gong in their ears.

If no one else thought of that, The Shadow would take care of the matter, when he returned as Cranston. For the present, he was no longer Cranston. From a special sliding drawer beneath the rear seat of Moe's cab, The Shadow had extracted his familiar garb of black. Ready with his automatics, he was prepared to blast the hearse as soon as Moe overtook it.

Shiwan Khan provided for everything. He had probably arranged this getaway, if forced to hide at Twindell's. Perhaps the walls of his special hearse were of steel. The only way to find out was to test them. That opportunity depended upon Moe, the man at the wheel, and also on the cab.

Like Shiwan Khan s special vehicle, The Shadow's cab was geared for speed, and demonstrated it. Away in back, The Shadow could hear the wail of sirens fade. The fact did not surprise him, for the hearse had tried some twisty tactics that only Moe had managed to follow, partly by The Shadow's guidance.

They were on a cross street and the hearse was only a few blocks ahead, making straight for a downtown pier. Ahead loomed a yawning entrance; beyond that, the dock itself. The Shadow urged Moe to a greater show of speed. It was given just in time.

As the hearse sped through the pier opening, a big steel door began to slide shut. Moe whisked to the other side and whipped through with inches to spare. The hearse did not slacken speed. It reached the outer end of the pier and scaled off into the river!

Only The Shadow saw two figures dive from the front seat as the vehicle disappeared into the water. One was the driver, probably Hoang Khu; the other, Shiwan Khan, who had come through to the front seat. Moe did not see those flying shapes; he was watching the pier itself.

Brakes jammed, the cab did a nerve-racking skid right to the brink. The door on that side flew open and The Shadow launched himself into space. He did not know what lay beneath, but Shiwan Khan and the other man had found it. That was why The Shadow took the same leap.

HAD he delayed, even a few seconds, The Shadow would have missed his chance. He landed on the very stern of a long, rakish speedboat, just as it roared out from beneath the pier.

Clutching the stern rail with one hand, The Shadow aimed an automatic toward two figures that were driving at him.

The stabs of the gun showed the faces of two Mongol fighters. Their knives slashed The Shadow's cloak, skimming his flesh with it. His first shots were wide, but the next ones took effect. Lurching forward, ripping his cloak from the knives that pinned it to the narrow deck, The Shadow made a hard swing with his empty gun.

That stroke clashed the blade that Hoang Khu was thrusting for The Shadow's heart. Two Mongols eliminated, The Shadow had reached the last of the brawny killers in Shiwan Khan's depleted crew.

The Shadow had guessed right; Hoang Khu had been the hearse driver. Judging from his actions, he hoped to make the boat a dead wagon, with a real corpse in it—The Shadow's.

His crippled arm recovered, Hoang Khu held The Shadow in a rib-cracking grip that prevented him from getting at the extra automatic which he had stowed beneath his cloak. All the while, knife jabs were coming, and The Shadow was fencing them off with slashes from his empty gun.

During that flaying struggle, Shiwan Khan was watching calmly from near the bow. Clad in the dark, baggy clothes that he had worn beneath his golden robe, the Oriental crime master was patiently depending upon his most capable Mongol to succeed where many others, Shan Juchi included, had failed.

There was nothing else that Shiwan Khan could do. The Shadow had not forgotten him. At no time did enough of a cloaked form display itself for Shiwan Khan to fire, if he had held a gun in readiness. But Shiwan Khan did not have a gun. His only weapon was his brain.

Leaving a scudding wake behind it, the rakish speedboat was driving far out into the harbor. Coolly, Shiwan Khan stepped up beside the man who stood at the wheel. The pilot was Mitchell Dorron; he had provided the speedboat at his accepted master's command.

Away ahead, Shiwan Khan saw the glimmer of searchlights upon a squatty vessel that was being towed into port vessel that was being towed to port by two tugs.

Words dropped from slitted lips: "The *Aritoba.*"

Dorron nodded. His lips showed a grimace. He was angry because the freighter had been halted and turned back with its cargo. But Shiwan Khan was not angry.

"Bear straight for the *Aritoba,*" he commanded. "Do not change your course."

"But she's loaded with munitions—"

"I have commanded!" Shiwan Khan's green eyes glared coldly into Dorron's, as the man turned his face. "You have heard. You shall obey!"

Dorron obeyed, while Shiwan Khan turned toward the stern. He could hear the muffled shots of an automatic and knew that The Shadow had managed to draw his other gun.

Hoang Khu was evidently fighting to ward away the muzzle, for although the shots continued, Shiwan Khan could still see the sway of the Mongol's looming body.

Counting the shots, Shiwan Khan heard one that brought a chortle from his slitted lips. It was The Shadow's last bullet. Hoang Khu had won.

So the master plotter thought, as he saw his strongest fighter lunge. Then, from the sag of Hoang Khu's body, Shiwan Khan learned for once that he was wrong.

The Shadow had won! Letting Hoang Khu's bullet-laden body fall aside, the cloaked victor was waiting for Shiwan Khan to move. This was the moment that The Shadow had long awaited, when Shiwan Khan would have no other choice than conflict, without the aid of hypnotizing lights, vibrating gongs, or protecting Mongols.

SHIWAN KHAN met the test. During his stay in Tibet, he must have made some side trips to the jungle, to learn the ways of beasts as well as men. For the spring that he gave had all the swiftness and the power of a tiger's lunge.

Shiwan Khan met The Shadow near the stern, flung him back against the rail. Hands that made steel seem pliable went for The Shadow's throat.

Shiwan Khan's fingertips failed to get their wanted grip. Twisting from the vise that would have meant sure death, The Shadow thrust his own hands for Shiwan Khan's neck. The man who sought mastery of all the world was to learn of conquest delivered by a single foe. The Shadow's clutch was velvet, with solid steel beneath!

Half across the stern rail, The Shadow was dragging Shiwan Khan into total submission. He could feel a neck that throbbed under his own choking fingers. His head bobbing, The Shadow was weaving away from Shiwan Khan's weakening grabs, actually elbowing aside the hands that had at first been more powerful than his own.

Shiwan Khan was sinking steadily,

when across his foeman's bowing head The Shadow saw two scudding tugs cut clear from a looming hulk that was rising dead ahead. It was the *Aritoba,* with only a dozen seconds to go before the speedboat reached her!

Giving Shiwan Khan a twisty fling, The Shadow rolled across the stern rail. As he went, two hands shot after him. Fingers, recuperating with a giant's strength, caught The Shadow's torn cloak. Lashing his overbalanced weight, The Shadow ripped free.

As he struck the water, he saw the face of Shiwan Khan, long arms outstretched beside it, making a great lunge across the rail.

Then came the blast that shook the harbor. Hurtled forward by its stiffened pilot, Dorron, the speedboat gored the hulk of the *Aritoba,* drove itself deep into the munition-stocked hold and became the spark that set off a vast explosion.

The freighter split apart, gushing a mass of flame that seemed to scorch the sky. Pieces of aircraft skyrocketed with the bombs that they would never carry. Echoes of the blast still roared when flame had vanished, like the freighter and its cargo.

Swimming steadily, The Shadow reached the stern of a crippled tug with a coal tow. Rolling upon the deck, he lay in darkness while the engine resumed its laboring poundings, to take the sinking towboat into dock.

Other craft were visible near where

the *Aritoba* had gone down They were using searchlights to hunt for survivors.

Seaplanes were zooming out from shore. One settled like a tired bird, its motor still throbbing. As the sweep of a searchlight glistened from its wings, the seaplane plowed the water. The Shadow saw it lift and take off.

With the plane's fading drone, The Shadow recognized that the brief landing could have been more than the pilot's whim. The ways of Shiwan Khan were many, as were those who served him. It was possible that the master plotter was alive; that the plane was beginning a trip to Sinkiang and the ancient city of Xanadu!

Such was crime's final riddle. Had Shiwan Khan, the conquered, survived his conflict with The Shadow? Or had he gone to the watery depths that swallowed the products of his lost ambitions?

The Shadow would know—if Shiwan Khan returned!

THE END.

NEXT ISSUE:—

Shiwan Khan has made his escape—he will be back again. But in the meantime, other crimes are brewing; The Shadow has other battles to fight. A very thrilling and unusual one will be given you in "Castle of Crime," in the next issue. Big things; bigger than the average criminal could imagine. Big enough to make The Shadow risk his life to break into the "Castle of Crime." Don't forget the next issue of

10 Cents—Twice a Month

SHIWAN KHAN
Returns

HIGHLIGHTS on the SHADOW

HERE he is again—Shiwan Khan, that menace from the Orient, who has once met The Shadow and escaped without harm, although his evil scheme was smashed. Clever enough to make dupes do his dirty work, Shiwan Khan is able to stay in a safe zone during most of his operations. He comes back, in this issue's complete novel, to match wits with The Shadow again, and believe us, the story is really something to talk about. All you have to do is start the first few pages, and you'll not stop until you've finished every bit of it!

If you live in or near New York, take advantage of the opportunity offered in the coupon on this page to see the broadcast of The Shadow program. Mail in the coupon, and we will send the tickets as soon as we reach your name on the list. Note, however, that it is necessary to use the coupon. We have received requests without it, and since we have more requests than we can handle easily, we naturally give first preference to those who make their application in the proper manner.

There is an excellent novel coming up in the next issue of The Shadow. Its central character is an elderly woman, living alone in the family mansion in the heart of New York, with a fortune at her control. Strange things happen in the dark house behind its dismal wall; strange things which require all the skill and daring of The Shadow to solve. The ending of this novel will certainly find you entirely unprepared for it.

Lack of space here has prevented us from giving you more information about The Shadow movie being produced by Columbia Pictures. In another issue or so, however, we expect to have all the details complete, and will give you the announcement. Watch for it.

THE SHADOW,
Radio Editor,
79 Seventh Ave., New York, N. Y.

Please send me two tickets to The Shadow broadcast, at the Mutual system's playhouse in New York City. I understand requests are filled in order of receipt, and that no specified dates can be filled.

Name ....

Street and No. ....

City and State ....

Produced by JOE KAUFMAN 25
Directed by PHIL ROSEN

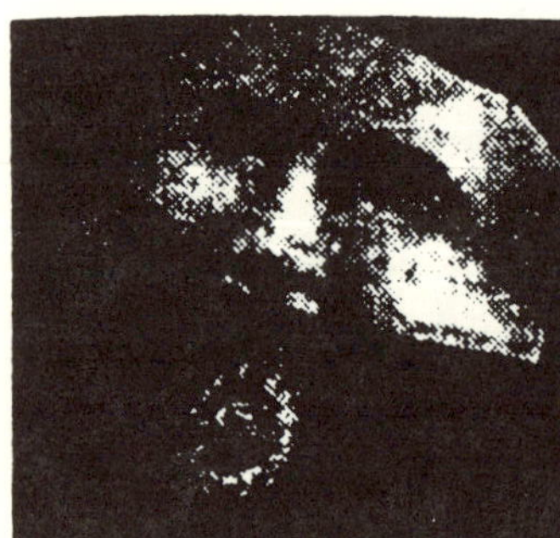

THE SHADOW MASK, a perfect disguise that will fool even your closest friends.......................... 10c

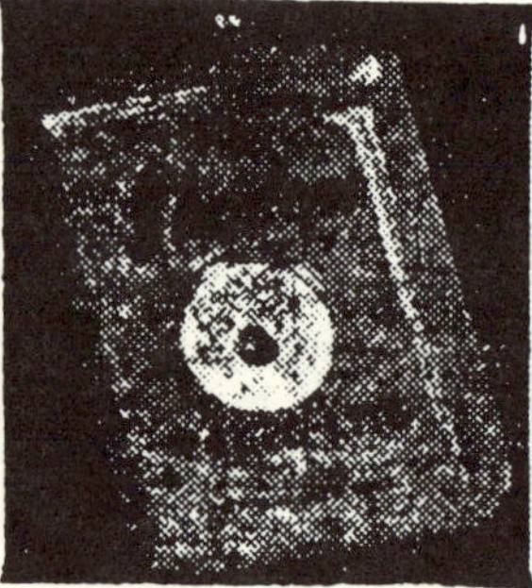

THE SHADOW TEC-TO-LITE, a powerful 2¼" x 1¾" flashlight. Hide it in the palm of your hand.............50c

SHADOW BIG LITTLE BOOKS, grand stories and pictures. Buy them at your 5 & 10c store.............10c

THE SHADOW HOLSTER SET, gun, holster, belt, Shadow mask, handcuffs, Shadow's whistle and The Shadow flashlight $1

OFFICIAL SHADOW STATIONERY & ENVELOPES, with Shadow Club insignia embossed in black and red 20c

THE SHADOW GAME, size 20" x 20", printed in beautiful colors. A pair of dice, 4 colored tokens, play money, 4 Shadow "black hats," dice cups and colored disks $1

SHADOW OFFICIAL HAT & CAPE, black hat (indicate size: large or small), and 36" red-lined, black cape $1

SHIWAN KHAN RETURNS

A Complete Book-length Novel from the Private Annals of The Shadow, as told to

MAXWELL GRANT

SHIWAN KHAN, MASTER OF THE ORIENT, AGAIN MEETS THE SHADOW, MASTER OVER CRIME!

CHAPTER I.

WORD TO THE SHADOW.

THE thing that stood in the center of the old garage looked like a crazed man's dream. It was intended to be an automobile, that much was certain; but it looked like a flashback to the experimental days of motor cars, rather than anything that belonged to the present century.

In the center of a short, broad-beamed chassis, the mechanical brainstorm had a squatty V-type motor hung low in a metal square. From each corner of the motor, a shaft ran to a wheel. In their turn, the wheels were pointed at different angles, giving the whole contrivance a wabbly, disjointed appearance.

Beside the distorted device stood a man whose expression marked him as mad as his creation. He was dressed in good clothes, but they were rumpled, soiled with grime and grease. His face, though youthful, had a haggard look that went with age. He was unshaven and his face, like his light-brown hair, was streaked with the same grime that ruined his clothes.

Few of the man's many acquaintances would have recognized him as Howard Felber, recently heralded as the most promising of young automotive engineers.

Near Felber stood two men in overalls: his mechanics, Casey and Jim. They, alone, had been allowed to join Felber in this squalid old garage. Located in a rundown section of Manhattan, the place was the only workshop that Felber could afford. He had exhausted most of his accumulated earnings buying the expensive materials that now lay discarded along the walls.

Felber trusted his two mechanics, and from their solemn expressions, they regarded the trust as a heavy burden. It wasn't just a case of sharing the secret of a new invention. Jim and Casey felt that they were looking out for Felber, keeping his madness a thing unknown to the world.

Watching him steadily, they finally turned to exchange hopeful glances. Felber looked tired, ready to quit. Perhaps his mood had passed.

Then came an outside roar: the approaching rattle of an elevated train. It rumbled overhead, above the street that fronted the garage. Felber's sudden triumphant shriek was drowned by the train's tumult, but his actions told that his mind had taken another of its crazy spurts.

Frantically, he set to work with a huge monkey wrench, detaching one of the shafts that ran from the motor to a wheel. Once the rod was loose, it slid into three sections. It consisted of a solid shaft inside a hollow tube, with a still larger tube girdling the inner portions.

Felber spent the next few minutes rearranging those tubes, turning them end over end. He was trying unsuccessfully to fit them back in place, when a light rap sounded at the small rear door of the garage.

"It's Miss Cragg," whispered Casey. "She must have come down on the el train."

"Better let her in," undertoned Jim. "She's the only person who can reason with him."

Casey opened the door. A slender, dark-haired girl stepped into the garage. Gowned in light blue, she brightened the dull setting, though her face turned solemn the moment that she noticed Felber.

It was a lovely face, though, well-rounded and perfect of profile. Forcing a smile, the girl managed to make it look genuine as she approached Felber and in a beautiful contralto voice said:

"Hello, Howard."

"Hello, Marjorie," returned Felber, seriously. "I'm coming along finely with my four-wheel drive. See those shafts along the wall? The ones of different lengths?"

Marjorie nodded.

"I made them work," affirmed Felber. "But not as well as I wanted. I'm testing shorter ones, on the motor. Three shafts for each wheel"—he was sliding rod and tubes as he spoke—"and each shaft handles a different speed. A new idea in gears. This car will do anything, when I've finished with it!"

Another el train came crashing by, out front. Felber clapped his hand to his forehead; his blue eyes took a half-crazed gleam. Darting from the chassis, he reached the wall and began to tinker with the rods of assorted lengths.

Joining Jim and Casey, Marjorie requested their opinions. Both shook their heads.

"It's those el trains," argued Casey. "Every now and then one bangs by and jars him from his senses."

"We can't help it, Miss Cragg," added Jim. "We tried to get Mr. Felber settled in a quiet place, but he wouldn't stand for it."

"He just ranted around," added Casey. "He kept telling what his new car would do if he could get the right man to test it. He kept saying it would go anywhere, if he could get back here to finish it."

Slowly, Marjorie nodded. She was familiar with Felber's obsession. Knowing his genius for invention, she was in a quandary. Jim and Casey, earnest though they were, might be lacking in the imagination necessary to understand Felber's final goal.

From her purse, the girl drew a letter; she opened it, let the mechanics read it. Careful not to touch the letter with their grimy fingers, the men noted its brief lines. The letter was addressed to a Mr. Lamont Cranston; it was simply a request, on Marjorie's part, for an interview on a subject that might prove of importance to him.

"Mr. Cranston is wealthy," explained the girl, "and he is an explorer. If anyone needs a type of vehicle that would travel anywhere, he is the person. Would it be all right for me to send him this letter?"

For answer, Jim thrust a clean glove on his dirty hand, took the envelope after the girl had replaced the note in it. Jim gave a solemn nod to Casey.

"I'll mail it," said Jim, starting for the door. "I'm going uptown to get those special tires, though I can't figure why Mr. Felber needs them. You talk to Miss Cragg awhile, Casey."

Casey did talk, after Jim had left. He used a guarded undertone, so that Felber couldn't hear him, though the precaution was scarcely necessary. Felber was rattling rods and other gadgets at a great rate, muttering, sometimes loudly, as he passed back and forth from his invention to the wall.

Only when an elevated train went by did he pause. On those occasions, he stood with wide eyes fixed in a far-away gaze, as though the discordant rumbles were music to his whirling brain.

"All those parts cost like blazes," confided Casey, solemnly. "They're made of some alloy that's lighter than aluminum and tougher than steel, so Mr. Felber says. I wouldn't have believed him, if I hadn't hefted those rods myself and watched the way he whacks them."

Mentally, Marjorie decided that the information would be a sales argument with Cranston. Her mechanical knowledge was very meager, but she could at least declare that Felber used costly materials.

"Maybe the thing's too deep for me," admitted Casey, "but I'd say that if Mr. Felber got over this three-shaft idea of his, he might get somewhere. He hasn't figured yet how he's going to steer the car or brake it. But you can't argue with him."

"Do you think he'd welcome a visit from Mr. Cranston?"

"If you brought Mr. Cranston here—yes," decided Casey, after considering Marjorie's question. "Mr. Felber trusts you, just like he trusts Jim and me."

GLANCING at her wrist watch, Marjorie decided that it was time to leave. She broached another subject to Casey, speaking very firmly.

"I'm going to talk to Dr. Buffton," said Marjorie, as they were walking to the door. "I've mentioned Howard's case to him and he is quite willing to help us. Howard's mental condition may be the whole trouble, you know."

Casey nodded his agreement.

"Mr. Cranston should receive my note this afternoon," added the girl, "so I can hope to hear from him this evening. I'm all booked for a cruise; I am supposed to go on the boat this evening. But if anything can be done for Howard, I shall cancel the trip."

Outside the garage, Marjorie saw a dingy cigar store across the little street. Pausing, she looked inside the place and observed a telephone. After a quick glance about her, the girl entered the store. Marjorie had gained the momentary impression that eyes were watching her.

They were. Dark eyes that belonged to darkish faces. Two men, crouched in a parked coupé, had noticed the girl leave the garage. They held muttered conversation in a foreign dialect. One slid from the car and entered the cigar store.

In peculiar broken English, the darkish man was asking for cigarettes at the counter when Marjorie made her call at the open phone. He understood English better than he could speak it, for the fellow's saffron lips showed a smile beneath his smudge-black mustache, as he listened.

"Dr. Buffton is not there?" Marjorie was saying. "Yes, this is Miss Cragg. . . . Not until seven o'clock, you say. . . . Very well, I shall expect a call from him then. . . . Yes, at my apartment. . . ."

The darkish man was back in the car when Marjorie came out to the street. He and his companion were exchanging guttural mutters, as they watched the girl walk toward the elevated station. The glitter of their ugly eyes, the fangish expressions of their leering mouths, were those that hunters might give when sighting a choice and helpless prey.

Savages both, despite their ability to travel freely in New York, the villainous pair were confident that they could wait for an easier opportunity to pluck Marjorie Cragg from circulation. Their calculations told that they had until seven o'clock that evening, at which time darkness would favor them.

The men waited, motionless, in their car, until they heard the heavy roar of an elevated train. Their faces firmed, their eyes glistened like fireballs, bulging in a sightless stare.

When the clatter had faded, the two strange men relaxed. The one at the wheel started the car, while the other gazed curiously from the window, much interested in observing the peculiar customs of Manhattan dwellers that they passed.

With all their vigilance, the spies had failed to notice the letter that Jim carried when he left the old garage. Coming out through the door, the mechanic had thrust the small envelope into one pocket, his glove in the other. Marjorie's letter, slight though the facts it gave, was on the way to Mr. Lamont Cranston.

A girl in danger, as Marjorie

Cragg definitely was, could have chosen no better person with whom to correspond. Though noted for his remarkable experiences in many foreign lands, Cranston had a habit of finding still greater adventures in New York. Any shred of mystery or intrigue became his cue for action.

On those occasions, Lamont Cranston frequently disappeared. In his place, there roved a singular being known as The Shadow!

CHAPTER II.

SEVEN O'CLOCK.

MARJORIE CRAGG was punctual, when it came to keeping appointments. She had to be; otherwise, her profession would have suffered. Marjorie wasn't really famous as a vocalist, but she had made some fairly profitable concert tours through the Middle West.

Certain persons had enthused quite highly, regarding the merits of Marjorie's contralto voice. One was Howard Felber, but Marjorie had long ago decided that his opinions were not based on her voice alone. Otherwise, he wouldn't have traveled many miles to see her, on nights when he couldn't arrive until the concert was over.

Howard Felber was ambitious, and so was Marjorie Cragg. Perhaps that was why they had never really talked of love. Each recognized that the other had a career ahead; that not until success had been individually attained would they talk of sharing it together.

Pure coincidence had brought them to New York. Howard had come to discuss the commercial possibilities of new automotive developments, while Marjorie had been attracted by a short-term radio contract.

Once in New York, they had stayed on—Howard, to work on a new invention; Marjorie, to accept a singing engagement on a cruise ship. Then Marjorie had learned of Howard's strange mental turn.

How it began, and why, she did not know; but it perturbed her. She hoped that his brain, and his invention, both, would prove sound; that Buffton, the physician, would certify one, and Cranston, the financier, would approve the other.

She was willing, in the emergency, to sacrifice her future for Howard. All day, she went about her shopping, pretending that she was going to take the cruise; but she made it a point to dine early, and reach her little apartment ahead of seven o'clock.

She knew she would hear from Buffton, perhaps from Cranston. If either insisted that she remain in town to further Howard's welfare, the cruise ship could leave without her.

The apartment looked quite pathetic when Marjorie reached it. Her luggage formed an unsightly stack, featured by the huge but almost empty trunk that was to hold the many costumes which were being sent to the boat.

With an entertainment scheduled for nearly every night of the three-week cruise, Marjorie had decided to vary her performances with the aid of costumes. In fact, she was being advertised as the "International Songstress," and there would probably be considerable speculation regarding her actual nationality.

Around the trunk lay suitcases; one was open for last-minute packing. Though she was tense with worry about Howard, Marjorie decided to pack the articles that she had brought back from her shopping tour. She was piling bundles on the trunk, studying the suitcase to see if all would fit in it, when she gave a sudden gasp.

The aeolian harp was gone!

Of all articles that Marjorie prized, the aeolian harp rated first. She had obtained it literally for a song. Someone who liked her radio singing had sent it to the studio, as a token of appreciation. The harp was a ten-stringed instrument, shaped like a long, shallow box; but no skill was required to play it.

That was, no skill except nature's own. When the harp was placed in a breeze, the air currents themselves would play it, sometimes producing most remarkable harmonies.

HER hand pressed to her forehead, Marjorie tried to think clearly. Her head was aching from worry over Howard; she wondered if she could have put the wind harp in the trunk or in another suitcase.

Not wanting to unlock and open all the luggage, she was hoping for some clue to the missing instrument when the harp itself supplied one.

Vaguely at first, then with gusts of sweeping melody, the tunes of the rare instrument reached Marjorie's ears.

She turned to the window, gave a happy sigh. The aeolian harp was on the window sill, where she must have left it. The window, too, was open, though she thought that she had closed it when she left the apartment before noon. Outside, a night breeze was stirring, its fitful impulse gaining a steady strength.

The spirit of the breeze was registered by the harp. The twang of the strings came louder. They faded into a fairylike pianissimo, to which Marjorie's fancy could add the tinkle of sylvan bells. Then, to the accompaniment of a powerful gust, the harp produced an imposing forte that strengthened the girl's fiber.

From the window, Marjorie saw the lights of Manhattan—a myriad array of forceful glow that seemed in keeping with the harp's proud melody. Then they were gnome lights dancing in the distance, as the easing breeze swept lighter music.

Eyes half closed, Marjorie caught the dreamy lilt of vague and distant song. It faded; she listened, intent, hoping it would return.

Then came the voice.

It was a voice that spoke, each word tuned to a twang of a harp string. A tone that was at moments kind; at others, commanding. It spoke her name, ordering her to listen; then its gentle words soothed her, much like the cooling breeze.

The voice spoke thought-words.

They were in no language, yet she understood them. The voice was telling her to wait, to let her problems rest. Should other things distract her, she was to pause and contemplate. The voice would answer.

Into that lovely mental harmony came a discord: the ringing of the telephone bell. It grated on Marjorie; she drew her body taut and clenched her fists. She wanted to hear the voice again. It came. Striking a mighty beat from the harp, it said:

"Answer!"

Marjorie found the telephone, lifted the receiver and gave a detached hello. Over the wire came a precise tone that she recognized as belonging to Dr. Buffton. He was asking about Howard Felber. He had to repeat the question, for Marjorie didn't answer.

Letting her lips relax, Marjorie waited for the mental voice to tell her what to do. Almost before she realized, she was speaking into the telephone.

"Howard Felber?" Marjorie gave a musical laugh, that she caught from the rippling harp strings. "He's quite all right, doctor. I called you to tell you so."

Came more questions, that Marjorie heard but did not weigh. Some other mind had taken command of hers. Its vibrant music gave her words to say—words that she echoed in a tone not quite her own.

"I'm leaving tonight on the cruise

Firing as he whirled from doorway to doorway, The Shadow was looking for some path to safety.

ship," said Marjorie. "We can see Howard together, when I return. Thank you so much, doctor, for offering to help."

There were other words, that Marjorie answered; then the *click* of a receiver that she did not hear. Her hand drifted downward to place her own receiver on the hook. The telephone was like a weightless plume as she rested it lightly on the table.

From the harp came a happy melody of triumph, which Marjorie felt she shared. The music seemed to inspire the breeze, rather than be governed by it. Under the fascination of complete hypnosis, Marjorie waited dreamily for the next command.

The telephone bell began to ring again. The girl did not even notice it. A lighter sound, however, attracted her full attention. It was a slow, repeated rap at the door. Automatically, Marjorie spoke the word:

"Come!"

The door opened in a drifting fashion. On the threshold stood a tall, darkish man, who bowed.

"We are ready, Miss Cragg," he announced in choppy tone. "The cab is waiting downstairs, to take you to the ship."

THOUGHTS of the luggage did not bother Marjorie. Her only reluctance was that of leaving the music behind her.

Curiously, the harp faded of its own accord. Trying to catch some haunting recollection of the melody, Marjorie walked mechanically from the room and toward the stairway.

She passed other men that she did not notice. They waited, while the one who had entered leaned above the aeolian harp in the window. The strings were twanging jerkily, its tones as jarring as the telephone bell, which kept up its persistent ringing. The dark man at the window spoke, in English:

"It is I—Suji. I have word, Kha Khan."

His gleamy eyes fixed in a rigid stare, as if his brain were ejecting full news of Marjorie's departure and the unanswered telephone call. Then the dark face lighted, as if receiving answer. Curling lips announced:

"It shall be done, Kha Khan!"

To his darkish fellows, Suji gave orders in a guttural tongue. They finished packing the baggage, adding the aeolian harp. To the accompaniment of the telephone bell's jangle, they cleared the room of luggage in a single trip.

Only Suji waited; his lips formed a satisfied sneer as the ringing ceased. Extinguishing the lights, he departed.

In a cab that she had found awaiting her, Marjorie had begun a trip that seemed to carry her through circular paths of light and darkness. She had no way to judge the time it took, for she was solely concerned with humming the last bars of a strange melody that she did not want to lose.

She lost count of the times she hummed it. Still singing softly to herself, the girl alighted when the cab stopped. A dark-faced driver guided her into an obscure doorway, which, to Marjorie, in her present mental state, might have represented anything, even the gangway of an ocean liner.

Next, she was on an elevator, trying to fit its constant *thrum-thrum* to the haunting tune that she hoped never to lose. Exiting from the elevator, she followed a corridor, lured by the tone of the harp itself!

Ahead was an open doorway, a maid waiting beside it, but Marjorie did not notice her. Entering, Marjorie merely realized that the door had closed behind her and that she was alone.

The harp was on the window sill; the sash was slightly raised, to admit the wafting breeze that strummed the strings. All about was Marjorie's baggage, carefully arranged. Some of her things had been unpacked; the bed was turned down, and her pajamas were lying on a chair, along with slippers and dressing gown.

Marjorie decided that she had been assigned to a very lovely stateroom.

Her voice vibrating softly to the lilt of the aeolian harp, she undressed. She didn't notice her wrist watch as she removed it. Much had happened in a very short space of time. Dr. Buffton had phoned the apartment at seven o'clock, and the watch, still running, registered only quarter past that hour!

Nor did Marjorie realize that she was retiring at a surprisingly early time. She was intrigued by the way her clothes seemed to float away as she touched them, until they were all gone. She drifted into the pajamas, then found herself in bed. Her hand found the lamp above her head, extinguished it with a lazy touch.

With the lulling notes of the harp, Marjorie heard the deep moan of a steamship whistle. It was distant, but her impressions of space were as vague as those of time.

Totally unaware of the fantastic experience that had overtaken her, Marjorie sank into a deep, comfortable sleep, undisturbed by any dreams that might have furnished an inkling of her plight.

CHAPTER III.

KHYBER KILLERS.

Riding in the rear seat of his luxurious limousine, Lamont Cranston again studied the letter that he had received from Marjórie Cragg. The passing lights of the avenue showed Cranston's features to be masklike, but of a singularly hawkish mold.

His eyes were suited to his profile. Sharp orbs of burning power, they scanned each line of the letter, as if ferreting out some hidden meaning from the penmanship alone.

The letter was unusual. In stating little, it said much. A simple request for an interview, from a young lady named Marjorie Cragg, was slight in itself; but the reference to a "matter that might prove of importance" meant much when written by the girl in question.

Though Cranston had never met Marjorie, he recognized that the matter which she mentioned could be vitally important to some third person, whose name was not stated. Unwittingly, Marjorie Cragg had written her own personality into the letter.

The rounded curves of the writing, with wide margins at the ends of the lines, were clues to an artistic temperament. Slight separations in the midst of words were signs of intuition, produced by lifting pauses of the hand. There was sincerity in the vertical formation of the letters. Whatever favor that writer might request, it would not be for herself.

More than that, if some risk should be involved, Marjorie would be willing to share it. Whether or not the risk already existed was a fact unrevealed, but there was a circumstance that made it seem most likely.

The letter had been addressed to the Cobalt Club; arriving there at seven, Cranston had received it and had promptly called Marjorie's telephone number.

The line had given a busy signal; when it cleared, Cranston's call had remained unanswered. Obviously, some sudden occurrence had been responsible. After a second attempted call had failed, Cranston had promptly left the club and ordered his chauffeur to take him to Marjorie's address.

As the big car swung from the avenue, Cranston reached beneath the rear seat, drew out a hidden drawer that was fitted under it. From the drawer he brought a black cloak, a slouch hat, and a pair of .45-caliber automatics.

He was attired in the black garb, his guns were beneath his cloak, when he reached for the speaking tube and spoke in calm, leisurely tone:

"This will do, Stanley. Wait here five minutes, then return to the club."

Those words were the final token of Cranston. The figure that glided from the limousine was not the dinner-jacketed form of the jaunty clubman. It was a blot of blackness—a strange, sinister shape that had the ability to blend with gloom.

Lamont Cranston had become The Shadow!

THE apartment house where Marjorie Cragg lived was in a secluded neighborhood, about two blocks from where the limousine had stopped. The path that The Shadow followed to reach his destination was untraceable.

Avoiding the front entrance, he entered a rear courtyard, scaled to a hallway window on the high first floor. Finding the stairway gloomy, he ascended it.

Marjorie's apartment was number 3C. Past the doorway, merged with blackness at the end of the hall, The Shadow stretched a gloved hand to the knob, found the door latched. His next move was to produce a small tool shaped like a gimlet. Its shaft no thicker than a needle, The Shadow bored the point straight through the old woodwork, slanting pressure against the latch.

The door slid open from the jogging pressure of a black-cloaked elbow. After a dozen seconds of absolute silence, The Shadow entered, closing the door behind him. He used a flashlight guardedly, keeping its beam shrouded in the folds of his cloak.

Brief inspection showed the tiny apartment to be furnished, but untenanted. The only sign of recent occupancy was the open window. Above a roof on the opposite side of the courtyard—the roof was on a level with this window—The Shadow could see a considerable portion of Manhattan's skyline.

Superficially, the situation could represent either a hoax or a trap. More careful consideration indicated that it was neither. Marjorie's letter was neither a jest nor a lure; not with the sober, troubled indications that The Shadow had observed in it. If someone else had taken a hand in the matter, it was too trivial to be a hoax. As for a trap—

The Shadow interrupted a rapid chain of thought. He had just about decided on the verdict that a trap, to be worthy of the name, would have some features to occupy his full attention. This apartment lacked any such; yet it *was* a trap. The Shadow had seen the proof of it.

A thin slice of light had disappeared. It was the dim streak of glow that showed beneath the doorway from the hall. Blocked partly by a rug, the disappearance of that

He was backing toward the stairway door when arms grabbed him.

faint token would not have been noticed by anyone standing in the apartment. It happened that The Shadow, in making his rounds, was keeping to a crouched position below the window level.

The question was: how had The Shadow's entry been detected? No one had seen him enter the building; there had been no lurkers in the hallway when he opened the apartment door. Chances favored the supposition that the arrivals did not know their prey had arrived. They might be coming here to put the place up to the standard of a proper trap.

Before The Shadow could carry the question further, the door was opened. The Shadow sensed the fact from the slight breeze that stirred in from the window, only to cease as promptly as it had begun. Whoever these entrants, they had closed the door behind them, and they were experts in ways of stealth.

Two of them. The Shadow sensed that, also, as he worked toward the door. Their breathing was barely audible, yet more pronounced than The Shadow's. He was shoulder to shoulder—first with one, then with the other.

Crouched low, they were working inward from the door, yet taking turns at crossing the path to that outlet. They acted as if they expected to find someone. The Shadow decided to let them.

With a quick sweep, he drove toward the man on his right, expecting to floor him, then whirl on the other. The Shadow shot one hand for an invisible throat; in the other fist, he clenched an automatic, prepared to use it as a cudgel. The swiftness of his surge took his opponent almost off guard; not quite.

The result was a real surprise.

Instead of striking a rising human form, The Shadow struck a thing that whirled. Hands sliced in past his own; The Shadow's gun stroke overreached. Hoisting shoulders came up in corkscrew fashion, aided by a twisting, butting head.

Lifted from his feet, The Shadow was hurled into a sideward fling as if recoiled from a cannon!

In the midst of that half sprawl, he recognized the mode of battle; one that belonged to a clime far different from Manhattan. Coming to one hand and knee, The Shadow made a quick spin of his own to meet the second foe, in whose direction he had been tossed.

The clash came instantly; this time, it was equalized. As The Shadow's whirling figure met that of a revolving opponent, they locked like two jamming cogwheels out of gear. Lashing arms hooked tight, but The Shadow's spin was the one that carried the greater power.

Twisting his foeman with him, The Shadow drove straight for the man who had supplied the first fling. Fresh arms grappled; all three were in the struggle.

The Shadow recognized the breed of his enemies. They were Afghans, killers of the sort that stalked the Khyber Pass. They used these twisty tactics not only for attack, but as a means of wriggling free when outnumbered. Holding the odds, they weren't thinking of getting loose. They were working hands free merely to draw their favorite weapons: knives.

They were depending too much on their own game. It didn't work for them. It took two arms to hold The Shadow's one. His free fist was slashing with its heavy gun, making the Afghans duck, striking down the hands that tried to haul out long-bladed knives.

They were snarling in their native language, Pukhtu, and The Shadow understood the jargon. The pair wanted to get their troublesome foe over by the window.

Apparently, they were afraid of knifing each other by mistake. Their butting tactics, too, would serve them better if they could ever combine beside the window, for in that case The Shadow would go out across the sill.

Each was calling the other by name: one was Suji; his pal was Kuli. In the midst of the whirl, The Shadow soon lost track of which was which.

He was letting them swing him toward the window. He knew that when they reached it, they would think to trap him unawares. A swing, half across the ledge, would give The Shadow a backhand sweep at their heads. It would be tough for either Afghan who tried to hoist his shoulders or draw a knife. In either case, the fellow would have to straighten, which was what The Shadow wanted.

The whirl reached the window; The Shadow feinted with a tricky lunge. Again, the Afghans did the unexpected. Kuli used both hands to hang onto the one cloaked arm that they already had. Suji made a high, sweeping grab for The Shadow's gun wrist and caught it. They were hauling him back, trying to pin his arms behind him, keeping his cloaked form directly toward the window.

As they made that effort, the pair raised an outcry, far louder than their former babble. Together, they shouted a name:

"Ahmed!"

Faced toward the window, The Shadow saw a figure rise from the low parapet of the opposite roof. It was the tall, lithe figure of an Afghan warrior, lifting himself from ambush as coolly as if he had sprung from a mountain rock on his native soil. It was the way such Afghans rose when they felt that their prey was sure.

Usually, their targets were visible. In this case, Ahmed was simply picking the blackened square of a window, confident that Suji and Kuli would perform their part.

Ahmed's lifting hand raised high above his head, drew back, clutching the most formidable of Afghan weapons, a war spear.

His limber figure poised, then slung forward. From his fist, with all the power that could score a bull's-eye shot at fifty yards or more, Ahmed launched the mighty shaft straight for the square black target that held a waiting victim, The Shadow!

CHAPTER IV.

MEN OF THE DARK.

DESPITE the power of his arm and the accuracy of his aim, Ahmed the Afghan had overlooked one factor regarding an invisible mark. He had forgotten the time element, or perhaps he had never known that such a thing existed.

In aiming spears from mountain passes, at men or beasts that he could see, Ahmed, like all others of his ilk, instinctively sped their aim, or deviated it, according to the chance movement of the prey.

This was the first time that Ahmed had ever depended upon a blind hurl. In pausing for a straight, hard thrust at short range, he had left too much to Suji and Kuli.

The Shadow had seen Ahmed, the instant that the spearman rose. He, too, had gone on the move, in a fashion that neither of his grapplers expected. Braced between their forward-shoving arms, The Shadow had flung his feet ahead of him, against the window sill. Timed to the lift of Ahmed's spear, The Shadow supplied a mighty recoil.

Three figures were slashing backward in the dark, as Ahmed made his poise. Wildly, Suji and Kuli were trying to keep The Shadow in the spear path as the shaft whizzed toward the window. They were slashing with their knives, to force The Shadow to his feet, a thing in which they succeeded; but they couldn't stop his whirl.

Whipping at an inward angle, The Shadow struck the inner wall of the room just as the spear arrived there.

It skimmed him as it struck; then, burrowing like a mighty arrow, the weapon finished deep in the wall, quivering its full length.

Hearing the challenge of a sinister laugh, the closer Afghans knew the thrust had failed. They dived for obscure corners of the room, to be away from the threat of The Shadow's gun. Their scramble was unnecessary; the automatic wasn't pointed their way.

Dropping his arm along the spear that ran beneath it, The Shadow aimed his .45 along the rooted shaft. The weight of the automatic brought the wooden brace to level as he fired. This time, the targets were reversed, as were the conditions. The Shadow was picking Ahmed, a target that he could see.

Half over the edge of the opposite parapet, Ahmed jerked upright with the spurt of The Shadow's gun. The impact of the bullet jarred him as it struck his chest; then, his balance thrusting forward, Ahmed toppled from the brink. His throat voiced a shrill, meaningless shriek as he made that nonstop journey to the cement courtyard.

In dropping Ahmed, The Shadow settled the riddle of the trap. Ahmed had served as watchman, prior to taking over a murderer's task. He had seen a slight light from the doorway, when The Shadow had entered the apartment. By a signal to Suji and Kuli, lurking somewhere below, Ahmed had brought up the two who were to bring The Shadow into his range of power.

WITH Ahmed gone, the others were thinking only of escape. They hurled their knives wildly as they flung themselves for the door, thinking to balk The Shadow's aim.

Shots blasted after them, but did not score. They had dead Ahmed to thank for that luck. His spear had done them one favor.

Skimming The Shadow's ribs, the pointed shaft had bundled the black-clad fighter's coat along with his cloak, actually pinning him to the wall. The Shadow's side had received a painful gouge, but that was a minor problem. With garments skewered to the wall, he had managed his straight aim at Ahmed; but twists to reach the others were impossible.

The Shadow's shots were meant to spur their flight, no more. As the slamming door told of the double exit, The Shadow set to work to free himself.

Grabbing the spear, he tried to loosen it, but failed for lack of leverage. Trying opposite tactics, he kept his grip and made a powerful sideward twist, that brought him free at the sacrifice of coat and cloak.

Ripped from sleeve to hem, the cloak gave the effect of a wide-spreading V, as it caught the breeze when The Shadow yanked open the door to start below. The hallway was dark, as the Afghans had left it, and there was no sign of the two fugitives.

Sidling rapidly across to the stairway, The Shadow took up a position there. He knew the tricky ways of these Khyber killers. Having identified them for what they were, he used the proper tactics to offset them.

On the chance that they had dodged into hiding places on the third floor, he waited, keeping his gun moving in a slow, sweeping arc. Then, when no sounds stirred the hallway, The Shadow began a slow descent by the stairs.

Stealth masked his departure. So did blackness, until he reached the second floor. From there downward, it was a case of watching all doorways and other hiding spots. On journeys to Kabul, the capital of Afghanistan, The Shadow had often watched wary natives dodge from sight, vanishing into spots that seemed no larger than big rabbit holes.

If either Suji or Kuli tried such methods hereabouts, they would be due for trouble when The Shadow neared them. His probing gaze picked out every cranny along the second floor.

Starting down the final flight of stairs, The Shadow was prepared to repeat his stalking process, when a clatter from the front street told him of a new development.

Reaching the first floor, The Shadow sighted men in uniform hammering at the front door. Someone in an apartment pushed a buzzer to admit them.

The noise of The Shadow's gunfire had alarmed the tenants. They had summoned the police.

One officer must have caught a glimpse of The Shadow whisking to the window at the rear of the hallway, for a shout came from the front door. Vaulting through the open window, The Shadow landed lightly in the courtyard, just as bullets began to whiz through the space above.

Knowing that the bark of the police guns would rouse any lurkers, The Shadow came to a crouch and began a rapid spin. The move was opportune. In from darkened spots about the gloomy court came a surge of whirling attackers: reserve Afghans, who had crept into this vantage spot, to remain while others went upstairs.

THE SHADOW's free hand was plucking wrists that swung through the air, warding away the strokes of slashing knives. His gun was spouting return thrusts more dangerous than the slashes that the Afghans attempted.

Twisty as ever, the darkish men scattered. Their own rapid thrusts had failed, but they were quick enough to scoot away amid the first blind shots that The Shadow fired.

The cloaked fighter had revolved across the courtyard. Back to the farther wall, he drew his second gun and made three fan-spread jabs in the darkness, to spur the flight of his routed opponents. With the echo of the last shot, The Shadow caught a sound from above. He pointed his gun toward a dark window and fired.

There was a scream: Kuli's. He and Suji had lurked on the third floor and returned to the apartment. Hearing the gunfire below, Kuli had yanked Ahmed's spear from the wall and leaped to the window. Spotting the three jabs from The Shadow's gun, Kuli had tried to make amends for Ahmed's miss.

The Shadow's shot clipped Kuli in the midst of his throw. It jolted him backward, giving his arm an upward jerk. The spear struck the wall above The Shadow's head, took an angled bounce and clattered across the courtyard.

Vague light showed the window empty. Kuli was out of harm's way, dragged back to safety by his sidekick, Suji.

Other weapons were in action. Guns were talking from the window in the lower hall. Bullets from Police Positives flattened against the wall where The Shadow had been. The cops had seen the cloaked fighter's final shot. Taking him for an invisible foe, they were trying to drop him in the darkness. But The Shadow hadn't waited for that mistaken attack.

He was out, through the mouth of a narrow alley by which the Afghan mob had fled. Brief seconds, though, had changed the nature of that route. It was no longer clear. A trio of patrolmen was surging in, with flashlights. As one gleam took a sweep, The Shadow saw a fourth officer picking himself up from the curb.

Evidently one cop had encountered a twisty, fleeing Afghan, so all were coming through to look for more. The Shadow decided to let them think that they had found one. Before the first flashlight revealed him, he hurdled forward, smothering its glow. Guns cloaked, he went into a dervish spin, flinging his arms for the man with the flashlight.

The Shadow cut a tornado path right through the converging officers. Their flashlights went clattering, their guns spouted off at angles. They were grabbing for him one-handed, too late. Ripping from fingers that clawed his cloak, The Shadow stumbled across the curb, found his footing, and dodged away in darkness.

He had won his escape, but he was serving the Afghans as well as himself. Four vengeful cops were spreading, spattering wild shots, in an effort to flank the swift fugitive that they had scarcely seen. Attracted by the fire, the police in the apartment house dropped out through the window and joined in the chase.

The next ten minutes were strained ones for The Shadow. He couldn't seem to shake the trailing police.

They didn't see him, but they heard him. There were times when he had to reach for fire escapes and climb upward, to get across the blocking ends of blind alleys. The neighborhood was full of cul-de-sacs, that afforded all sorts of complications.

Once, The Shadow was momentarily spotted by an arriving police car, as he sped across the street in the path of its approaching lights. A siren's wail brought pursuers in that direction, forcing The Shadow to a roundabout change of course.

He was trying to pick up the path of the scattered Afghans, but it couldn't be done. Like The Shadow, they were men of the dark. Given a scant head start, they were able to veer their own course away from the sounds of pursuit.

PICKING an opportunity that at last came his way, The Shadow dropped from a fire escape, cut across a street at an angle. Waiting in a doorway as a police car rolled by, he took another angle back across the street and sped through a narrow passage that he remembered.

Another crossing, a quick path in the dark—he was back in the courtyard behind Marjorie's apartment house.

That scene of rapid battle had become a quiet center in the midst of a storm of circling police. It had been that way ever since The Shadow's flight had begun, fully ten minutes ago. All was silent when The Shadow snapped on his flashlight, keeping its glow close to the ground.

The sweeping beam showed vacancy. Ahmed's body was gone; so was the Kafir spear that had twice been flung The Shadow's way. Three floors above, The Shadow saw the glint of a closed window in Marjorie's apartment. The grim silence mocked The Shadow.

It meant that the tricky Afghans had reversed their own course during the ten minutes that The Shadow had wasted dodging the police. Bobbing back, they had removed Ahmed and his weapon; probably, they had also helped Suji take away the wounded Kuli. They had covered their tracks in skillful style, but at last The Shadow's laugh came whispered in the darkness.

In the outlet from the courtyard, he had found a trail: slight blobs of blood, that showed at intervals under the flashlight's probing gleam. He traced that course across the street, through an opposite alleyway, along a zigzag path of a hundred yards, before he realized what it really meant.

The trail was The Shadow's own!

For the first time, he felt the painful gash that Ahmed's scraping spear had given him. His energetic progress had caused the wound to bleed; the torn edges of the cloak were well stained with blood. At present, the flow from the gash had lessened and could be easily stanched.

Sounds told that disgruntled police were returning to the source of their chase. Silently, The Shadow worked out through the loosely closing cordon. On his way, off into darkness, he issued a low, sinister laugh, its tone repressed.

Crime lay behind the vanished Afghans. Hidden crime, that involved the disappearance of a girl named Marjorie Cragg, who, like dark-faced fighters, had left no trail. An arduous campaign awaited The Shadow; one in which he would have to mask every move, since many lives—like Marjorie's—might be at stake.

Behind this mystery, involving the fighters imported from Afghanistan, The Shadow could picture the machinations of an insidious brain. It belonged to a master criminal of gigantic mental prowess; one that the world thought dead.

The Shadow, however, had never agreed with that view. He had long been alert to the prospect of a returning menace, in the person of a master plotter known as Shiwan Khan.

When last they had met, The Shadow had won victory over the genius of evil; had seen his vicious foe disappear beneath the waters of New York Bay. But that event had been no proof that Shiwan Khan had died.

The ways of the master mind were devious; his followers were many. Even self-destruction could be a sham with Shiwan Khan: a scheme of pretended death to throw trackers off his trail. Nor was Shiwan Khan, monstrous creature of the Orient, a person who would ever admit defeat.

Shiwan Khan was the sort whose taste of failure would whet his appetite for success. His schemes might change, when he discarded old for new, but Shiwan Khan would never lose his urge to acquire mighty power.

The Shadow knew!

CHAPTER V.

THE MAN FROM PERSIA.

When Marjorie Cragg awakened in the morning, she found herself quite bewildered. The room in which she had slept was not part of her apartment, nor could it be a steamship cabin.

Looking from the window, she recognized the New York skyline; then, from the position of the landmarks, she suddenly realized that she was only a few blocks from her own apartment.

Her present room was much higher up, certainly thirty stories above the street. That fact, and the absence of a building that reared quite close to her apartment house, enabled her to realize where she was. She happened to be in the missing building, the Hotel Monolith.

Marjorie wondered if there had been a fire in her apartment, or if she had missed the boat. Either catastrophe could be a reason why she had come to the nearby Hotel Monolith. Somehow, the events of the previous evening were a blank. Marjorie decided to get dressed and go back to the apartment.

She looked for her clothes; they were gone. In their place she found a Persian costume, much finer than any of the theatrical apparel that she had sent to the boat.

It consisted chiefly of long silk pantaloons, a jeweled girdle, and a gorgeously embroidered jacket, which Marjorie later learned was called a caftan. In addition, the girl found a pair of slippers with upward-curving points.

Purple was the predominating hue of the colorful gear. Discarding her pajamas, Marjorie attired herself in the Persian trappings, then surveyed the effect in a full-length mirror. The jeweled costume was gorgeous, but it simply wouldn't do for street wear in New York. Not even when Marjorie added a golden sash that she found hanging from the chair back.

The sash made up for the high cut of the caftan; but portions of the costume were thin, like gossamer, producing a peekaboo effect. Though preferable to slippers and dressing gown, the Persian attire would still be too conspicuous for a daylight venture through Manhattan.

Nevertheless, the costume pleased her. Its silk had a shimmery flow, that made it comfortable as well as beautiful. Time floated dreamily, as Marjorie posed before the mirror; then an enchanting melody gripped her.

The tune came from the window, where a light breeze had plucked the strings of the aeolian harp. Her thoughts tuned to the mood of the previous evening, Marjorie turned toward a connecting door. Responding to a mental command, she opened the door and stepped into the adjoining apartment.

The room that she entered was lavish in Oriental splendor. Persian rugs overlapped themselves upon the floor. Gorgeous tapestries hung from the walls. It was a palace chamber from old Persia, transferred to America. In the room was a bowing dark-skinned maid, dressed in a costume similar to Marjorie's, but of a plainer sort.

A soft rap came from another door. Responding to the command that accompanied the harp's thrum, Marjorie spoke: "Come!" The door opened, a man stood on the threshold.

Bowing, he swept his hand toward a rug-decorated divan. With a gracious smile, Marjorie draped herself upon the Oriental coach and watched the visitor enter.

He was the most singular man that Marjorie had ever met. Wide at the forehead, his face tapered toward a pointed chin. The center of that triangular visage was a straight-marked nose, as definite as a ruled line. His eyebrows were thin curves of black that ran almost to his temples. His lips formed a thin, straight streak of brown, set against a saffron background. There were also a thin mustache and a dab of chin whisker, in the Oriental style.

Most amazing of all his features were his eyes. They were green, catlike in their glow. Yet, to Marjorie, as her own gaze met them, those eyes had the deep gleam of emeralds. When the man's lips opened, words seemed to drip from

Hulagu was handling The Shadow as a St. Bernard would treat a poodle.

them, like the tone of the aeolian harp.

"I am Shah Nikwan," he stated. "You are welcome here, Princess Dunyazad."

Marjorie smiled. She was sure that Shah Nikwan was a Persian. He was wearing a golden tunic, with a tight-fitting turban of the same hue. In the center of the turban glistened a star composed of diamonds, evidently the symbol of high rank. But she thought that his reference to her as a princess was merely a jest.

Shah Nikwan observed the girl's smile. He spoke again, in his musical tone.

"You are to be the Princess Dunyazad," he declared, "when you have learned the language of my country. Later, you shall be known as the Persian nightingale, most beautiful of all song makers! Come!"

He led Marjorie along the corridor. Ahead, the girl could hear the muffled thump of the elevator; its mechanism seemed constantly in motion. They passed long rows of doors; when they reached the elevator, Shah Nikwan pressed a button. Soon, the elevator stopped.

They entered it and went one story up, but the elevator mechanism continued to run after they had left it.

They were on the top floor of the hotel, and there Marjorie saw a huge room with a dome-shaped roof, painted dark blue, with tiny white bulbs for stars, and an artificial moon. Below the center of the vaulted ceiling was a square platform, raised a few feet from the floor.

A recollection came to Marjorie; perhaps the thoughts of Shah Nikwan inspired it.

"Why, this is the Moonlight Café!" exclaimed the girl. "It was all built and ready to open, when the owner of the Hotel Monolith committed suicide because of financial troubles."

Shah Nikwan bowed acknowledgment of the statement.

"I begin to understand," added Marjorie. "You intend to open the Moonlight Café, don't you, Shah Nikwan? This is where you will want me to sing."

"Your discernment is excellent," returned Shah Nikwan. "I have decided upon such a venture. But this room"—he indicated it with the sweep of a long-fingered hand—"will not be the Moonlight Café. It will be styled the Garden of Omar."

Marjorie's eyes brightened. She could picture herself, as Princess Dunyazad, singing Oriental melodies in a room resembling a Persian garden, with artificial moonlight overhead. Unquestionably, Shah Nikwan had heard of her as the "International Songstress," and had chosen her as the star attraction for his future night club.

It did not surprise her that this man from the Orient should be entering a commercial venture. Such things occurred frequently in New York.

Shah Nikwan stated that the decorations of the forthcoming garden would arrive in a few days. In a few weeks, the place would open; meanwhile, Marjorie could learn new lyrics, and from her maid acquire a smattering of Persian.

"We shall call you Princess Dunyazad," he said, smiling wisely as he spoke. "You must try to believe that you are Princess Dunyazad. It will be helpful to us both. Very shortly, I shall announce your arrival in America. After that, there will be interviews."

Marjorie nodded. It was all good showmanship, a thing which she approved as legitimate in the theatrical business. Shah Nikwan was offering her a chance to become famous; it would be her part to cooperate.

As they left the domed roof garden, the girl kept repeating her new name to herself.

THEY stopped at Shah Nikwan's apartments, which occupied most of the floor below. Dark-faced men were there, as servants, and Marjorie was delighted by the magnificence of the place. As they passed an end room where the door was open, Marjorie had a view off through an opened window.

She saw an elevated train and heard vaguely its approaching rumble. She felt a sudden surge of jarring memories; then Shah Nikwan spoke a harsh order to a servant. The fellow promptly closed the door, to cut off the sound.

A sudden mistrust had gripped Marjorie. It ended as they reached another room. There, a window was open, facing in another direction. On the sill was an aeolian harp, exactly matching Marjorie's. The strum of the wind-plucked strings soothed her. She smiled again, as she gazed toward Shah Nikwan.

"Our thoughts are in tune, Princess Dunyazad," he said smoothly. "We must let such harmony continue. My servants will conduct you to your own quarters, which are even more lavish than these."

Marjorie was pleased. What Shah Nikwan said was true. His own apartment, of many rooms, was done in Oriental style; but none of its furnishings were so distinctly Persian as those of her own new abode. Shah Nikwan had reserved the best for Princess Dunyazad.

It was strange, how the new name gripped her. Repeating it, the girl actually felt that it was her own. By the time she reached her suite, where the maid waited, she couldn't quite remember what her former name had been.

Then, pleased with her costume and the luxurious surroundings, Marjorie sank to the divan and decided to forget that she had ever had another name.

Back in his own maze of rooms, Shah Nikwan stopped at a door and listened to the sound of a steady buzz that came from beyond it. His green eyes glistened; at moments, they showed a brilliant flash. Thoughts were passing from the brain of Shah Nikwan, to be picked up by some distant person whose mind had tuned to that vibrating buzz.

Farther along the inner hallway, Shah Nikwan paused again. He was catching the steady pounding of the elevator, that kept running up and down its shaft. His saffron face darkened. He could not gain the mental contact that he wanted. Clapping his hands, Shah Nikwan gave a sharp call:

"Hulagu!"

The man who responded was a giant Mongol, compared to whom the tall Afghan servants looked puny. Towering close to seven feet, he had to stoop almost to his knees as he came through the doorway. Proportionately wide, Hulagu was forced to make a sidewise twist, to work his shoulders through the opening.

"Order them to stop the elevator," commanded Shah Nikwan, in English. "It is useless to keep running it, at present."

Bowing, the giant Hulagu boomed the reply: "It shall be done, Kha Khan."

His lips curving into a slitted smile, Shah Nikwan stepped into the room that opened toward the elevated. He took a chair beside the window; leaning back, he closed his eyes and entered a state of powerful concentration.

That face, with its vicious smile —a curve of brown, etched upon yellow—was one that The Shadow would have recognized, could he have viewed it. But its owner was not titled Shah Nikwan. The name, like the man's promises, was a sham.

This strange man from the Orient was Shiwan Khan. His ways were unfathomable, even to those persons that he controlled. When Shiwan Khan plotted evil, innocent persons became his tools. From this lair, high in Manhattan, he was at work upon a mysterious scheme involving many helpless dupes.

For, like his ancestor, Genghis Khan, it was Shiwan Khan's desire to rule the world!

His brain could work afar, as he had demonstrated. Howard Felber, like other deluded persons, was swayed by his mental control. Should persons interfere with his machinations, as Marjorie Cragg had unwittingly done, Shiwan Khan knew how to rule them and make them useful to his plans.

It was all part of a gigantic game, gauged to a final purpose that would eventually be revealed. During the process, Shiwan Khan intended to deal with human beings as puny pawns, discarding them when he was through with them.

The smile that was fixed to Shiwan Khan's saffron face was proof that he feared opposition from no one.

Not even from The Shadow!

CHAPTER VI.

BAIT FOR THE SHADOW.

FROM a single fact, The Shadow had decided that Shiwan Khan was again in New York; namely, because of the Afghan fighters who had invaded Marjorie's apartment. The last time that Shiwan Khan had come to America he had brought Mongol warriors, letting some of them reside in Chinatown, which had enabled The Shadow to trace them.*

* Note: See "The Golden Master," Vol. XXXI, No. 2.

Profiting from that mistake, Shiwan Khan had produced a different breed of tribesmen, and was probably keeping them at his own headquarters. The fact that the Afghans roamed at large in New York was of very little help to The Shadow.

If seen, they would simply pass as unusual foreigners; but Afghans had a habit of not being seen at all. To them, the alleyways and buildings of New York were a happy hunting ground, compared to the rocks and ravines in their own land. Clever as well as murderous, the Afghans could hold their own in any terrain.

Working from the assumption that he had to deal with Shiwan Khan, The Shadow analyzed Marjorie's disappearance. Another girl had vanished during Shiwan Khan's previous sojourn in Manhattan. Posing as a Chinese maiden, Marjorie had unwittingly served as Shiwan Khan's messenger.

A similar situation could exist in Marjorie's case. There was also a strong possibility—as in the other instance—that Marjorie had some connection with a person who had become the prey of Shiwan Khan. The Shadow's belief that Marjorie had the interests of a friend at heart was something to strengthen the theory.

It was all part of Shiwan Khan's craft; his game of turning people against the very ones they sought to aid. The secret of his strange ability was his power of thought transference, or telepathy, which he had learned while living in Tibet.

The Shadow was also skilled in that line. Like Shiwan Khan, he worked from hypnotism as a basis, having learned that thoughts passed more readily from mind to mind when both were under a mesmeric influence. Knowledge of such principles, however, was not enough to accomplish the gigantic marvels of which Shiwan Khan was capable.

While The Shadow had been spending years in training himself to physical combat against crime, his rival had devoted that same period to a system of continued mental concentration. Thus, each was equipped in a different way for the warfare that they had actually resumed.

Just as The Shadow could baffle the fighting skill of Shiwan Khan's Afghan warriors, so could Shiwan Khan snatch victims like Marjorie Cragg from The Shadow's protection, leaving no clue to tell where they had gone. In Marjorie's case, The Shadow felt sure the girl would be safe until Shiwan Khan's purposes were gained, but after that there would be no guarantee.

Why had Shiwan Khan returned to America?

There lay a mystery in itself. On his previous visit, he had tried to acquire huge supplies, chiefly bombs and airplanes, to start a world-wide conquest from his base in the heart of Asia, the underground city of Xanadu.

Defeated in that effort by The Shadow, Shiwan Khan had become a known menace. Every factory that turned out military equipment was keeping close watch on its workers, to see that none developed peculiar mental symptoms.

As for military secrets and the men who devised them, such things were already under surveillance of the Feds. Spies were prevalent in America, and many ways had been designed to thwart them. It seemed a certainty that any thrust by Shiwan Khan would at least be detected and reported.

Yet The Shadow felt that such was Shiwan Khan's most likely move. Merely to spread a warning would be worse than useless. It would simply tip off Shiwan Khan and cause him to switch to some alternative measure. Under such circumstances, The Shadow's only course was first to learn exactly what Shiwan Khan intended, then give the real alarm.

FROM his own headquarters, a hidden sanctum in the heart of Manhattan that even Shiwan Khan could not locate, The Shadow sent orders to various of his secret agents, through his contact man, Burbank. They were to learn all that they could concerning Marjorie Cragg, taking care to keep their investigations covered. The Shadow, alone, was impervious to Shiwan Khan's measures of remote hypnotic suggestion; no one else could be regarded as safe.

During two days the agents had investigated, and brought back certain facts. Their reports included data concerning Marjorie's career as a singer, as well as photographs of the girl herself.

She was supposed to be cruising the Caribbean on the steamship *Atlantis;* but radio messages to that liner, guised as offers of future concert engagements, brought back the news that Marjorie was not on board the ship.

Such information proved that Marjorie had been abducted, but that was all. As for her acquaintances in New York, it appeared that Marjorie had none, except some professional friends, who could not be targets of Shiwan Khan. Nevertheless, The Shadow had instructed his agents to keep on checking facts regarding Marjorie Cragg.

For news of the vanished Afghans, The Shadow was depending on the police—with little luck.

The law had gone blank on that score. No one had been able to describe the missing trouble makers, nor even guess why they had entered the apartment house. In fact, the people who reported the gunfire did not know in which apartment it had begun.

Dining at the Cobalt Club in the guise of Lamont Cranston, with his friend Ralph Weston, The Shadow had sought shreds of information. Since Weston happened to be New York's police commissioner, he was the one man who should have been able to supply any news of roving Afghans. But Weston was merely annoyed by Cranston's occasional references to the mystery of two nights ago.

"There's no mystery to it!" insisted Weston, brusquely, as they sipped their coffee in the grillroom. "I've told you that a dozen times, Cranston. If we tried to investigate every minor mob skirmish, the department would have no time for handling important matters."

"Odd how those chaps disappeared," mused The Shadow in Cranston's leisurely style. "Right from the center of a police cordon, so I understand."

"Bah! You've been reading the *Classic!*" snapped Weston. "I'm glad the club doesn't allow that scurvy scandal sheet to be among the newspapers in the library."

Cranston smiled. The *Classic,* a tabloid newspaper dealing in sensational and exaggerated news, was a constant thorn to the self-important police commissioner.

While they were finishing their coffee, Weston continued to look annoyed. Finally, he clashed his empty cup into its saucer and exclaimed:

"Your persistence has won out, Cranston! I still think there's no mystery in the case, but I can't get it out of my head. Wait here while I call Inspector Cardona and get him to repeat the details of his report."

The Shadow waited willingly. It was more than persistence that had won for him. He had been using Shiwan Khan's tactics of mental concentration, constantly keeping his mind fixed on one point while he gazed at Weston. The influence had finally taken full effect. It was to produce results, too.

Returning, the commissioner announced:

"The thing has been bothering Cardona, too. He admits that he has been having patrolmen question everyone along their beats, regarding persons seen near that apartment house."

"What have they learned?"

"A lot of hodgepodge." Weston tossed some notations to his friend. "Not a thing of any consequence."

THE list did appear to be a drab one. It included such items as a shoemaker giving a two-dollar bill as change, in mistake for a one; an argument between two boys over ownership of a stray dog; a geranium pot falling from a window and smashing the derby hat of a patron entering a barber shop.

Nearly a dozen items in all—but among them one that interested The Shadow, though it meant nothing to the police commissioner. Someone had called headquarters to report that a truck belonging to the Integrity Transfer Co. had been seen in the neighborhood of the apartment house shortly before seven o'clock.

Inasmuch as no trouble had begun until after seven, at which time the truck had been gone, Cardona had considered that item the most foolish of them all. Nothing had been reported stolen from the apartment house; no truck had figured in the flight of the men who had indulged in gunfire. Weston's mind, therefore, was at ease; he hoped that Cranston's would become the same.

It did. Soon afterward, Cranston left the Cobalt Club. Riding to Times Square in his limousine, he alighted and sent the big car home. Picking a taxi that stood on a side street, he gave low-voiced instructions to the driver. The cab headed eastward.

From a drawer beneath the rear seat, Cranston produced black garments, identical with those that he carried in the limousine. Putting on the cloak and hat, he became The Shadow. This cab was his own; its driver, Moe Shrevnitz, one of his secret agents.

Two blocks from a squarish garage that belonged to the Integrity Transfer Co., The Shadow left the cab. As he approached the garage under sheltering darkness, he suspected the presence of watching eyes that could have been in any one of several cars parked along the street.

The garage was well filled with cars; dropping his cloak and hat between two light trucks, The Shadow strolled into a room marked "Office." A beefy man looked up from a battered desk. Sight of a well-dressed visitor like Cranston rather surprised him. His eyes took on a sudden squint when The Shadow quietly asked if the company rented trucks.

"Yeah, we do," the man admitted. "Only when business gets slack, though. There's one we rented out, on the streets right now. What did it do"—his tone was anxious—"run into your car somewhere?"

"My chauffeur had an argument with the driver," was Cranston's reply. "Nothing more. Only, the fellow seemed rather surly. He was a dark, scowling fellow who talked broken English."

The beefy man nodded.

"That's one of them, all right," he said. "Anyway, the truck is insured, and they paid a good price for the rental. I'm sorry, mister—"

"You've had other trouble?"

The beefy man looked startled; then, caught off guard, he forced a nod. The eyes that met his were persuasive. He said more.

"They were loading the truck at this address"—the beefy man shoved a slip of paper across the desk—"and they must have bashed some fellow's fender. He called up a while ago and made a squawk. Wouldn't give his name; just said we'd hear from him later."

Assuring the man that his own complaint was merely a minor one, The Shadow left, picking up his cloak and hat when he passed the parked trucks. Skirting the garage, he noted the light in the little office. The beefy man's desk was away from the window, but the fellow's silhouette showed plainly against the wall.

Evidently, The Shadow's own profile had been outlined, too, in shaded form. Any outside observers could have seen it. From the circumstances that The Shadow had learned, it was quite possible that spies had been on lookout duty, to check on persons visiting the garage.

It was impossible, though, that they could have overheard his chat with the garage man. Nor could they have observed his entry and departure. Apparently, the address mentioned by the garage man was one where the truck had been, and would not return—another place like Marjorie's apartment.

Reaching the cab, The Shadow told the driver, Moe Shrevnitz, to follow a roundabout course to the neighborhood of the new address, which was on the West Side. As they rode, The Shadow kept on the lookout for trailers. There were none.

Within the cab, The Shadow voiced a laugh. It was a whispered tone, mocking in its mirth, though it denoted only partial satisfaction. At least, The Shadow had gotten another trail to the Afghan followers who served Shiwan Khan.

Perhaps it might prove a dead trail, like the one of two nights ago. Yet, in this case, there had been no tumult; therefore, darkish departers might have been less careful in covering their tracks. Until he investigated it, The Shadow could not pronounce the present trail as useless.

Anything might develop, when dealing with Shiwan Khan. The Shadow had learned that in the past. He was to find it out again in the very immediate future!

CHAPTER VII.

FRIENDS OF SHIWAN KHAN.

MOE's cab stopped in an old-fashioned neighborhood, where great, grim brownstone houses etched their misshapen roofs against the glow of Manhattan's sky. It was one of those districts where progress had marked time since the beginning of the present century.

Built to last for many years, the houses had fulfilled expectations, but their original owners had long since abandoned them as antiquated. With rentals cheapening, the area had become shabby. Its only future lay in the removal of the out-of-date structures, which no one had as yet attempted.

The address given by the garage man lay near the middle of a block that was suited precisely to The Shadow's needs. He reached the house, found it quite as dark as the gloomy walls that had hidden his advance. The windows had no boardings, however, which indicated the house was occupied.

Choosing the basement as the best place to enter, The Shadow picked the lock on an old door that was sheltered beneath the brownstone steps. Inside the house, he locked the door behind him and began a probing tour. The basement was poorly furnished, but the first floor was better.

The rooms showed fairly modern furniture, and a considerable amount of it; but silence stayed complete. Keeping the rays of his flashlight guarded, The Shadow started for the second floor. He was halfway up the stairs when he detected the first tokens of life in the place.

From high above, somewhere on the third floor, came a steady whirring sound that formed a peculiar buzz. It seemed like the mingling of several sounds, all in concert, yet very much alike.

Passing closed doors, The Shadow crept toward the third floor, extinguishing his light completely. The buzz was louder; he could tell where it came from. A quick glimmer of the flashlight showed him the right door.

Quite different from the other doors in the house, this one was new and closely fitted. It was made of heavy wood and there was no crack beneath it to emit light from the room within. Reaching the door, The Shadow tried it, found it tightly bolted.

He tried to analyze the buzzing sound. There were at least twenty variations of the hum, though the average listener would have detected only a half dozen. The Shadow's ears were trained to pick up sounds, particularly in complete darkness, which again existed, for he had turned off the flashlight.

Moreover, The Shadow was skilled at noting remote sounds, even when those close by attracted him. That was why he caught the slight, shuffling noises that came from the lower floors that he had left.

Swinging about, The Shadow descended to the second floor. At the head of the stairway leading down to the first floor he heard the sounds more clearly, the scrape of many feet.

Someone began pressing light switches. The cavernous hallways glowed. Men faced toward the stairway and looking upward, saw The Shadow. They raised a shout as he wheeled away. There was a rear stairway; the cloaked intruder made for it, only to be blocked by other oncoming trappers.

Diving for an open room, The Shadow ducked from sight just as his first pursuers saw him. They were shouting for him to halt; when he didn't, they blasted loose with guns.

Flashlights burned into the room, showed an open window, with a cloaked form wedging through. Again, revolvers barked—too late. The Shadow was dropping when his trappers fired.

He took a hard fall into a cement passage; one that brought a sharp pang to his ribs, healing from the spear wound. Diving for the rear street, The Shadow reached it while men above were blazing shots from the window. Their fire was useless in one sense, important in another. No bullets came anywhere near The Shadow, but the shots served as an alarm.

Big-beamed flashlights swept the rear street, coming from half a dozen spots. Caught in the glare, The Shadow became an actual target as he zigzagged across the street. The playing flashlights made his running form grotesque—a long, warped streak of blackness that might have been anything from man to monster.

The Shadow had encountered friends of Shiwan Khan; the same friends whose aid the world empire builder had enlisted two nights before. Again, The Shadow was dodging the police!

Craftily, Shiwan Khan had kept his precious Afghans out of it. He had no need to sacrifice them, or clutter the battleground with men who might divert the trail. Shiwan Khan had simply arranged matters to put The Shadow at temporary odds with the law. Odds which might prove fatal to The Shadow.

Firing as he whirled from doorway to doorway, The Shadow was looking for some path to safety. He was shooting over the heads of the police, even though every man he spared might be the one to drop him. The Shadow's shots were close, for he wanted his assailants to duck—which they did, as their bad aim proved.

But this street, of all streets in Manhattan, was about the worst when it came to finding an exit. On both sides, the old buildings reared for an unbroken block.

Smashing a basement window, The Shadow dived through, disregarding the glass that slashed his cloak. Speeding through, he came to a rear courtyard, the hue and cry right after him, interspersed with gunshots. Flashlights appeared with the pursuing cops; again, The Shadow was ducking beams, some of which flickered away when he whistled shots above them.

This would prove a worse trap than the street—a fatal one, if he did not leave it in a hurry. But The Shadow was sure that the courtyard had some outlet. He found one, on the opposite side. With bullets thudding against the brick walls about him, The Shadow made for the next street.

A mad dash for the corner brought him to a secluded avenue, with bullets buzzing about like hornets. Zigzagging across the avenue, The Shadow hoped that Moe would hear the shots and head in their direction.

Making for the next side street, he dropped to a sheltering doorway, to let the first police go by. Others were in the distance, coming from the opposite direction.

When they met, they would know that they had been tricked. Meanwhile, The Shadow would merely encounter trouble if he reversed his course. Peering past the corner, he saw police spreading across the avenue. He heard them shout, and knew the answer. It was Moe's cab, wheeling through.

Moe took the corner, rather than stop to argue with the cops. He took it on two wheels, and the tilt of the cab found The Shadow just beneath it. With a quick-paced stride, the black-cloaked fugitive caught the door handle. Flipping the door open, The Shadow rolled inside, letting the cab slam the door itself, as its wheels jounced back to normal.

Seeing police ahead blaring their whistles at him, Moe decided to stop. He had slackened speed and officers were almost to the running board when a whispered voice stabbed a command in Moe's ear.

His foot jamming the accelerator pedal, Moe whipped away from the astonished cluster of cops, took the next corner on the other pair of wheels, just as revolvers began to blast.

The Shadow saw the front of the old house as they roared past the corner beyond it. A lot of cars were drawn up in front, and plenty of flashlights were sweeping the street. Moe didn't notice the house; he was looking straight ahead along the avenue that they followed. Turning his peaked face, he gave bad news.

Patrol cars were looming up ahead. The mirror showed another in the rear. Maybe a side street would offer some chance at a getaway; but, from all appearances, the cab would soon be boxed.

From then on, The Shadow directed things. Moe simply handled the wheel, but he did his part well.

It was a cat-and-mouse chase that seemed more hopeless to Moe the farther they went with it. They were circling the same blocks over and over, in a sort of pretzel course, that took them away from trouble and got them back into it. Spying a straight route, The Shadow at last gave orders to take it. The cab was out of one mess, but Moe knew that they would find another.

They did, a few blocks ahead. As The Shadow called for Moe to turn a corner, a police car whined into sight, spotting them just after they made the swing.

Whistles shrilled from the next block, were answered from a side street. The cab had found the opposite side of the cordon, which the police had rapidly been forming, ever since the start of gunfire in the old house.

THE SHADOW called for Moe to wheel back toward the center of the net. Moe obliged; but, for once, he couldn't see how his chief intended to get out of it.

If they crossed the encircled area, they would only be back with their old friends, who were still looking for them. But it wasn't The Shad-

1. On the trail of an Afghan-manned truck carrying an invention stolen by Shiwan Khan's natives, The Shadow's taxi follows it to a strangely constructed alleyway. Slipping from the cab, The Shadow is about to launch an attack on the natives, when he is pounced upon by . . .
2. . . . Hulagu, giant Mongol aid of Shiwan Khan. In a terrific battle between the two men The Shadow is nearly killed, and only through the assistance of his agent, Moe Shrevnitz, does he manage an escape. Crawling into the . . .
3. . . . alleyway, looking for a place to barricade himself in case of the Mongol's return, The Shadow finds an old door in the wall, through which he enters—and again finds himself facing terrible peril!
3
2
1

ow's intention to let two groups of pursuers meet.

He guided Moe along a zigzag route, with the chase getting hotter every moment. Then, of a sudden, they wheeled right into the thick of things, along the street in front of the old house where all the cars stood outside!

Police were leaping out into the street, shouting, brandishing revolvers. Moe dropped low behind the wheel, knowing that this might be the last blockade that they would ever try to run. Then, before a single shot was fired, he heard The Shadow's calm command:

"Pull up!"

Moe swung to a stop beside a large official car. The pursuing patrol cars arrived; their occupants leaped out, to join the officers who were already on the cab's running board.

Cops were dragging Moe away from the wheel, hauling him out by the collar. Others were thrusting revolvers in through the windows, growling for all passengers to surrender.

A brawny police sergeant yanked open the door on the curb side. He was waiting with his gun, when a lone passenger came out, smiling, with upraised hands. Straightening, he made a tall figure, immaculately clad in evening clothes.

Ignoring the police who were frisking him for guns, he looked up toward the house steps and called out in leisurely voice:

"Good evening again, commissioner!"

From the steps, Commissioner Weston blinked; then, in an astounded voice, he exclaimed:

"Why, it's Cranston!"

Then Weston was down the steps, bawling orders at the officers who were in the cab, searching it. They came out empty-handed, for The Shadow's cloak and hat were safely stowed beneath the trick rear seat, along with his guns.

Their looks turned sheepish, as they saw the irate commissioner gesturing both hands. On the steps was the man that they had captured, free of covering guns. There The Shadow, transformed into Lamont Cranston, was shaking hands with a swarthy, stocky man: Inspector Joe Cardona.

Explanations were in order, along with apologies. Weston took it that Cranston had returned to the Cobalt Club, and had come here from there. Since Cranston was busy talking to Cardona, the commissioner accepted his own theory and added to it.

Cranston's cab had tangled with the cordon while entering it. Being a friend of the commissioner, Cranston had done the right thing in keeping right on to his destination. The only men to blame for this commotion were the officers themselves.

In that surmise, Commissioner Weston was completely mistaken. The police had played a part in the disturbance; so had Lamont Cranston, while guised as The Shadow. But the fault for the whole affair belonged with a crafty plotter who had not appeared in it at all.

Only The Shadow could have named him: Shiwan Khan!

CHAPTER VIII.

DEATH BY DESIGN.

WITH matters nicely smoothed, Commissioner Weston gave heed to the whimpers of a pasty-faced man who stood beside the house steps. The fellow was repeating a plea to "Remember poor Mr. Maybrell." Weston nodded, then said to the whimpering man:

"All right, Jennings. Lead the way."

They started up into the house, The Shadow hearing details from Joe Cardona. The house belonged to an old inventor named Clifford Maybrell, who had gained some repute in designing air-cooling systems.

"Tonight," declared Cardona, in a matter-of-fact tone, "Maybrell went nuts. He began yelling that there were burglars around the place, and he locked himself in the fan room."

Cranston's eyebrows lifted in query, as he asked where the fan room was.

"On the third floor," stated Cardona. "Maybrell kept howling through the door at Jennings, his servant, telling him to get the police and bring a lot of them.

"By that time, Jennings was pretty near nuts himself. He ran out and got to a telephone—it's two blocks to the nearest one around here—and kicked up such a holler when he talked to me that I thought the whole neighborhood must be going to pot.

"So I sent a squad to pick up Jennings and let him take them to the house. I'd just been talking to the commissioner, a little while before. Since he was at the club, I called him up, figuring he'd want to be here."

They were at the second floor. Up ahead, Jennings was volubly insisting that there *had* been burglars in the house. Cardona turned to Cranston, spoke in a confidential tone.

"The squad did run into somebody," he said, "and lost their heads about it. But, from all reports, it wasn't a bunch of burglars, but just one person. He got away—and all for the better, because"—Cardona was speaking close to Cranston's ear —"my hunch is that the guy was The Shadow!"

From experience, Inspector Cardona knew that The Shadow was more than a figure of mystery; that the black-cloaked investigator had more than once turned results in the law's favor, when the scales were balancing heavily toward crime.

But Commissioner Weston still tried to class The Shadow as a myth, from the official standpoint, so Cardona had to be careful what he said within the hearing of his superior.

Headquarters men were waiting on the third floor, outside the room that produced the incessant buzz. Jennings was explaining that Maybrell had started the fans for another test, which proved that he must have been suffering mentally.

"He shipped the new fans this afternoon," declared the servant. "They were the important ones, made of the special metal. I can't understand why he started the old ones going, all of them at once!"

Men were hammering at the door, but getting no response. Jennings produced a fire ax; fearful of fires, Maybrell had it in the house, along with fire extinguishers. Using the ax, Cardona hewed a hole through the stout door, then thrust his hand inside, to reach the bolt.

The door swung open. The sight within halted everyone upon the threshold. The room was shuttered tightly, so as to allow no light to leave it. Bright bulbs were glowing in sockets on the walls. Everywhere were fans, dozens of them, swift-spinning blades propelled by electricity. They covered walls and ceiling, except for a hollow gap above: a trapdoor that led to a small attic.

Below that space lay Clifford Maybrell, an aged man with wrinkled face and smooth bald head. His hands were stretched beside him, the clawlike fingers clenched. His lips wore a fearful, frenzied grin, which had become a fixture on his face, like the pallid bulbous eyes that projected from their sockets.

Clifford Maybrell was quite dead.

GAZING suspiciously at the gap in the ceiling, Inspector Cardona reached for his gun. It was Cranston who stopped him. In calm tone, he offered Joe a suggestion.

"Step to the center of the room," said The Shadow. "Stand right beside the body, then look toward the ceiling."

Joe did as directed. They watched him squinting upward, pointing his gun. His swarthy face began to tighten, particularly at the lips. As Cardona winced, his eyes bulged. Weston gave a sharp cry as the police inspector wavered.

The Shadow swung to the wall, pressed a row of switches that he saw there. Cardona had caught himself; he took deep breaths of air, as the whirling fans ceased their combined humming and dwindled their speed to a silent stop.

"I couldn't breathe!" gasped Cardona. "Do you know what those fans did? They sucked the air right up into the attic! Maybrell suffocated himself in this air-tight room! Being off his nut, I guess he didn't realize what would happen."

With death on actual display, Commissioner Weston decided to sift all details in the case. He asked for facts, and Jennings gave them, very earnestly. According to the servant, Maybrell had been acting oddly for weks. Even his experiments had indicated the workings of a deluded mind.

It had all begun one day while Maybrell was in the workshop testing an air-conditioning appliance. There were only two fans in the place at that time; both had been running steadily, as Jennings remembered it. Then, Maybrell had been seized with a brainstorm. He wanted more fans, dozens of them.

Jennings ordered them, fans of all sorts and sizes, and helped his master install them. Maybrell kept running them in shifts; never was there a time when all were stopped. He termed the workshop the fan room, and declared that with new principles of alternating air currents he would revolutionize the science of air conditioning.

Experts had come to the house, at Maybrell's request; all had left shaking their heads. Their doubts of Maybrell's theory had egged him on further. He needed speedier fans, he claimed, so he ordered them, made specially of light-weight metal.

"They sang with a high pitch, those fans," specified Jennings, soberly. "A maddening tone, that reminded me of gnats. Mr. Maybrell developed the speed he wanted; then became dissatisfied. He began replacing the light fans with the heavy ones."

Weston asked if the lighter fans were the ones that had left the house that afternoon. Jennings said that they were. Angered because they had not suited his expectations, Maybrell had disposed of them as junk, at a fraction of their original cost.

"He was starting all over again," declared Jennings, wearily. "As fast as he put the old fans up, he turned on the switches that controlled them. He kept shrieking that he would succeed, but that he would have to hurry. He liked the drone of the heavy fans, and wanted it louder—louder—louder—"

Jennings was lifting his hands, clenching them, as if his own nerves were shattered. Finally gaining control of himself, he relaxed and completed his story.

"Every fan was in operation," said Jennings. "It was the first time that Mr. Maybrell ever ran all of them at once. The noise seemed to craze him, for he drove me from the room, telling me to search the house for burglars.

"When I came back, the door was bolted. I knocked, and Mr. Maybrell heard me. He kept screaming to get the police before the burglars found him. Before I knew it"—the servant's tone was earnest—"I was hearing sounds myself. By the time I had gone downstairs again, they were creeping all around me!"

No one doubted the testimony. It wasn't surprising that the servant's own nerves should have cracked. Besides, as Commissioner Weston reminded, there actually had been someone in the house when the police arrived.

The commissioner had just one question: he wanted to know why Jennings had not foreseen that the fans would suck the air from the closed room.

"They never did before," explained Jennings. "Of course, Mr. Maybrell never operated all of them at once, until tonight. Besides, he always alternated the fans."

Stepping to the wall, the servant pressed one switch upward, the next one downward. Fans began to spin in opposite directions, forming a cross current of air. Gesturing along the row of switches, Jennings kept moving his finger up and down.

"That's how they were when I left, commissioner," he said. "The fans were alternating their currents, as they always did. Mr. Maybrell must have changed the odd switches, after he bolted himself in here."

Commissioner Weston pondered. He was wondering whether the tragedy was the result of some new idea that had occurred to Maybrell, or an actual attempt at suicide on the part of the inventor. In either case, the demented condition of Maybrell's mind could be held responsible.

"Death through misadventure," was Weston's verdict. "A case for the medical examiner to worry about. We'll investigate the burglary angle, but it can scarcely have a bearing on Maybrell's death. If he wouldn't open the door to admit Jennings, it is unlikely that he would have responded to the knock of an intruder.

"Besides, Maybrell would have had to bolt the door again himself, if he let anyone in or out. The blame for Maybrell's death lay with his own mental state."

What Weston said was true, but

it was only half the story. The Shadow considered the other half of it, while he was riding back to the Cobalt Club. He knew where the real blame rested: with Shiwan Khan. It was that genius of supercrime who had inspired Maybrell's death.

Shiwan Khan could thrust his mighty will into remote and guarded spots, forcing persons to follow his commands, even to their own destruction. Provided only that he could attune the victim's mind to his, through some vibratory influence that would produce the same mental wave.

In Maybrell's case, Shiwan Khan had controlled the inventor's mind, forcing Maybrell to unwitting suicide. But that was merely the climax of a well-planned purpose. Shiwan Khan had wanted more than Maybrell's death, and had gained all that he sought.

To trace the details that lay behind the tragedy was The Shadow's present and most pressing problem.

CHAPTER IX.

MOVES IN THE DARK.

LATE that same night, Lamont Cranston played chess with a friend named Rutledge Mann. They formed a serious, but contrasting, pair as they sat above the chessboard in a secluded nook of the Cobalt Club.

Cranston's hawkish, masklike countenance was one of absolute calm that hid an adventurous personality. Mann, a round-faced man with owlish expression, was exactly what he appeared to be: a man deliberate in everything, precise in all affairs, yet fond of ease and comfort.

As a person of reputed wealth, it was logical that Cranston should be acquainted with Mann. Cranston needed someone to watch the fluctuations of the stock market, and Mann was an investment broker by profession. Yet, behind that business acquaintance lay a stronger friendship.

Behind the guise of Cranston lay the personality of The Shadow, and Mann was one of The Shadow's trusted secret agents.

There were moments when the chess game was forgotten. During those intervals, The Shadow spoke. His tone had Cranston's calmness, yet it was reduced to a singular whisper. The Shadow was piecing facts that he wanted Mann to know.

"You will remember," said The Shadow, "that Shiwan Khan exerted hypnotic influence upon his victims, when first we encountered him. His previous method involved the use of lights. Persons saw them flashing, in the exact fashion of duplicate lights at Shiwan Khan's hidden headquarters."

Mann nodded very soberly. This business of mutual hypnotism between Shiwan Khan and victims rather awed him. It meant that the stronger mind would dominate, as Shiwan Khan had consistently demonstrated.

"Shiwan Khan has chosen another method," continued The Shadow. "He is using sound, instead of light. Not only is the process more difficult to uncover; it enables him to reach remote places, such as Maybrell's workshop.

"We can trace the case back to the day when Maybrell first became inspired with a mania for new invention. Jennings said that fans were running in the workshop on that day. We may assume that Shiwan Khan had reproduced the same sound elsewhere. Finally catching the right pitch, he projected his thoughts to Maybrell."

Again, Mann nodded. Weighing other details that Cranston had told him regarding Maybrell's death, Mann remarked:

"If Shiwan Khan merely intended to dispose of Maybrell, he took a long while doing it. I would say—"

Mann paused, observing Cranston's smile. He realized that The Shadow had already figured out the answer.

"Shiwan Khan first wanted Maybrell to complete certain experiments," declared The Shadow. "Of all Maybrell's crazy whims, his purchase of light-weight electric fans and the high-speed tests he gave them seem to be the maddest. His disposal of those special fans, as junk, has been classed as another quirk of his demented mind.

"Peculiarly, tragedy reached Maybrell soon after those discarded fans had been shipped away. In that fact lies our answer. Maybrell designed those special fans at the bidding of Shiwan Khan; he disposed of them at the bidding of his mental master.

"Wherever Shiwan Khan may be"—The Shadow's gaze was piercing, as though seeking to view some hidden, distant scene—"he has received the products of Maybrell's creative workmanship.

"For some reason, Shiwan Khan requires high-speed fans of light-weight metal. He chose Maybrell as the man to design them. The work done, Shiwan Khan disposed of Maybrell."

There was silence. Like The Shadow, Mann was picturing the ways of Shiwan Khan. Tonight, Shiwan Khan had baited The Shadow into visiting Maybrell's house. The inventor's howl about burglars, a fever which Jennings had caught, had come from the projected thoughts of Shiwan Khan. It explained how the master plotter had brought in the police, as trappers of The Shadow.

The trail of the truck would be useless in the future. Taking it once, The Shadow had almost met disaster. From now on, he would use his own leads in seeking Shiwan Khan.

"One mad invention," remarked The Shadow, "may mean others. Our next move is to find more men like Maybrell. I have already started a campaign that may bring results."

EARLY the next afternoon, Mann saw evidence of The Shadow's campaign. It appeared in the New York *Classic*, where a story appeared under the by-line of Clyde Burke. Though Clyde worked as a reporter on the *Classic*, he was also an agent of The Shadow. In making news, Clyde often served his chief.

This was one such instance. Where other newspapers treated Maybrell's death as a strange accident, the *Classic* played it up as the result of a madman's crazed disappointment. With a story was a picture of Jennings, his pasty face distorted with alarm.

Clyde got that shot with the aid of a photographer, who puffed a flash bulb within a few feet of Jennings while the servant was staring at the camera. The picture gave every evidence of terror, the sort that might come from living with a madman.

There were two men who pondered over that copy of the *Classic:* Jim and Casey, the mechanics who worked for Howard Felber. It worried both of them.

Alone, either man might have decided that Felber's mania for inventing a car with a four-wheel, triple-shafted drive ought to be reported to the authorities before Felber went off his nut like Maybrell.

However, since they were two to Felber's one, the mechanics decided to wait awhile, keeping careful watch over their afflicted employer.

In his headquarters high in the Hotel Monolith, Shiwan Khan studied a copy of the *Classic*. It was dusk, yet fading light from the window showed the glower that came to Shiwan Khan's saffron face. There was no evidence to connect the *Classic* story with The Shadow; nevertheless, Shiwan Khan did not like it.

Shiwan Khan laid the newspaper aside. Concentrating, he waited by the window while an elevated train rumbled by below. Brown lips were slitted in a smile as the mental master left that isolated room. Stopping by the door that had formerly emitted a steady buzz, Shiwan Khan smirked again.

The buzz from that room was ended, no longer needed. But Shiwan Khan found reason for annoyance when he stopped near the shaft of the ever-moving elevator. Though his eyes focused into a fixed, distant stare, Shiwan Khan was unable to pick up thoughts accompanying the pounding *thump-thump* of the elevator.

Placing the starred turban on his head, he adopted the bland pose of Shah Nikwan. Passing patrolling Afghans, he left his spacious apartment, to knock at the door of Marjorie's suite. The girl's musical voice invited him to enter; the words were spoken in Persian.

Marjorie had progressed as Princess Dunyazad. She appeared quite as Persian as the maid, Hayat, who attended her. Greeting Shah Nikwan in phrases that she had learned from Hayat, the girl waited for his reply.

Shiwan Khan spoke in English, using the smooth, bland tone that suited the polite Shah Nikwan.

"There is a mission, princess," he stated, "which I trust you can accomplish. A message must be carried to a certain man. I cannot visit him; therefore, I must rely upon someone, like yourself, to meet him and return with his reply."

The prospect pleased Marjorie. She liked being Princess Dunyazad, but it was rather boring, having no one to chat with except Hayat. Her nod showed her acceptance.

Beside the divan was a narghile, a Persian pipe consisting of a bowl above a water jar, with a stemmed hose attached. Placing the hose to her lips, Marjorie puffed tobacco smoke that passed through cool-scented rose water.

Gazing into the emerald eyes of Shah Nikwan, she heard the instructions that he spoke. His voice, like his gaze, had a hypnotic force. Resplendent in her jeweled Persian costume, Marjorie arose from the divan and walked toward the door.

Hayat pushed a Persian cat from the divan and picked up the caftan jacket which was lying there. She saw Shah Nikwan shake his head. Hayat hung the jacket in the closet, along with some of Marjorie's American clothes.

From the doorway, Shiwan Khan watched Marjorie walk toward the elevator. She seemed a character from the "Arabian Nights"; her appearance would probably impress the whirling, bewildered brain of the man who was to receive her message.

Shiwan Khan, alias Shah Nikwan, was depending upon Marjorie Cragg—otherwise Princess Dunyazad—to smooth an unanticipated difficulty that threatened his important plans.

DOWNSTAIRS, a car was waiting at the secluded side door of the ho-

Her hand tightened; her finger found the trigger and pressed it.

tel. Its darkish driver opened the door for Princess Dunyazad, and began a twisty trip through darkened streets.

The Persian-garbed passenger sat motionless. Her eyes fixed straight ahead, Marjorie's lips were repeating the instructions given her by Shah Nikwan.

It was an hour before the girl returned. She had hardly entered her suite before Shah Nikwan appeared.

The eyes that met the greenish gaze were blank. The princess had delivered the message, but had received no reply.

Snapping his fingers, Shah Nikwan brought Princess Dunyazad from the depths of her trance. Purring a polite good night, he departed.

Reaching his own apartment, Shiwan Khan flung away the turban that went with his Persian masquerade. He clapped his hands, to summon Hulagu. The big Mongol was the one man in whom Shiwan Khan confided; therefore, Hulagu seemed to understand the trouble.

"I must have contact!" declared Shiwan Khan, in a harsh tone. "The girl took the message, but apparently Orlio would not listen. I shall send *you* next time, Hulagu."

The giant Mongol looked pleased.

"Tomorrow night," decided Shiwan Khan. "We shall wait until an hour after sundown. If contact is not restored by then—"

Shiwan Khan saw no need to complete his statement. Hulagu's vast leer told that the giant understood.

CHAPTER X.

THE SCARED MAN.

ONE day's story had created such a sensation that the New York *Classic* decided to run a second article pertaining to the Maybrell case. It was Clyde Burke who supplied the new material, at the suggestion of The Shadow.

The story was wild, yet plausible.

In his article, Clyde maintained that some forms of mania occurred like epidemics, and that men of genius—and particularly inventors—were peculiarly susceptible to such plagues.

He cited statistics to prove it: facts from the files of the *Classic*. Reviewing old cases of suicide and startling instances of violent insanity, Clyde showed that they had come in clusters.

When the afternoon editions of the *Classic* reached the street, they were bought as quickly as people could grab them. It wasn't until late in the afternoon, when the furor was lessening, that Commissioner Weston saw a copy of the tabloid.

The person who supplied it was Cranston. He had smuggled one of the banned scandal sheets into the sanctimonious preserves of the Cobalt Club.

"Outrageous!" stormed Weston. "Do you know what this ridiculous stuff will do? It will bring dozens of people to headquarters, claiming that they know crazy inventors who have been bitten by the bug!"

The Shadow smiled. That was exactly what he hoped would occur. But there was something else he wanted. His expression became serious.

"I think you are right, commissioner," he agreed, in Cranston's most solemn style. "Therefore, this is your chance to prove just how much harm a ridiculous newspaper story can produce."

"How can I manage that?" asked Weston, eagerly.

"Have all complaints sent directly to Inspector Cardona," returned The Shadow. "Instruct him to communicate with you whenever anyone comes in with a report of a mad inventor. Make it a point to interview the persons yourself."

"A great deal of trouble, Cranston—"

"But trouble well worth while, commissioner. Every time you run down a rumor and show it empty, you will add a spike to the indictment that you are building against the *Classic*."

Intrigued by the prospect, the

commissioner decided to concentrate on the suggested plan. No other business was pressing him, and Cranston's suggestion offered a chance to silence pesky tabloid newspapers like the *Classic*.

In fact, if it worked out as well as Weston began to hope, there might be a chance for the police to take legal action against the owners of the *Classic*.

Weston was further pleased when Cranston declared that he would stay on hand, to see how the plan developed. The commissioner didn't realize that his friend was expecting real kernels in the chaff.

THE one man who didn't like the idea at all was Inspector Joe Cardona. He received word of his new appointment just as he was leaving his office for the day. Slamming the telephone on his desk, Cardona stared from the window and glowered at the sunset.

Then he took it out on Markham, who was unlucky enough to be present. Markham was the detective sergeant who had yanked Cranston from the cab, up at Maybrell's house.

"I'm slated for twenty-four-hour duty," stormed Joe, "so you're elected, too, Markham! One of us has got to get some sleep between times."

Hearing what the job was to be, Markham couldn't understand why a constant vigil was necessary. He asked if the commissioner had ordered it.

"No, he didn't," returned Cardona, "but people don't pick reasonable hours when they go screwy. From the way the commish talked, people are liable to barge in here any time of the day or night, yelling that they've found some whacky inventor.

"Even the precincts will be steering them our way, because a general order has been sent out. Where would I stand, if the commish got wind of a case before I reported it? That's why we're going to stick right here, one or the other of us."

With that, Joe sent Markham out to get supper and bring back sandwiches and coffee. Calming as he sat at his desk, the ace inspector began to hope that things *would* happen at odd hours of the night. Joe relished the thought of waking the commissioner with frequent calls from midnight until dawn.

It was dusk when Markham returned with sandwiches and coffee. Cardona had a mouthful of ham on rye when the telephone bell rang. He gestured for Markham to answer the call.

"First customer," stated Markham, as he hung up. "A guy named Truman dropped in at Smitty's precinct. Says he can tell us all about a batty inventor. They're sending Truman down here. He ought to show up in about five minutes."

Arriving with two uniformed policemen, Truman proved to be a tall, drab-faced man, who looked somewhat nervous every time he tried to smile.

Cardona invited him to make himself comfortable. After the drab man had begun to smoke a cigarette, Joe remarked:

"Who's this inventor that you're worried about? Will we find him so dangerous that we ought to take along a net?"

Truman gave a genuine grin.

"He's Professor Orlio," he said. "Richard Orlio. He invents diving equipment. He's crawled into his bathysphere and won't come out of it."

"The bathy—which?"

"The bathysphere." Truman gave a circling gesture with his arms.

"It's a big ball, ten feet in diameter. They use it to go down to the bottom of the ocean."

"Where has Orlio got the thing?" queried Cardona. "In a drydock?"

Truman shook his head.

"It's upstairs in a storeroom," he said. "Over a printing shop."

Cardona had heard of cranks who built boats in their back yards, and then couldn't get them to the water. Orlio's case sounded similar. After making a few notes, Joe commented:

"I guess this Orlio is nuts, all right."

"You bet he's nuts!" exclaimed Truman, eagerly. "Do you know what he made the bathysphere out of? Beryllium!"

Cardona had heard the term before, but couldn't quite place it. Truman explained that beryllium was the lightest of all metals, including aluminum.

"Orlio made it light," snorted Truman, "so it could be transported easily. But it's got to be heavy, so it will sink. How do you think he intends to manage that? I'll tell you. He's got four holes in the top of the sphere, and he's going to pump compressed air into it, to give it weight!"

"Won't there be people in the thing?"

"Of course there will," returned Truman. "But old Orlio hasn't thought of what's going to happen to them. That's just another proof that he's gone nuts."

Cardona completed his notations. He was reaching for the telephone, to call the commissioner. Pausing, he asked in afterthought:

"Anything else?"

"Plenty!" assured Truman. "I told you that Orlio is in the bathysphere. Well, he's been in there four days. He crawled into the thing because the printers went on strike. He won't come out until they get back to work."

CARDONA shot a look at Truman, as the fellow paused to light a second cigarette from the first. Glancing at Markham, Joe saw the burly detective sergeant rub his chin. Both Joe and Markham were swinging to the same idea: that perhaps Truman was a bit crazy himself.

"Tell me some more about Orlio," suggested Cardona. "Didn't you try to reason with him?"

"Yes, but it wasn't any use," returned Truman. "He wouldn't even listen to the princess, when she came around last night."

"What princess?"

"The Persian princess. Boy, was she something! She pleaded with old Orlio, begging him to finish his work. He just dug deeper into the bathysphere. If the thing had a cellar, he'd have headed for it."

Cardona's face was solemn, almost sympathetic, as he nodded. Then, soothingly, he remarked:

"Tell me some more about this Persian princess. Have you seen a lot of her?"

"Pretty near all of her," chortled Truman. "She was wearing a skirt with purple leggings, about as thick as cobwebs. She had strings of jewels around her chest. Her shoes were sort of like slippers and curled up at the tips."

"Did she talk to you, too?"

"No. Only to the professor." Again, Truman grinned. "I don't think she even saw me. What do you think of that?"

Cardona had his own thoughts about it. He reached over and clapped Truman on the shoulder.

"Thanks a lot, old man," said Joe. "Tell you what. You start ahead; I'll be right along. I want to see what this nut Orlio looks like inside his bathysphere."

The two officers caught Cardona's signal as Truman arose. They kept close to him as he went from the office, ready to grab him if he tried to make a break. As soon as the three were out of earshot, Cardona turned to Markham.

"No use in calling the commissioner yet," said Joe. "This guy Truman is the one that's nuts! There probably isn't any inventor named Professor Orlio. I'm going to check on it, though, just to make sure. I know that the commissioner expects me to report first and investigate later. But how can I do that, until I know there's something to report?"

Fifteen minutes after Cardona had gone, Markham received an unexpected call from Weston. The commissioner wanted to talk to Cardona. In a quandary, Markham finally stated that the inspector had just left, which caused Weston to ask why.

Muddled by the question, Markham decided to explain where Cardona had gone. He emphasized that Truman probably was crazy, but he gave the address of Orlio's place, which Cardona had learned while questioning Truman.

At the phone booth in the Cobalt Club, Commissioner Weston repeated the details to Lamont Cranston. He mentioned that Cardona had just left headquarters, not knowing that Markham had misgauged the time. When Weston named Orlio's address, Cranston's eyes took a sudden glint.

"We can get there first, commissioner," suggested The Shadow. "Why not take a cab out front, and be on hand when Cardona arrives?"

The idea pleased the commissioner. They left the club promptly and stepped into a cab that Cranston hailed. Soon, they were speeding to their destination, where Commissioner Weston expected some interesting developments.

The Shadow expected more. He foresaw the situation as a grim one, upon which life depended. Not just one life, but many. The curious case of Professor Orlio might bring exactly what The Shadow sought: a chance to thwart the schemes of Shiwan Khan!

CHAPTER XI.

A TRAGEDY OF ERRORS.

With fifteen minutes' start, Cardona arrived at Orlio's ahead of The Shadow and Commissioner Weston, even though Joe's trip was some twenty blocks longer. The police inspector wasn't wasting any time. He wanted to find out whether or not Truman was crazy, so as to deal with the fellow accordingly.

As they swung the final corner, Cardona saw that Truman had informed him correctly on one point. The printers who worked in the shop on the ground floor were having some sort of strike. Men who wore big placards were standing on the sidewalk staring in through the window at others on the inside.

Alighting first, Cardona observed two types of pickets. Apparently, the printers themselves were engaged in a dispute over whether the strike was authorized. It must have been going on for a few days, as Truman specified, for most of the arguing pickets had unshaven faces.

The men inside looked worried. They were all ready to start the presses; a foreman was urging them to go ahead. But they wanted to see what happened outside, first. Too many men were picking up bricks, as if ready to heave them through the window.

Scuffles were starting among the arguing pickets. Cardona shoved a pair of men aside and started for the steps that led up to Orlio's place. He beckoned for Truman to follow him, and the fellow did. The two officers clambered from the car, remembering Cardona's order not to let Truman get away.

Sight of the uniforms brought yells from the strikers. They thought that the cops had come to scatter them. Instantly, brawling was forgotten. Both brands of pickets scattered of their own accord. Inside the printing shop, the insistent foreman won his point. The presses began to move.

They were thumping steadily, those presses, as Cardona and his companions went up the steep stairs to Orlio's premises. For a moment, Cardona thought the pounding sound came from an elevator; then one of the cops informed him what had happened below.

Cardona chuckled. Perhaps it was well that he did. Joe wasn't going to run into anything else that was funny; not for quite a while.

Truman pointed the way through a musty storeroom to a doorway. He said that the bathysphere was in the room beyond. Convinced that maybe he was going to see a bathysphere Cardona shouldered ahead and found one.

It was quite like Truman had described it—a hollow metal ball, ten feet in diameter. It glistened with a silvery tint, and above it Cardona saw the holes that had been mentioned. They were gouged upright, like corners of a square, a few feet below the summit of the great sphere.

The room itself wasn't much larger than the bathysphere. It had a small, square window in the opposite wall; but the only light in the room came from the large storeroom where Cardona stood, for darkness had settled out of doors.

Before Cardona could approach the metal ball, a door flipped downward from its side and a scrawny man popped into sight. He was white-haired, with unkempt beard, and his actions were very wild. Springing to the floor, he clapped both hands to his forehead and shrieked in high-piped tone:

"I can work again! Eureka! I can work again and my task is almost finished! I remember!"

Like an ape, he scrambled around the bathysphere, snatching at the gadgets on the top. He was tightening them, shrilling constantly:

"Wait—wait—give me a few minutes more!"

Cardona gave Orlio the few minutes that he wanted. Knowing that the scrawny professor had been cooped up for several days, he decided that the man would soon exhaust himself.

Cardona's hunch seemed justified, when Orlio slid down to the floor and flipped the metal door shut. Backing away from the bathysphere, he sagged, murmuring happily.

Catching Orlio, Cardona heard the man murmur:

"It is finished!"

"All right, professor," approved Joe, in a humoring tone. "You've done a good job. What you want is something to eat and a place to rest. Come along."

CARDONA was steering Orlio toward Truman and the waiting officers, when the man's scrawny figure went rigid. It seemed to swell, like a bundle of tightening muscles. Clapping his hands to his head, Orlio wrenched away.

It seemed as if his jerky actions were inspired by the thumps of the presses below.

"It's finished!" he screeched. "Finished, I tell you! Why do you ask me? Can't you hear me answer?"

Sharp eyes were staring from the scrawny face. Orlio's gaze was distant. The mad expression of his features indicated that he actually saw something, far away. Taking a look, Cardona spied only a brick wall, almost in front of the professor's nose.

Cackling gleefully, Orlio swept his arms wide and bounded about as he had before. He acted as if he had heard an answer to his shrieks.

"He's nuts, all right!"

With that assertion, Cardona grabbed for the human jumping jack. Slippery as an eel, Orlio twisted away. Bouncing from the bathysphere, he darted out into the larger room.

The cops tangled with him; despite his puny weight, Orlio dragged them along. Then, with a dipping dive, he was free of them. Wheeling toward the outer doorway, he shouted again:

"I hear! I shall obey!"

With that, Orlio thrust his hand behind his hip and yanked out a big, old-fashioned revolver. He flourished the antique weapon as he backed toward the door. His tone was a cackled threat, more than a warning.

"Don't try to stop me! You will regret it!"

He was backing toward the stairway door when arms grabbed him. Truman had sneaked to the exit ahead of Orlio. Valiantly, the man was trying to suppress the maddened inventor. The officers drove forward to help. Orlio's gun came wagging upward at them.

Cardona yanked the cord of the dangling light that illuminated the room. The move was timely. The cops were diving for the floor, with Orlio trying to spot them as he struggled in Truman's clutch.

Thanks to the darkness that Cardona supplied, Orlio fired wide. Joe was making a low drive for the doorway when another shot came, muffled.

Something went thudding down the stairs. Halted by the door, groping vainly for Orlio, Cardona heard a chortle very close to him. The professor's tone was gleeful.

"It is done!" gloated Orlio. "My life work is completed! Where are the fools who said that I could not accomplish it? One is gone"—the words were chuckled—"and I shall find the others!"

Cardona knew the one that Orlio meant: Truman. It was the grappler's body that had thudded down the stairs. Orlio had managed to turn the gun on him and deliver a fatal shot. Loose again, the mad professor was looking for more victims.

He was sneaking somewhere, very close at hand. Cardona couldn't see him, for, quite oddly, the clanking of the presses seemed closer. The heavy *thud-thud* could have been in this very room; but, as Cardona groped about, it gradually dwindled.

Against the dimness of the little window in the next room, Cardona suddenly saw Orlio and made a grab for him. The officers sprang to their feet and joined the mad struggle. They could tell where it was by the sounds, but the darkness handicapped them later.

Orlio was slashing about with his revolver, shrieking that he would need his bullets later. No hands could stop that scrawny, lashing arm, that seemed inspired by some strength greater than the professor's own.

Cardona was managing to dodge the strokes, but the cops were taking them. Joe felt them drop away, though he couldn't hear them fall.

Cardona's head was pounding with a rising *thud-thud-thud,* louder than the presses below, which hadn't stopped. They made so much noise, those presses, that the printers couldn't hear the gunfire. Then the thudding ended. Only the presses kept up a steady throb.

Struggling furiously with the wiry professor, Cardona heard footsteps coming up the stairs.

Reeling across the floor, Cardona propelled Orlio to the inner door that opened into the bathysphere room. It was there that the professor landed a glancing blow, gave a gleeful cackle as Cardona staggered. Groggily rising on hands and knees, Joe heard a gloat, knew that Orlio had spotted him in the darkness.

A bullet was scheduled next. Cardona expected it, but the shot did not come. Instead, Orlio gave a frenzied shriek. Cardona heard the crazed professor stagger backward, held in the grip of an arriving foe.

Low, whispered, and sinister came an accompaniment to Orlio's disappointed screams. Cardona recognized it, knew that rescue had arrived.

It was the laugh of The Shadow!

CHAPTER XII.

THE VANISHED TRAIL.

FACTS were pounding themselves through Cardona's head; details that jammed themselves into brief seconds. Truman had said that Orlio quit working when the printing shop had closed. He'd told the truth, as in everything else, Truman had.

Whatever his mania, Orlio gained the inspiration from the thumping presses. The first error in a tragic series was the mistake on the part of the pickets, when they thought the police were after them.

They had let the presses start again, and Orlio had gone back to work. Lacking only a few minutes to complete his crazy bathysphere, he had found the time he needed. No wonder he had gone berserk and tried o murder all intruders.

It didn't occur to Cardona that all of Orlio's actions were inspired by the restored control of Shiwan Khan. The chance closing of the printing shop had furnished a snag for the master mind who had made allowances for everything else. The thumping elevator in the Hotel Monolith was tuned to the pounding of the presses below Orlio's storeroom!

Cardona had something else to think about at the end of those crowded seconds. The Shadow was struggling with Orlio, trying to capture him alive. Knowing that even The Shadow might find difficulty with the crazed inventor, Cardona made for the little room.

At that moment, a flashlight glimered. It belonged to Commissioner Weston; he turned the beam from the stairway door. Seeing the hanging bulb that Cardona had extinguished, Weston dashed forward and tugged the cord.

The glow showed the window in the little room. Orlio had reached it, was thrusting his scrawny body through. Weston saw Cranston trying to haul him back, with Cardona stumbling up to aid in the process.

Others saw that struggle, too, thanks to Weston's mistake in turning on the light.

Guns barked from outside. Orlio's body writhed, then slid back into the little room. Wheeling away from the sprawling figure of the inventor, The Shadow grabbed Cardona and hurled him to the floor, just as more shots blasted. Then, crouched low, Cranston stooped above Orlio's body.

The gaze that The Shadow turned toward Weston told that the bearded inventor was dead.

Cardona was staring about, totally amazed. He saw neither Cranston nor Weston. He was looking for something that should be in this room, but wasn't.

"The bathysphere!" he gulped. "It's gone!"

From the way his eyes went upward, Cardona apparently expected to see something the size of a young elephant. Blinking, he looked toward the little window and shook his head.

"Ten feet high," muttered Joe, "and ten feet wide. A big ball, made of metal. It couldn't have gone out through there."

Joe was too bewildered to connect the louder thumps that he had heard with the disappearance of the beryllium bathysphere. But The Shadow, looking round and about, saw immediately how the thing had gone.

This little room was an elevator. Someone had pushed an automatic switch, taking it to the ground floor while the fight was going on in the big room. The bathysphere had been rolled out into the rear alley, below the little window.

The elevator had been sent up again, arriving just before Cardona reeled Orlio toward the little room.

"Turn out the light, commissioner," said The Shadow, quietly. "We may see something interesting from the little window."

THE commissioner extinguished the light and crept into the elevator. Lifting his head, he peered out through the window. For a dozen seconds, he studied the darkness below; then he heard a rumble. A truck suddenly shot into sight, to swing for the corner. Street lights showed a bulky, rounded object in the center of the open truck.

The thing was the bathysphere, covered with a large sheet of canvas. Men were crouched beside it, staring back at the building they had left.

Shots rang from below. The men on the truck answered with quick-spurting guns. The truck was around the corner, away from immediate danger, but a cab was taking up the trail. Weston thought that there must be three men in the cab, from the rapidity with which shots issued from it.

"Come on, Cranston!" shouted Weston. "Let's get down there and dash after them!"

Hurrying for the stairs, Weston reached the bottom. He hurdled Truman's body and yelled at a patrol car that was pulling up. Climbing into the rear seat, the commissioner saw another man come dashing from the doorway and yanked him into the car, thinking it was Cranston.

It wasn't until the patrol car was on the move that Weston discovered his companion to be Joe Cardona. By then, they were around the corner and in the middle of another block. Regretfully, the commissioner decided that it was too late to go back and pick up Cranston.

They heard distant shooting, but lost it after several blocks. Realizing that the trail had vanished, Weston decided to return to Orlio's, anyway, and give the general alarm from there. The patrol car whisked them back to their starting point. As they neared the rear alley, they came across two groggy cops.

The officers were the pair who had taken the battering from Orlio's gun. They had come downstairs, and found a rear way through to the alley. Weston gave a rueful grunt.

"That's the route we should have taken," he said to Cardona. "But it's too late. The trail is lost. Go into that printing shop, Cardona, and phone out an alarm. And tell those fools their presses are making so much noise that they didn't know when murder was happening right over their heads!"

Looking for Cranston, the commissioner discovered that his friend was gone. So was the cab that had brought them from the Cobalt Club. Weston hadn't told Cardona that it was Cranston who had rushed to Joe's rescue.

In the first place, Weston thought that Cardona knew who it was. Again, the commissioner did not realize how much Cranston's aid had meant to the ace inspector. Not only had The Shadow handled Orlio in the darkness; Weston had still been on the stairs when it happened.

There was still another reason why the commissioner let the Cranston matter drop. He was somewhat disappointed in his friend. He supposed that Cranston, somewhat overexerted, and perhaps alarmed by gunfire, had taken the cab and returned to the club or gone home.

Weston knew that Cranston enjoyed hunting big game; but elephants and tigers didn't fire back at people, the way crooks did. Cranston couldn't be blamed, if he didn't consider crook hunting as fun.

IT never occurred to Weston that Cranston had started downstairs ahead of him, and had found the

Continued on page 70

Recognition

Practically every city has an annual event at which time the various police and fire employees are given recognition for brave deeds done during the previous year. In many cases these citations are given to the relatives of those who have given their lives in the service; in others, fortunately, to those still living.

It is a fine custom, and it certainly does its share to hold up the reputation of our police and fire employees, and to make them feel that they have a job to which they should be ready and willing to give everything, if necessary. But there is an even finer custom in many cities; one that might well be followed by every municipality in the country. This is the custom of awarding honors to people not on the police force or in the fire department, but who did not hesitate, when the time came, to help these departments perform their work.

A policeman or fireman is paid to do his job. He understands the risks that might come up when he takes his job, and it is therefore his duty to perform his task with bravery when necessary. Such occasions do not come too often, of course, to most of the men. But to people who are engaged in other work; to whom the enforcement of the law, for example, is only something distant as represented by the uniform of an officer, it is something else entirely when they are willing to take the risk of personal injury, possibly even death, in order to help the law.

These people should be rewarded in as fitting a manner as possible. The reward need not be money; after all, that is not what they expect. But they should be given public recognition, so that others who may, at some time or other, have occasion to help the law, will know that a good example has been set for them to follow.

Members of The Shadow Club, all of whom make aid to the law a part of their lives, might do a very fine

Join The Shadow Club!

If you are interested in observing the law, and doing all you can to make others observe it, then it is your duty to join The Shadow Club. It costs you nothing to join; it costs you nothing to remain a member. You can be one of the tens of thousands all over the world who are in this tremendous movement for justice. Sign and mail this pledge and you will become a member:

"I promise to bend all my efforts to give my moral, and when called upon, actual support to uphold law and order and down crooks."

Name ....

Street and No. ....

City and State ....

If you wish to wear the emblem of The Shadow Club—actual size shown, in nickel-silver—inclose ten cents to help pay for part of cost of manufacture and mailing.

The Shadow rubber stamp, an exact duplicate of the emblem, with the word "Member" added, is also available. The price is 10 cents.

thing if they would see to it that their own community would set up some such system of recognition for those who are willing to give their physical assistance to the law. Sometimes a small medal serves the purpose well; other times, different organizations are willing to set up monetary awards; at all times, it should be possible to arrange for a public presentation, with city and police officials presiding, and showing all the people in the community how important it is to give the police your physical as well as moral support at all times.

Coin Racket

Most of us have, at one time or other, felt the urge to make a fortune by finding a coin that, supposedly, is worth thousands of dollars. Hardly a year passes by without someone pointing out that this or that series of bills, for example, lack some point which appears on all other bills; the inference being, of course, that this particular series will become a collectors' item.

Of course, there are many coins worth thousands upon thousands of dollars, and new ones are being discovered right along. But those new ones rarely are found in the exchange of money in business; they are mostly coins of ancient nations, so rare that they bring a big price.

When you hear of some current coin that is supposed to be worth a great deal and start looking for it, remember that thousands of other people probably heard the same thing, and they're all looking for such coins. Very many times there's nothing to the report to begin with.

In the rare-coin field, however, there are pieces worth quite a bit, and as a result there is a specialized criminal field which operates just in this circle. The recent robbery of a number of rare Greek coins from the Pennsylvania Academy of Fine Arts, in Philadelphia, shows that such crimes have not ceased.

Crooks who specialize in that kind of work spend a great deal of time in studying ways and means to commit the thefts. First, they must either do them while the museum is open to the public, which means they must be ready for any occasional intruder; or they must sneak into the museum at night—and museums are pretty well protected by alarm systems. The Philadelphia robbery, for example, was accomplished at noon! About an hour passed between the time the coins were last seen in place and the time their loss was noticed.

CODES

by Henry Lysing

Author of "Secret Writing: How to Code and Decode," "The Cryptogram Book," "Men Against Crime," etc.

CODES, CIPHERS, CRYPTOGRAMS AND SECRET INKS FOR THE EXPERT OR THE NOVICE.

ANSWER TO PROBLEM XX

In case you haven't been able to solve the problem given you in the previous answer, here's the solution:

"There are some people adapted to solving a code like this one. Others like a single substitution. Still others have uncanny ability for solving transpositional codes. Many people, those in the first group, will be very quick at solving this. Those in the second group will get it eventually, but with a little trouble. Well, good luck to all who attempt it!"

How was the solution reached? Simply by the use of three codes, using them one letter after another. The first letter, the code is A for B; the second letter, A for C; the third letter, A for D. Then you repeat on the next three letters, and so on.

SECRET INKS

Here are additional secret inks, which you can add to the list already published in this department in order to keep your record complete.

21. Manganous chloride and manganous sulphate, each make a fine sympathetic ink of their own. The chloride can be seen under the ultraviolet light slightly; the sulphate is quite legible under the same light. The chloride can be developed by means of heat, silver nitrate and light, hydrogen or ammonium sulphide, or iodine fumes. The sulphate will respond to hydrogen or ammonium sulphate.

22. Go to your druggist and ask him to make up some oil of lemon for you. This can be seen by means of ultra-violet light.

23. Ordinary storage-battery acid is a good secret ink. This is nothing more than a weak form of sulphuric acid, and it can be revealed by ultra-violet light, or by heat.

24. A solution of soap and water, mixed to the right consistency, will give you a colorless writing fluid is revealed by means of heat, iodine fumes, or ultra-violet light.

25. A gold-chloride solution (get that from your druggist, too) will respond to heat or ultra-violet light.

26. Hydrochloric acid is still another good ink to use for secret purposes. This can be brought out by means of silver nitrate and light, by heat, and the ultraviolet light.

27. Copper sulphate and copper chloride are both good. The chloride can be brought out by means of heat or ultraviolet light; the sulphate by heat, ultraviolet light, iodine fumes, or hydrogen or ammonium sulphide.

28. Tannin, or tannic acid, as it is most often known, will be only faintly seen under the ultraviolet light, but will come out strongly in response to a ferric-chloride solution.

Continued from page 54

rear door to the alley. It would have surprised the commissioner further, had he known that their cab was the one in the alley.

It had gone there as soon as the shots sounded from that spot, and had picked up Cranston as a passenger.

In fact, the three men in the cab had all been Cranston. The commissioner's estimate was a most complimentary one. Weston had never guessed that Cranston was The Shadow.

Nor had Joe Cardona. Finished with his telephone calls, the police inspector decided to keep certain facts to himself. There would be no use saying that The Shadow had sprung in to the rescue. The commissioner wouldn't believe it.

Funny, thought Joe, the way The Shadow had disappeared so rapidly. Yet Cardona had a good idea where he had gone.

Joe's hunch involved the cab that had pursued the crooks. He figured that The Shadow was in that cab; that he had stayed close enough to keep on the trail of the murderers who had stolen Orlio's bathysphere. It was a double hunch, and both guesses were correct.

Many blocks away, a light truck was dodging in and out of narrow streets, trying to shake off a cab that pursued it. In the truck was a huge hollow sphere. Though made of metal, it was light enough to roll every time the truck swung a corner.

Darkish men who formed the truck's crew were busy keeping the stolen bathysphere underneath its canvas. At the same time, they were taking turns to guard against attacks from the rear.

The cab did not overtake them. Purposely, it lagged behind, to make the Afghans think that it had lost sight of them. So far as the law was concerned, the trail of the truck had vanished. So had the trail of The Shadow.

He was no longer Cranston. The cab in which he rode was Moe's; it han been in readiness outside the Cobalt Club. Having managed to leave the police commissioner at Orlio's, The Shadow had produced his black garb from beneath the rear seat. Wearing cloak and hat, he was ready to leave the cab after the truck stopped and take up the trail on foot.

Vengeance against the Afghans could wait. The Shadow wanted them to reach their appointed destination and deliver Orlio's bathysphere. There was only one place where that valued prize could go: to the headquarters of Shiwan Khan.

Like Maybrell's high-speed fans, Orlio's huge sphere was something that Shiwan Khan wanted; would intrust to no one else. Trail's end promised to bring The Shadow face to face with the unfathomable Shiwan Khan!

CHAPTER XIII.

STRANGE SNARES.

DURING his canny pursuit of the Afghan-manned truck, The Shadow kept on constant lookout for other cars that might close in about him. He knew the ways of Shiwan Khan; how the Oriental crime wizard took tricky precautions to cover every evil deed.

Possessed of limitless wealth, Shiwan Khan could buy all the help he needed. It was possible that he had bands of New York mobsters on the move, to intercept pursuers like The Shadow.

As the chase progressed, however, it became apparent that such was not the case. It followed, therefore, that Shiwan Khan had not expected his Afghans to encounter trouble.

He had probably sent the truck to Orlio's to pick up the bathysphere, whether it was completed or not. Unacquainted with Truman's visit to police headquarters, Shiwan Khan's messengers had arrived when they did through sheer coincidence.

They might have remained befuddled in the alleyway, if the printing presses hadn't started. Regaining contact with Orlio, Shiwan Khan had caught some mental picture of the trouble, and had responded with telepathic orders that caused the professor to behave in murderous fashion.

Through his victim, Shiwan Khan had tipped off his workers to hurry up their job!

The Afghans had killed Orlio and started their getaway. Shiwan Khan had faith in their ability to disappear when hunted. He was expecting overmuch, though, when he wanted them to dispose of a truck along with themselves, to say nothing of Orlio's bathysphere, which was bulky, despite its light weight.

From the way the truck was twisting, The Shadow knew that the Afghans were still trying to dodge away with it. They would have to do something smarter, if they wanted a clear path to Shiwan Khan's headquarters. A crisis was due, and The Shadow scented its immediate arrival when the truck swung from a side street into an alleyway, where its sides almost scraped the walls.

Moe extinguished the cab lights at The Shadow's order. As the cab nosed into the darkened alley, The Shadow saw another peculiarity. The buildings on either side had a connection overhead—a high brick archway, that the bathysphere must have grazed when it went beneath.

The fact betokened previous calculations on the part of Shiwan Khan. Ahead was the truck, halted in the depths of the alley, where Afghans were frantically trying to open an old gate, so that the truck could pass through.

The Shadow's gloved hand clamped Moe's shoulder, an order for the cabby to stop.

It was all too easy, up ahead. If these had been ordinary thugs, The Shadow would have told Moe to speed straight for the truck, while his cloaked chief opened fire. But it was better, in this case, to let the Afghans think that they were safe and untrailed.

They couldn't see the cab, where it had stopped in the shelter of the looming archway. The Shadow decided to fare ahead alone; to spring a surprise attack in the very midst of the darkish murderers. Silently, he swung from the cab.

The Shadow was past the front of the cab when something dropped from the archway. It must have dangled before it fell, for it landed with a very slight *plop*. In fact, the sound did not reach The Shadow, up ahead; but Moe heard it, for the thing struck just outside the window at his elbow.

Peering down into the space beside the cab, Moe made out a roundish shape that he almost mistook for the bathysphere, until the thing stretched toward him.

An instant later, the mammoth hands of a seven-foot giant were stretching into the cab. One came through the front window, the other through the back.

The huge Mongol, Hulagu, was on the job. He had come along with the truck.

So huge were Hulagu's fists, so confident was he of his prowess, that he thought nothing of tackling two adversaries at once, even with The Shadow included in the pair. But his crunching grip found only one: Moe Shrevnitz.

With a twisting wrench, Hulagu swung Moe out from behind the wheel and hauled him through the open window. The one hand that performed the move clutched clear around Moe's neck. The cabby couldn't even gargle a warning to The Shadow.

Moe did the best he could, though, and it was good enough. He kicked hard as he came through the window; his flaying feet rattled a tattoo against the cab door. Hearing the sound, Hulagu uttered a deep but muffled bellow, just as The Shadow lunged around from in front of the cab.

A spotlight gleamed from the truck. Its glare showed The Shadow, but Hulagu and Moe were out of sight. In a moment, The Shadow would also have been gone, if Hulagu hadn't found a way to stop him.

The Shadow was aiming an automatic, holding his fire temporarily, to avoid hitting Moe. Hulagu decided that if The Shadow wanted Moe, he could have him.

Crumpling the helpless cabby, the giant hurled him like a bag of straw, straight for the black-cloaked rescuer. The Shadow hadn't a chance to side-step that human missile. Nor did he attempt to do so. He wanted to break the force of the hurl, on Moe's account.

Though he spied Hulagu and noted the man's great bulk, The Shadow underestimated the force of the fling. Hulagu had hurled Moe with about three times the power that The Shadow considered humanly possible.

Hitting his chief, Moe's figure lifted The Shadow clear from the ground and landed him face up in the alley. Moe himself rolled a dozen feet beyond, but the force of his smash was broken.

Guns spat from the truck. The shots were wide. Indifferent gunners, the Afghans had settled Orlio with a volley, when he was framed in a lighted window. But it was a different matter, finding the blackened shape of The Shadow as it lay below the fringe of the spotlight's glow.

The Shadow told them where he was, but he sent the message with bullets. Half groggy, he had his head tilted back, his arms lying beyond. But even in a dazed condition, The Shadow could not ignore so obvious a target as the big, shining eye of a spotlight. As for shooting overhead, that was a method in which he was long trained.

When The Shadow shattered the spotlight with his third bullet, he settled the Afghan problem. Fearing for their own hides, worried lest shots would dent the valued bathysphere, the tribesmen did not linger. The gate was open; the truck roared through.

Hulagu was left alone to finish off The Shadow.

His catlike approach a contrast to his elephantine size, the Mongol crept toward where The Shadow lay. Guns silenced, The Shadow, too, was on the move, rising to hands and knees. He shook his head a few times to relieve the daze, then turned to listen for Hulagu. He sensed the Mongol's approach and lunged.

It was too late. Though gloved fingers were on gun triggers, shots were rendered futile when Hulagu's great paws drove The Shadow's fists straight upward. Bullets nicked the bricks on the archway, nothing more. Then Hulagu was handling The Shadow as a St. Bernard would treat a poodle.

CONTORTED in the giant's tremendous arms, The Shadow felt Hulagu's fingers pluck away the guns. The Mongol had a grip like a python; wrenching out of it was impossible. His only course was to clutch at his foe's throat—a remarkable achievement in itself, considering the way The Shadow's arms were skewed about.

The counterattack surprised Hulagu, especially when he found he could not shake it away. Though he twisted The Shadow right and left, and nearly managed to tie him in a knot, those fingers wouldn't leave Hulagu's windpipe.

The Shadow's grip was his only chance for life. He clung to it, despite the torture that Hulagu provided.

At last, the giant had enough of the choking tactics. He clamped his own hands upon The Shadow's, with a grip that threatened to break the cloaked fighter's wrists and render his clutch useless.

As Hulagu relaxed his fists to get a firmer hold, The Shadow saw a chance to get away. Jamming his feet against Hulagu's knees, he made a backward flip, clear from the Mongol's grasp.

Hulagu was pouncing after him, pawing the darkness. The Shadow managed to stumble away from him; coming across a gun, he picked it up and fired its remaining shots. The cartridges did no more harm than blanks.

The Shadow hadn't an idea where Hulagu was. The shots gave him respite, though, for Hulagu, knowing that bullets could bite, made a distant scramble into the depths of the alley.

Someone was stirring close by. It was Moe Shrevnitz. He was whispering hoarsely that he had found a gun, which happened to be The Shadow's second weapon. Moe heard a sibilant laugh, weary of tone and forced. The Shadow had reached the cab and was summoning the driver.

Hopping to the wheel, Moe heard The Shadow mutter something about resuming the chase. Rather dazed himself, Moe thought that his chief was all right.

Tossing the gun into the back seat, Moe shoved the cab into reverse, backed it unsteadily out beneath the arch. At the street, he turned on the headlights.

The glare showed the alley. From the depths, Moe saw Hulagu hurtling forward. So immense did the giant seem, that Moe actually thought his forward crouch was necessary to get him underneath the arch. Moe gargled a warning, but The Shadow did not heed it. No shots came from the rear seat.

Remembering the former order, realizing that he couldn't battle Hulagu alone, Moe gave the cab a last jab backward, swung the wheel and shoved into low gear. He heard the door slam just before he started and thought that The Shadow had pulled it shut from within.

Then the cab was away, just as Hulagu lunged with both arms for the open window. The Mongol's previous tactics did not work. The whip of the cab was too speedy, too sudden. The windows caught Hulagu's arms and handled them like levers.

Spun away from the cab, the giant went whirling like a human windmill, across the curb.

He didn't give up the chase. Wrenching a chunk of broken stone from a house step, Hulagu hurled it as he would a pebble. The heavy missile caved in the back of the cab.

Hopping along the street with great strides, Hulagu snatched up an ash can and tossed it forty feet. It landed, clattering, just behind the cab.

Rounding one corner, Moe swung for the next one. He caught a last glance of Hulagu, a block behind, tearing a fire plug from its moorings. Hulagu didn't have a chance to use his new ammunition, for Moe sped out of sight.

Valiantly, the cabby tried to pick up the truck's trail, not realizing how good a start the Afghans had gained. Moe threaded through scores of blocks, scarcely seeing red lights when he ran right past them. Sagging at last through sheer exhaustion, Moe stopped the cab in the middle of a block.

Dizzy all during the drive, he hadn't an idea where he was, nor where he had come from. Everything was chaos in Moe's mind, except the fact that The Shadow was a passenger. Staggering out from behind the wheel, Moe tottered to the rear door and yanked it open.

The sallow light of a street lamp showed only a loose gun lying on the floor. There was no sign of a passenger, though the whole rear seat was revealed.

Moe had made that frantic trip without The Shadow!

CHAPTER XIV.

THE MISSING SHADOW.

BACK in the blackened alley, a figure was crawling painfully beneath the archway. It was The Shadow, and his creeping progress was actually a limp. Racked by the wrenching hands of Hulagu, his limbs seemed out of socket, his ribs constricted so tightly that he could hardly breathe.

The Shadow's condition explained why he was where he was. He had actually gotten into the cab, but had lacked the strength to stay there. Moe's quick-jolted reverse had tumbled The Shadow through the unlatched door, just before the cab had pulled away past the mouth of the alley.

Slamming automatically with the cab's motion, the door had given Moe the impression that his chief was with him. Hulagu had held to the same idea when he chased the cab. Pursuit failing, the disgruntled Mongol had returned to Shiwan Khan without taking a route past the alley.

Those circumstances were unknown to The Shadow. Anticipating Hulagu's return, he was trying to get to some place where he could barricade himself. At intervals, The Shadow fumbled with the gun he carried, hoping to reload it. His hands were too numb to do the work.

Reaching the gate, The Shadow found it open and crawled into the space beyond. It was a little court, wide enough for a truck to pass, with street lights shining ahead. Avoiding the glow, The Shadow found an old door in the wall. Managing to thrust his gun beneath his cloak, he gripped the doorknob with both hands and squeezed.

The door gave. Half crawling, half rolling, The Shadow entered in a little room, found a table in the darkness and dragged himself to his feet. As he came entirely clear of the door, it went shut on a spring hinge. As the door latch clicked, the room flooded with light.

Cobwebbed walls, dust on the plain furnishings, indicated that the room was a janitor's office, fallen into disuse. Its self-closing door, with the automatic light switch, proved that it had been converted to some other purpose.

Only one person could have so devised it: Shiwan Khan. This room was the superplotter's trap for The Shadow, in case Hulagu failed. Shiwan Khan had taken the most likely place where The Shadow, if crippled, would seek refuge, and had turned it into a potential murder chamber.

He had supplied the murderer, of course. Shiwan Khan was a stickler when it came to details.

Facing The Shadow was a gorgeous girl, shapely and alluring in the scanty Persian costume that she wore. Her beauty, however, did not intrigue The Shadow. He could reasonably have regarded the girl as hideous, for she had come here to be The Shadow's executioner.

In her hand the girl held a silver-barreled pistol, which glimmered dully, compared to the jeweled girdle which encircled her slender body. Gold sash, purple pantaloons and curled slippers completed her Oriental costume.

She could well have been a Persian princess, the product of an age when savage motives could inspire the most civilized of ladies. For her eyes were fixed upon The Shadow with a hateful glare. Her lips were set with a tight determination, matched by the tension of her slender trigger finger.

She was waiting, ready to fire the fatal shot the moment that The Shadow moved. Like a hunter trapped by a ferocious jungle cat, her cloaked prey realized that a gesture would mean death. This girl was under the control of Shiwan Khan; set, like a human mechanism, to act with clockwork precision when the cue arrived.

His muscles weakening, The Shadow knew that he would soon waver, and thereby give his own death signal. Keeping his hands pressed wide against the wall, he tried to prevent his coming sway. His thoughts came clearer as the moments passed. For the first time, he actually studied the girl.

She was not a Persian. Her face looked darkish, because her back was toward the light. But her shoulders and her arms were whiter; so were the hips that showed above the fringe of the loosely tied gold sash.

His face obscured by the shading brim of his slouch hat, The Shadow showed no visible motion of his lips as he pronounced the name:

"Marjorie Cragg!"

A GLEAM came to the girl's fixed eyes, a quiver rippled her statuesque body. It was as if she had heard a voice from far away—a ghostly tone creeping out of the forgotten past.

Again, The Shadow spoke the name. His tone was louder, almost sinister. It had the touch of a rebuke. The girl's finger relaxed; her lips opened as she tried to speak.

"You are Marjorie Cragg—"

"Yes!" The girl trembled violently. "Yes! I am!" She paused, her shudders indicating her effort to discard an acquired personality. "I am—"

At that moment, The Shadow's strength failed him. His hands slipped from the wall. His sagging motion jolted the girl mentally back into the character of Princess Dunyazad. Her hand tightened; her finger found the trigger and pressed it.

Had she been wholly Princess Dunyazad, Marjorie would not have heard the gunshot that echoed through the room. When she came here, she had been totally under the influence of Shiwan Khan. The Shadow had broken the mental shackles that held her, except for the one cue that forced her action.

The shot delivered, Marjorie was her own self again. The roar of the pistol completed the work that The Shadow had commenced.

A very horrified girl was staring at a smoking gun that lay loosely in her trembling hand. The silver pistol clattered to the floor, as Marjorie's eyes turned toward the wall and saw a huddled, motionless figure in black.

"I killed him!"

It was Marjorie's voice; not the forced tone of Princess Dunyazad. Stumbling forward, Marjorie sank to her knees beside the victim. As she sobbed, tears streaked her face. The blur that came to her eyes made the whole scene shimmer. She thought that the black-cloaked figure had moved. Marjorie gave a joyous gasp.

At that moment, The Shadow did move. He propped himself upon one elbow and managed to speak. He wanted to learn Marjorie's story, to learn the clues that she could give. But the effort was too much. The Shadow sagged.

By then, the girl had spied a bullet hole in the wall. Hazily remembering her action with the gun, she realized that The Shadow had collapsed before she fired. He had spoken to her then, had called her by name. That was why she had delayed her shot. The Shadow had dropped below the gun level when Marjorie pressed the trigger.

The shock of the experience helped her. She was able to recall bits of the false part that she had played, as Princess Dunyazad. Eyes half shut, Marjorie could picture the sallow face of Shah Nikwan floating in front of her. She shuddered, wondering why she had not detested the man.

Marjorie's thoughts went to The Shadow.

She knew that Shah Nikwan—if such his name chanced to be—had plotted the death of The Shadow. She was to have been the instrument in murder. As amends, she must find some way to get The Shadow to safety.

Marjorie couldn't remember how she had reached this room. She looked at the door that The Shadow had entered, then shook her head. Across the room, she saw another door. It was the right one.

When she helped The Shadow to his feet, he responded. He still had strength, but he needed guidance. She piloted him out through the far door; it swung shut after they passed, and from the *click* that sounded Marjorie knew that the lights had been automatically extinguished.

They were in a little courtyard, similar to the one from which The Shadow had entered.

Letting The Shadow lean against a wall, Marjorie stepped slowly toward the street. She felt terribly conspicuous in her featherweight costume, for she could feel the cool night breeze sweeping from her shoulders to her hips. Marjorie paused, clenching her hands tightly.

She found that she was carrying the pistol. She had picked it up, probably inspired by the fact that The Shadow clutched a gun. Tucking the silvery weapon into her sash, Marjorie took a few steps forward.

She drew back as a car wheeled toward her. It swung into the alley; pressed against the wall, she hoped she would not be seen. Then came the driver's voice, in a peculiarly foreign accent:

"I have come for you, princess!"

MARJORIE stepped toward the car, wondering what to do next. She repressed a scream as a hand clutched her arm. She realized almost instantly that the hand was The Shadow's.

As she opened the door, he released his grip and eased into the rear of the car, where he settled silently upon the floor.

As soon as Marjorie was in the car, it backed from the little court. After a trip of about a dozen blocks, the car stopped by an entrance to a tall building.

Marjorie watched the driver; he did not budge. She opened the door felt The Shadow's shoulder graze her ankles as he worked out into the darkness. Marjorie followed. The car pulled away.

The outside air had strengthened The Shadow. Marjorie helped him into the building; an elevator was waiting. Deciding that she was to take it, she guided The Shadow along. At moments she hesitated, wondering if the course would be the best one. It was The Shadow who ended her hesitation. He kept urging her forward.

Starting when Marjorie closed the door, the elevator carried its passengers up to a high floor. The door slid open; Marjorie saw a deserted corridor and recognized it as something in a dream, particularly because of the open door that waited at the other end.

Supporting The Shadow as he stepped along, Marjorie reached the open room and closed the door behind them.

She knew this room.

It was where she had lived for days as Princess Dunyazad, with a maid named Hayat, who, fortunately, was absent. Next to it was another room, an ordinary hotel room, that was not furnished in this lavish Persian style. She urged The Shadow toward the connecting door. It opened.

The room beyond was black. The Shadow seemed to welcome it. He paused, though, steadying himself against the doorway. In weary tone, he asked:

"What place is this?"

"The Hotel Monolith," replied Marjorie. "But a dangerous man controls everyone who lives here. He calls himself Shah Nikwan."

The Shadow responded with a whispered laugh.

"His name," he told Marjorie, "is Shiwan Khan! Be careful what you say to him. If you meet with danger, summon me."

The door closed, but Marjorie could see The Shadow waver as he shut it. Alone in the Persian room, she was tempted to knock and learn if he needed aid. With the pistol in one hand, she raised the other. Hesitating before she rapped, she was startled to hear knockings!

But not from the connecting door. Marjorie suddenly realized that the raps were from the hallway. Fearfully, she crossed the room; gathering nerve, she pulled the door wide.

On the threshold stood the very man she did not want to meet. She had hoped that it was Hayat who had knocked, but luck was against her. Marjorie Cragg was faced by Shiwan Khan!

CHAPTER XV.

INTO THE PAST.

Of all the times when the pretended Shah Nikwan had called on the so-called Princess Dunyazad, this was the only one when his keen vision was lacking. The girl knew that he was Shiwan Khan; it was logical that he should have recognized her as the old Marjorie Cragg.

Instead, he missed the self-betraying expression on Marjorie's face. Believing her still to be a dupe, Shiwan Khan grabbed the first thing that caught his eye: the pistol that Marjorie carried. Cracking it open, he saw that its single cartridge had been fired.

"You killed him!" exclaimed Shiwan Khan, gleefully. "You have done well, Princess Dunyazad!"

By the time the compliment was spoken, Marjorie had gained a sham composure. Spared the ordeal of meeting Shiwan Khan's gaze, she rallied to her part.

"I obeyed your order," said Marjorie, forcing her tone. "I shall always obey your orders, Shah Nikwan."

Their eyes met. Marjorie was steeled for it. The greenish gleam in Shiwan Khan's eyes was something monstrous, but it expressed elation. He was too enthused to indulge in his usual sharp scrutiny, whereby he studied the innermost thoughts of his dupes.

"I leave you, princess," stated Shiwan Khan, with a bow. "There are matters to which I must attend. After that, I shall return."

Bowing in the smug manner of Shah Nikwan, the master plotter left, taking the pistol with him. Returning to his own apartments, he gave orders to his Afghan servants, then entered a room that was draped with golden curtains.

Hulagu was there, looking very glum. Shiwan Khan addressed the huge Mongol, with a tinkly chuckle.

"You were wrong, Hulagu," said Shiwan Khan. "The Shadow did *not* escape in the cab. He tricked you and remained in the alley. I was sure that he must have, from your description of the way you treated him."

A furious glare swept over Hulagu's face. He wished that he had treated The Shadow even worse.

"It worked as I planned," continued Shiwan Khan, displaying the pistol. He gave his hand a graceful gesture, as if in a farewell. "We have solved the problem of The Shadow."

He stepped to a corner, raised a curtain, and drew out two oblong boxes of fine mahogany. Each box measured about a foot across, and they matched perfectly. Shiwan Khan set them on a taboret.

"These are needed for tomorrow," declared Shiwan Khan, "after we have dealt with Felber as we did with Maybrell and Orlio. Our real task is just ahead, Hulagu. I shall need you."

The Mongol's glum expression faded.

"You will share my glory," continued Shiwan Khan. "The others, they are nothing. But you are my right arm, Hulagu, and my sword, as well. It is the sword that strikes down, as you struck down our enemy, The Shadow.

"After the sword, the poniard. It takes the dagger, Hulagu, to end the life of the vanquished foe. Princess Dunyazad was the dagger; that was all. We shall let them find The Shadow, in the death room where he lies. They will not discover him until long after we have left here, Hulagu."

For the first time, Hulagu spoke,

in his ugly, muffled tone. His glary eyes showed malice, as he asked:

"We shall take the princess with us?"

"No, Hulagu," replied Shiwan Khan. "We shall let them find her, also. Dead, by her own hand! But not until after we have completed our real task. Until then, I still may need her."

UNAWARE of Shiwan Khan's new plans concerning her, Marjorie was pacing the Persian room, stopping at the windows, where she gazed at the lights of the city. For the first time since she had become Princess Dunyazad, she wanted freedom.

All that kept her here was her hope that she could protect The Shadow; but with the passing minutes, Marjorie realized that she could do but little, if a crisis came. It would be better, she finally decided, if she attempted an escape.

If she succeeded in leaving the hotel, she could bring aid. If not, her attempt would at least be helpful to The Shadow. It might give him a chance to stagger to freedom, while Shiwan Khan's men were capturing her.

She couldn't leave in this Oriental garb. Her plan was to find a way to the floor below, then go down through the hotel, instead of by Shiwan Khan's private route. Fortunately, one of her suitcases was in the closet of this room; she had seen Hayat put it there.

It was an unlocked suitcase. They had taken the keys to all the others. Luckily, it contained the clothes that Marjorie needed. She stepped to the closet to get it; paused there, listening to sounds beyond the outer door, which was close by.

Men were in the corridor, moving something. At times, the sounds came closer; at last they dwindled. Marjorie decided to hurry. Eagerly, she removed her Persian trappings, which did not take her long.

She felt a surge of freedom, the moment she was relieved of those garments. Pushing them aside, she tugged the closet door. She found the suitcase and opened it.

The suitcase was quite empty.

Kneeling beside the closet door, Marjorie realized how she had been tricked. This was Shiwan Khan's way of telling her that escape was useless. Listlessly, she reached for the Persian costume. The mere touch of the garments harrowed her. Shrinking away, she stared at the jeweled decorations.

Emeralds predominated. They reminded her of the green, evil eyes that belonged to Shiwan Khan.

Marjorie realized her full plight, designed by Shiwan Khan. As herself, she would never have courage to put on those flimsy garments, once she had discarded them, for they belonged to Princess Dunyazad.

When Shiwan Khan returned, Marjorie could not answer his rap. He would send Hayat in, to find her in the midst of scattered proof that she was no longer a dupe.

That learned, Shiwan Khan would doubt everything, including the supposed death of The Shadow. Steeling herself, Marjorie tried to gather up the exotic costume. Her will power weakened instantly. It would be impossible to resume that hated garb.

Unless she could again believe that she was Princess Dunyazad! The inspiration horrified her; nevertheless, it was the only way. The opportunity was present, for the aeolian harp lay beside the window, which was closed.

She had nerve enough to open the window; rising, she stepped toward it and raised the sash. A breeze stirred the harp strings.

There was rapture in the rising rhythm of those chords. They drifted dreamily; fading, they produced a delicate harmony. Turning from the window, Marjorie gathered up the Oriental costume.

Never had silk seemed so lovely, jewels so brilliant. Adorning herself with the splendid trappings, Marjorie sought the divan and reached for the narghile.

She was smoking the pipe contentedly when Shiwan Khan rapped at the door. It was Princess Dunyazad who graciously requested Shah Nikwan to enter. She spoke in the language of Persia.

A SLITTED smile was present on the face of Shiwan Khan when he made his entering bow. He was pleased when he heard the strains of the wind harp. He thought the playing of that instrument to be the idea of Princess Dunyazad; not of Marjorie Cragg.

No wonder. It was Princess Dunyazad who returned his smile. Marjorie's brief respite from that strange part was ended. Voluntarily, she had returned to the servitude of Shiwan Khan. Her memory of a brief escape from mental bondage had effaced itself.

Shiwan Khan had brought the silver pistol. He showed the princess that the gun was loaded, then gave her the weapon. Meeting the girl's fixed, wide-eyed gaze, Shiwan Khan spoke slow, emphatic words:

"Keep this pistol always. The time shall come when you will need it. Then you will respond to my command. Remember!"

Marjorie did not nod. Her eyes retained their hypnotic stare as she repeated:

"Remember. Yes, Shah Nikwan I shall remember."

The interview completed, Shiwan Khan departed, still wearing his pleased smile. He had accomplished exactly what he wanted, so he believed. He expressed that opinion to Hulagu, who awaited him in the golden room.

"The Persians," affirmed Shiwan Khan, "have a civilization which is merely skin-deep. In it, the barbarian, even the savage, sleeps but lightly beneath the cloak of culture. I am glad"—he chuckled dryly—"that Princess Dunyazad is a Persian. It will serve well in the future."

It happened that Princess Dunyazad was thinking of the past. Alone in the sumptuous room that fitted her assumed character, Marjorie had risen from the divan. Holding the pistol, she spoke the words:

"I shall remember."

Stepping to the connecting door, the girl opened it. Every vestige of Marjorie's true personality had vanished. She was every inch barbarian—a savage princess bent upon redeeming a forgotten cause.

Against the glow from the room behind her, she was a revelation of shapely beauty, her clinging raiment a mere haze that intensified her alluring figure. Soft was the voice of Princess Dunyazad. Her eyes sparkled as she turned them toward the light; her lips wore a sweet smile above her uplifted chin.

Her left hand was resting against the doorway. Her right pressed lightly toward her graceful hip. Partly hidden, that hand was slipping downward, carrying her sash with it. A totally unconscious action, so it seemed, until the loosened sash fell away.

That moment was designed. The girl whirled in from the doorway, swinging to the left, where her toying fingers had found the light switch. Her right hand swept into sight with the silver-barreled pistol, which had been hidden in the sash.

The entire room was within the view of her glaring eyes, with the pistol muzzle following her gaze. No victim, lulled by the sight of unfolding loveliness, could possibly have anticipated that change from beauty to savagery.

Doom was due, except for an existing victim. Halting her whirl, the murderous girl stood rigid. The flare faded from her eyes; their gaze became fixed. Lips that spread for a triumphant snarl became straight and expressionless.

This wasn't the scene that Princess Dunyazad expected. Instead of a hotel room cluttered with luggage, the place was a Persian boudoir fitted with rugs and cushions. Marjorie's trunk and suitcases were gone, so was the wearied, black-cloaked fighter that the girl had hidden here.

SHIWAN KHAN had ordered his Afghans to change the decorations in this room. They were the men that Marjorie had heard moving about, providing new furnishings to enlarge the suite assigned to Princess Dunyazad.

It was a reward from Shah Nikwan, a token of pretended esteem because Princess Dunyazad had settled the problem of The Shadow.

By that action, Shiwan Khan had further preserved the life of the foe that he already regarded dead. Forced to some move by the arrival of the Afghans, The Shadow had somehow managed to disappear along with the furniture and luggage.

In the newly arranged room, there wasn't a spot where The Shadow might lie hidden. No crannies of any size existed; none even large enough to suit a creature so small as the Persian cat that came strolling in from the other room, to rub itself against Marjorie's silk-draped ankles.

Not being herself, Marjorie was unamazed. As Princess Dunyazad, she picked up the fallen sash, tied it about her smooth waist and tucked the unfired pistol in its folds.

Again, The Shadow had melted away in darkness, to avoid a seeking killer inspired by Shiwan Khan!

CHAPTER XVI.

PATHS UNSHADOWED.

THE tragic death of a second crazed inventor was meat for the New York *Classic*. Added to the story was the angle of positive crime. Maybrell's death could still be classed as accident or suicide. Not Orlio's, however.

Perhaps chance had brought those shots from the alley. The police were hunting up the pickets who had fled from the printing shop, arresting them on a murder charge. Most of them had been gathered in, all swearing innocence.

In handling the story for the *Classic*, Clyde Burke supplied the gravy that went with the meat. He poured it on thick. Murder or what not, Richard Orlio had brought it on himself, by his madness. The claim that an epidemic of deranged genius had struck New York was something that people could actually believe.

The *Classic* had published descriptions of Maybrell's high-speed fans, with statements from experts, who could see no purpose in such lightweight devices. But Orlio's bathysphere offered greater scope.

A sketch of it appeared with detailed diagrams, with a caption en-

Continued on page 84

KANE RICHMOND BARBARA REED
A MONOGRAM PICTURE

It's going to be a **SHADOW CHRISTMAS**

● For Christmas all the stores will be featuring The Shadow merchandise pictured here. If you can't buy it at your local store, send direct to us the amount which each item costs and we will have it mailed to you without additional charge.

This year you can wear The Shadow Hat and Cape and melt into the shadows. You can hide your face in The Shadow Mask. You can disguise yourself as a Chinaman, porter, or ranger. Write letters in invisible ink or in code on your own Shadow Stationery. Strap on The Shadow Official Holster Set, use the keen Shadow Tectolite, which you can hide in the palm of your hand. Write in the dark with the Pencil Lite just as The Shadow makes his notes. And play The Shadow Game—the finest fun.

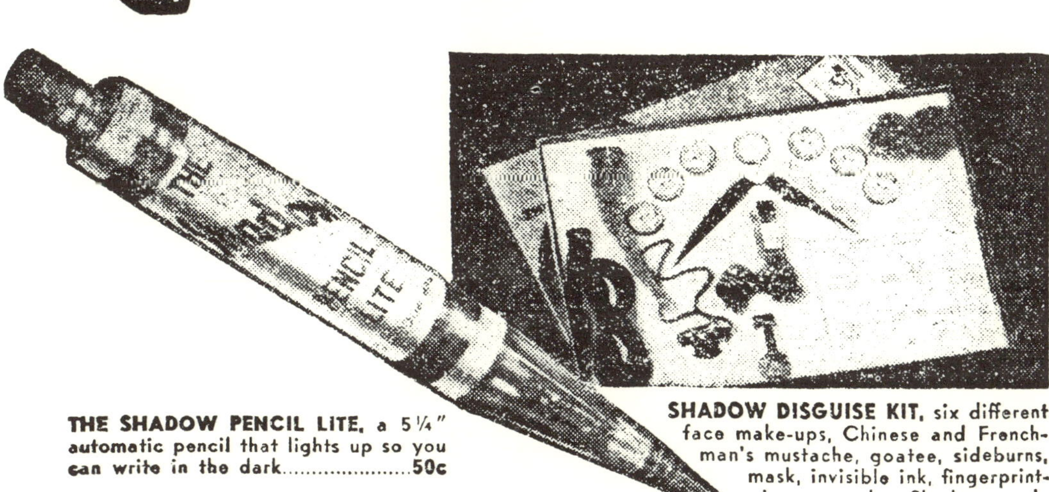

THE SHADOW PENCIL LITE, a 5¼" automatic pencil that lights up so you can write in the dark......................50c

SHADOW DISGUISE KIT, six different face make-ups, Chinese and Frenchman's mustache, goatee, sideburns, mask, invisible ink, fingerprinting records, Shadow code book............$1

Continued from page 81

titling the bathysphere as "Orlio's Folly." A beryllium globe, light enough to float on the ocean like a rubber ball, could not feasibly be used for exploring the ocean's depths. Even if it were hung with tons of weights, its thin shell couldn't stand the strain when submerged.

More conservative newspapers were advancing the theory that Orlio was experimenting with the tensile strength of beryllium; that he wanted to prove the wonder metal could resist the pressure of deep-sea journeys. Such a theory did not have a chance. The *Classic* spiked it in a later edition.

Why, the *Classic* asked, had Orlio constructed a complete bathysphere, equipped to carry human observers, if he merely wanted to test the metal used? The bathysphere had a watertight door and windows, according to Cardona's firsthand description of the thing.

Who had stolen the bathysphere?

Someone as crazy as Orlio, according to the article that Clyde Burke wrote. Another mad inventor was probably in the picture. The epidemic was spreading to the point where crazed men were declaring open season on their fellows.

No one could dispute that point; not with the slender evidence at hand. It actually was the best portion of Clyde's story, for it served a hidden purpose.

It kept the trail away from Shiwan Khan.

Until they heard from The Shadow, Clyde and other agents were doing their utmost to stifle any talk of a mysterious figure from the Orient, who might have uses for such crackpot inventions as Maybrell's electric fans and Orlio's bathysphere.

The agents knew that their chief was missing. His life, if he still possessed it, might depend upon their ability to maintain the existing situation.

Yet the agents could not remain idle. They knew that other lives were threatened. Unable to link Marjorie with either Maybrell or Orlio, they came to the correct conclusion that another inventor must be somewhere in the picture; that his life, like the girl's, might soon be terminated by Shiwan Khan.

It was their hope to find the trail, and with it gain some way to reach The Shadow, the only person who could hope to fully block the schemes of Shiwan Khan.

APPOINTING himself as a committee of one, Rutledge Mann went to the Cobalt Club and sought out Commissioner Weston. They had met before; Weston knew that Mann was Cranston's broker.

When Mann stated that Cranston had not called at the office to complete the purchase of some important bonds, Weston began to wonder what had happened to his friend.

The commissioner took Mann into his confidence, was telling him all angles of the Orlio case, when another visitor was announced. The arrival was Vic Marquette, a Federal agent, in from Washington.

A mustached man with an expressionless face, Marquette was taciturn, until he learned that Weston and Mann were talking about Cranston. Then Vic spoke his piece.

"Cranston is the man I've come to see," said the Fed. "I'm here at the suggestion of Senator Releston. Some time ago, Cranston helped us prevent the theft of some important military secrets. We may need his services again."

Weston ventured a question. "Do you mean that Maybrell and Orlio were working upon inventions that could be used in warfare?"

Marquette shook his head.

"Not a chance!" he said. "I've talked with experts who say that both those guys were crazy. What bothers us"—he was drawing a copy of the *Classic* from his pocket—"is this epidemic stuff. We're afraid it may be real, wild though it seems. We're worried about certain persons who have invented things of actual value.

"Suppose that one of them should go nuts"—from Vic's tone, it was apparent that he was thinking of a particular person—"and let out something that nobody is supposed to know. We'd have real trouble on our hands. Trouble so bad that we might not be able to rectify it."

Sitting back, Vic pondered. He hadn't stated the most important reason why he wanted to talk to Lamont Cranston. It was Vic's intention to enlist The Shadow's aid in a most important matter. He knew, from past experience, that Cranston was one man who had some way of communicating with The Shadow.

"I don't know where you can find Cranston," declared Weston, soberly. "He was with me last night, at Orlio's, and he disappeared immediately after the trouble there. From what Mann tells me, it appears that Cranston may be missing. Mann"—Weston gestured toward his companion—"happens to be Cranston's broker."

There was silence, while Vic's eyes showed prolonged meditation. Suddenly, the Fed swung to Mann with the question:

"Do you know a chap named Harry Vincent?"

Mann nodded. Harry was one of The Shadow's agents; the oldest, in point of service. Only Burbank, the contact man who played a passive part, had been with The Shadow longer than Harry.

"Where can I reach Vincent?"

"At the Hotel Metrolite," replied Mann, in answer to Vic's question. "I am quite positive that he is in town."

VIC MARQUETTE made an abrupt departure. Rutledge Mann knew why. The Fed had learned one fact that very few people knew: namely, that Harry Vincent worked for The Shadow. Often, Vic's path had crossed Harry's, in cases where The Shadow had co-operated with the law.

Unable to find Cranston, Marquette had decided to see Vincent, the only other person—so far as Vic knew—who might be able to reach The Shadow.

Rather impressed with Mann, Commissioner Weston invited the investment broker to have dinner with him. They had just finished their meal, when Joe Cardona appeared, accompanied by a serious-faced man who wore large gold-rimmed spectacles. Mann started to take his leave, but Weston told him to stay.

Cardona introduced the serious man as Dr. Philip Buffton, a nerve specialist. He let the physician do the talking.

"I have come in reference to the subject of crazed inventors," declared Buffton, importantly. "All talk of an epidemic is tommyrot, but very regrettable. It is quite possible that it may influence persons already on the border line of insanity, should they hear of it."

"Do you know of any such cases?" asked Weston, quickly. "We are anxious to learn of them."

"I have heard of one," declared Buffton. "A young man named Howard Felber is working on some sort of automotive device that has perplexed his associates. A while ago, they were worried over his mental condition."

"Do you know where Felber is?"

Dr. Buffton nodded.

"We shall have to stop at my office," he stated. "My secretary has left, and the address is in my files. I didn't happen to think of Felber's case until I was driving downtown. The newsboys were shouting about another mad inventor. Their cries stimulated my recollection."

The commissioner decided that they would go to Buffton's office. He asked Mann to go along; the broker hesitated, not wanting to overdo his new acquaintance with Weston. Then Buffton made a statement that settled the matter. After hearing it, Mann had to go along.

"According to the last report," stated the physician, "Felber had improved. But that was before this so-called epidemic started. Since then, it has been impossible for me to learn more about the case, because the person who informed me has gone away.

"I preferred to wait until she returned, as she did not tell Felber that she was consulting me. But she has gone on a three-week cruise, and the time may be too long. Perhaps you have heard of the young lady in question. She is a radio singer—Miss Marjorie Cragg."

The Shadow's newspaper campaign had worked. Through Clyde's articles in the *Classic,* the needed link had turned up. Crime's coming threat was known in advance.

But The Shadow was not here to learn it!

The thought distressed Rutledge Mann, but it steeled him to a purpose. He knew that he would have to do what little he could, to make up for The Shadow's absence. How soon the stroke would come, Mann could not guess.

Only one person could have told him.

By a window, high in the Hotel Monolith, Shiwan Khan was engaged in deep concentration. His green eyes dilated as an elevated train rumbled below. Rising, he let his hideous features relax into calmness, then summoned Hulagu.

"All is ready," announced Shiwan Khan. "Send out the Afghans, Hulagu; then remain here. Do not disturb me, as further concentration will be needed at important moments. I shall continue to use the thought control that I have so perfectly established."

Relaxed by the window, Shiwan Khan eyed a squatty, tight-closed building far below. It was the sealed garage where the Afghans kept the hired truck. Even Shiwan Khan could not spy the creeping dark men as they approached the place, but he saw the truck wheel from the squatty building and roll away beneath the elevated structure.

Another expedition was on its way; in this, the third of his peculiar enterprises, Shiwan Khan expected no opposition. If his Afghans met with a challenging figure in black, they would know it for a ghost and nothing more.

The ghost of The Shadow!

CHAPTER XVII.

SCHEME OF DEATH.

Howard Felber was standing beside the chassis of the crazy-looking motor vehicle that still occupied the center of his garage workshop.

He was more haggard than ever; his clothes, hands and hair were a mass of grime. So was the light-hued beard that sprouted from his face. Those grease-streaked whiskers were nearing full-fledged proportions.

Casey and Jim were watching him from a corner beside a junk pile. Their faces were beard-stubbly, too. Their taut nerves had reached the limit of endurance. Felber's constant mutters drowned the whispers of the mechanics. Between them, Casey and Jim were agreeing that it was time the farce should end.

Creeping from the corner, they approached Felber, hoping to trap him unawares. The thing that stopped them was the rumble of a passing el train. During that roar, Felber clapped both greasy hands to his forehead and stared upward with wild, bulging eyes.

"Hold it," advised Jim, gripping Casey's arm. "He's having another fit. Better wait until he calms."

With that, a strange thing happened. Felber drew both grimy hands down across his face. Pressure seemed to ease his eyes back into their sockets. His hands wiped the haggard expression from his features. Drawn past his chin, those hands dropped to his sides as Felber's whole frame relaxed.

Turning about, Felber saw Jim and Casey, gave them a mild smile through his beard. He greeted them as if seeing them for the first time after a long absence.

"Hello, boys!"

The mechanics gawked. Felber's return to normalcy surprised them more than his strange actions. They had become used to his crazed behavior.

"Something went wrong with me," declared Felber, stroking his forehead. "But I've snapped out of it. Say"—he was rubbing his whiskers, dubiously—"I must have been goofy for a long while, wasn't I?"

It was Jim who gulped the answer: "A couple of weeks, boss."

Felber shook his head. He gazed curiously at the chassis, with its four wheels askew at different angles. Half laughing, he asked:

"Was this thing *my* idea?"

The mechanics nodded. Apparently, Felber had no recollection of his invention. Together, Jim and Casey explained the intricacies of the four-wheel drive, with the triple shafts that went to each wheel.

"I must have been woozy," declared Felber, ruefully. "Does the thing run?"

"It ought to," said Jim. "But if you ever got it started, there'd be no way to stop it!"

FELBER strolled over toward the wall. There, he saw another motor, an array of shafts, like those on the chassis. Handling the light-weight rods, he exclaimed:

"These are a beryllium alloy! The stuff costs like all blazes! Who bought it?"

The mechanics told him that he had.

"Don't worry, boys," decided Felber. "I'll get most of my money back. This isn't ordinary junk."

He picked up a large hollow shaft. He noted that it was about four feet long, that there were several others like it in the stack. He looked at the chassis and nodded. These outer shafts were the right length.

He was puzzled, though, to find that shafts of the next diameter were longer, approximately eight feet. As for the slender, solid shafts that lay in the discarded pile, they were a dozen feet in length.

"Why did I get these extra lengths?" inquired Felber. "Did I intend to cut them shorter?"

"We figured you did," replied Casey. "You had them spread all over the place, testing them. But when you got working on the motor, you shoved this whole batch aside and began to work with standard-sized shafts."

"You kept talking about strain," added Jim, "and you said a lot about torque. There's a lot of other gadgets in this junk pile, too. Stuff that you fooled with, then chucked away."

Felber wasn't surprised. His success as an automotive engineer depended largely on his love for experimental work, in which he discarded much, before choosing little. Evidently, his ingenuity had been working at par or better during his period of mental chaos.

He was frowning, trying to catch a few thoughts from the whirl that had dominated him. Seating himself on the chassis, he rested his chin in both hands and stared toward the junk pile. His eyes lighted up as an elevated train rolled by.

The uneasy mechanics were ready to grab him if his former mood returned. But Felber showed no signs of reverting to his mania. Instead, he seemed to have captured the thoughts he sought.

"I remember," he said slowly. "I am to send the unused parts away, along with the extra motor. As for this creation"—he gestured to the chassis—"I shall keep it. How would you boys like to test it some day?"

"Good enough," returned Jim, with a grin, "if we ship it out to the middle of a prairie, first. We couldn't run it around the block, the way you wanted."

"We talked you out of that idea, boss," added Casey. "Jim kept stalling while he filled the gas tank, and I argued with you about other things until you forgot that you wanted a test."

"You must have had to humor me a lot," decided Felber. "But that's all over. I don't know where I picked up this fool idea, but it's out of my system."

He strode across the garage, opened the little door at the back wall.

"Truckmen are coming for the junk," he said. "Give them a hand with it."

Both mechanics stared. They couldn't remember any time when Felber had left the garage to call up truckmen. Felber was smiling, though, quite normally, as the mechanics stared at each other. It was their turn to scratch their heads.

"I arranged for the truck to come," declared Felber. "Don't you remember? Let me see"—he was stroking his chin—"well, I can't just recall when I did it, but the truck ought to show up very soon. You'll see."

Jim and Casey heard before they saw. Returning to the chassis, Felber had scarcely seated himself before a clatter sounded in the alley. Through the doorway, the mechanics saw the lights of a truck.

Tall, darkish men entered the garage, bringing a load of luggage. Two were handling a heavy trunk; others were burdened with stacks of suitcases. Complacently, Felber gestured toward the front of the garage, told them to stack the stuff there.

That done, the darkish men gathered the discarded shafts that Felber was sending away, along with all stray parts and gadgets. Two of them picked up the extra motor. They formed a procession, starting out through the little door in the back of the garage.

During that process, two onlookers stood totally amazed: Casey and Jim. Muttering to each other, they wondered if they were the ones who had gone crazy.

"Maybe it *is* an epidemic," expressed Jim. "Felber was took with it, and got over it; but we could have caught the bug from him."

"We can't both be nuts," argued Casey. "It don't seem logical. Only when a guy goes whacky he don't know what's logical, anyway."

If those two had looked behind them, their speculations as to their sanity would have ended. Each mechanic would have been convinced that the mania had actually seized him. For, in contrast to the normal behavior of the truckmen, who were carrying burdens in normal style, something very unusual was occurring at the front of the garage.

The big trunk had opened. Its lock, though broken, had appeared quite tight, until the trunk lid lifted. Through a four-inch space peered eyes that reflected the garage lights with a burning glow. Beside those fiery eyes appeared the muzzle of an automatic, trained for the darkish men who were filing out through the rear door.

Those were the eyes of The Shadow. He had left the Hotel Monolith in Marjorie's trunk, which had contained only a few theatrical costumes. Recuperated after a day's rest in the tight-locked building where Shiwan Khan kept the hired truck, The Shadow had made this trip with the crew of Afghans.

The fact that they had brought Marjorie's luggage to this old garage, was proof that some disaster was intended after the Afghans left with another stolen invention.

Whatever happened later would probably be blamed on Felber, as it had with Maybrell and Orlio. Marjorie's luggage, found here, would indicate that Felber had abducted the girl.

As usual, Shiwan Khan was covering everything; but the master plotter had missed one angle. The Shadow was still alive; moreover, he was in a perfect vantage spot. He was waiting only until the Afghans were through the doorway. Then they would hear from him.

A fling of the trunk lid, a spring across the garage—The Shadow could overtake the men who served Shiwan Khan and catch them off guard before they reached their truck.

Such a move, performed in The Shadow's swift style, would place him between the Afghans and men like Felber, Jim and Casey, who had no weapons for their own defense.

There might be trouble from Felber, but The Shadow's tactics would give Jim and Casey a chance to handle the inventor. The Shadow's plan seemed perfect. In fact, it would have been, had he been allowed a dozen seconds more.

But something was already on its way, to steal those needed moments from The Shadow and give them to Shiwan Khan.

The approaching rattle of an elevated train grew suddenly into a terrific rumble that quivered the walls of the old garage. Eyes toward the Afghans, The Shadow could no longer see Felber, as the inventor clapped both hands to his forehead.

Above the roar of the passing train came a curdling shriek from Felber's lips, a cry that marked the ruin of The Shadow's present strategy. Felber's brain had caught the tuned command from Shiwan Khan: the signal that was to loose a scheme of tragedy more potent than any launched before!

CHAPTER XVIII.

DEATH ON THE LOOSE.

FELBER'S harrowing yell put everyone in action. Jim and Casey forgot their stupor, made a mad dash to grab the berserk inventor. The Afghans who crammed the doorway pushed hurriedly out into the alley with the burdens they lugged.

The Shadow hurled the lid of the trunk wide open, vaulted into sight with a long lunge, to begin his planned pursuit.

His muscles, still stiffened from battle with Hulagu, and cramped by a long stay in the trunk, were not equal to the need. The Shadow's foot tripped on the trunk edge; he took a long sprawl across the floor.

He was up, though, with his gun, as the Afghans slammed the rear door. He still saw a chance to reach it before they could bar the door from the other side.

It was Felber who blocked The Shadow's effort. Acting with greater speed than anyone else, the inventor had flung himself into a narrow seat that crossed the chassis of his crazily built car. He had started his jump as he screamed; he was completing his move when Jim and Casey reached him.

Turning a switch and kicking a starter, all in one action, Felber rammed home a gear that put the vehicle in motion. Instantly, the machine was a thing as wild as the madman who handled it. The crazy car was headed toward the door that The Shadow had chosen as his own objective.

Only an amazing effort could have saved The Shadow. He made it, and this time his muscles served him true. Flinging himself full about in the middle of a stride, he hit the floor shoulder first and took a quick flip along the floor, away from the hurtling car.

Big wheels almost skimmed his body as they matted down the stray folds of his cloak.

Rolling over, The Shadow came to hands and knees just in time to make another spring for safety. Responding to Felber's handling, the four wheels of the car had slashed sideways, to whirl it full about.

Felber was steering the thing by throwing power to separate wheels—a wild, haphazard process. There wasn't any method of braking the car, except by turning off the ignition, something that Felber did not intend to do.

Screeching his high-pitched glee, he bore down on Jim and Casey. Each dived in an opposite direction.

The roaring car went into a whirl, as Felber yanked levers and pushed pedals. It was a juggernaut on the

The Shadow tops them all!

● What is the leading dramatic show in America?

What is the leading daytime show in America?

What is the proven favorite of young America?

THE SHADOW!

This famous program is now heard on the following stations:

WCAE	Pittsburgh, Pennsylvania
KGFL	Roswell, New Mexico
KHJ	Los Angeles, California
KFRC	San Francisco, California
WTAR	Phoenix, Arizona
KTSM	El Paso, Texas
WGRC	Louisville, Kentucky
WKRC	Cincinnati, Ohio
WQAM	Miami, Florida
WSIX	Nashville, Tennessee
KOH	Reno, Nevada
KGU	Honolulu, Hawaii
WDNC	Durham, North Carolina
WGH	Newport News, Virginia

You can hear THE SHADOW in your own city if you'll get in touch with your local station now! It's the most thrilling dramatic show of all time . . . as proven by ten years' leadership in the Crossley and other polls!

loose; what little control it had was a matter of the crazed driver's whim. Felber, it seemed, was bent upon destroying everything in the place.

Slashing along the front wall, the crazy car smashed Marjorie's luggage into shreds. Glancing from a corner, it veered back toward The Shadow, blocking him from the rear door. A long dive across an approaching front wheel saved The Shadow. When he came up beside the wall, the car was past him.

Jim wasn't so lucky. He and Casey were again the threatened ones, and Jim gave his pal a needed shove to safety. Hit by a wheel, Jim was thrown to the wall, where he crumpled. Fortunately, the wheel did not pass over him; but he sagged weakly when he tried to get to his feet.

The car was slashing away again, taking The Shadow as its target, while Casey tried to get the front door open. Casey had no luck; the door was nailed tight. Seeing The Shadow tugging at the rear door, Casey realized that the truckers had by this time barred it.

Instinctively, The Shadow guessed the direction of the car's next veer, for he flung himself in the opposite direction, escaping death by inches. His gun shoved away, he whirled across the center of the floor under the very nose of the returning juggernaut, to reach Jim.

Whipping the disabled man into a corner, The Shadow performed another rescue as he swept about and bowled Casey away from the front door. Felber had swung the death car full about, and was again on the trail of victims.

He almost clipped The Shadow, after Casey's rescue. Only by flattening himself against the door did The Shadow avoid the onrush of the mechanical avalanche.

All wheels slanted at a sharp sidewise angle, the crazy car went into a rapid revolution. Struck by the passing chassis, Casey was thrown a dozen feet away. The best he could do was crawl to a corner, like the one that Jim had found. Both men were too groggy to save themselves further.

The whirl of the car revealed Felber's ultimate purpose, as dictated by Shiwan Khan. Each revolution was carrying him closer to the walls, where he would eventually crush all human obstacles. After that, there could be only one result: the complete wreckage of the car, with the destruction of its driver.

OUTSIDE, the Afghans had pulled away with their load of freight: the motor and special shafts that Shiwan Khan desired.

The Afghans knew they wouldn't be needed back in the garage. Shiwan Khan deemed death a certainty for anyone trapped in the place. It was he, the mental master, who actually controlled the course of the flaying juggernaut.

Sweeping like a whirlwind, the murderous chassis left only one spot of certain safety: the center of the floor, about which it revolved. To reach that zone meant crossing the path of the metallic cyclone, which was sweeping about so rapidly that it looked like nothing more than a vast blur.

A matter of split seconds, such an attempt—but The Shadow was practiced in that sort of speed. Just as the blur skimmed close to him, he flung himself straight at it. The whirling car was gone before he reached it. Almost instantly, as Jim and Casey viewed it, the thing was full around again.

The seeming instant was enough. The Shadow had passed the car before it reached him on its swing. He had ended his dive abruptly, in the middle of the floor. The Shadow was safe, for Felber hadn't even seen him.

Still, tragedy loomed ahead for Jim and Casey; eventually, it would gulp Felber, also, if nothing intervened. If self-preservation had been The Shadow's only motive, he would not have come to this garage at all.

He was here to save other lives; so far, he had managed a pair of temporary rescues. And dangerous though the prospect was, he intended to put an end to the thing that threatened death.

Rising in the central calm, The Shadow could follow the whizzing car with his eyes, for now he had a better angle of view. Gauging its speed was impossible, but precise calculation was not necessary. The Shadow had gained his required vantage point; having very little time to spare, he started his all-important move.

Beginning a rapid spin, The Shadow carried his own whirl as close as possible to the revolving chassis. It was making three trips to his one, although he had the inside track, and the radio further favored the metallic monster as The Shadow's circle widened.

Then came the moment when The Shadow felt singeing burn, as the whole length of the chassis grazed his shoulder. An interval, while The Shadow drew a breath; again, the metal mass skimmed him.

Another breath; The Shadow was flinging outward. His own dash helped, for the machine overtook him at an angle. Off his feet, The Shadow was spinning in the air, clawing for any hold that he could get. His hand bashed a lever, lost it, only to strike another.

Twisted about, The Shadow made a mad effort to better that skimpy grip. His free hand made a sweep and found substance on which to cling. Instead of clamping another hold upon a portion of the car, The Shadow had grabbed the driver.

SWAYING, shouting as he crouched low on the seat, Felber was no longer bothering with the controls. His brain, whirling as rapidly as the car, was telling him to let destruction ride. He was conscious, though, that something had flung in from space to molest him.

Violently, Felber grappled, and thereby served The Shadow. Anchored safely in the center of the chassis, the inventor indulged in bone-crushing tactics that drew his attacker down beside him. Once secure, The Shadow began to fight off Felber's grip.

They sagged as they struggled, until both were scorched by the red-hot motor just below the seat. Gauged according to the revolutions of the car, the fight was a long one; in a matter of minutes, it was very brief.

With all his maniacal power, Felber was yielding to The Shadow's strength. They bent forward toward the crude cross brace that served as dashboard for the hoodless car. The Shadow's hand, working despite the pluck of Felber's fingers, managed to reach the ignition switch.

In its wider revolutions, the car was nearing the corners that Jim and Casey had tried to reach. A few more rounds would doom that crippled pair. Felber didn't know it; he had forgotten the unfortunate mechanics entirely. All he wanted was to keep the car in its mad motion.

He gave a tug that wrenched The Shadow's hand from the ignition switch, but lost his own grip as he made the pull. The Shadow's fingers plucked for the switch, while Felber grabbed for the first thing that might serve him as a weapon. It proved to be a lever. Felber yanked it.

The lever didn't come loose, as Felber was crazed enough to think it might. Instead, it changed the speed of one rear wheel. The car took a flying skid as The Shadow's fingers pressed the switch. The power was off, but the course of the car was altered.

The front wheels were cutting to the left, but the rear ones formed an outward V which caused one wheel to act as a drag.

Like a great stone flung from a catapult, the machine left its circular course and hurtled straight for the wall. The distance was too short for the stalling motor to halt it, but the crash was greatly lessened.

If it hadn't been, the garage would have crumpled into ruins, for the shock that did occur was sufficient to crunch a big chunk from the wall. The chassis telescoped; two figures shot forward, along with the motor, which broke loose from the bolts that moored it.

There was a huge spatter of gasoline, a flare of flame that showed two forms rolling from the wreckage, still struggling. As they rolled toward the spreading flames, one fighter lost a cloak that had entangled with a twisted crossbar. The Shadow's slouch hat had already gone with the crash.

The strugglers weakened through sheer inertia. Rolling apart, they were lying in the path of the fire, their garments oil-soaked, ready to add fuel to the flames. Shiwan Khan's design of doom would still have functioned, had it not been for Casey.

There was a fire extinguisher in Casey's corner. He had strength enough to get the big cylinder and spray the chemicals on the fire, keeping its blaze away from Felber and The Shadow.

Jim was trying to get another extinguisher, but couldn't make the grade. Casey was turning to help him, when other rescuers arrived.

The door from the alley was flung open by a man who had unbarred it from the other side. Joe Cardona rushed into the garage, followed by Commissioner Weston. Behind them were Dr. Buffton and Rutledge Mann.

They extinguished the flames, then looked to the victims. Casey and Jim were telling them who Felber was. It was Commissioner Weston who announced the identity of the other stunned survivor, whose face was recognizable despite its fire-blackened grime.

"It's Cranston!"

MANN heard the commissioner's ejaculation. He stood by, watching solemnly, while Cardona and Buffton carried the unconscious forms to the car.

Casey was aiding Jim, and Weston was watching both, when Mann stepped to the mass of steel and battered beryllium that lay against the wall.

From the wreckage, Mann extricated a torn cloak and a flattened slouch hat. Taking off his topcoat, Mann placed The Shadow's garments in its folds, then laid the cloak across his arm.

Whatever else might come, Mann, as an agent of The Shadow, had preserved his chief's identity. An important precaution, considering the fact that The Shadow, for the present, lay helpless. A question of mere identity might mean life or death, where The Shadow was concerned.

From all accounts that Mann had heard, Shiwan Khan was practical, rather than vengeful. If his death thrusts failed in the case of minor victims, the master plotter followed the policy of letting them live awhile, rather than make the misstep of showing his own hand too soon.

That rule, Mann knew, would never apply, should Shiwan Khan discover that Lamont Cranston was The Shadow.

CHAPTER XIX.

MARQUETTE'S MISSION.

Two men were seated in a far corner of a small café near Times Square. Their luncheon finished, they were chatting in low tones that no one could overhear. One man was Vic Marquette, as dour-faced as ever. The other was Harry Vincent, agent of The Shadow.

So far, Vic had mentioned The Shadow, but had not stated definitely why he wanted to see him. Matters had reached a point, however, where Vic was ready to talk.

"I just came from Buffton's place," said Vic. "I wanted to talk to Cranston, but no luck. He isn't in shape yet. He and that fellow Felber got pretty well banged up last night."

Harry nodded. From his expression, Vic could tell that Harry was deeply concerned over Cranston's condition.

"I wanted to have Cranston contact The Shadow," declared Vic. "But since he can't, I'm going to put it up to you, Vincent. How soon do you think you could reach The Shadow?"

"I don't know," returned Harry, frankly. "I can pass the word along, but it all depends upon when The Shadow is ready to see me. That's the way it always works."

Marquette didn't catch the connection between the fact that Lamont Cranston was out of circulation and Harry's inability to promise an immediate response from The Shadow. Figuring that Harry would do his best, Vic decided to proceed.

"It's these crazy inventors," declared the Fed. "First Maybrell, then Orlio. Last night, Felber. There's a lot behind it, Vincent. Not any epidemic hokum. That stuff is all bunk!"

"I suppose it is," agreed Harry. "Nevertheless, the inventions were crazy, if the inventors weren't. From all appearances, the man who stole those inventions could be crazy, too. What does anybody want with high-speed fans, a beryllium bathysphere, and a motor with a four-wheel, triple-shafted drive?"

"There's one man who might figure some use for that junk," returned Vic. "His name is Shiwan Khan."

Harry's face went rigid. He hadn't supposed that anyone, other than The Shadow, knew of Shiwan Khan's presence in America. Vic saw the alarm that Harry tried to repress, but the Fed didn't catch its full significance.

"Right here in New York," said Vic, looking about to make sure that no persons were within earshot, "is a man who could supply Shiwan Khan with the most powerful weapon ever designed for warfare! The man is a chemist. His name is Hiram Bixley.

"He has developed a compressed gas that is both poisonous and inflammable. A bomb load of it, dropped in a small town, would spread all over the place. Not only would it kill off the inhabitants; it would ignite the moment it encountered a spark or a flame.

"The stuff is heavier than air. It can work down into bombproof shelters. Its fumes are even more poisonous than the gas itself, and they stick around. If Shiwan Khan gets a sample of that gas, Vincent, he'll he ready to start conquering the world tomorrow morning."

Harry was thoroughly impressed, as Vic expected him to be. Having revealed the main issue, Marquette decided to embellish it with complete details.

"We'll go up to see Bixley," decided the Fed. "After you've seen the place and know what it's all about, you'll be able to give The Shadow a full report on it. What we want him to do is find out if there's any loophole, any chance of a slip, in the precautions that we've taken in regard to Bixley."

THE house where the remarkable chemist lived looked very much like any other brownstone house. Harry noted, though, that several alert men were in the vinicity and was quite sure that they were Feds.

When Vic knocked at the basement door, the man who admitted the visitors had a badge showing beneath the edge of his coat.

On the second floor, they found Bixley in his laboratory. The chemist was a benign, white-haired man, who talked quite freely about his invention when Vic introduced Harry and said it would be all right.

"Here are the components of the gas," said Bixley, as he pointed to a row of beakers, containing liquids of different colors. "The 'terror gas,' we call it, and it is my hope that it will never be used in warfare. I have developed it in the belief that its existence will encourage peace, so long as it remains the sole property of a nation like our own."

Going to another table, Bixley pointed out the apparatus with which he manufactured the gas. Harry saw Bunsen burners, hydrometer jars, spiral tubes of glass, all leading to a metal cylinder that projected from a heavy wall bracket.

Marquette tested the bracket, found it solid. It was supported by an old water pipe that ran up beside the wall. Vic nodded his approval.

"I'm glad you let Torron fix that," declared Vic. "If that tank ever fell and cracked open, you'd have a lot of gas loose in the place."

As they left the lab, Harry observed that a Fed was on guard outside the door. On the way downstairs, Harry asked Vic who Torron was. He learned that George Torron was one of Bixley's assistants, of whom there were several.

"None of them know the formula," stated Marquette. "It's locked in Bixley's brain. We always have a man on duty to see that Bixley doesn't talk to any of them. We've been watching Bixley more than ever, lately"—Vic's tone became emphatic—"because of Shiwan Khan!"

Harry understood, fully. Shiwan Khan's ability at thought transference was a known fact. But, as Vic proceeded to assert, there were always definite symptoms when any brain came under Shiwan Khan's control.

"Those nut inventors," declared Vic, "could have gone gaga because Shiwan Khan was working on them. It's beyond me how he does it, but we've got plenty of evidence in our files to prove what I say."

Harry remembered that full reports of Shiwan Khan's former campaign had become part of the government records, with the testimony of persons who had been under Shiwan Khan's influence.

The New York police had figured in those cases, too, but only from the local angle. It wasn't surprising that they had not linked Shiwan Khan with present happenings.

"Understand this, Vincent," said Marquette. "I'm not saying that Shiwan Khan *is* in this business. I'm only saying that he *could* be. You've seen Bixley. What do you think of him?"

"He seems quite normal."

"That's my opinion, too," nodded Vic. "I'd say he's safe. But that's partly what bothers me. He looks *too* safe."

"How often does he leave the house?"

"Never! We let Torron and the others go out, because they don't know the secret. But we watch them like hawks whenever they go in the lab. We won't even let a thimbleful of that terror gas go out of the place."

Harry asked if Bixley minded the shut-in life that he led. Vic replied that the chemist actually liked it. He was free to take a vacation, should he need one, under the surveillance of Feds, but so far Bixley hadn't used the privilege.

By that time, the two investigators were in the basement. From a rear room, they could hear the plaintive tinkle of an old-fashioned music box. Vic smiled.

"It's Torron," he said. "He collects music boxes. He has some that play a dozen different tunes. Quite a hobby. I guess he spends most of his spare cash on it."

Vic knocked at the door from which the music came. It was opened by a solemn-faced man, whose narrow, curving chin and roundish bald head reminded Harry of an egg balanced on its small end.

"Hello, Torron!" greeted Vic. "Meet Mr. Vincent."

Torron shook hands cordially, but did not speak. He sat down in a corner, beside the playing music box. Vic looked at the little cabinet, admiring its mahogany finish.

"A new one, Torron?"

"Yes," replied the man, in a drawling tone. "It arrived this morning.

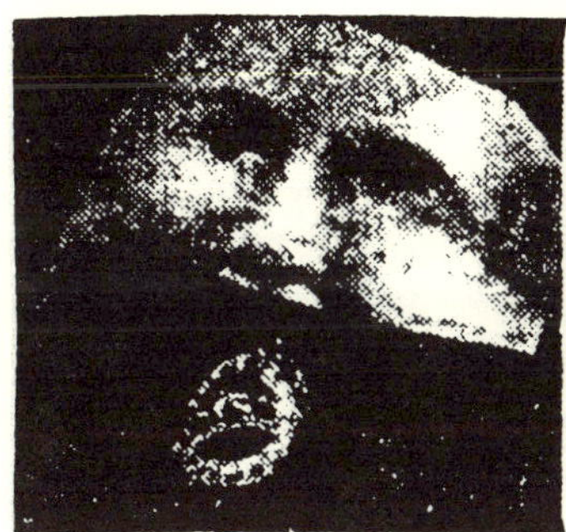

THE SHADOW MASK, a perfect disguise that will fool even your closest friends 10c

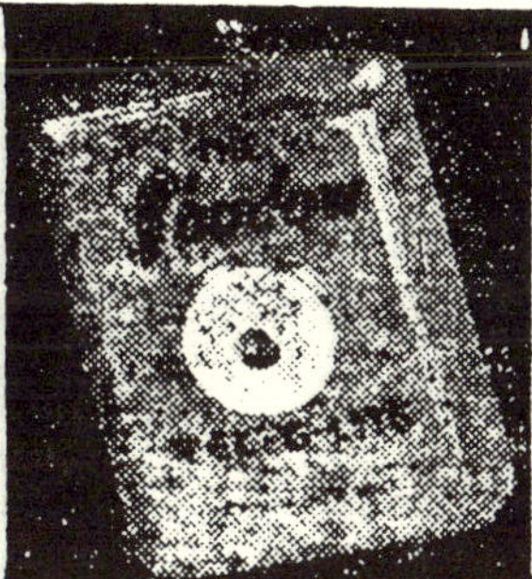

THE SHADOW TEC-TO-LITE, a powerful 2¼" x 1¾" flashlight. Hide it in the palm of your hand **50c**

SHADOW BIG LITTLE BOOKS, grand stories and pictures. Buy them at your 5 & 10c store **10c**

THE SHADOW HOLSTER SET, gun, holster, belt, Shadow mask, handcuffs, Shadow's whistle and The Shadow flashlight **$1**

OFFICIAL SHADOW STATIONERY & ENVELOPES, with Shadow Club insignia embossed in black and red **20c**

THE SHADOW GAME, size 20" x 20", printed in beautiful colors. A pair of dice, 4 colored tokens, play money, 4 Shadow "black hats," dice cups and colored disks **$1**

SHADOW OFFICIAL HAT & CAPE, black hat (indicate size: large or small), and 36" red-lined, black cape **$1**

It is a fine piece of workmanship."

There were other music boxes about the room. Torron did not seem to mind if they were handled. He preferred to sit and listen to the new one; when its tune had finished, he started it over again.

Meanwhile, Vic began to operate others, including the one that played a dozen tunes. The room became a medley of jangling tunes, but Torron was not annoyed. He kept playing the new music box, watching it with his chin in his hand, as if its tune reached his ears alone.

Leaving Torron's room, they went up to the first floor, where Vic ushered Harry into a comfortable library.

"An odd chap—Torron," declared Vic, "but he's consistent. As long as he sticks with his music boxes, he's normal. He's free to leave the place whenever he wants, provided he notifies us first. We've got to be careful, though, with anybody who comes in here. Those are the regulations."

"I suppose," remarked Harry, with a smile, "that the regulations now apply to me?"

"I guess they do," returned Vic. "Tell me this, Vincent: How do you expect to contact The Shadow —by telephone?"

"Very probably."

"Why don't you stay here, then? You can make all the calls you want, in private. You'll have a chance to see Bixley at work, and you can look the whole place over, if you want. I'd like The Shadow to get a full report as soon as possible; so the more you can tell him, the better. It will save time after you reach him."

Alone in the library, Harry telephoned Burbank. He learned that Mann was going to visit Buffton's later in the afternoon, with the police commissioner, to learn how Cranston was progressing.

Meanwhile, Burbank agreed, Harry's best course was to stay at Bixley's, since it would please Marquette.

Finished with his call, Harry gazed from the window while he awaited Vic's return. Noting the Feds in the offing, he wondered whether this house would become the scene of Shiwan Khan's most important thrust.

Somehow, the place seemed very peaceful and secure; almost too much so, as Marquette had put it. Imbued with the calmness, Harry found himself humming the strain of a short, lilting tune. Odd, he thought, that he should remember the melody played by Torron's new music box, out of all the others that he had heard.

Had Harry regarded that fact as an actual riddle, and pondered on its possible significance, he might have gotten the answer to a coming problem.

Without realizing it, The Shadow's agent had found the key to Shiwan Khan's main move, the subtle stroke through which crime's master genius intended to acquire the famous terror gas that would make world conquest simple!

CHAPTER XX.

CRIME'S GREAT STROKE.

It was dusk when the commissioner's car stopped at Dr. Buffton's office. Three passengers alighted; Weston was one; the others, Cardona and Mann. Looking about, the commissioner saw policemen on duty and gave an approving nod.

He had preferred to leave Cranston and Felber at Buffton's, rather than at a hospital. Here, they could be under special guard.

Much would depend upon the testimony of the two patients, when they recovered from last night's brutal experience. Neither Jim nor Casey had been able to supply the law with any worth-while information.

But Felber, certainly, was a victim of some peculiar mania, like Maybrell and Orlio. Perhaps he could describe some of the sensations that had held him during the past few weeks.

As for Cranston, he had definitely forestalled disaster when Felber's crazy car ran amuck. Weston was confident that his friend, back from the missing, could relate facts of value to the law.

So far, only one thing was established. Felber's invention, as wild an idea as anything produced by Maybrell or Orlio, had been shipped away, perhaps to reach mysterious hands.

True, the model of the finished car had been left in the old garage, but duplicate parts, motor included, had been loaded into a truck and carried away.

The visitors found Buffton in his office; the nerve specialist had a worried look. He took them to a room where a detective stood on guard. Cranston and Felber were lying there on cots. Both were asleep.

"I can't quite understand these cases," declared Buffton. "Both men have recuperated physically. They needed nourishment, and it was given them. Felber's mania seems to have passed, and Cranston has suffered no apparent harm.

"Yet they seem subdued. Any attempt at questioning tires them. It would be no use to wake them. I have tried and found that their response does not improve. I suppose their lethargy is the result of the strain they underwent last night.

"Felber acted like a madman and is suffering as a consequence. As for Cranston"—Buffton shook his head—"I can only presume that he deliberately threw himself into a similar state, in order to cope with Felber. In dealing with erratic individuals, I have often observed that the persons who handle them become quite as exhausted as the patients."

BUFFTON spoke quite sincerely—enough so to impress Weston and Cardona. The only one who doubted was Rutledge Mann. Methodical to the extreme. Mann was looking for a flaw in the argument. He felt a lurking suspicion of Buffton.

To test it, Mann remained in the sickroom when the others left it. His roundish face was very solemn as he gazed at the recumbent form of Cranston. The quietness of the room impressed him, until he heard a distant jangle.

It was a telephone bell, ringing in an apartment across the courtyard. Mann tilted his head and listened. He remembered that the bell had rung while Buffton was talking. Two minutes passed; Mann heard the bell again. He left the room and went to Buffton's office.

Weston and Cardona were gone. Buffton was quite surprised when Mann appeared.

"We thought you had left," said the physician. "The commissioner said that you had an appointment and intended to take a cab. So he didn't wait—"

"The appointment does not matter," interrupted Mann, his tone unusually abrupt. "Tell me, doctor, why is that telephone bell ringing in the apartment across the court."

"You mean it's still ringing?" queried Buffton. "Why, I thought it had stopped hours ago."

"Who lives there?"

"No one. The people left a month ago. I suppose they forgot to have the phone removed."

Buffton went to the sickroom to listen for the disturbing bell. Mann headed for the courtyard, where he was stopped by a patrolling officer. Explaining, satisfactorily, that he had come with the commissioner, Mann inquired about the telephone next door.

"That bell's been ringing ever since I came on duty," declared the cop. "I didn't think it was important. What's it doing, disturbing the patients?"

Mann nodded.

"I'll fix that," the officer assured him. "If nobody's living there, nobody's going to squawk if I climb in and take the receiver off the hook."

By the time Mann had returned to the room where the patients were, the telephone's jangle had ended. While he was gazing at Cranston's cot, Mann saw the patient stir. So did Buffton.

"A good sign!" exclaimed the physician. "I must call the commissioner and inform him."

Knowing that it would be some minutes before Buffton could locate Weston at the club, Mann remained in the sickroom. Seated beside Cranston's bed, Mann met his chief's eyes when they opened. A murmur came from The Shadow's lips:

"Shiwan Khan?"

Mann nodded. The Shadow came up to one elbow, holding his hand to his forehead.

"I recognized it," he said. "It had the same effect as the astral call bell, the mental sound that the mystics of India produce when they wish to communicate with one another. People believe that the telephone bell is a modern invention. Instead"—The Shadow chuckled—"it dates back to antiquity!

"It is the sound that commands attention. No mind, when weary, can think of anything else, when concentrated on that sound. Shiwan Khan has learned that Felber was brought here, and has been ringing that number constantly, to keep him lulled.

"Unfortunately, it has the same effect on me. I couldn't shake it off, Mann, not after the ordeal I had undergone. Every time I tried to speak, it halted me. The intervals were perfectly spaced. You did well to have it stopped."

Resting back upon the pillows, The Shadow closed his eyes. Then, dropping the tone of Cranston, he spoke one word in his own weird whisper:

"Report!"

Mann told what he had learned from Burbank. News of the terror gas and its inventor, Bixley, roused The Shadow.

"There is no time to lose," he decided. "Get my clothes, then summon the special cab. After that, have Burbank contact Vincent."

WHILE Mann was obeying those instructions, events were taking place at Bixley's house. The elderly chemist was conducting one of his scheduled experiments, with Vic Marquette and Harry Vincent standing by. Liquids were bubbling in their jars; vapors were passing through the gas coils into the metal tank above, forced there by pressure.

"We ship the tanks under guard," explained Vic to Harry, "so that the gas can be tested. Its results vary, according to the quantities of the component parts."

Torron entered while Vic was speaking. A solemn look upon his egg-shaped face, the baldish assistant walked directly to Bixley's table. Marquette stepped close to check on whatever Torron said. Reaching past the tank, Torron carefully tightened the new wall bracket.

"If everything is satisfactory, sir,"

he said to Bixley, "I should like your permission to leave. I am going away for a few days, you know."

Bixley nodded. "Good-by, Torron," he said. "Have a good trip."

Noting nothing unusual, Marquette stepped back to let Torron pass. Vic's eyes were on Bixley; it was Harry who watched the assistant's departure.

It seemed to Harry that Torron was moving in a very mechanical style, almost as if in a trance. But from what he had seen of Torron, Harry supposed that was the man's usual manner.

A few minutes passed, while liquids bubbled and gases of vivid colors ran through the glass coils. Then Bixley turned about, his face quite troubled.

"I can't understand it," he said. "Look at that gauge, Mr. Marquette."

"It's working, isn't it?" queried Vic. "It says half full."

"It has stayed at that point," replied Bixley, "ever since Torron left here. Yet the gas has been flowing steadily. Ah! The gauge has started again."

Vic shot an alarmed look at Harry, then shot the words: "Let's go!"

They dashed down the stairs to Torron's room. When Vic yanked open the door, they were greeted by the tinkle of a music box. Torron was gone, but he had left evidence behind him. A table was pulled out from the wall. The space revealed the bottom end of a water pipe, plugged with a steel screw cap.

"The bracket in the lab!" exclaimed Vic. "It must be hollow! Torron drilled a hole into the water pipe and fitted it with a screw valve. That's why he fooled with the bracket tonight.

"He came down here and opened the screw cap. He's drained half a tank load of the terror gas, and has taken it with him. He's on his way to Shiwan Khan!"

THE music box had stopped, but the tinkle was still running through Harry's brain. He knew who had sent that curio to Torron. It was a gift from Shiwan Khan.

Too clever to work upon Bixley, whose peculiarities were being watched, Shiwan Khan had chosen Torron as his instrument. Their minds tuned to the same vibration, Shiwan Khan had inspired the chemist's assistant to a deed of crafty theft.

Through the old disused water pipe, Torron had drawn off a supply of the deadly gas while Bixley was manufacturing it. Marquette was right: the dupe was on his way to Shiwan Khan!

Dashing to the front of the basement, Marquette shouted at the Feds stationed there. He learned that Torron had taken a cab and was carrying a heavy suitecase. Having been told to pass Torron through without question, the Feds had let him go.

They had noted the direction that the cab had taken. Jumping into a car, Marquette started on the trail, shouting for Harry to follow in another automobile. But Harry was gone, with a purpose of his own. He was dashing up to the library to reach the telephone.

He heard the bell start to ring while he was on his way. Snatching the receiver, Harry heard Burbank's voice. Quickly, Harry gave the details regarding Torron. Burbank told him to stand by for instructions.

A sample of that vapor in his possession, Shiwan Khan would have the requirement for world conquest, as Vic Marquette had declared.

Victory was in the grasp of Shiwan Khan. Only one being could pluck the triumph from him.

That being was The Shadow!

CHAPTER XXI.

BLOCKED VICTORY.

SEATED in his golden room, Shiwan Khan smiled as he heard the final tinkles from a little music box. Closing the mahogany case, he handed it to Hulagu.

"Dispose of it," ordered Shiwan Khan. "I go to meet our new guest, Mr. Torron."

There was a button on the table. Shiwan Khan gave it a final press, timed to an exact interval.

"Our last call to Felber," he told Hulagu. "He will rouse soon, when he hears the ringing bell no longer. But it will not matter. By the time that he has told his hazy story to the physician, we shall be gone."

Apparently, Shiwan Khan did not consider Lamont Cranston as a factor. That was not surprising, since the newspapers had merely stated that the commissioner's friend had aided in Felber's rescue. The Afghans, fortunately, had brought no word of The Shadow's reappearance.

The thing that had hurried the darkish truckmen out from Felber's garage had been the scream that the inventor gave. In reporting to Shiwan Khan, the Afghans had stated that all had operated according to their master's plan; at least, up to the moment when they had made their rapid exit.

Strolling from his many-roomed apartment, Shiwan Khan heard the elevator coming upward. He waited until it stopped; then stepped toward the opening door.

Torron came from the elevator, carrying a suitcase. Shiwan Khan plucked it from Torron's hands, opened it and found a small, sealed tank within.

In response to Shiwan Khan's evil

gloat, Torron smiled. Under a strange control that he had been unable to explain, the dupe was finding this reception to his liking. When Shiwan Khan beckoned, Torron followed.

Shiwan Khan led the way to a spiral staircase that led to the floor above. They reached the closed door of the Moonlight Café, which Shiwan Khan had stated he would change into a Persian garden. There, Shiwan Khan placed the little tank in Torron's custody.

"I shall take you with me," declared Shiwan Khan, in a tone that carried the tinkly rhythm of the music box. "Yes, Torron, I shall need you, because of your experience with Bixley. You shall leave tonight, with myself and Hulagu."

As he finished the statement, Shiwan Khan lifted one yellow, long-nailed hand and spoke the word:

"Listen!"

From far away came the sound of sirens, the *clang* of bells. Police had joined the Feds, in an effort to trace Torron. The sounds jarred the long-faced man. He spoke pleadingly to Shiwan Khan.

"I did as you ordered, master," claimed Torron. "I took the first cab I saw and came here. But I was afraid that they would follow—"

"I knew that they would follow," interposed Shiwan Khan, in his bell-like tone. "I foresaw that it would be impossible to acquire Bixley's gas without raising a huge alarm. They have found our lair"—he turned to Hulagu, with a smile—"now let them trap us!

"It will occur to them that Shah Nikwan and Shiwan Khan are one. They will be unable to use my private elevator. Forced to batter their way up from the floor below, they will meet my faithful Afghans, fighters who consider death in battle to be life's greatest privilege.

"With all those obstacles conquered, they will come for us, only to find that we have gone. How, they will never guess. Our strange departure will remain a mystery."

DRAWING a large key from his tunic, Shiwan Khan turned to unlock the door of the hidden Persian garden. He paused, smiling as he recalled a former time when he had opened that same door.

"I must not forget Princess Dunyazad," declared Shiwan Khan. "It is too bad"—he was clucking his disappointment—"that we cannot take her with us to Xanadu. She is very beautiful, but she is not important.

"Princess Dunyazad still awaits my command. She has a mission; it is only right that I should allow her to complete it. Remain here, both of you, until I return."

Hulagu was holding Shiwan Khan's turban. Taking it, Shiwan Khan put on the headpiece, to play the part of Shah Nikwan. He descended by the spiral staircase, leaving Torron with Hulagu.

When Shiwan Khan had gone, Torron became nervous. This talk of going to a place called Xanadu had sounded glorious while Shiwan Khan was present. But when Torron gazed at his traveling companion, Hulagu, he found himself ill at ease. The Mongol glared in Torron's direction; the long-faced man stiffened, clutching the gas tank tightly.

Reaching the floor below, Shiwan Khan passed two rows of stolid Afghans. Each row had its leader. Suji was one; Kuli, conspicuous because of a bandaged shoulder, was the other. Shiwan Khan spoke to them in their Pukhtu dialect. The tribal warriors clasped their fists to the long daggers that they carried.

They could hear the siren shrieks, the *clang* of bells, much closer than before. They were pleased at the thought of coming battle. They loved death, as Shiwan Khan had said; yet they loved life, too, a fact that he had not specified.

Not one of the wily Afghans knew of the sacrifice that was to be their lot. Confident in the power of Shiwan Khan, they supposed that he included them in his future plans and had therefore made arrangements for their safe departure.

Passing the Afghans, Shiwan Khan knocked at the door of Marjorie's boudoir. A voice, speaking Persian words, requested him to enter. Shiwan Khan stepped in and closed the door.

As he had said, Princess Dunyazad was beautiful. Since her return to mental bondage, Marjorie had reveled in the part she played. Her eyes were languid, her smile voluptuous, as she rose to greet Shah Nikwan.

Meeting her gaze, Shiwan Khan wondered if she would balk at the test to come. Her thought was life; not death, as with the Afghans. But Princess Dunyazad would relish death if melody came with it. Pointing toward the window, Shiwan Khan spoke in smooth Persian. Marjorie understood.

With slowly undulating stride, Marjorie strolled to the window and opened it. Her eyes lighted with a joyous recollection as the wind stroked the strings of the aeolian harp. There was ecstasy in her gaze as she turned to face Shiwan Khan.

Green eyes bored into Marjorie's. Her face froze in all its loveliness. Fascinated by Shiwan Khan's hypnotic power, entranced by the strum of the vibrating harp, the girl was ready for any command.

Shiwan Khan could have controlled her by thoughts alone; but he spoke, to give emphasis. His voice chimed with the chords from the harp:

"The pistol!"

Sliding the golden sash from her hip, Marjorie lifted the silver gun. Again, Shiwan Khan gave an order:

"Place it to your heart!"

The girl obeyed. Riveted by Shiwan Khan's gaze, she did not feel the coldness of the gun muzzle as it pressed her flesh below the jeweled girdle. Her finger was on the trigger, awaiting the word to fire.

This was to be death as Shiwan Khan enjoyed it. He lingered, as the moments oozed, holding the final word until the wavering harp notes should rise to a crescendo. The tone was swelling, almost to the needed pitch, when suddenly strings clanged with discord.

Shiwan Khan's eyes sped to the window. So did Marjorie's; the girl's lips gave a horrified gasp at the sound of the jarring interruption. A single string twanged sourly. With that last false note, the harp was silent.

A hand had stifled the plucking sweep of the intermittent breeze. A gloved hand, that reached across the sill and clamped itself upon the strings. The notes of the harp were replaced by a weird whisper that Marjorie had heard before, but never with such mockery.

A head came above the sill. Burning eyes glowed from beneath a slouch hat. Lips were hidden, however, as they voiced the eerie taunt still louder. That mockery was meant for Shiwan Khan, the plotter who had never expected to hear its challenge again.

The laugh of The Shadow!

CHAPTER XXII.

CRIME'S FLIGHT.

They were face to face, old enemies who had met before, each at a disadvantage of his own manufacture. Shiwan Khan had come here weaponless, fearing no opposition from a foe. The Shadow, climbing from a floor below, had stretched his hand to the limit, to gain a hold upon the dooming harp.

Though the fate of civilization rested in their coming duel, the present moment offered controversy over a single person. Marjorie Cragg was the person for whom they fought. She held the balance, thanks to the silver pistol. Already, the startled girl had withdrawn the weapon from her breast.

Marjorie's next move with the gun was to be a deciding factor in a struggle between two titanic wills.

Green eyes glaring, his voice babbling swift persuasion, Shiwan Khan tried to regain his sway over Marjorie. He was telling her to give death where it belonged: to The Shadow.

Remembering a previous mission, Marjorie swung about. She met the burn of The Shadow's eyes, heard his laugh quiver its strident peal. The girl aimed, but her finger did not press upon the trigger. Then, as the mirth reached its crescendo, Marjorie yielded to its strains.

No words were needed. Marjorie understood the command and obeyed. Wheeling, she pointed the pistol for Shiwan Khan.

Green eyes saw the death threat coming. With a forward bound, Shiwan Khan grabbed at Marjorie's slender wrist, struck it upward as she fired. The bullet whistled past the turbaned head, burned a path through a rare tapestry hanging on the wall.

With a fling, Shiwan Khan sent Marjorie sprawling across the divan; recoiling, he fled for the door.

Startled Afghans spread away as they saw their vaunted leader's rush.

They spied The Shadow in pursuit, but not a hand went to a knife. Darkish faces were bobbing back and forth, watching the amazing sight.

Behind The Shadow came Marjorie, carrying the pistol. Though she wore the attire of Princess Dunyazad, the girl was herself again. She had caught the spirit of bravery from The Shadow's challenge to Shiwan Khan. She was ready to throw her frail strength to The Shadow's aid, no matter what the danger.

Shiwan Khan had reached the spiral stairs. There, he banked everything on a desperate stroke. Wheeling to face the Afghans, he spread his hands, empty, shouting that he was weaponless.

The Afghans did not realize that Shiwan Khan had gained boldness because he was temporarily away from The Shadow's aim. They saw only that he halted, turned about to meet death face to face.

WITH one accord, the Afghans sprang for The Shadow. He was in their midst, whirling before they could start their own spinning tactics. His guns were pumping, spilling those who tried to draw their dirks. The only ones who reached him were those who fought with bare hands, clutching for The Shadow's throat.

Passing the black-centered whirl, Marjorie saw Shiwan Khan start up the stairway, and shouted to The Shadow. Slugging away a pair of clawing Afghans, The Shadow gestured toward the elevator, then followed Shiwan Khan.

Grabbing a dagger that lay beside a sprawled Afghan, Marjorie reached the elevator. As she pulled the door aside, she swung about defiantly, ready to meet any attacking Afghans, blade to blade. In her other hand was the gun. None were in sight, except the flattened ones. The rest had gone for the stairs.

Inside the elevator, Marjorie slammed the door, started a downward trip, for aid.

On the top floor, The Shadow met Hulagu coming in full stride. He didn't aim at the huge Mongol; an instant's pause would have been too much. It would take a lot of bullets to stop Hulagu, and meanwhile, the Afghans would arrive. Side-stepping, The Shadow let Hulagu end his surge against the wall.

Shiwan Khan was unlocking the door of the former Moonlight Café. Instead of taking the Unfathomable as a target, The Shadow swooped upon Torron, who still clutched the tank of death gas. Pressing Torron to the wall, The Shadow placed a gun muzzle against the metal container.

A shrill order came from Shiwan Khan. It stopped a lunge from Hulagu, and halted a squad of Afghans at the stairway top. Shiwan Khan knew what a shot would mean: death to all, himself included.

Words dripped from those slitted lips, as Shiwan Khan proposed terms to The Shadow. All the while, the green eyes were darting beady looks toward Hulagu and the Afghans. Imperceptibly, they were working closer to The Shadow.

Shiwan Khan was trying to gauge a moment for attack. He didn't know that The Shadow, in his turn, was calculating the time it would take Marjorie to return. Shiwan Khan had opened the door to the Moonlight Café; inch by inch, he was working past it, ready for a slippery move if all else failed.

Amid the increasing tension, The Shadow heard a faint *clang* from below. It must have reached Shiwan Khan, also, for the master schemer shouted an order. Instantly, Afghans were surging for The Shadow, while Shiwan Khan was diving into the Moonlight Café.

Instead of blasting the death tank,

The Shadow wheeled away. Worming past the clutches of dark hands, the slashes of hastily swung knives, he reached the door of the Moonlight Café.

With a hard swing, The Shadow whipped the door into the faces of the nearest Afghans and went through. Flung blades, aimed for The Shadow, found the door instead.

There wasn't time to look for Shiwan Khan. One fighter had reached The Shadow. The pursuer was the giant Hulagu. Again, it was a case of combat between the cloaked battler and the giantlike killer from Mongolia.

SWINGING both guns, The Shadow drove for Hulagu. The giant performed his usual trick. His big paws thrust out, grabbing for wrists, to twist away the guns from hands that clutched them. Hulagu missed that grab, as The Shadow's hands flung aside.

Hurling one gun squarely in the monstrous Mongol's face, The Shadow lunged as the giant staggered. Clamping his free hand upon Hulagu's shoulder, the black-cloaked fighter vaulted to his foeman's neck. He wrapped a choking grip there, not with his hands but with his knees.

Slashing with his gun, he beat off the big hands as Hulagu tried to raise them. Then, swinging downward, The Shadow hooked one massive arm with his own and wrenched it behind Hulagu's back.

Hulagu couldn't reach The Shadow. Choking, he was unable to bellow as he reeled. Astride those huge shoulders, The Shadow jabbed bullets at the Afghans, sent them diving for the stairs.

There, as they tried to rally, gunfire greeted them. The Shadow's agents had come to the proper door, in accordance with instructions that their chief had given to Rutledge Mann. Marjorie had brought the valiant squad up by the elevator.

Hulagu was sagging to his knees. Twisting furiously, he gained a grip on The Shadow. They were tangled in a solid grapple, but The Shadow's locked legs still kept their strangle hold on Hulagu's neck.

Working to wrest his gun hand wholly free, The Shadow took another look for Shiwan Khan. He saw the master plotter, standing by the strangest machine that human eyes had ever viewed.

The contraption was mounted on the great plaform in the center of the room. It looked like a giant mechanical octopus, with its rounded body and long, thin arms. The body was Orlio s beryllium bathysphere. The arms were the three-length shafts left over from Felber's motor.

Wherever inner shafts poked from the outer, the larger ones had one of Maybrell's fans geared to it. The four holes in the top of the bathysphere were also equipped with shafts, each carrying one of the propeller fans.

Crazy inventions when taken singly, those brainstorms had been combined into a complete machine. The contrivance was a helicopter, built for flight through the air. Its propellers, set on the horizontal, were equipped to lift it in a straight, upward flight.

There wasn't a doubt that it would work. Such machines had been devised before, with successful results. This craft of Shiwan Khan's had features that none of the previous models possessed. With sixteen blades to lift it, made of the lightest of all metals, beryllium, it was the aircraft of the future.

How Shiwan Khan intended to fly it was another question. The domed roof had the helicopter cooped in. Meanwhile, Shiwan Khan was shouting encouragement to Hulagu, urging him to dispose of The Shadow and bring the precious gas tank.

Hulagu didn't respond. Instead, The Shadow did. His gun hand swung toward Shiwan Khan. Ducking into the bathysphere, the cornered conqueror reappeared with a revolver. By then, The Shadow and Hulagu were no longer tangled.

RISING above the half-choked giant, The Shadow aimed for Shiwan Khan, who returned the favor. Both guns spouted, starting a new deal. Neither marksman found his target.

Hulagu had grabbed The Shadow, ruining his aim; but in hauling the cloaked fighter downward, the giant had dragged him from Shiwan Khan's path of fire.

Lashing with Hulagu, The Shadow swung toward the wall, to keep his huge foe still blocking any shots from Shiwan Khan. Hulagu was groggy, but he still had power. The Shadow let him waste it, giving way as fast as Hulagu surged.

As they reached the wall, the Mongol made a lunge. The Shadow side-stepped, but Hulagu's paw came ahead. Over the cloaked shoulder, it clamped upon a lever and dragged it downward, hard. A rumble came from the roof of the Moonlight Cafe.

Looking upward, The Shadow saw the great dome spread apart, to reveal the sky above. Designed by Shiwan Khan, built by a man that he controlled, that special roof had been provided for this moment.

The name of the Moonlight Cafe was singularly appropriate. With the dome spread apart, real moonlight shone from above, visible despite the glow of the Manhattan sky.

The blades of the helicopter's propellers were whirling dizzily. Inside the body, Shiwan Khan was handling the controls beside the purring motor.

Geared differently, because of the varied shafts, the horizontal blades were lifting the arm ends first; those long rods seemed to hoist the body before its propellers had reached their full whirl.

With a sudden rise, the whole contrivance took off for the open dome, just as The Shadow reached the platform. It was clear of the roof as The Shadow opened fire. Bullets were useless in stopping a take-off with the speed of that one.

The Shadow's agents were through the door, a sprawled mass of Afghans behind them. Hulagu, on his feet, was making a surge for The Shadow, only to be blocked by a huge African not nearly his own size, but big enough.

The new fighter was Jericho Druke, a handy man in mass conflict. Harry Vincent had brought him along with other agents.

Jericho had long been looking for a foeman bigger than himself, and he had found one. He and the revived Mongol reeled to the very roof edge, where Jericho showed that he could use footwork with his brawn.

Wresting clear of Hulagu, Jericho twisted in again, to meet the rival giant's lunge. As they rammed, Jericho side-stepped, to take a strangle hold.

He missed it. Hulagu had started a dive that couldn't be stopped. Tripping across a low rail, the Mongol was on his way to the street. He ended that thirty-story plunge with a smash that cracked the sidewalk.

Gazing down from above, Jericho let his broad grin dwindle. He was sorry that Hulagu hadn't stayed to make it a finish fight.

The Shadow held the same sentiments regarding Shiwan Khan. From the doorway, others watched him. Beside Harry and accompanying agents stood Torron, clutching the precious gas tank, blubbering that he would take it back to Bixley.

Marjorie was there, too. Unconscious of the fact that she was still attired in the minimum of costume, even for a former Persian princess, the girl was staring toward the sky, her gaze fascinated by a sight that The Shadow also viewed.

Tiny against the moonlight was a silvery speck, heading off over the sea. Whether that strange ship of the air would come to a safe landing, where it might find haven, were questions that only the future could answer.

Its pilot had escaped with nothing except the chance of continuing his own evil existence. Perhaps, with that mighty brain of his, Shiwan Khan could catch the echo of a weird, pursuing sound that came from a rooftop thousands of feet below.

It was the laugh of The Shadow. Victor in the final fray, the cloaked fighter was sounding his triumph over Shiwan Khan, the vanquished man who called himself a conqueror.

With that weird farewell, The Shadow voiced his invitation to return, that he might put a final end to the career of Shiwan Khan.

THE END.